"I DO!"
LOVE STORIES

BY JOHN A. REID

BOOK COVER & INTERIOR PAGE DESIGN BY THE AUTHOR

iUniverse, Inc.
Bloomington

"I Do!"
Love Stories

iUniverse books may be ordered through booksellers or by contacting:

iUniverse
1663 Liberty Drive
Bloomington, IN 47403
www.iuniverse.com
1-800-Authors (1-800-288-4677)

ISBN: 978-1-4502-9370-9 (pbk)
ISBN: 978-1-4502-9371-6 (cloth)
ISBN: 978-1-4502-9372-3 (ebk)

Library of Congress Control Number: 2011901157

Printed in the United States of America

iUniverse rev. date: 3/15/2011

INDEX

The Romance Of Rosanna Tucciano

The intoxicating aromas swept into her nostrils and swirled in glee around her thoughts, making Rosanna feel both lightheaded and ebullient.

Every stall along the cobblestone street taunted her with promised ecstasy, and the windows of shops she passed were laden with marvelous arrays of foods crying out to her: "Place your lips close to me! Lick my excitement! Take me into your body and let our souls mingle in glorious satisfaction!"

Plump loins, succulent and many-spiced sausages, and a tempting profusion of chubby, luscious meat rolls pleading to be sliced and placed on fresh-baked bread beckoned her from butcher shops. Drying spices hung about wagons, thrilling Rosanna's senses with a titillating medley of pungent whispers.

Her appetite along with the weight of her shopping basket grew with almost every step she took through the marketplace. Would-be suitors handed her roses that Rosanna either placed in her hair, or laid on top of the purchases in her shopping basket.

All the young men stood up and held their breath when Rosanna looked around the flowered outdoor cafe as she contemplated which table to sit at.

Murmurs of admiration from the young men drifted around her like an erotic, exotic silk cloak while she cast her smile in all directions, then she sat down and bit into a juicy, golden plum.

Green shadows of envy washed over her being as the young women seated at other tables compared her beauty to theirs. Cecilia arrived, and as she walked across the patio, she was immediately aware of the usual constant attention Rosanna was receiving from all the patrons.

She sat down across the table from the beautiful Rosanna Tucciano, and then Cecilia smiled and said: "Sorry I'm late, but the bakery was crammed. Marcello! Iced tea, please! Those roses are so lovely."

"Thank you," said Rosanna. "Every rose an offering of undying devotion and a promise of love and marriage, but it's absolute hell not getting the attention I *really* want from...Oh, I feel so...So unappealing."

"You? The most desirable woman in the entire village?"

"That seems to be true, however, there is one heart that doesn't flutter for me, and *that* leaves me feeling so unfulfilled."

Marcello, the waiter, rushed to their table, and now he waited breathlessly for Rosanna's sweet lips to form her lunch request that he desperately wished to fulfill. He'd already served Rosanna her usual cold drink when she'd graced the restaurant with her presence, and now Marcello stole a glance at her while serving Cecilia the glass of iced tea.

"You still haven't told me who this man is that is torturing your soul. Grazie, Marcello," said Cecilia, looking up at him.

"Me? No man is torturing my soul," he said, wide-eyed.

"No, not you. I was talking to Rosanna."

"Oh, uh, sorry. How is your iced tea?" he asked.

"Perfect, as usual. Grazie, Marcello," replied Cecilia.

"And you can bring me another pineapple-lemon squish and your pastry tray, Marcello," said Rosanna. "And...hmmm, a sandwich of assorted cold cuts. I find a sandwich before any meal whets the appetite, admirably. You can surprise me with your selection of a salad and a bowl of soup, but I'll have a pastry first, and while eating my sandwich and soup, and the salad, I'll need you handy with the pastry tray now and then. Oh, yes, and a small plate of chocolates, as well. Please? Grazie, Marcello."

"Certainly, Rosanna. Right away. You look so lovely today. I hope you enjoy the pastries we have today. And the soup. My mother's favorite recipe. The cold cuts are...Uh, forgive me. I'll hurry. Oh! Cecilia? Anything to eat for you?"

"Yes, please. I'll have a small plate of the primavera pasta. Wait! This veal dish looks interesting. Hmmm, yes, I'll have that. Hmmm, and the soup, too. Now, for dessert, I'll have...hmmm, a slice of pecan and banana cake with gelato. Oh, I didn't notice the stuffed chicken breast special. Yes, I'll have that, too, and plenty of your always so tasty baked rolls, with extra bowls of whipped butter. Grazie, Marcello."

"Of course, right away," he said before rushing away.

"Are you dieting?" Rosanna asked her.

"No, it's just that I'm not very hungry right now. I'll have a bite to eat before dinner."

"Oh-oh. Man trouble again. What's Paolo complaining about *this* time? As if I should ask, but he has to wait until *after* he marries you. *Such heat,*" said Rosanna, clucking her tongue.

"It's not him. It's his mother. You know how he wants to marry me, but as always, she wants him to wait because I've seen the way she grins at you. She thinks if Paolo puts off marriage long enough, he might cast me aside for you."

"So, she's trying to cause problems between you two again."

"Exactly," said Cecilia. "That woman never lets up. I say hello to her and she looks past me and waves at somebody behind me. The last time I looked behind me to see who she was waving at, it was a chair. Sometimes she asks Paolo why he's sitting home alone, and yet I'm right there, standing beside him."

"Still hinting about your weight, huh?"

"It's like she's screaming it down my throat. She keeps...Oh, grazie, Marcello. That looks wonderful," said Cecilia, smiling.

Marcello served the ladies their luncheon requests, then he felt so pleased when he saw the delighted expressions on their faces after they tasted the food, and then he hurried away.

"As I was saying, Paolo's mother keeps showing me pictures of her family and pointing out that none of them look like me, and then she shakes her head, clasps her hands to her bosom, and moans, and then she says it's so sad that I have such a terrible problem with my figure, then she holds a hanky to her face, sobs, and walks away."

"For her, that's not being dramatic," said Rosanna. "Not like when she sings in church at weddings."

"Oh, I know," said Cecilia. "She gets down on her knees and grabs the hands of the bride and groom as she's singing and soaking the bride's gown with her tears. Although, that's what people look forward to at every wedding because they find her performance hilarious. Then she's always helped away by two men as she's sobbing and yelling out to the bride and groom that she hopes they have thirty or forty children. Mama mia!"

"She should stop hoping other newlyweds such bliss, and let you and Paolo marry and have many children," said Rosanna.

"Hah! She'll never agree to that!"

"You must be more forceful with Paolo to pull him away from his mama. You can do it, Cecilia. But be careful. Remember that women are strong, and men are so fragile. Be gentle with him. Just tell Paolo that he's not a real man unless he ignores his mother and marries you. He says he loves you, so, tell him to prove it or you'll leave him for a *real* man, and then you'll see how fast he'll change his...Oh, yes, Marcello. Such a delightful array. Hmmm, not enough cream in that one."

Marcello had brought them another pastry tray, and his heart was beating faster as he watched the lovely Rosanna Tucciano pouting a bit while trying to decide which pastries to choose.

"Ahhhh, yes, the chocolate and lemon tart looks tempting. Hold it. And the raspberry puff. Grazie, Marcello."

"A perfect decision, as always, Rosanna," he said, grinning.

"As I was saying, he'll change his tune. Oh, of course, his mother will feign a long, very painful death, but just step over her wailing body as you walk out of the house with Paolo, then she'll shut up as soon as you're pregnant. And Paolo's father will kiss your feet for that."

"I'm sure you're right, Rosanna," said Cecilia. "I'll tell him that when I see him to...Oh, that lemon tart looks yummy. And one custard. Grazie, Marcello. I'm seeing Paolo after dinner and I'll tell him that it's either me and babies or his mother and complaints. Listen to me going on about my love life when you feel so distressed about yours. I'm so sorry. Have you made any progress? You won' tell me who it is. You suffer in silence, and I wish you'd let me ease your anxiety by telling me who this man is who has perturbed you so. But I don't know of one unmarried man who doesn't want you to look his way, so, you're the last person in the world I'd ever expect to be at a loss for a man's love. After all, you're young, vibrant, beautiful, with personality for days."

"Well, it doesn't seem to be enough for the man of my heart because I've never seen him show interest in me. I saw him smiling right at me one day, but I was in a crowd, so, it could've been anyone else in the crowd he was smiling at. Oh, Cecilia, I find him so exciting. So masculine, yet at the same time there's a slight hint of sweet vulnerability. I can't tell you who he is because I want to hold this magic gift that is him away from the eyes of the world so that I may fondle it with the gentle fingers of my weeping soul until an angel kisses that gift and it will grow lovely, golden wings that'll send our magical love soaring to the stars! Oh, if I could only let you know how much I like him. No, love him. Yes, Cecilia, I love him. Oh, I know that is a reckless statement because I haven't dated him yet, but I feel it. I know it."

"Nobody could ever call you reckless in word or action. You've just given me advice that I'm sure will bring about my marriage to Paolo, so, as your best friend, I'm asking you to consider taking a tidbit of advice from *me,* now."

"I'm almost at my wits end, Cecilia, so, I might dare baring my soul to get some advice from you. Hmmm, oh, my heart is pounding. Oh, decision! Do or don't? I gasp as I walk along the precipice above the void of uncertainty! Oh! Do I dare?"

"Please try? I desperately want to help you see your happiness fully realized. We've shared so many deep secrets. Wept together.

Laughed in sunshine and in rain. I've suffered with your every pain as you have mine. We are friends that people could only hope that they...The soup was fabulous, Marcello. Your mother is a genius. Mmmmm, oh, and this chicken looks marvelous."

Marcello smiled at Rosanna as he removed Cecilia's empty soup bowl, and he felt slightly giddy from the aroma wafting up into his nostrils from the many roses that were stuffed into Rosanna's hair.

"Please take just a smidgen of my advice? No, not you, Marcello. Let me help you, Rosanna. Grazie, Marcello."

"Prego, Cecilia. Rosanna? A pastry?" he asked, smiling and wishing she were his.

"Hmmm, just three pastries for now, grazie, Marcello. I must commend you on that sandwich because it was beyond my expectations. You amaze me with your culinary skills. Some would say only a sandwich, but I say, art. Mastery. Genius. So, I've decided to have another one. But this time, a veal cutlet sandwich with a small splash of your special sauce, a slice of roasted eggplant on it, about a tablespoon of sour cream, a slice of

Swiss cheese, two strips of crispy bacon, and one leaf of romaine

lettuce. Please," Rosanna said before she bit into a pastry.

"Immediately," said Marcello, grinning as he hurried away.

"Are you thinking about taking a touch of my advice?"

"I've already thought it over, Cecilia, and I've decided yes.

I'm sure it'll help lift away this burden I've endured too long on

my shoulders."

"Oh, wonderful!"

"Please begin."

"Grazie," said Cecilia, smiling. "Well, what I want to suggest

is that knowing the overwhelming and spectacular effect you have

on men, that perhaps he feels he doesn't have a chance because

you rarely allow yourself to be escorted anywhere, or of course, it

may look as though you *are* being constantly escorted because you

are always surrounded by many men, so, he might have the idea

you're flippant about serious relationships. That you laugh at love.

Oh, we both know that's not true, but he may not. Now, I'm not

saying he's stupid for not knowing that by just looking at you and

how you exude the very essence of true love, but you know how sometimes you have to tell a man what he wants, and he's grateful for it. So, why don't I feel him out? Don't look at me that way, Rosanna! I only meant, I'd ask him, in my most subtle manner, what he thinks of you. I'd casually ask...You have sauce on your chin. Yes, right there."

"Oh, how clumsy of me. Did I get it all?" asked Rosanna, patting her napkin on her chin.

"Yes, you got all the sauce on your chin, but there's a tiny bit on the end of your nose."

"Oh. Hmmm, and now?" Rosanna asked her.

"Perfect. Then he might say something about *you*. About how he feels, or thinks about you."

"And it would be subtle? It has to be subtle. I wouldn't want him to think I'm, well, groveling for his affection. Not until after we're married. Oh, if *only*! Me! Married! And pregnant! Yes! Yes, yes, yes! Cecilia, you're brilliant. I adore you. Your advice has brought me such hope. Paolo is a fool for not pleading with you to marry him in the very next moment his gaze falls upon you. How can he not see that his life is not a life at all until he...Marcello!

Please bring me the pastry tray again? Until he sees you in the same light as I do. Shine on him more. You absolutely must."

"I will. I'll follow your advice as I'm ecstatic that you've decided to follow mine. Look at that street, Rosanna! Can't you just envision you and I pushing prams together with a giggle of our children prancing alongside us? It could be a reality within sudden years. So, who is he?"

"Lean closer so that I can whisper the name of my hope."

"I'm ready. Not now, Marcello. Grazie," said Cecilia.

"Giorgio Tomasino," whispered Rosanna.

"Him? That shop of his is a gold mine! Not that money should ever play a part in love, but it helps to feather a nest. Giorgio is their youngest son and the only son to take an interest in the family business. He's actually improved the business. He has excellent taste, too. Well, it's obvious that you do, as well, for selecting him."

"But if only *he* would select *me*. He's always smiling and laughing. Every woman I know has walked away from him totally satisfied because Giorgio certainly knows material, patterns and colors. He can just look at a woman and know what would suit her best. But I can't go into his shop. I can't. If I did, and he came up to me and said, 'May I help you, today?' I'd panic and say, 'Yes, marry me!' Oh! His smile! His eyes! His hair! And he's intelligent. With a future, too. His father retired last year and handed the business over to *him*. It could be ours. Together. Every day I could watch him flipping out lengths of material for women to admire. Women standing before a mirror as he drapes marvelous material around them to prove his genius in the selection of what would make them look like goddesses. Be still my heart! Such fantasy! Marcello! The bill! Please!"

"Rosanna! You must breathe deeper!" exclaimed Cecilia.

"My thoughts whirl! Ohhh, it happens every time I think of Giorgio! And that's almost every moment of every day. I'm an excitable woman as all men must fantasize I am. Please tell me about this subtle approach you mentioned. Make this day an enchanted memory for me that I can look back on with complete happiness and remember that on this very day, I stepped closer to the altar with Giorgio."

"Well, after we leave here, we walk over to his shop, and you stand across the street from it. You look nonchalant. You smile. Not at him, of course, but away at perhaps a lamppost. Every now and then you casually inspect the contents of your shopping basket. You're coy. Meanwhile, I'm inside his shop. Giorgio will ask me if I'm uncertain about a pattern or color of material I want, then I tell him that I admire the color of your dress, and I point you out to him. He glances out the window at you standing across the street so that he can examine the color of your dress, then I ask him if it suits your coloring. If it brings out your stunning beauty or if it hides it. Takes away from it. Then, while he's looking at you closer, I'll ask him if personality is a determining factor in reaching a decision on what color, fabric, or style of dress a woman should wear and if he would suggest any changes in the style or color of the dress you're wearing. You see? He'll offer his opinion, then you'll know a little of what he thinks of you. Then, the following day, you go into his shop and express your opinion of what I told you he said. And so, a conversation has begun!"

"Oh, I'm beginning to tremble! How brilliant! Whew! I can

hardly breathe. There. I'll leave Marcello half my change and let him see me kiss a rose and lay it on the tray with the change. Of course, the rose he'll cherish as the biggest tip he got today. Oh, it's so tragic how so many hearts will be broken when I marry Giorgio. That's the burden of beauty. Guilt. Over unintentional crimes of the heart," said Rosanna, then she sighed.

"But! You must have the courage to walk into his shop in order to carry through this plan. You can do it and I know you'll do it with finesse, as you do with all things. I've always admired your strength, Rosanna. If Paolo had an ounce of your strength, he could have told his mother he was marrying me, ten years ago."

"I'll do it. Oh, I hope Giorgio tells you that he finds me ravishing. Let's go. You walk ahead of me so that I can drop a rose or two behind me that I've plucked from my shining hair. I won't kiss the roses because that would surely crush Marcello's heart. He's such a tragic figure, as well as an excellent cook and waiter," said Rosanna as she tossed roses and blew farewell kisses to young men as they tried catching them in midair.

· · · · · · · ❀❖❀ · · · · · ·

Giorgio looked over at the shop door when the bell jingled, and he saw Cecilia enter, then begin admiring bolts of material.

Mrs. Lamantia agreed with his suggestion, of course, then Giorgio cut the length she required, packaged it, and then after being paid for it, he hurried to the door to open it for her while smiling and thanking her again.

Cecilia lingered by the shop window with a frown, which was Giorgio's immediate cue to approach her so that he could solve her indecision with finesse.

"May I help you, Cecilia?"

"I hope so. I feel so distressed because I've been to three shops and sorted through every bolt of material on display and in their stockrooms, but I can't find the color I want."

"I have the largest selection in the village, but if I don't have what you're looking for, I can order it in. Did you bring a swatch of the color you'd like?"

"Well, no, but I'm looking for exactly the same color as that dress my friend Rosanna is wearing now. Her aunt sent it to her from America. She's standing right across the street. See?"

Giorgio turned his head to look out the shop window, and when he saw Rosanna, he said: "Oh, yes. So beautiful."

"I meant the color of her dress," said Cecilia.

"Why, that's what I meant, too."

"Oh. Hmmm, I'm curious. Do you think *that* color would suit *me*? I mean, my personality, as well? Do you think that color *she*'s wearing, compliments her?"

"Almost any color would look good on her because of her black hair and the color of her skin."

"I see. Hmmm, I was wondering if that color of red signified something about the person wearing it," said Cecilia.

"Well, there are many reds, you know, which makes it difficult to sense a particular thing about the person wearing a red, but the color of red Rosanna's wearing would also suit *you*. Actually, I have a bolt of material put aside for her because I thought the color would look wonderful on Rosanna. It's a remarkable yellow with a very nice pattern, so, I felt that it'd be perfect for her, however, she never comes in here. Why don't you come in again tomorrow, and by then I'll have had time to search my stockroom for a similar red as the one that Rosanna is wearing, now?"

"So, what you're saying is that I could wear that red color, and that you've been saving some material for Rosanna to consider."

"Yes."

"Fine. I'll come back tomorrow and I'll tell Rosanna about the yellow material, and you never know, it might pique her interest. Ciao, Giorgio."

"Ciao, Cecilia."

She hurried across the street, took Rosanna's arm, then they walked out of sight of Giorgio's shop before they stopped to talk about what he'd said.

"And he's been saving it for *me*?" asked Rosanna, wide-eyed.

"Yes, he said just for you."

"Oh, this could mean more than simply material, Cecilia! He *has* noticed me with at least *some* interest! He's pictured me in yellow! My body clad in the material he's chosen! Yes! Clinging to my fabulous form! How intimate! Dare I think he's naughty? Oh! Virginity perches on my shoulder, ready to take wing the moment he kisses my bared shoulder!"

"Oh, no! Rosanna! Quick! Control yourself! Think of your spotless reputation!"

"Ahhhhhhh, and he speaks my name."

"Thank heavens you didn't scrape your knees when you fell to the ground. That's it, you just prop yourself up against the wall and I'll fan you with my purse. Now you can see what love does to you, Rosanna. What I've felt for too long. Paolo feels the same. He soaks my blouse with his tears when I tell him, 'No, you can't put your hand inside my blouse, Paolo.' And 'No, Paolo, I don't feel right about you walking me all the way home with your hand on my buttocks.' Oh, sweet, true love. It causes so much confusion. Yes, and much frustration, as well. Now you and I suffer together. Paolo, too, of course."

"Tomorrow. Oh, I can't bear the wait!" Rosanna exclaimed.

"You mean you're going to start dieting tomorrow? But why? There's absolutely nothing wrong with your weight."

"No! Waiting to walk into Giorgio's shop tomorrow."

"When you do, I'm sure you'll win his heart," said Cecilia. "I know so well the effects of love. Love slows hours when you're waiting, and at other times it speeds them when you're with the one you love. Love has so many forms. Right now it's a teardrop teetering on your eyelid. Ready to leap away from the wailing of your lonely heart. Love can be so many tears. Love can be so wet."

"Wet. Oh-oh! Help me up, Cecilia. I have to find a washroom to tinkle in."

Was is it possible? Could it have been some clever ruse by an emissary? 'No, it couldn't be,' thought Giorgio. Cecilia had only walked into his shop to hopefully find a color of red similar to the red of Rosanna's dress.

If she'd been truly interested in him, Rosanna would have accompanied Cecilia, instead of standing across the street looking as beautiful as always. It just couldn't be that she was shy. She who had every unmarried man's heart beating faster the instant she appeared before them.

Rosanna could have her choice of any man in the village. Men with much more money than him to lavish luxury upon luxury at her feet. Giorgio wondered if he'd been too bold when he'd told

Cecilia that he was saving a bolt of material for Rosanna. Tomorrow, Cecilia would probably come into the shop and tell him that Rosanna didn't like yellow.

Giorgio fretted for the rest of the day about his feeble attempt to entice Rosanna into his shop, then later in the day, his mother sat beside him at the table, her arm around him as she stared into his eyes and asked him why he wasn't able to eat his dinner.

She'd wept when she had thought the dinner she had prepared had lacked something; perhaps too much of a certain spice, or not enough of it. Giorgio had kissed her hands and told her that it wasn't the food; that he wasn't hungry, but his mother couldn't be placated as she laid her head on his chest and sobbed.

His father had thrown up his hands and left the table as he told her that the dinner was perfect and that Giorgio's loss of appetite was probably because he was in love.

His mother had grasped Giorgio's cheeks, then laughed with joy, and then she'd asked him whom had stolen his heart. But Giorgio was afraid to speak Rosanna's name because his mother might tell him that Rosanna Tucciano was beyond his reach, and then he wouldn't have been able to bear the pain.

He thought he'd never sleep that night. The countless, shimmering stars were singing too loudly. The moon seemed to be like a gigantic, magical balloon attached to a long string that was clutched in Rosanna's sweet, dimpled hand, and because it was her holding the string, the moon was swelling larger and larger until Giorgio thought it would burst with pride and joy.

He closed his eyes because he was becoming dizzier from watching the stars spinning, then shooting like fantastic fireworks across the deep purple sky, and then he opened his eyes to brilliant gold sunlight caressing his tingling body.

He sat up quickly, rushed to the window, threw it open, and then listened to the birds twittering and jabbering as he looked out at this new day that had opened like a beautiful, headily scented, yellow rose.

Yellow. The color of the fabric that he hoped Rosanna would love and wear and thank him for saving it just for her to adorn her sensuous, stupendous frame with. He readied himself for the day, then almost skipped downstairs and into the kitchen, and then he smiled and said: "Buon giorno! Mama, I'm starving."

"Thank God! The blessed virgin! All the saints! At last your appetite has returned! Oh, I've been so worried because I thought...I thought that...Oh, Giorgio! What would you like?"

"Six eggs. Sausages and more sausages. Ham. Fruit. It's today. A day that I will treasure for the rest of my life. A day of hope. This is the day that the woman I love might walk into my shop."

"*Might*? My son, what woman would be mad enough not to marry you? You're so handsome and bright and so talented, and successful, too. Look at our home. Four empty bedrooms. Room enough for six or more children, and I have piles of baby clothes, blankets and diapers. Why *wouldn't* she come into your shop?"

"Because she has her choice of any man in the village. But today, she might be standing across from me as I hold in my hands the material she could never know is an offering of my undying admiration of her being."

"No! You mean? Is it...Yes! Only one woman answers that description! It can only be Rosanna Tucciano!"

"Yes! Such intuition! You're psychic! Mama! Am I reaching beyond my grasp? Am I a fool for hoping?"

"A perfect match! You both have impeccable taste. You're both young and pure of heart. No, my son, fear not. Go to your shop and I sense that Rosanna will appear there today. Now you must eat so that you will look your best when she sees you. Rosanna Tucciano! Oh, Giorgio!"

Rosanna bit her knuckles as she stared at the dresses she'd laid out on her bed. Which one? Which dress would hypnotize Giorgio? Cecilia had told her that Giorgio had said that any color would suit her. Or did he say *compliment* her? Was that a subtle compliment from him about more than just her dress?

Time had sprouted wings and she had to make a decision soon. Rosanna's heart was fluttering like the wings of fleeting time as she contemplated which dress to wear. And her hair. Was it as perfect as always, or had her anxiety rubbed the sheen from it?

None of those dresses, after all! Her pleated, chartreuse skirt with the purple silk blouse! The amethyst brooch pinned in the center of the bodice would not only be tasteful, but it would draw Giorgio's attention to her luscious breasts. But would that appear wanton? Oh, dear. So daring!

Rosanna finished dressing, then munched on a sandwich as she gazed at her reflection in the mirror, and then she raised her chin and walked downstairs, and into the kitchen.

"Oh, Rosanna! You look wonderful! Stunning! But it's so early in the day for...Ahhhhh! Never have you looked so happy! Your eyes glow! Now you've blushed! It must be! Rosanna, is it time? Have you reached a decision about which man will be blessed with your hand in marriage?"

"Oh, mama, I've fallen in love with a man who seems to show no love interest in me. I know that sounds unbelievable, but there is that possibility. I may be too beautiful. Too wonderful. Too perfect. Yes, perfection may be my greatest flaw."

"But the flaw could be that you haven't considered that he may be extremely shy, or he may think that you are too perfect. Yes,

Rosanna, he might feel he isn't perfect enough for you. Worthy of you. You know that all men feel that way about you."

"Yes, that's true about men, but I hope that the man of my heart will feel daring enough to tell me if there is or isn't just the spark of love in his heart for me. Now I will walk out of this house, and I will have hope. I will confront him, but I will be subtle. I'm sorry I was too nervous to eat all of my breakfast, mama. I could only finish half that chicken and eat two sandwiches, but if *he* smiles at me, I'll eat almost all the menu at a restaurant for lunch. Perhaps two restaurants. Oh, mama, I feel so happy, yet at the same time, terrified! No! I can be brave. I'll face come what may. I'll suffer rejection, then someday, I will try again to find another man as wonderful as him. I go now. Into that great uncertainty. I, Rosanna Tucciano."

"*The* Rosanna Tucciano! My daughter! Good luck in your venture, and goodbye!"

"Goodbye, mama! I love you! Oh, God!"

The jingling of the bell on the door of Giorgio's shop startled

Rosanna as she stepped inside. She turned her back to Giorgio, lowered her sunglasses, practiced the right smile, then she turned around, walked slowly by him, and toyed with some fabric on display as she felt her heart pounding.

Giorgio fumbled through the sale to Mrs. Balmetti, and thanked his lucky stars that it was close to lunch hour and most of his customers had settled somewhere to dine, leaving him alone in the shop with the sensational Rosanna Tucciano.

He sucked in his breath, said a silent prayer, then ventured over to her, and then standing beside her, he felt that the floor seemed to lift as if it would carry them up to the clouds where they could sit and stare into each other's eyes for countless time.

"My friend, Cecilia, told me that you wanted to show me a fabric. Something yellow," said Rosanna.

"Yes. May I show it to you?" asked Giorgio.

"Please do. I trust your taste. Your reputation for fine taste rings throughout the village like hundreds of bells announcing a stupendously happy, memorable and historical event that will resound beyond the most distant horizon."

"Your presence in my shop has swayed those bells to peal. My clientele will increase when it is known that you deigned to be a customer of mine because you're the best-dressed woman in the village, so, I feel so humbled that you're in my shop. I will rush away to retrieve what I hope you will find suitable."

"Grazie, Giorgio. I shall await in excited anticipation," said Rosanna, daring a wider smile.

He rushed away to the stockroom, then lifted the bolt of yellow fabric into his arms, and then hugged it, kissed it, and sighed. He was just about to walk out of the stockroom when he stopped, hurried back, laid the bolt back down, and combed his hair again.

Rosanna swirled fabrics up into the air and let them float down around her as she stood in front of the mirror to weigh the effects of the color and pattern draped on her splendid body.

She sensed Giorgio standing near her, so, she slowly turned around to face him, then they stared into each other's eyes for unknown, astoundingly silent moments before she took the first step in his direction.

Giorgio's heart was beating like the wings of a hummingbird

about to suck at a breathtakingly beautiful flower with the most
glorious nectar on earth as he took a step toward her.

"This yellow! It's sensational! I adore it!" cried Rosanna.

"Thank God! I was so worried you might not like it. I wasn't
sure. It was such a risk," said Giorgio.

"I'll take ten meters because I want to make a dress to wear to
Cecilia's wedding. I have a feeling that she and Paolo will be
making definite plans to marry, very soon."

"Oh? Uh, that's wonderful news. One day, perhaps soon, *you*
will be married, too."

"I have my dreams, and there is one man I hope will ask me to
marry him. He's handsome. Debonair. Clever. But he hasn't shown
interest in me," said Rosanna, pouting.

"I see. Well, one must realize that although something may
look delicious to some, others prefer another type of food. I have
an aunt who won't eat shellfish, whereas I love it, and I have a
cousin who breaks out in hives if he eats strawberries. I love
strawberries and luckily I don't get hives when I eat them. This
man you feel love for, may somehow and sadly prefer women with

blonde hair or red hair, so, it doesn't mean that you're lacking in beauty, but just that you're not to his particular taste. Please take heart that a compatible man will come your way someday soon."

"I suppose that could be possible. I mean, that he has different tastes. I've heard of those possibilities. Do you...hmmm. Do you close your shop for lunch?"

"No, I don't. My mother brings me lunch so that I can eat it here in case a customer comes in with an emergency."

"Hmmm, I hate eating alone," said Rosanna.

"*You*? Oh, I'm sure that won't happen because you are like a candle to dozens of handsome, eager moths. There, now your package is nicely wrapped, and I'll put it in a bag with handles for you. I'm sure you'll look marvelous in this fabric because the color seems to have been dyed especially with you in mind."

"Yes, it *is* enchanting. Well, grazie, Giorgio, and grazie too for putting this aside just for my delight. I'll definitely shop here again. Farewell."

"Farewell, Rosanna. Rosanna Tucciano."

Cecilia saw Rosanna walking toward her and she gasped when she noticed that Rosanna wasn't holding her head up and blowing kisses to all the young men who said hello to her.

Rosanna spoke a weak hello to her, sighed, beckoned Marcello to the table, and then ordered the pastry tray before she looked directly into Cecilia's eyes.

"Well?" asked Cecilia, excitedly.

"Hmmm, I'm not sure. My heart says yes, but there is a strange little bird pecking away at my hope."

"Oh? I see. Hmmm, it sounds to me like the name of that strange little bird is 'Uncertainty,' and it's not like you to not shoo that bird away because you're always so strong. So sure of...That chocolate covered custard tart with the cherry on it looks yummy. Oh, good, there's another one. Hmmm, and this one because I love pecans. Grazie, Marcello."

"Prego, Cecilia. Rosanna? A pastry?"

"Oh, yes, Marcello," she said, gazing at the pastry tray.

Marcello desperately hoped that Rosanna would glance up for even a split second from the tray.

"Are you going to show me the fabric? I'm dying to see the color he chose for you," said Cecilia.

"I'll tear open the end of the package, so you can have a peek. Look at the ribbon he used to tie it with. Hmmm, I'll have the lemon turnover. Oh, and it has ricotta cheese stuffed in it, as well. Just two for now, Marcello. Grazie. Lovely ribbons."

"Ribbons?" he asked. "Well, yes, the stripes of chocolate icing on that pastry do look like ribbons, I suppose."

"Oh, no, not on the pastries, Marcello," said Rosanna, smiling up at him.

His heart sank, but he was able to muster up a smile for her before he walked away with the pastry tray.

"Poor Marcello," said Rosanna. "You see how lovely the package has been wrapped? Giorgio usually uses simple string to wrap parcels with, but he used ribbon for mine. He's such a tease that it's driving me wild with frustration and desire. Well? Did you give Paolo an ultimatum last night?"

"Yes, I did. I told him exactly what you said about being a real man, and his eyes almost popped out of his head. He staggered back like I had stabbed him. Paolo pounded his fists against his head and his chest, and then he shouted as he wept. He fell to his knees, moaning and groaning. But Paolo's quite quick. He jumped to his feet and held his mother back as she tried to beat me with a broom for causing her son such anguish. But his father said, 'Ay!' And after he threw his newspaper away, he left the house mumbling and swearing. I've always known that his father was on my side. I just placed my hands on my hips, raised my chin and walked out of the house, listening to her screaming curses at me. Her son. Her baby, she screamed. Her *baby*? Paolo's miles beyond twenty-five. He'll be twenty-six in three weeks. He pounded on my door all last night. He was totally drenched by the fourth time he came back because every time he did, my father dumped a pail of water on him to get Paolo to go home, so, I didn't get to sleep 'til early this morning because Paolo was singing love songs to me. But they were hard to hear over the shouts of my mother."

"Good for you! It's about time you played hard to get. If he doesn't kill himself, there's a good chance he'll propose to you by the end of the week at the latest, and I wouldn't be surprised if he does it today. Men are so emotional. Well, except perhaps Giorgio. I'm not sure if he...I'll start with the soup, Marcello, then, hmmm, the fricassee tempts my soul, but pork or beef? Hmmm, yes, the beef fricassee, Marcello. Oh, and the stuffed pork loin looks interesting. Yes, a small portion of that, too, with extra sauce, and...hmmmm, what else? More decisions. Uh-huh, yes, and add six chicken wings and four potatoes. I'll have the, um...Oh, yes, the oven-roasted potatoes, instead of the mashed. Oh, and please bring the pastry tray back with my drink. Grazie, Marcello."

"Prego, Rosanna, I hope you...You're so...Oh, uh, please excuse me. I'll...Your selection is perfection," he told her.

Marcello hurried away to place Rosanna's order before taking Cecilia's, then on his way back to their table to ask Cecilia what she wanted, another customer beckoned him.

"Hmmm, I'm sure that he's slightly insecure," said Rosanna.

"Insecure? Giorgio? That's hard to believe. What makes you think so?"

"Because while I was making the purchase in his shop, he stood on a wooden box."

"I see. Yes, that does sound a bit insecure," said Cecilia.

"Cecilia?" asked Marcello, returning to the table.

"Hmmm, the fish in tomato sauce sounds nice. Okay, I'll have that and...hmmm, let me see. Yes, the sausage casserole, a beef pie, and mashed potatoes. And I might want to try the lemon and garlic chicken after that, Marcello. Grazie. On a box? I mean what does height have to do with love?" Cecilia asked her.

"Pardon?" asked Marcello.

"No, not you, Marcello."

He hurried away, and Marcello felt confused, as usual, because he often had difficulty determining whether they were referring to him, someone else, or the meal he'd served them as Rosanna and Cecilia chatted, however, he wished that sometime very soon he'd be the main topic of Rosanna's conversations.

"I don't know why he'd want to stand on a box because Giorgio's tall enough to reach your bosom. Well, slightly shorter than that, but what does it matter? Height doesn't come into play when you're lying down, so, it doesn't make sense that he should feel insecure," said Cecilia.

"I'm sure that's his only reason for not asking me for a date. At least I hope that's the only reason. I *am* very beautiful, so, it just can't be because I'm homely that he's not interested in me."

"You have to find some way to reassure him. Oh, if only that were the reason that Paolo is hesitant to marry me! But no, it's my figure. I mean, you know as well as I do that there's nothing wrong with my appetite because I eat as much as you do, but I can't seem to gain a pound. You wear food so well, too, and that's why Paolo's mother is so eager to have him marry you. All his family are robust. Oh, my problem would be solved if I had your perfect body. Why, you must be the size of two of Paolo's plumpest aunts. I envy you, Rosanna."

"Shush! Envy is a sin! *Now* who's sounding insecure? You have so many other wonderful qualities. Take your height for example. Do you know of another woman in this village as tall as you? No, none. And very few men. Paolo looks up to you in more ways than one."

"Well, he hasn't dated anyone else in the past ten years. It's just that mother of his. Ay! I've told her at least a hundred times that I have six brothers and seven sisters and that my mother has the same figure as I do. But no, she just won't listen. Well, once Paolo proposes to me, she'll see, because my family will be traveling here for our wedding, then once she sees my mother, that should shut her up. Hah! Such peace that will be, at last!"

Marcello returned with their lunch selections, then after he bowed, he rushed away.

"Here. See what Giorgio chose for me," said Rosanna, trying to smile.

"Oh! Oh, marvelous! Absolutely beyond sensational! Such a yellow! And the floral print on it! Oh!"

"Tiny roses. Pink and orange roses with a hint of hyacinth leaves. So lovely. Just think of the possibilities if I make a two-piece dress. A plain skirt of a complimentary color to go with a blouse of this material, or a plain blouse to go with the skirt. I plan to make a long jacket as well out of this, and I can wear it over another of my fabulous dresses. Giorgio's broadened my scope. His taste is breathtaking."

"What a striking couple you two would make. That you *will*

make. Just think about it. Rosanna and Giorgio Tomasino! The talk

of the village! It's so...Mmm, mmmmmmm, this sausage casserole is

divine. How is the fricassee?"

"Perfection. You know, twins run in my family. Wouldn't it be

wonderful if I had two or three sets of twins first? Oh! I tremble

when I think of Giorgio in a nightshirt! Hmmm, perhaps pajamas.

But then, I'm such a sensual woman, so, I'm now imagining him

in just his undershorts and socks."

"Rosanna! People can hear us!"

"Oops! See how I throw caution to the wind when I think of

him? It will take all my strength to remain intact while or if he's

courting me. I'm a woman of great passion, Cecilia. Yes, there's a

raging, out-of-control fire hidden behind my astounding beauty. I

am not as aloof as people may think. No, I am more than just a

pretty face with a body that drives all men wild with almost

uncontrollable desire. With all I have going for me, I could be

conceited, but that is something I could never be because I've

never been one to brag," said Rosanna, bowing her head.

"Oh, I know that so well, and I give a prayer of thanks every day that Paolo has poor taste and finds *me* more attractive than he does *you*."

"Yes, it *is* sad that Paolo has bad taste in women, but he has other qualities. One of them is that he likes my personality. That says *something* for your Paolo. You know, if I felt more confident, I wouldn't feel so devastated that Giorgio is obviously too shy or insecure to approach me, and that if I had confidence in myself, then I could approach *him*. I feel as if...Mmmmm, the fricassee is wonderful, but so is this. Here, have a taste of this stuffed pork loin, Cecelia. As if, well, as if I might be in some way unattractive to him," said Rosanna, patting her pout with her napkin.

"*You*? How could that be possible? He's a man, isn't he?"

"Well, he *did* happen to mention that some men are more interested in blondes or redheads."

"No!" exclaimed Cecilia in wide-eyed disbelief.

"Odd, isn't it? Almost perverse. Twisted. I mean, look at my glorious, shining, raven hair. And naturally wavy, too. I was such a beautiful child because I had a mass of sensational, black curls. A dark Shirley Temple. Slightly more talented than she was, though.

All my relatives loved my acting and singing, and I was my parents greatest pride. Unfortunately, I was a little too heavy to tap dance better than other girls, so, I had to rely on my beauty and my superior brains."

"And don't forget your high morals, Rosanna, and of course, your modesty. Women half as beautiful as you, boast about their looks, but you're so much more reserved. Unaffected. Paolo often remarks on your nose, too. It's regal. All your family have beautiful, large noses. The largest of anyone else's in the village. Your sense of smell is amazing. And your..."

"I just thought! I'm so impressed with this material and that Giorgio held it back from display until I looked at it, so, a simple thank you and one of my amazingly beautiful smiles isn't sufficient. I should take a bottle of wine as a gift to him for his generosity. A bottle of the best wine in the region. Yes! Cecilia, right after lunch, I'll buy gorgeous wrapping paper! Ribbons! A bow, or perhaps two! Oh! This could be the answer! Marcello! The pastry tray! Please! What do you think?" Rosanna asked her.

"Brilliant! I just know it'll work. I can see it now. His hands holding one end of the bottle and yours holding the other. Neither one of you can let go of the bottle as you gaze into each other's eyes. Time stands still. The only sound is the slight rustle of angel wings. Then you move closer, then closer, then you...Hmmm, I'll have the strawberry tart. Oh, and a piece of that hazelnut cream cake with gelato. *Lime* gelato. Grazie, Marcello. Then you say to him that this is just a very small token of your appreciation. That he's stirred your heart with beauty beyond comprehension."

"Rosanna? Cake?" asked Marcello, his heart fluttering.

"Yes. The chocolate and banana cream looks interesting. Grazie, Marcello."

"Like the...Uh, the cream of your...Immediately, Rosanna," said Marcello, blushing. He rushed away from their table before Rosanna and Cecilia could see him blush even deeper.

"Tragic. Poor, suffering Marcello," said Rosanna. "Oh, well, I knew ever since I was a child the devastating effect I would have on men. I only hope that if Giorgio asks me for a date, that half the men in the village don't slash their wrists. God only knows what will happen if and when I announce my *marriage*. I adore wearing bright colors, so, I'd hate having to wear black to all the funerals of men who had lost all their dreams of complete happiness with me. Unintentional crimes of the heart. So sad. So utterly tragic."

"Che sera, sera, Rosanna. As you said, beauty can be such a burden, especially a beauty such as yours. Matchless. I wish that I...It's Paolo! He looks as if he's seen a ghost! Oh, no! He's carrying flowers! Somebody's dead!"

"You can bet it isn't his mother. She's an ox. Yes, he *does* look like he's in deep shock. Perhaps there's been a train accident."

They stared out from the outdoor patio at Paolo walking toward them, carrying a large bouquet, and looking terrified. He made his way to their table, then he stood staring at Cecilia.

"Paolo?"

"Cecilia. I...Oh, Cecilia," he said, collapsing to his knees.

"Paolo! You'll ruin your best suit! And why are you *wearing* your best suit? Is it your father? An uncle or aunt? Who died? Speak to me!" cried Cecilia, gaping down at him, wide-eyed.

"I want...I...I want you to be the mother of my children. Oh, Cecilia! Marry me!"

"Ah! At last! At last!' shouted Cecilia, tumbling off her chair, and into his arms.

"Ohhhhh, Cecilia! My most precious love! Forgive me for waiting so long!"

"Hush! We'll have forever now, my love! Rosanna! Run and get that bottle of wine! We can have *two* weddings! Oh, Paolo! Paolo! Paolo!"

"Congratulations on your betrothal of wedded bliss! Oh, what joy I witness!" cried Rosanna. "Give Paolo the rest of my cake! I'm going now! To love! Oh, I *hope* to love! To realize my dreams! Pay the bill! Please!"

Rosanna grunted as she stepped around Cecilia and Paolo as they knelt on the ground, hugging, and when Marcello heard the loud moans and cries, he rushed out onto the patio, but Rosanna was already far down the street.

"Aw, Rosanna had to rush away. Oh, well, if I'm lucky, she'll be back tomorrow. Cecilia? Paolo? Coffee?" asked Marcello.

"No! Champagne! Champagne for everyone!" exclaimed Paolo, hugging a weeping Cecilia.

While Rosanna hurried from store to store for a bottle of wine and gift wrap, Giorgio anxiously paced his shop, stopping every few moments to heave a big sigh, as his mother served customers and worried about him.

She knew that he had fallen in love with the most desirable young woman in the village, and she felt proud of him for having the courage to challenge all other suitors who were hoping to have Rosanna Tucciano simply smile at them.

But would Giorgio take that leap toward Rosanna? Would Rosanna scoff at him? As the tension grew, Giorgio's mother bit down on her bottom lip while she counted out change to the customers, and she knew that Giorgio was about to explode because he'd spent months looking for the bolt of material he had hoped would bring him closer to Rosanna, and now it was in her possession at less than cost.

Giorgio recalled how he'd looked up beyond Rosanna's more than ample bosom and into her eyes when he'd been holding the bolt of yellow material in his arms, and he'd felt blessed.

· · · · · · · ❀✳❀ · · · · · · ·

Rosanna rushed into the florist shop and had them tie a small bouquet to the beautifully wrapped bottle of wine, and she wondered if she should buy an oval crystal bowl to lay the gift in.

She strutted down the street, the gift cradled in one arm like the baby she dreamed to be hers and Giorgio's, and Rosanna stopped several times to take a deep breath to gather her courage.

And then there it was. The door that might lead to love eternal. The jingle of the bell on the shop door sent tingles right down to her toes as Rosanna entered the shop.

Giorgio's mother rushed to the back of the shop to put the kettle on and to tell Giorgio that Rosanna Tucciano had deigned to enter their shop again.

Giorgio gasped, then he stepped nervously out from behind the curtains and hurried to assist Rosanna. His heart was jumping up and down with joy.

"What you did for me was astonishing. You knew that no other woman except I could do justice to that material. A verbal expletive is beyond insufficient. Something more tangible was needed, therefore, I have brought you a gift, and I hope with all my heart that you will find it to your liking. Perhaps not even this can express my gratitude. You have astounded me with your generosity and good taste," said Rosanna, handing him the gift.

"A gift from Rosanna Tucciano is priceless to anyone fortunate enough to be the recipient. Just to have the village know that you have graced my humble establishment is reward enough. How did you arrange to have angels wrap it? Such taste. Such a pity to destroy this exquisite objet d'art by tearing even a corner of the giftwrap to peek inside at the wonders that lay within."

"Oh, please do. Throw away your inhibitions. Be reckless. Besides, I value your opinion. If I leave without knowing that I have succeeded in repaying you with something barely touching adequate, I could never sleep this night," said Rosanna, smiling down at him.

"It is only at your insistence that I tear apart this precious giftwrap you've chosen for my delight. Hmmm, what can it be? Ah! Wine! And *you* selected it! Obviously, the vintners are blessed this day. Please don't think I'm being too familiar, but may we share a glass of this magical vine nectar?"

"I have no other engagements, so, perhaps just half the bottle if you say you wish to share it with me. It would please me."

"I'll put the closed sign on the door because an interruption would be in bad taste. Please excuse me while I open the bottle. That settee over there should be suitable for our purpose. To drink wine, I mean."

"Yes, that settee over there will be perfect. For sharing the wine, I mean," said Rosanna.

Giorgio raced to the back of the shop, then after kissing the neck of the wine bottle, he held it to his chest, threw back his head, and then sighed.

"Giorgio! Drinking during shop hours?"

"No, never! Mama! She wants to have wine with me! I've closed the shop!"

"Rosanna Tucciano and my son sharing wine? This is an omen! I sense the sound of a grandchild crying. Yours and..."

"Mama! This isn't even a date!"

"But it's still daring, Giorgio, to be so near her with love in your heart. Thank God I am here because with the shop closed, people might gossip. I can chaperone by peeking through the curtains. Oh, I trust *you*, but I'm not sure how a young woman even with a reputation as pure as Rosanna's might react alone with you, because of your tremendous charms."

"No, mama. She is beyond reproach. And her *control*. Why, the handsomest men in the village are constantly throwing themselves at her feet, but she is never tempted by lustful arousal, and that must be difficult for a woman such as she with raging hormones because she is perfectly ripe. At the very pinnacle of young womanhood. No, mama, it is I who may falter morally. But not with you here. If I stumble, I want you to rush out and slap my face until I regain my composure, then we can both beg her forgiveness at my audacity for presuming she might allow me to kiss her hand. Damn this cork. Hmmmff! Nnnff-ff, there! Mama, hand me the glasses. I'll try my best not to bring shame to our family name. But! God help me! Be on guard, mama!"

"God be with you, my son. I'll be watching you. Oh, dear, I must pray."

Rosanna had watched him hurry away with the bottle of wine,

then she had bitten down hard on her purse to stifle a cry of joy. She now sensed that he was slightly shy like herself, and if she fumbled this golden opportunity of almost a date with him, she knew she would regret it for the rest of her life. But just how much of her feminine wiles should she put into action?

Rosanna glanced down at the buttons on her blouse, then blushed at the urge that suddenly nudged her sense of modesty, causing it to teeter on the brink of lascivious thought.

She gasped. She closed her eyes and prayed as she undid two buttons, then three, and then she opened her eyes to observe her decadence. It was slight, but a tad enticing. She waited a few more moments before undoing one more button.

Giorgio rushed back out to the front of the shop, pulled a small, low table over to the settee, set the glasses down, then poured the wine.

He picked up the glasses, sat down on the settee at a polite distance away from her, then handed her a glass and choked out a whimper when he saw that her cleavage display had lengthened.

"Salute," said Giorgio, then he whispered, "Nnnnn, uhhh-ohhhh, mmmmm."

"Salute. Mmmmm, adequate," she said, after tasting the wine. "The wine *I* make is of course better."

"Your talents are legend. You are a remarkable seamstress, as well. So many professional pleats in your skirt."

"Another compliment. Grazie, Giorgio. A compliment from you I treasure because of your knowledge of fine fashion."

"Prego. Hmmm, I...I, um...So, uh-huh," he stammered.

They hesitated. They dallied over their wine. They fidgeted. The silence was deafening. Then a movement of their hands. A large gulp of wine and a sigh from each of them. The deadlock had been broken.

Another moment passed, then after Rosanna inhaled the aroma of the wine that wafted from the glass that she held close to her trembling, so sensual lips, she said: "Oh! I have fabulous news! Paolo proposed to Cecilia today!"

"Superb! I'm so happy for them. Uh, she's your best friend, so, this leaves you without her close companionship while they are away on their honeymoon. I'm happy for them, but I grieve at your temporary loneliness without the comfort of her company."

"My loneliness is temporary, but yours seems to have been for quite some time because I haven't seen you dating."

"The shop keeps me busy. You say your loneliness is temporary. Is it until after their honeymoon or have you had a marriage proposal, too?"

"No, I haven't. I'm waiting. Day after day, moment to moment. Tick-tock, tick-tock. Wait, wait, wait."

"Oh? So, you expect a proposal soon?" asked Giorgio.

"Yes, in my every prayer, day and night, I hope to hear those words of everlasting love spoken to me. Four words: 'Will you marry me?'"

"Huh? You're asking me to...Oh! Uh, yes, figuratively speaking. More wine?"

"Yes, please. That material you sold me is so beautiful, however, I'm unsure of what style of dress I should make to use it to its best advantage. This skirt I'm wearing is one of my favorite patterns. What do you think of it?"

"Well, hmmm, I like the way it flows when you walk."

"You do? Grazie. And do you like the number of buttons I put on my blouse?" asked Rosanna, getting shockingly bolder.

"They look...Um, well, they...Uh, seven buttons. Four of them are undone, and, uh, considering that there are seven buttons in all, that means that three buttons are not undone. The four buttons that are undone add...They, um...You...They're so...Excuse me. I'll make up a tray of biscuits and cheese."

"Oh, before you go, Giorgio, would you please finish critiquing my blouse?"

"It's sensational! They look wonderful! The buttons, I mean!"

"But what about my complete blouse, Giorgio?"

"They look wonderful, too! I mean, *it* looks...Oh, God!"

"Giorgio! You almost fell over! Here! I'll help you stand!"

"I...Oh, no!" he cried as Rosanna grabbed his shoulders.

"The wine has made you giddy. Now you come back and sit down. The cheese and biscuits can wait. Come on, now. There, you just sit right here on my lap until you catch your breath."

"Oh, God! I, uh...Ohhhhhhh," sighed Giorgio, fainting.

"Dear saints in heaven! What happened?" cried Giorgio's mother, rushing out from the back of the shop.

"Oh, Mrs. Tomasino! Giorgio fainted! It was the wine. He drank it too fast. Poor, poor Giorgio. Thank goodness my bosom is like a big, soft pillow. Awwwww," said Rosanna as she rocked him back and forth.

"He fits so well on you."

"Yes. I am sanctuary for a man's troubles. My warm beauty, a refuge from his weariness. My body is Giorgio's for...Oh, I should leave now so that he can recuperate from the wine. Samson's downfall was his hair, and I now know that Giorgio's is wine. It's his Achilles heel. But I am a woman, therefore, none of those unfortunate faults can effect me. Even the most powerful men like Giorgio have a weak spot, and that is why there is woman. We were created more perfect. Well, some of us are in ways weak, but not I. No, I am the paragon of femininity. Aw, poor Giorgio. Mrs. Tomasino, forgive me because I didn't know about the wine's effect on your son. I'll just lay him out here on the settee, and then I'll leave."

"Grazie, Rosanna. Your heart is even larger than your body. Please excuse me for a moment while I go get a damp cloth to lay on his forehead."

"An excellent remedy. I'll stand guard because he might roll off the settee," said Rosanna, authoritatively.

Mrs. Tomasino rushed away, dampened a cloth with cool water, and then she peeked through the curtains. Her hand flew to her mouth to silence a loud gasp when she saw Rosanna begin leaning over Giorgio.

Rosanna's head lowered slowly until her puckered lips pressed against Giorgio's forehead. There was a breathtaking moment that caused both women's hearts to beat faster, then Rosanna flung away all her moral reserve, and kissed him on the lips.

Rosanna jumped back as Mrs. Tomasino jumped forward. Giorgio stirred and moaned. Mrs. Tomasino rushed to him and laid the cloth on his forehead, then she looked up into Rosanna's face, and smiled as she said: "My son's eyelids fluttered."

"Good, he's awakening. How brave of him to put hospitality ahead of his own welfare. I feel so guilty for buying him a gift of a bottle of wine, so, please forgive me. Now I've destroyed any hope of being a friend to both of you. Goodbye, Mrs. Tomasino."

"Wait, Rosanna! It wasn't the wine!"

"No! I saw! I forced him to drink it! Now he'll never talk to me again! Oh, what lengths men will go to, just to please me! I'm heartless! Oh! Insensitive! Oh!"

"Rosanna! Please don't go! Oh, no. She's gone. Giorgio! Wake up! Giorgio!"

"Huh? Mama? Where's Rosanna?"

"She left. And in tears, too."

"Oh, no! I remember now! She sat me on her lap and I was overwhelmed by the magnificence of her beauty! Did I control myself while I was unconscious? Is our family name still intact? Have I soiled it? Oh, God!"

"My son, today I witnessed your future. Yes, today my dreams came true. From this day forward, I will be the envy of all other mothers in this village. Today, my son was blessed. Today, I..."

"Oh, my God, mama! How far did I go?"

* * * * * * ❧❀❧ * * * * *

Dogs barked and ran around in circles while every person in every street stopped to stare in astonishment as Rosanna's high heels clattered her rapidly away toward home.

After the slam of her front door closing, there was silence in the street, except for the occasional worried screeches from the neighborhood cats.

Rosanna stumbled upstairs and threw herself onto her bed, and then wept uncontrollably. Her bewildered and greatly concerned family gathered around her bed, wringing their hands, whispering, crying, and asking questions that went unanswered from either Rosanna or each other.

Her mother hurried downstairs and began cooking pounds of food to placate her grieving daughter. Her sisters followed their mother; busying themselves by preparing sauces and kneading pastry dough while the ground floor of their home was darkened by dozens of neighbors' faces pressed against the windows.

Evening tiptoed through the neighborhood that was astir with whispered gossip and the howling of forlorn dogs sitting around the front doorstep of Rosanna's home.

Dark clouds drifted in front of the moon, then after they'd passed, the street was lit by rays of moonlight that revealed a lone figure walking toward Rosanna's home.

After the sudden whoosh of the neighbors' breaths being sucked in, there was complete silence, except for the slow footsteps of one person, then the dogs hurried over to both accompany and sniff at the lone figure's legs.

Rosanna sat alone in her bedroom, surrounded by many sauce-stained empty plates as she stared up at the moon and sighed. Every burp brought a stream of fresh tears.

She had abandoned her morals because of the tremendous passion she felt for Giorgio, so, now she was close to being a ruined woman. Her guilt would never allow her to hold her chin up high again while walking through the village marketplace.

Suddenly, a serenade lifted into the air and into Rosanna's ears. She rose from her chair, opened the window wider, and looked down at the street. She saw Giorgio looking up at her, and many bouquets circled his feet. He was holding a guitar and smiling as he sang his love to her.

The evening air was soon filled with a chorus of neighbors' voices, which made Rosanna's heart swell with joy. Within moments, crowds holding candles began to gather around Giorgio, lighting the elated expression on his tearstained face as he crooned to his beloved Rosanna.

She rushed away from the window, down the stairs, then she opened the front door and whooped. Relieved, happy laughter filled the street as she lovingly picked up Giorgio, then carried him into her home, and into her heart forever.

Rosanna Tucciano would now become even more beautiful as Signora Rosanna Tomasino.

The End

So Many Portraits

It was near the end of May in 1960, and the rain looked as if it would never let up as Melanie and Brianna huddled in the doorway of Julio's beauty salon.

People hurried by them in both directions, looking for refuge in other doorways, and across the street from them, crowds stood under the canopies of Henderson's department store.

"Forty-five dollars for a new hairstyle, and then a flash rain. It wasn't supposed to rain today, and it was sunny all morning, but now look at it coming down," said Brianna.

"Maybe Mother Nature's out to get you because this happened the last time you had your hair done. Well, it's coming down quite hard, so that usually means it'll stop soon," Melanie told her.

"I sure as hell hope so. Damn! Look at the time! It's ten after twelve! I'll never get to Ciccone's by one!"

"Relax, okay? It's not raining as hard as it was, and it'll only take you ten minutes at the most to buy the blouse, then you can grab a cab and get to the restaurant in plenty of time."

"But the clerk put the blouse away in the stock room for me, and with my luck, when she gets it for me, all the change rooms'll be occupied, so, I might not have time to take the tags off the blouse, then put it on, and then get to Ciccone's on time."

"So, you'll be fashionably late. Ten minutes at the most. Besides, it's a lunch, not a job interview," said Melanie, smiling.

"Look at the huge puddles. My shoes'll get soaked unless we walk all the way to the end of the block to cross over."

"I can cross over to Henderson's and get the blouse for you, and then you can put it on in the salon."

"Oh, would you?" asked Brianna, frowning.

"Sure. I can towel-dry my hair in the salon, then either Julio or Meg can run a hairdryer over it. It dries in about two minutes."

"What about your shoes?"

"They're just an old pair, and I'm going straight home, anyway. It's not raining that hard. Okay, I'll be right back."

"Oh, thanks!" cried Brianna.

Melanie winced as she stepped off the sidewalk and down into a puddle, then she dodged traffic as she made her way across the street. By the time she'd bought the blouse, and then walked back out of the store, the sun was shining again.

Brianna thanked her profusely as she hurried into the back room of the salon to change into her new blouse, as Melanie dried her hair with a towel that one of the hairstylists had given her.

* * * * * * ⟶❋⟵ * * * * * *

Less than ten minutes later, the same hairstylist had blown-dry Melanie's hair, and she was sitting in a chair, glancing through a magazine, when Brianna walked out of the back room of the salon, and smiled as she said: "Well, I'm ready to go. What do you think of the blouse?"

"It looks wonderful on you," said Melanie. "We'll hail a cab, then after I drop you off at Ciccone's, I'll take it home."

After they walked outside, Brianna was becoming more anxious when every cab that passed by had already been hired. Melanie glanced across the street, then she smiled and waved.

"Who were you waving at?" Brianna asked her.

"I don't know his name, but I know him in a way."

"From where?"

"He used to live near me when I was around seven or eight years old. I never knew exactly where, though. We probably went to the same school, and that's why I saw him once in awhile. His parents must've had a cottage near ours, too, because I'd sometimes see him during the summer, through the years," said Melanie. "I didn't see him again until years later, and then I was so surprised when he was in Acapulco at the same time as me. I was walking down a street when I looked across at the other side of it, and there he was, walking in the opposite direction. When he saw me, he waved and smiled, just like we always do whenever we see each other."

"You should say hello to him the next time you see him."

"I would, but he's never been on the same side of the street as me at anytime I've ever seen him. Other times, I've seen him passing by me on a bicycle, or in a crowd, then he just mixes in with the crowd, and then that's it. Gone."

"And you can't remember his name?" asked Brianna.

"No, but I don't think I ever did know it. You know how it is when you see people you went to school with, and all the time you were at school, you never got to meet them. I've seen him quite often since the time I was about eight years old, and every time I have, he was either across the street from me, or just walking away into a crowd, or into a store. But every time, just after I see him again, and before I lose sight of him, we always see each other, then wave and smile. When I first moved here from Kildonan, I was surprised when I saw him again, so, he must've moved here around the same time I did because I saw him the first week I was here, and a few times since then."

"Oh? Well, Kildonan's not *that* big. I'll bet that sometime you go back there for a weekend, and you asked people if they knew him, some of them must know who he is, and then you...Oh, thank God! There's a free cab!" exclaimed Brianna, hailing it down.

"Good. See? Your luck's changing," said Melanie, smiling.

When the cab pulled up in front of Ciccone's, Douglas was walking toward the restaurant, carrying a small, clear plastic box with a ribbon on it, which Melanie realized was a corsage.

She knew that Douglas had planned the luncheon so that he could propose marriage to Brianna, and Melanie hadn't told her about the surprise.

She waved at Douglas and Brianna as the taxi drove away, taking her home. Melanie entered the house, walked through to the kitchen and put the kettle on for tea, then she went upstairs to put on dry shoes.

She looked into her mother's bedroom suite, and saw her working at the sewing machine, so, she knocked on the open door.

"Hi, mother."

"Oh, hello, dear. Well? Did Brianna suspect anything?"

"*I* would've, but she didn't. I'm sure Douglas is sweating at the moment while he's trying to think of the best way to ask her to marry him. He bought her a corsage. It was lunch, not a dance he was taking her to, or a club, but then, when you think about it, a marriage proposal rates a corsage."

"And an engagement ring."

"I hope he remembered to buy one. You should've seen him. He looked terrified," Melanie said as she laughed.

"It's taken him almost a year to propose to her. Are you still thinking about having a double wedding ceremony?"

"Yes, but they may want to get married back in her home town. Keith and Douglas are close friends, and Brianna and I have become much closer friends in the past year, so, if she doesn't want to get married back home, I thought the four of us could go to the same place to get married and have our honeymoons. Brianna will probably be calling me in an hour to tell me that Douglas proposed to her, then we can discuss our plans, but that's only if she hasn't fainted."

"She might want to wait 'til after *you're* married first, so that you can attend her wedding back home."

"Perhaps. Then again, Keith and I could postpone our honeymoon so they can come with us to Bermuda."

"Keith's still thinking about getting married there?"

"Yes, he is, but I told him about so many of our relatives wanting to attend the wedding, here," said Melanie.

"Oh, to hell with relatives. There's enough weddings a year, here. Dorothy, Jean, and Marjorie were married this year, and

Kirk, Hilary, and Lorraine are planning to get married soon. Besides, your father and I'd love to spend a week in Bermuda enjoying the lovely scenery and beaches. Keith's parents will be there, too, and Tom and Barbara, as well as his sister."

"You never told me that before. Would you really want to?"

"You bet I would. I'm sure Brianna and Douglas would love a trip to Bermuda, too. And who knows? It just might push their marriage ahead, then there'd be a double wedding. I'm sure her parents would love it, and Brianna's an only child, too, so, I know they'll agree to anywhere she wishes to marry. Well, within reason. So, suggest it to her. After you speak with Keith first, of course."

"I don't have to," said Melanie. "He's already said he likes the idea of a double wedding. Keith's looking forward to being married in Bermuda because of the beaches, and the scuba diving and other things, and I have a feeling that Brianna will think it's a great idea, too. I won't mention it when she calls me because she'll agree to anything in the mood she'll be in now that she's engaged. I'll wait until the four of us get together, then she and Douglas can think it over in the next while, and decide whether they want to get married in Bermuda with Keith and I. Well, I'd better get downstairs because I put the kettle on medium-low when I came in, so it'll be boiling by now. Would you like a cup of tea?"

"Love it. I'll be right down. I just want to finish this sleeve."

Melanie continued on to her bedroom, put on a dry pair of shoes and walked across the room to look at her latest painting. She'd started painting the view outside her bedroom window, and it was a scene of the backyard with her mother sitting in a lawn chair by the garden.

She flipped through canvases that were leaning against the wall, then paused when she saw a portrait she had painted about a month ago.

Melanie thought it was odd that for so many years she had felt almost compelled to paint so many portraits of that blond young man whom she'd never met, so, she had never been able to finish painting any of the portraits because she still didn't know the color of his eyes.

She heard the whistle of the kettle, so, she leaned the canvases back against the wall, and went downstairs. Her mother walked into the kitchen just as Melanie had finished pouring the tea, and then they sat down at the table.

"Mother, you know that young man I told you about? The one I keep running into? I mean, not run into, because I always see him on the other side of the street? That guy I've been seeing for years back in Kildonan, and now here?"

"Oh, yes. The boy, or I should say young man, now. The one you find so intriguing, so, you've been painting his portrait since you were...Oh, I'd say about twelve or so."

"Well, I saw him again today. Brianna and I were standing across the street from Henderson's, waiting for a cab, when I saw him again. He noticed me, then he smiled and waved at me, just like he always does. I tried to point him out to Brianna, but by the time she looked over to where I was pointing, he'd already gone. He must've gone into Henderson's.

"Oh? You pointed him out to me once, remember? We were at the cottage, and you were thirteen at the time. But he was in a crowd at the beach, so, I couldn't determine which boy you were pointing at. He certainly seemed to fascinate you because you were always sketching or painting him from memory. You must have what? At least three dozen paintings of him, and I don't know how many drawings."

"Yes. The last time I started painting his portrait again was about a month ago, but I stopped again, just like I always do when I can't decide what color to paint his eyes. I feel I just have to paint them the right color, but he's never been close enough to me at anytime so that I could see the color of his eyes."

"You said he's blond, so, I imagine his eyes are blue."

"Hmmm, no, I can't be sure of that. They could be green or gray. Even brown. Dad's blond and his eyes are brown, so, see what I mean?"

"Yes, that's true. Same as your brother's."

"So that's why I can't paint in the color of his eyes in the paintings I keep doing of him. For some reason I don't understand, I feel I have to get the color of his eyes exactly right."

"And so you keep sketching and painting him over and over. You know, even after all the portraits you've done of him, I'll bet if you got very close to him, you'd find out that he'd look much different. Many artists, when they create a setting, like say, to illustrate a historical event for instance, they often put some of themselves into it. Like that painting you did of a family of settlers about four, maybe five years ago. I could see some of *your* features in at least two of the family members. Such as their chins and noses. Other features, too."

"I know. I don't see it, but other people do," said Melanie.

"So, you see what I mean about him perhaps not looking quite like your depictions of him on paper or canvas?"

"I can see your point, but I'm sure he looks very close to what I've painted. I mean, after all, I've been painting his portrait for so many years. Granted, his features have changed as he's matured, but I still feel that even my recent portraits of him in the past few years, are close to accurate."

"I wonder what Keith would think of your preoccupation with painting a strange young man so often?"

"Oh, it's not like that at all, because I'm not attracted to him, although he *is* quite handsome, but I just feel there's something about him. And this may sound odd, but something very familiar, and...Well, *warm* in a way. It's hard to describe how close I feel to him. I don't know anything about him because we've never met, yet somehow I feel...I'm not sure if *close* is the right word to use, but I feel that if we met someday, we'd be very good friends."

"Are you going to continue painting him after you're married?"

"I may do because I've been painting him for years. That's what I'm going to do later. Try to add more to the last painting I was working on while his features are still clear in my mind."

"And I want to get that jacket finished, too. You're so talented. I love the outfit you've designed for me to wear to your wedding. When I'm finished the jacket, I've been thinking about making some sort of hat to go with it. What do you think? Something very small, and very tasteful. Just as an accent to the outfit. Oh, well, I'll leave the decision up to you because I know whatever you design will be lovely."

"Thanks, and I'll make sure it's *very* lovely. I'll work on something tomorrow," said Melanie, smiling.

Their Bermuda wedding plans changed because Douglas had a cousin who worked for a travel agency, and he was able to get a substantial discount at a hotel resort in The Bahamas for both couples and their parents.

They had arranged a month's vacation, and Keith, Melanie, Brianna and Douglas had decided to arrive in The Bahamas two weeks before their weddings, then spend the other two weeks honeymooning, and their parents were to arrive a few days before the weddings, and then return home six days later.

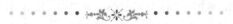

The day after they arrived at their resort hotel, they went on a boat tour, during which Melanie and Brianna chatted about their weddings that would take place in two weeks.

Later that afternoon, Melanie and Brianna were strolling along a street, carrying several purchases while looking in store windows, then seeing a small cafe with a patio, they decided to rest for awhile.

"This is a nice table. Close to the sidewalk, and a pretty vase of flowers on the table," said Melanie as she smiled.

"Yes, it is, and our waiter seemed fast and efficient, too. Oh, and he *is* fast. Here he comes with our drinks, already."

The waiter served them their cold drinks, and then as they began drinking, Melanie and Brianna talked about the people walking by on the street, then Brianna asked her: "What are you wearing dinner?"

"My white dress with the tiny green and blue flowers. I'm sure Keith'll be wearing shorts and a short-sleeved shirt with a very colorful floral pattern on it."

"I'm getting butterflies in my stomach every time I think about the wedding," said Brianna.

"I'll bet Douglas had them for weeks before he asked you to marry him. Now that he has, he's much more relaxed."

"If he hadn't asked me within another month, I'd've asked *him* to marry *me*. I just don't understand why men are so nervous about asking a girl to...Who are you waving at?"

"That young man," replied Melanie, smiling. "Oh, now I can't see him because he's just mixed in with the crowd. I'm positive it was him."

"Him, who?"

"Remember I told you about him? That guy I keep seeing since I was a little girl? The last time I saw him was when you and I were outside Julio's salon waiting for a cab so that you could meet Douglas at Ciccone's."

"Oh? Hmmm. Oh, yes, you said he was rather handsome, if I remember correctly."

"Yes, he's quite handsome," said Melanie.

"Did you ever, or do you remember his name, yet?"

"No, I don't. It's so odd. I told you before that the last time I was on vacation in Acapulco, I saw him again. Just like now. Across the street from me. It *was* him again this time. I'm certain of that. For so many years, I keep seeing him, and when I do, we always smile and wave at each other."

"Oh, it was probably somebody who just looked liked him."

"But it was the way he walked. He has the most distinctive way of walking that I'm sure I'd recognize him even if I saw him walking away from me. That young man I just saw was around the same height as him, too. Same build, and same quite striking blond, wavy hair, too, so, I'm so sure it was him," said Melanie.

"Well, this is a popular vacation spot, so, it could've been him. Does it bother you? I mean, do you think he's stalking you?"

"No, I've never felt that there was anything dangerous about him. He seems to exude a very pleasant, familiar feeling. As if we *were* friends. Very close friends. Hmmm, it's just that it's such a coincidence, and I always see him at a distance."

"Well, no matter how friendly you sense he is, he might actually be stalking you, so, it'd be a good idea to *keep* him at a distance. But then if he's never approached you in all these years, then he probably isn't stalking you."

"No, I'm sure he's not. He's around the same age as me, and since the time we were children, I'd see him...Oh, I'd say once or twice a year, and he never seemed unusual or strange. Just very nice, and always smiling at me."

"You know, I knew a girl once who I ran into on three vacations, and we waved and smiled at each other, but we never stopped to talk because we weren't really friends. But you've never even met that guy in all the years you've seen him. I suppose that because he's now grown up to be a handsome young man, and you still see him at times, a person could jump to the wrong conclusions. But in this case, he's just passing by when you see him. He's never stopped to talk to you?" asked Brianna.

"No, and I see him every six months or so. Oh, there he is, now, getting into that car!"

"You're sure?"

"Yes, because he has the same blond, wavy hair."

"Too late," said Brianna, frowning. "I didn't see him before he got into the car, and it's going in the other direction. If he's here, we might see him at the beach, or somewhere else. He might be on *his* honeymoon, too. Hmmm, no, because if he is, then he'd have been with his wife."

"Not necessarily. After all, we're not with Keith and Douglas, so, you never know, his wife could be shopping somewhere, just like we are. Or something like that."

"Do you want another drink, or look in a few more shops?"

"No, I think I've had enough shopping for one day, so, let's head back to the hotel. I'll just bet Keith and Douglas are having a great time lying on the beach and looking at all those gorgeous women wearing bikinis," said Melanie, smiling.

"Uh-uh. They're probably watching that film being made. The female lead is Brigitte Martineau. I saw her photo in a magazine, and I've seen one of her films, too. But of course, the guys are more interested in her body, than they are her talent."

"It's a French film, right?"

"Yes, it is. Oh, I forgot to tell you! The stars and the film crew are having dinner at our hotel this evening."

"Oh? The men'll love seeing a real live close-up of Brigitte Martineau, if she's as pretty as you say she is."

"She *is*," said Brianna. "The lead actor, Yves Lemieux, is so amazingly handsome. I saw one of his films, and believe me, I sure didn't read much of the subtitles because I was staring at *him*. He's such a hunk. Tall, dark and handsome, *and* with muscles, too. He has a neatly trimmed beard and mustache that makes him look very sophisticated. Mmmm, and his hair. *It* looks so great, too. It's almost black, so it sure accents his sexy eyes. Mmmm, he has the most remarkable blue eyes. Such a beautiful color of blue."

"Really? Well, while the boys are looking at Miss Martineau this evening at dinner, we can giggle like little girls and wave at Yves Lemieux," said Melanie, then she laughed.

"We just might get to meet him. Her, too."

"How old is he?"

"I'm not sure. Hmmm, I saw him in that one movie and that was...Oh, about two months ago. It was made about a year ago, and in that, he looked about twenty-five or so. Well, he could be younger without the beard and mustache."

"Was Brigitte the bombshell in that one, too?"

"Yes, she was. I wonder if they're an item? Could be. Shooting two movies in such a short time, and being on location together every day, well, that *does* tend to bring people together. They probably don't have much time to date other people."

"Some actors take their wives with them when they're working, or I've read where their wives or girlfriends visit them often on the set. I'm sure that Brigitte's boyfriend isn't going to let her spend too much time alone with this Yves character, unless he and Brigitte *are* involved," said Melanie.

"True. I think it's exciting having movie stars so close to us every day. We're going to be here for a month, so, there's a very good chance that we'll get to meet him. I mean, both of them."

"Hey, you're getting married soon. Remember?"

"Don't be silly. I'm just looking. Don't tell me that Douglas isn't gawking at Brigitte Martineau every time he sees her somewhere, especially on the beach. Bet he'll suggest we spend time wherever they go to shoot various parts of the film because he's hoping that she spends most of the time in a bikini. You know how men are," said Brianna, smiling.

"What sort of film do you think they're making?"

"I'm sure it's a romance. You know, for dinner this evening, maybe I should wear something a little more...Well, hmmm."

"Uh-huh, sure, and then you'll waltz over to their table and ask for an autograph."

"Well, of course. I mean, Douglas is probably too shy to ask Brigitte for her autograph," said Brianna, then she winked.

"Oh, yeah, right. Are you ready to go?"

"Yup. I'm going to have a long shower when we get back to the hotel, then I'll put on my swimsuit. Are you coming to the beach?"

"I certainly am because I've got to distract Keith's attention away from lovely Brigitte, *and* her bikini. Blonde?"

"Blonde. And she's almost flawless."

"Well, I'm a brunette, and that seems to be the color of hair that Keith likes."

"Don't be so sure. Men like *any* color of hair, depending on what's attached to it," said Brianna, then they both laughed.

Brianna had decided to wear a full-length, buttercup-yellow dress with very little bodice and back to it, and Melanie knew that dress was to impress Yves Lemieux more than Douglas.

At 6:30 p.m, Douglas and Keith arrived at their suite to escort them to dinner, and Melanie liked Keith's ivory colored suit, and his blue and pale orange striped tie.

Brianna was excited when they were seated at a table near the film crew, then she almost dropped her martini glass when the stars and the director walked into the dining room.

Keith and Douglas rose slightly out of their chairs when

Brigitte Martineau smiled and nodded at them as she passed by, then they grinned as they watched her until she sat down.

"Her dress is stunning," said Brianna.

"In all the right places, too," said Keith.

"It almost looks like she's wearing just white suspenders. And that very long slit in her dress is...hmmm," said Melanie.

"That's a slit? I thought she was wearing half of her dress at the front, and the other half at the back," said Douglas, grinning.

"Or she might be a very sloppy eater, so, she decided to wear two rather long napkins to dinner," Melanie suggested.

"Well, I think it's rather elegant, in a daring way," said Brianna.

"You know, I think I might have seen Yves Lemieux in a movie. That's if he's been in an American movie. No, maybe not. It's probably because he looks somewhat like some tall, dark and handsome Hollywood actor I've seen sometime in a movie. Just like I've seen so many blonde, Hollywood starlets like Brigitte Martineau," said Melanie. "Uh-huh, just as I thought. They *are* an item because Yves Lemieux just kissed her cheek. Hmmm, you never know; maybe they're planning to get married here, too."

"I'm going to wait until they've had dinner, and then I'll ask them for their autographs," Brianna told Melanie.

"You and everyone else in here," said Douglas.

"He's...Well, *sort* of attractive, don't you think? You know what I mean? Like the sort of looks most women find very exciting. Of course, I don't, though," lied Brianna.

"He's not my type, either," said Douglas, grinning.

"Right. You prefer blondes like Brigitte," said Brianna.

Their dinner conversation centered on the leading actors across the room, and after dinner, Brianna took the pad and pen from her purse, walked over to Yves Lemieux and Brigitte Martineau's table, and then Melanie was surprised when they asked Brianna to sit with them as they answered her request for an autograph.

Ten minutes later, Brianna was smiling broadly as she returned to the table, holding her pad to her chest.

"They're wonderful!" cried Brianna. "They've invited us for a drink on the patio tomorrow at noon!"

"They're not working on the film tomorrow?" asked Keith.

"No, they said something about a two-day delay because their schedule's been so heavy that they needed a break."

"Mmmm, and I like where *she's* so heavy," said Keith, smiling.

"Probably implants, sweetheart," Melanie told him.

"And I think they *are* in love. I just feel it," said Brianna.

"Lucky guy," said Douglas. "Well, not as lucky as me, though."

"Thanks, honey," said Brianna, kissing him. "Oh, I almost forgot to tell you! They told me that this movie they're making is a sequel to the first one, and it's a murder mystery. It's like those movies where the murderer is supposedly dead at the end, but in the next one, he reappears, and then he comes after them again."

"Part two, then part three, and so on. It either did well at the box office, or else this is a second try," said Keith.

"It wasn't *that* bad. In the first movie, the man who played the killer fell off a bridge into a river, and then he was swept away, so, obviously, they can make a sequel," said Brianna.

"Yes, obviously. And in the first movie, the killer was probably bumped off the bridge by Brigitte's boobs," said Melanie.

Her remark caused much laughter amongst the four of them,

and the movie stars smiled and nodded at them, which made Melanie laugh harder.

* * * * * * * ❊ * * * * * *

The following day, they sat at a patio table with the actors and the director, and Melanie noticed that most of the time Douglas and Keith stared at Brigitte Martineau's cleavage.

Half an hour later, Brigitte's costar, Yves Lemieux, apologized for having to leave so soon, and he explained that he had to drive into town to pick up a suit at the dry cleaners. Keith and Douglas, however, didn't seem to hear what Yves had said because they were smiling at Brigitte.

Melanie was becoming annoyed as the time passed because Keith and Douglas continued to pay avid attention to every word Brigitte spoke. Melanie wasn't jealous, but slightly angry at Keith because he seemed to have forgotten that she was sitting beside him, especially considering that they were being married soon.

The movie director, Bernard Marchand, seemed to find Brianna charming, but Melanie found her to be too gaga over meeting and chatting with film people, who were really just working people like themselves, although with a little fame to their credit. She became even more annoyed when everyone wanted to spend a longer time drinking and chatting because they were getting a little inebriated, except for Melanie, who was slowly coming to a boil from both boredom and Keith's obvious adoration of Brigitte.

When Bernard Marchand invited them for a cruise on his yacht, Melanie declined as she feigned a terrible headache caused by the drinks she hadn't had, and from the bright sunlight, which she hadn't been sitting in.

To her chagrin, Keith accepted the director's invitation, and then Keith told Melanie that he hoped she felt better by dinner. Melanie forced a smile as she bid them farewell, then she walked back inside the hotel, and went upstairs to her room.

She paced the room for awhile, tried to concentrate on reading a book, then she changed into her swimsuit and went back downstairs to the beach. She was far enough away from them not to be noticed as Bernard Marchand, Brigitte Martineau, Brianna, Douglas and Keith boarded the yacht.

Melanie laid back in the chaisse deck chair, trying to think pleasant thoughts, but she kept wondering if she should tell Keith to go to hell when he returned from his four or five-hour excursion with the voluptuous Brigitte Martineau.

Melanie reclined in the chaisse deck chair, making mental comparisons between herself and Brigitte, and she felt sure that she was just as beautiful as a brunette as Brigitte was as a blonde, so, she couldn't understand why Keith couldn't seem to stop gawking at Brigitte.

She disliked beauty pageants, so, Melanie had refused to compete in them all through school, and so many people had told her that she should think of a career in modeling, yet just because Brigitte had blonde hair, rather big boobs, and she was a not-so-famous movie star, Keith was mesmerized by her.

Melanie applied suntan lotion to her arms and legs, then she laid back in the chair again, checked her watch, and then after she closed her eyes, she fumed about what could possibly be happening on the yacht.

"Pardon moi, mademoiselle."

She opened her eyes, looked up, and saw Yves Lemieux smiling down at her, so, Melanie sat up and tried to smile.

"Oh, hi," she said.

"I returned and I find my friends have gone. Your friends, too. Did they go into the village?" asked Yves.

"No, they went sailing on Mister Marchand's yacht."

"Oh? Oh. Hmmm, I have bad news for Brigitte. Her mother is now in the hospital. How long have they been gone?"

"About half an hour or so. They should be back in I think I was told about three hours."

"Brigitte's mother has been quite ill. Brigitte asked to be told if there was a change in her condition. We have been expecting her to leave if her mother became worse in her condition. Brigitte has telephoned home every day. Which direction did they go?"

"That way. Toward those islands."

"I see. I promised to tell her immediately if a telephone call came to the hotel. This is terrible," said Yves, frowning.

"Why not rent a boat? Then you'd be able to find her, and give her the news," said Melanie, thinking about Keith with Brigitte.

"Oui, of course. Would you help, please?"

"Help?"

"With renting a boat. We have made arrangements with the hotel, but not with the marina. Bernard is...*Managering*? All our costs, and so I am without funds. I would pay you immediately when Bernard returns to the hotel."

"I, um, sure, of course. After all, it *is* an emergency. Give me ten minutes while I get my purse from the hotel, and then I'll meet you at the marina. Okay?"

"Thank you very much."

Melanie felt sure that when they reached the yacht, Keith would be even more inebriated and nibbling on Brigitte's ear, or shoulder, or worse. She then suddenly felt ashamed of herself for thinking about her situation with Keith, when Brigitte's mother was seriously ill in the hospital.

Melanie hurried from the hotel to the marina, met Yves, and then they went from dock to dock, trying to find a boat that was available to rent.

Every watercraft had been rented, but they were told that there was another dock about half a mile along the beach, so, they hurried toward it.

When they reached the dock, there was a small motorboat for rent, and then after Melanie paid the man, Yves started the outboard motor and they sped away from the dock.

* * * * * * * ⚜ ❈ ⚜ * * * * * *

Melanie looked back at the dock, watching it slowly getting smaller as the outboard motor of their boat roared very loudly. Over ten minutes later, Melanie looked down at her feet after she felt them getting wet, and then she noticed a puddle of water in the bottom of the boat.

The old outboard motor was making so much noise that Melanie had to lean forward, then shout to Yves: "I hope this puddle of water is from the rain, and not a leak! Well, if it *is* a leak, at least there's a big plastic bowl over there that I can use to bail the water out of the boat!"

"Pardon?" shouted Yves.

She made her way to the center of the boat, then shouted at him again: "I said, I hope this is rain and not...This motor is so loud!"

"Oui! Much noise! There is water in the boat!"

"I know! I'll use this old bowl!"

"Oui! Old boat!" shouted Yves.

"No! I said, *bowl*! Old *bowl*!

"I know! That is why water is coming into it!"

"No! *Bowl*, not boat!...Wait a minute!"

She made her way closer to him, then she held up the plastic bowl in her right hand and pointed to it with her left index finger.

"Ici!" yelled Melanie.

"Ahhhh, oui! Très bon!"

"Yes! Oui! It's all they had!...Okay! I'll start bailing!"

Melanie had scrunched up her nose when she'd been close to Yves because of the smoke coming off the loud outboard motor, then she smirked as she began bailing water while thinking about the large, luxury yacht that the others were on.

She'd definitely decided that when she and Yves reached the yacht, she'd stay in the small motor boat. She looked up occasionally at small islands they were passing and Melanie wondered if they'd find the yacht amidst them.

Half an hour later, Yves had steered the boat around five more small islands, but there hadn't been another boat in sight, then the motor started sputtering and Yves shouted to her, so, she crawled back toward him to hear what he was saying.

"Bring the tank! The motor needs petrol!"

"Okay!" shouted Melanie, then she moved back again.

She reached for the gasoline tank, hoping it wouldn't be too heavy for her to carry back to Yves, then her eyes widened and her jaw dropped when she found that it was empty.

"It's empty!" Melanie shouted.

"Bon! Bring it here!...Ici!...Oui!"

"I said it's empty!...*Empty!*"

"I will help you!" yelled Yves while shutting off the motor.

"The can is empty. *Now* what? Damn!" she exclaimed.

"It is empty? Hmmm. Ahhh, then we'll use the oars."

"Oars? There aren't any oars. Oh, God!"

"Oh, hmmm. We are near to that island. One moment."

Yves turned away from her and began taking off his shirt, then after taking off his shoes and socks, he removed his pants and dove into the water. He began kicking his legs as he held onto the boat, so, Melanie removed her light jacket she'd worn over her swimsuit, and jumped over the side of the boat to help him propel it toward the island.

Fifteen minutes later, they reached the island and tugged the almost half-waterlogged boat up onto the beach. After they tipped over the boat to drain the water out of it, they sat down beside it.

"Well, we won't be able to tell Brigitte about her mother unless they sail around this way," said Melanie.

"Oui. I was told you came here to marry. I am pleased for you. Congratulations."

"Thank you. Both of us are getting married."

"But of course," said Yves, smiling.

"No, I meant, our friends are getting married with us."

"Oh! *Two* weddings."

"Yes. So, are you and Brigitte, well, so, um, are you *together*?"

"No, Brigitte has a lover. I am sure they will marry soon."

"How nice for her. I'm sure they'll both be very happy. Have you ever been to The United States?" asked Melanie.

"No, but I am planning to go."

"I see. I thought perhaps you had. I mean, played in a movie there. I haven't seen any of the movies that you've been in, but the reason I asked if you'd been to the States is because you look sort of familiar. I mean, well, I thought I might've seen you in an American movie."

"No, but very soon. My agent is making negotiations now."

"That's wonderful. Good luck. Or as you say, bon chance."

"Thank you. Perhaps two Hollywood movies before I go back to France and no acting for me."

"Oh? You mean they won't want you to act in anymore French movies because you were in American ones?"

"Oh, no. No, I want to make my own movies."

"So, you're going stop being an actor and become a director."

"Oui."

"Well, you'd know a lot about how movies are made because you've acted in quite a few of them. I'll make sure I see the American movies you'll be acting in, and then I'd like to see the first movie you direct. I'll work hard at learning French, then hopefully by the time I see the first movie you direct, I'll be able to...Oh. Where are you going?"

"To the other side of this island to look for boats. If you signal one from here, you come tell me, and if I see one, I will come back here where we are now, and tell you."

"Good idea. Bye," said Melanie.

"Bye."

She stood up and walked to the edge of the water while hoping that a boat would sail by soon so that they could get to the yacht and tell Brigitte about her mother.

Melanie strolled along the beach, picking up shells, examining them, and thinking about Keith. She walked to the palm trees she saw far down the beach, then turned around, walked back along the beach to the palms trees far past the boat. After doing that several times, and not seeing a boat sailing by out on the ocean, she sat beside the boat.

· · · · · · · ⊱⋆⋅⋆⋅⋆⊰ · · · · · · ·

Yves scanned the landscape while wondering how far it was to the next island that he could see to his far right, or to the other island he could see to his far left, and he wondered if either he or Melanie might be attacked by sharks if they swam beside their overturned, leaky boat to get to one of the other islands.

The island they were on appeared to be rather big, so, he decided to walk along the beach to see what lay beyond the curve in the distance.

Twenty minutes later, he saw a large and rather nice cabin, then nearing it, he was surprised to see two small, Caucasian children run out onto the beach. The children saw him walking toward them, so, they started running to meet him.

"Hi!" exclaimed the children in unison.

"Hello. Our boat is out of petrol. It is on the other side of the island. There," said Yves, pointing his finger.

"Do you want something to drink?" asked the boy.

"Oh, yes, please. Thank you."

"C'mon!" cried the little girl as she and the small boy began running toward the big cabin.

He hurried after them, and as they neared the cabin, Yves saw a young couple sitting on the porch. They introduced themselves as

Joan and Scott Johnson, then invited him inside for a drink.

"Not many boats come by our way," said Scott.

"Oh, hmmm. Can you sell us some petrol?" asked Yves.

"Afraid not. No gas, either," replied Scott, grinning.

They explained to Yves that another American couple was renting a cabin on the island, and they'd gone to the mainland to fill the gas tanks for their boats, and they wouldn't be returning until after dinner.

Yves told them that he and Melanie had run out of gas while trying to locate a friend's yacht. Scott and Joan told him that if their friends didn't arrive back on the island soon with the full tanks of gas, and if Yves and Melanie couldn't get a lift back to the mainland by someone passing by in a boat, then they'd be welcome to have dinner with them.

Yves said he felt sure that another boat would pass by soon, and then he thanked them for their hospitality.

"Tracy! Kevin! I'll have the kids run over there and tell her how to get here. She must be dying of thirst," said Joan.

"What?" asked Kevin as he ran into the cabin.

"I want you to go over to the other side of the island and ask the lady to come back here. Okay? I'd like you kids to play there for awhile, and if you see a boat, hail it, because these people have to get back to the mainland," Joan told her son.

"Okay. I'll go get Tracy. Bye!" cried Kevin as he ran away.

"Well, I hope a boat *does* come by soon, although this is far off the usual path they take. Last time I saw a boat was an hour before Tim and Judy left here for the mainland," Scott told him.

"Oh? Well, perhaps we will see another very soon," said Yves.

They sat on the porch, talking about Brigitte, whom Joan and Scott had seen on television, being interviewed at a gala premiere for one of her films. Scott grinned when he mentioned that he'd seen a few pictures of Brigitte taken at a beach during the filming of her last movie. They asked Yves if he and Melanie were romantically involved.

"Oh, uh, we are meeting, or is it *met*? Pardon my English."

"It's a hundred times better than our French," said Joan.

"Ah, thank you. So, we are here now to film a movie."

"That sounds great. Well, your outing is turning out to be much more romantic than you'd planned," said Scott, winking.

"Uh, well, I...Uh, we..." stammered Yves.

"Oh, there she is now," said Scott. "She's a very beautiful young woman. *Very* beautiful. You're a lucky man."

"I'll go to her," Yves said as he hurried away.

Melanie saw Yves running toward her from a cabin, and she hoped that the couple she saw on the porch would be taking them back to the mainland, or to Bernard Marchand's yacht.

"Melanie, I have some bad news. These people say that they are unable to sell us petrol and that not many boats come this way. It may be another hour before we can leave."

"I see. Oh, well, considering that Brigitte is concerned about her mother, she may have asked that they return to the mainland by now. Thank heavens there's people on this island. I'm so thirsty."

"Come, and I'll introduce you to our hosts. Yes, I think you are right. Brigitte has probably asked Bernard to take her back."

An hour later, they sat on the beach, waiting for a boat to sail by while the children played on the other side of the island where

Yves and Melanie had left the leaky boat.

"It was very nice of Joan and Scott to have invited us for dinner if we can't wave down a boat," said Melanie. "Even if we see one, they either might not see us or they might think that we're just waving a greeting to them."

"Oui. Hmmm, I like this peace here. When we are at the hotel, and working, there are so many people around."

"Yes, I suppose you don't get much time to relax. Shooting all day, and then spending time with the crew after. And of course, so many people wanting to meet Brigitte. You, as well."

"She is beautiful, so, men ask for her autograph. Brigitte loves the attention, and I don't mind waiting until she signs all the autographs because I also have to please people who want to meet us because it is good for publicity. The people who want to say hello, and to ask for autographs, are very nice, but it is tiring to not be alone until it is time to sleep. Women like Brigitte and you cause much attention from men. Brigitte loves it. Do you?"

"Me? I'm not famous at all, and I'm not a voluptuous blonde movie star like Brigitte. She's quite pretty."

"Ah, but you are so beautiful. Your hair is dark like mine and Brigitte's is blonde. In my family, we are blonde and we are brunette. Some are beautiful and some are not, and so, blonde hair on a woman is not the only thing that makes her beautiful."

"Okay, I agree, because my family is the same. Both my brother and my father are blond and they're quite handsome. It's just that men seem to find blonde women like Brigitte much more appealing. Blondes like Marilyn Monroe," said Melanie.

"There are many beautiful movie stars with dark hair. Elizabeth Taylor, Vivien Leigh, Joan Collins. Many, many."

"Oh, Elizabeth Taylor. I don't think she'll ever be anything but beautiful. Vivien Leigh, too. But me, well, some men find me attractive, and I've been told I should get a job as a fashion model, but that really doesn't interest me because I don't think I could be just a clothes hanger for fashion designers. And besides, I love eating too much," said Melanie, smiling.

"I do, too. So far, the food agrees with you, very well indeed."

"Oh? Thank you. But then I do spend an hour a day at the gym. If I didn't, I'd probably be *twice* this size."

"I am sure you'd still be very beautiful at twice your size. I think much more beautiful than Brigitte."

"Hah! Tell that to all the men around her," said Melanie.

"They would do the same with you if you were a movie star. I am sure that if Brigitte was not in movies, men would simply walk by her. Just another beautiful woman like so many others."

"Keith doesn't seem to think so."

"Keith?"

"My fiancé. The man I'm marrying soon, and the same man like other men here who think that Brigitte is so gorgeous. Well, I suppose they're right, if they're only interested in cleav...All her pretty features."

"You are mistaken. It is only infatuation. Brigitte has a name, but she is not well-known in many countries. She is very nice, and that I am sure is why many of the men find her attractive. Brigitte may marry and not be in another movie again."

"Perhaps, but for now, she sure has my fiancé's head spinning."

"No! I cannot believe that!" exclaimed Yves, frowning.

"Oh, no? From the time we sat down at the table with you,

Brigitte, and the others, he acted like I didn't exist."

"Oh, I see. I am sorry. He is blind to beauty and sees only the false light of stardom and the makeup that Brigitte wears. I had to leave the hotel today and I told everyone I had to go to the dry cleaners in the village, but I lied."

"You did? Well, I suppose watching more men drool over Brigitte must've been quite boring for you," said Melanie.

"No. I saw you at dinner last night, then today. I had to leave for the village because I...I learned that you were to be married."

"I think Keith has forgotten about that for awhile. He's done that before, but the woman he was, as you say, *infatuated* with, was married. I've never understood what he found so attractive about *that* woman, either. Oh, well, I suppose that'll change once we're married. Right?"

"Hmmm, if that is what you think," said Yves, frowning.

They fell silent, and looked out at the water while Melanie thought about Keith making a fool of himself over Brigitte.

From the moment she'd first seen Yves, Melanie had felt quite sexually attracted to him, however, she was trying her best to suppress those feelings because she had promised to marry Keith.

She felt that Keith should also try not to show how sexually attracted he was to Brigitte, and she felt pleased that Yves had told her that Keith shouldn't be ogling Brigitte.

Melanie then recalled Yves telling her why he'd had to leave the table when she'd been out on the hotel patio with Keith, Brigitte, Bernard, Douglas and Brianna. Yves had explained that he'd had to leave the table because he'd found out that she was going to marry Keith.

She felt sure that if she hadn't been engaged to marry Keith, then Yves would have wanted to start dating her. Melanie smiled while wondering what Keith would think when he learned that she'd spent most of the day with a very handsome, friendly and sensitive man, who found her to be more attractive than Brigitte.

Melanie decided to ask Yves if he had a girlfriend back in France, then after turning her head to look at him, her heart leapt when she saw that he was looking at her with those remarkable blue eyes that made her entire body and mind tingle with sexual excitement, and she knew that she could fall deeply in love with him if she didn't constantly remind herself that she'd be marrying Keith soon.

"Uh, do you have somebody you're in love with?"

"Yes, recently," Yves replied. "Do you believe in how you say, love when you first see a person?"

"Oh, I believe that can happen sometimes. Is that how you fell in love with the woman you're with now?"

"Oui, but she is already taken. She will be married soon."

"Oh? That must make you feel so hurt and disappointed. Well, I suppose we're in the same boat, so to speak," then she laughed and said: "You fell in love at first sight with a woman who is going to marry somebody else, unless she gets divorced after a few years, and I'm marrying a man who I've known for many years before we decided to marry, but he has a bit of a wandering eye."

"It is what they say, a dilemma. One I find most difficult to understand because it would be very difficult for a man to let his eyes wander away from you."

"Thank you. I'll tell that to Keith. Not that it'll help."

"Hmmm, perhaps his eyes wander away from you because he

cannot see how you truly are. He should not need to be told that you are very beautiful, and so nice a person."

"And a person who loves to eat, and I'm very hungry right now, so, let's hope that Joan and Scott will offer us some lunch, even though they've already eaten," said Melanie, smiling.

"I'll ask them. I'd love to dine with you because I like talking with you. I find you quite charming."

"I'm enjoying *your* company, too. I was thinking about how it seems that I've known you for many years," said Melanie.

"I feel as *you* do. You're so very...uh...Hungry."

"Oh, Yves! Look!"

He looked in the direction Melanie had pointed to, and Yves grinned when he saw Joan walking toward them, carrying a tray laden with sandwiches, fruit, and cold drinks.

"I figured you two lovebirds couldn't live on love alone, so, I brought you something to eat," said Joan, smiling.

"Oh, thank you. I was just telling Yves that I was hungry. You're so kind. That looks wonderful."

"Yes, this is much more than lovebirds could eat. You are so generous, and gracious," said Yves, smiling.

"Thanks, guys. I hope you enjoy this. Now I can tell all my friends that Scott and I were visited by a handsome movie star and his beautiful girlfriend. And maybe soon-to-be bride?" asked Joan, then she winked at them.

"Yes, she wants to be married very soon," replied Yves.

"In less than two weeks," said Melanie. "But sometimes he can be...Well, I won't say what I'm thinking at the moment."

"Men love to tease, don't they?" said Joan, smiling.

"Mom!...Hey, mom!" shouted Kevin and Tracy.

"They must've sighted a boat," said Joan as they ran to her.

"Mom! We waved to a big boat and they came over to us! I asked them if they'd take Melanie and Yves to the mainland, and they said they would!" exclaimed Tracy.

"You two are in luck," Joan told Yves and Melanie.

"But you can eat your lunch first 'cause the people are looking for some shells. They told me to tell you they'd be leaving in over half an hour or a bit more," said Kevin.

"Oh, good. You can finish your lunch, now," said Joan. "And

Melanie, you can freshen up a bit in the cabin before you go. We have a septic tank."

"Oh, uh, thanks," said Melanie, blushing.

"When Melanie returns, I would like to...*Freshen* your septic tank, too, please," said Yves, smiling.

After Joan and the children walked away, Melanie and Yves laughed when he asked her if she thought the septic tank would be as refreshing as Joan had said, because if it was, then they could start a new line of colognes.

When Melanie came back out of the cabin, she didn't see Yves, so, she thought he might've gone over to speak with the people who had moored on the other side of the island, and thank them for assisting them.

She then began talking with Joan and Scott, thanking them for the refreshments and lunch, when she heard the children laughing in the distance.

Melanie saw Yves and the children walking toward the porch, and she suddenly imagined that he was returning home to her. She blushed while feeling as though she were sitting on the porch of the home she and Yves had lived in for years. When he began walking up the porch steps, Melanie's breath quickened as she looked into his eyes that seemed to reflect all her dreams and wishful thoughts.

"Ah! Your face looks radiant. The sun has given a beautiful color to your very lovely face," Yves told her as he smiled.

"Um, thank you. I...you...I've freshened up, so, you're next. You got some sun, too. You look so wonderf...Um, nice."

"I must hurry. We do not want to miss the boat."

"I think I almost did. Oh! I mean, yes," said Melanie.

She watched him walking away, and then she felt a sensation very similar to panic as she imagined that he was walking out of her life and taking a great part of her with him.

Melanie couldn't understand how knowing him for such a brief time could almost bring her to the verge of tears at the thought of never seeing him again.

"I really like Yves," said Joan. "He's not at all like I thought a movie star would be. You know, sort of above the crowd because of their popularity. But Yves is so friendly, and very down to earth. Very handsome, too, although he's not the least bit affected by that. You're both quite a bit alike because you're both very nice people. Not like many of the tourists we've met, who are so distant and sometimes snooty, but then, Scott and I are tourists, too. But you know what I mean."

"Yes, I think I do. Yves *is* very different. Hmmm. Well, it's time to say goodbye for now. Sometime you're on the mainland, you, Scott and the children must come to the hotel I'm staying at. The Golden Sails. I'd love to treat you to dinner. Your children are so sweet and cute, and I've enjoyed my time here with them. I'd like to visit you here a few more times before I leave for home."

"That sounds lovely, dear, but next time, make sure you rent a more reliable boat. And don't forget that you and Yves promised to spend tomorrow afternoon with us, and have dinner here with us, too. Tracy and Kevin love both of you. You two have such a way with children," said Joan.

"I promise we'll be here tomorrow afternoon. I've enjoyed you and your family very much."

Yves returned, and stood at the bottom of the porch steps, smiling up at them as he held his hand out to Melanie. She and Joan walked down the steps to him, but Melanie felt too excited to take his hand.

"We'll see you tomorrow, Yves," said Joan. "Scott looks forward to spending more time with you because he wants to hear all about how they make movies, and so on."

"You have been so good to us. I will very much enjoy tomorrow. I will bring wine and steaks," said Yves.

"Perfect. Scott can set up a barbecue and we can place the table out on the beach. It'll be so romantic. Scott! Yves and Melanie are leaving now!" she shouted.

Scott hurried over to them, holding his children's hands, and then after Melanie and Yves said goodbye to Joan, then Scott and the children walked with them to the other side of the island.

Yves and Melanie waved goodbye as the boat began sailing away to the mainland, and then Melanie began having doubts about marrying Keith.

* * * * * * * * * * * * * * * *

"Hi! I heard you got marooned on an island with Yves Lemieux. It's a good thing there was a family there," said Keith.

"Yes, wasn't it? How was *your* afternoon?" asked Melanie.

"Just great, thanks. Bernard told us he'd take Doug and me fishing tomorrow. You're still the best-looking chick I've ever known, and I see no worse for wear, considering that you were almost lost to us forever."

"Yes. I hope Brigitte's mother isn't doing too badly. I must ask Brigitte when I see her," said Melanie, looking away from him.

"We'll be seeing her at dinner. Your island castaway buddy won't be joining us, though. I think he said something about going into town because of some date he has with one of his fans. But you know guys like Yves. They have their choice of any woman they want. By the way, Brigitte's leaving for a few days, and they're taking a break until she comes back."

"They'll need a break for a few days because they've been shooting that film every day for so long," said Melanie.

"Yeah, that's why Bernard invited us to go fishing with him. Yves might back out though. He said he was very interested in that young woman he met. The one he's seeing in town tomorrow. Yeah, sure, interested for a few hours, right? He said he's having dinner with her family, too. They should watch that he doesn't just use their daughter, then throw her away."

"He's not like that! At least, not from what I've seen."

"That's because you see him as a polite movie star, but I know what those guys are really like behind all their suave facades. Yves is probably hoping this babe's parents'll go for a long walk after dinner so that he can get their daughter into her bedroom. All these movie stars are alike, sweetheart."

"Oh? I'm wondering what would've happened if Brigitte had invited you into *her* bedroom," said Melanie.

"I'm engaged to you, so, I wouldn't even think about it. I mean, she's not bad-looking, but c'mon, I'd never be interested in her in that way. Oh, I see what you're getting at now. Just because I went on the yacht with her today, you think I was attracted to her. Right? But you forget that Doug and Brianna were with me, and her director, Bernard, and I only went with them because I found *him* interesting. I asked him about his movies, and things like that.

Melanie, I'm surprised at you. Do you really think I'm like that Yves Lemieux guy?"

"No, I don't. He's not like you, at all."

"Well, there you are," said Keith, smiling. "What are you and Brianna going to do while we're out fishing tomorrow?"

"Oh, maybe tour the shops in town again, or I might just walk along the beach and do some sketching because I'd like to be alone for awhile."

"That sounds nice. By the way, don't forget your parents are arriving in three days. Won't they be surprised to find out that we've become good friends with a big director and two movie stars? Wait'll your father gets a load of Brigitte in a bathing suit. Talk about cleavage. Man oh, man. And her...Oh, here comes Doug and Brianna! Hi, guys!"

"Melanie!" exclaimed Brianna. "I heard you got stranded on a deserted island with Yves Lemieux! Just the two of you! How absolutely exciting! Did he make a pass at you?"

"No, he didn't because Keith told me that Yves is interested in...How did you put it?" Melanie asked him. "Oh, yes, you told me that he was interested in some *babe* in town. By the way, I wasn't stranded on a deserted island with Yves. There was a very nice couple there, with two adorable children. They gave us lunch, then we hitched a ride back to the mainland on a passing boat."

"Now that shows restraint on his part because you're every bit as gorgeous as Brigitte, except that she's a blonde and...Well, she's a bit bustier," said Douglas.

"And *me*?" asked Brianna, feigning a pout.

"You're making me the luckiest guy in the world. Yeah, and you're gorgeous, too," said Douglas, kissing her cheek.

Melanie had felt a pang of envy when Keith had told her that Yves had a date with a young woman in town. She felt disappointed that Yves had made a dinner appointment with Joan and Scott, when he'd obviously had every intention of having dinner with somebody else the following day.

Keith's lies about not being sexually attracted to Brigitte had annoyed her, and now Melanie felt upset while recalling what he'd said about very handsome actors like Yves having their choice of any adoring fan they wanted.

Tears blurred her vision as she felt that she'd been duped again by another man with a roving eye like Keith who could be right in his evaluation of Yves.

Melanie then recalled her afternoon with Yves, and she felt sure that Keith was wrong about him, however, that didn't explain Yves' date with a young woman in town.

The following morning, Brianna and Melanie were in the hotel room they shared, and Brianna had started asking her for more details about her time on the island with Yves.

"Are you sure Yves didn't make some sort of pass at you? I mean, you almost shot out of your chair to hurry away when Yves and the others came into the dining room for dinner last night. So? Did he make a pass at you on that island?"

"No, he didn't. Honest. I had to leave the dining room because I had a sudden earache from getting my ears clogged with salt water. I saw Brigitte rushing away early this morning, and I was so pleased to hear that her mother isn't as bad off as it seemed."

"She's lucky it's only a two-hour drive to the airport. We'll be alone for breakfast, I'll bet, because the boys partied late last night. They're having a great time here. Oh, I'd better hurry if I'm catching a ride into town with the Stevensons. You sure you don't want to come with us?" asked Brianna.

"I'm sure. I might join you for lunch, though. If I decide to do that, then I'll walk into town and meet you about one."

"Well, knowing you, you'll stop on the way to town to do some sketching. I love that drawing you did of Doug and me on the beach. Better than any postcard. There, now I'm ready to go downstairs. How about you?"

"Let's go," replied Melanie.

"Okay. Gee, you look as if you're dressed to go to a party, instead of breakfast."

"Well, I just felt like dressing up a bit, that's all."

Melanie planned to have breakfast, walk along the path beside the beach, do some sketching, then ask about hiring a boat to take her to visit Joan and Scott.

* * * * * * ☀ * * * * * *

As they ate breakfast and chatted, Melanie thought about what to take with her, then she decided to follow through with the plans Yves had now changed because of his date with the girl in town.

She planned to take steaks and perhaps two or three bottles of wine with her, and the best she could find, too. Yves had told Joan and Scott that he'd bring steaks and wine for dinner, so, Melanie felt sure that if Yves could do that, then she could, too.

She said goodbye to Brianna, then went to speak to the hotel manager about the wine and steaks. He was genially accommodating, and he mentioned that Yves Lemieux had also spoken to him about a similar request the night before.

Melanie then frowned while feeling sure that Yves was taking his steaks and bottles of wine into town for his dinner date with the young woman and her parents.

She was leaving the hotel manager's office when she saw Yves, Bernard, and a few members of the film crew on their way into the dining room for breakfast, so, she stepped behind a potted palm tree so that they wouldn't notice her.

She left the hotel and took the path along the beach past several docks with boats for hire. Melanie booked a boat tour, and the captain had agreed to drop her off at the island, and pick her back up again at ten o'clock that night.

She then returned to the hotel to get her pad and pencils. She made sure that she wasn't seen by Yves before she took the elevator up to her room, then returning to the lobby, she got off at the second floor, and took the stairs down to the lobby.

Melanie felt embarrassed and quite hurt because she'd foolishly thought that Yves was interested in her, but he was much more interested in a young woman in town.

She found it difficult to sketch because her thoughts were crowded with visions of Yves smiling while talking with her, and she realized she'd reacted in the same way to him as Keith had done, and still *was* acting toward Brigitte.

It made her feel so foolish. The only reason she'd had a sudden infatuation for him was because his eyes were a fascinating color of blue that mesmerized her, and made her feel very excited.

Thinking about Yves' eyes caused her to recall the young man whom she constantly drew or painted portraits of, and to wonder again what color his eyes really were. She wished that sometime soon she'd see that young man again when he was nearer to her, so that she could clearly see the color of his eyes.

She heaved a big sigh after deciding that she'd just have to continue painting so many portraits of that young man, without knowing what color to paint his eyes.

She then decided that the next time she saw him waving and smiling at her from across some street, she would immediately rush across that street to greet him, and then she would finally know the color of his eyes.

Melanie began thinking again about her impending marriage to Keith, and she wondered if she'd be making a terrible mistake because in the past two days, her feelings for him had waned.

He'd assured her that he wasn't sexually attracted to Brigitte, then almost in the next breath, Keith had said that when Melanie's father arrived, he'd also be quite taken by Brigitte's beauty when he saw her in a bathing suit.

Yves excited Melanie in a way that Keith never had, and he had seemed far more interested in her than Keith was, and Yves had

shown more respect for her, as well.

She then considered that it could be that French men were more

aware of what a woman wanted to hear, but that still didn't explain

why her heart beat faster every time she thought about him, and

she'd never reacted that way to a man before.

She realized that she had to stop thinking about Yves because

she'd be marrying Keith soon, and yet Melanie still felt that she

could be making a terrible mistake. She hoped that when her

mother arrived for the wedding, she'd reassure her that marrying

Keith was the right thing to do.

She kept glancing at her wristwatch and taking deep breaths to

relax whenever she thought about Yves while wondering what his

date in town looked like, and if that young woman was a blonde

like Brigitte.

* * * * * * * *🌺* * * * * * *

After returning from the beach, Melanie showered, dressed and

left the hotel while still trying not to think about Yves so much,

even as she walked to the nearby town.

Almost an hour later, she was seated at a table out on the patio of a small restaurant, and she'd only taken one small bite out of the sandwich she'd ordered, because she didn't feel hungry due to all her doubts about both Keith and Yves.

Melanie felt relieved that she hadn't sat out on the hotel patio to have a sandwich and cold drink, because now there wasn't the chance that Yves would see her, then smile at her as he walked away with Keith and Bernard to go fishing.

She felt that if Yves had seen her at a table on the hotel patio, and then casually ignored her, it would have heightened her embarrassment because she'd foolishly believed that he had really meant all the wonderful things he had said to her.

Melanie looked down at the uneaten sandwich on the plate, then she heaved a sigh, and left the patio of the restaurant. She walked back to the hotel, then picked up the food and wine from the hotel manager before she went down to the docks to take the large tour boat to visit Joan and Scott.

* * * * * * * ⟡⟡⟡ * * * * * * *

"Have you taken this tour before?" asked a woman on the boat.

"No, I haven't," replied Melanie. "Actually, I'm not taking the tour because I'm being dropped off at an island. I have friends who have a cabin on that island, and they spend their vacations there every year."

"That sounds wonderful. I see you must be spending the night."

"Oh, no. These bags are filled with groceries, wine, and a change of clothes. I also bought gifts for their children."

"I see. It looked like you were planning to stay awhile. The bags must be quite heavy, but those handles look strong enough."

"Yes, they are, and I won't have to carry these bags too far because Scott'll meet me at their dock," said Melanie, smiling.

"Thank goodness. Are you here alone, or with your husband? Is he coming along, later?" asked the elderly woman.

"I'm not married, and yes, I'm alone. Well, not really. I'm staying at The Golden Sails with my friend. She went into town to do some shopping."

"I'm having a lovely time. My husband gets seasick, so, he couldn't take the boat tour with me. There's so much happening this year, and they're making that French film here, too. I met the stars, you know, and that actor, Yves Lemieux, is so handsome, and so polite, too. Have you seen him?"

"Yes, we walked by while they were filming. Brigitte Martineau is rather beautiful, isn't she?"

"Is that her name? Yes, she *is* pretty. She doesn't wear much most of the time, but then I suppose that's for publicity purposes. It's nice to see a young woman like yourself who's every bit, if not more beautiful than her, but doesn't feel she has to bare it all."

"Oh? Thank you for the compliment, but from what I've seen, all the men gawk at her."

"Well, it's no wonder. Practically nude half the time, and I'll bet the men wouldn't be gaping at her if she were just another pretty girl on the beach, instead of a movie star of some sort."

"Somebody else said that same thing to me," said Melanie.

"There you are. You see? I'll bet you get your share of men looking at you. Why, you're far more attractive than her, and I know beauty because I spent years working as a modeling agent. Very few women have your type of beauty. Sort of exotic, and the type of beauty that not only lasts, but it seems to be a part of you. As they say, most beauty comes from within, so, I'm sure you must be a wonderful person to be so beautiful on the outside, as well. With your looks and personality, I'm sure you won't be single long, young lady."

"Thanks. I, uh, well, I *have* been thinking seriously about marriage. The friend I'm here on vacation with is being married soon, and that's why we're here. Her fiancé is here now, too."

"Oh, isn't that wonderful. Your hotel isn't far from ours. Is she being married at your hotel?"

"No, in town. There's a lovely chapel there."

"You'll have to tell me when the wedding is going to take place so that we can walk by during the..."

A tour employee suddenly appeared, and smiled as he interrupted their conversation.

"Excuse me, miss. We're ready to take you ashore."

"Oh, thanks, I'll be right with you," said Melanie.

"Those bags look so heavy," the elderly woman remarked.

"Oh, don't you worry because I can manage. Well, it was very nice meeting you, and I truly hope you have a wonderful time on your tour of the islands. Bye!" cried Melanie.

"Thank you! Bye! Have a nice time! Lovely day for it!"

Two young men helped her down into a small boat, then they rowed toward Joan and Scott's dock.

The children were waving at her as the rowboat approached, and they ran toward the dock. Scott hurried to the dock and helped carry the four bags of gifts, food, and wine while smiling and telling Melanie that she hadn't needed to bring so much with her.

Joan waved to them as she left the porch and walked over to meet them.

"Where's Yves?" Joan asked her.

"Oh, he, um...Something happened. I mean, he had something else he had to do, so, he won't be able to make it here."

"Look at this. Melanie must've bought out one of the stores."

"So, I see," said Joan. "You shouldn't have, dear, because we have plenty of groceries, and *we* invited *you*."

"Yes, but I love shopping at the stores in town, and I brought a few gifts for Tracy and Kevin, as well."

"Oh, that's so sweet of you. The children are going to love you even more than they do already. You kids run on ahead and pour a cold drink for Melanie, and be careful you don't spill it. It's too bad Yves couldn't come. He's such a nice guy. The kids loved him, and he loved them, too," said Joan.

"He had to work on the film, did he?" asked Scott.

"Something like that, yes."

"You're not smiling. Did you two have a spat?" asked Joan.

"No, I just...I...I feel so...I'm..." stammered Melanie.

"Time for girl talk. Scott, you make yourself scarce for awhile. Play Robinson Crusoe or Friday, okay?" Joan told him.

"I have a better idea. I'll play a hungry cannibal and eat the kids. I'll get 'em! Grrrrrrr!"

Scott ran ahead, then a few moments later, Tracy and Kevin came running out of the cabin, squealing and laughing as Scott chased them.

After she'd emptied the bags that Melanie had brought her,

Joan emptied a bit of the soft drinks out of their glasses, and then she winked at Melanie before adding a splash of vodka to each of their drinks. She nodded for Melanie to follow her out to the porch where they sat down and watched Scott and the children until they ran out of sight.

"I don't mean to pry, but if ever I've seen a woman on the verge of tears, it's you," said Joan, smiling at her.

"I'm all right. Really. It's just that...Um, my mother's arriving at the end of the week, and I have to talk to her."

"Uh-huh. But I'll bet you won't know what to say to her. Does she know about you and Yves?"

"There's no Yves and me. There never was. I'm getting married to another man. Keith. That's why we're here. We're supposed to be married soon. Very soon."

"Oh, really? I thought a flock of canaries was about to fly out of your mouth, singing love songs whenever you looked at Yves."

"No! You're mistaken! Really! I don't...I never have...I..."

Melanie began crying, and Joan moved her chair closer to her, then put her arm around her.

"You know, it's so strange how life works. You think you have everything sewn up in one perfect package, then suddenly all the threads break. You came here to marry this man, and you had no idea that Yves would be here. You thought that it was all set to go. Nice wedding and back home again. I'll bet Yves thought he was just coming here to make a film, but then he saw *you*. And I saw how he looked at you, and how you looked at him. Something's happened. I'll bet you didn't tell him you were coming here. Why, Melanie? Can you tell me? *Would* you tell me? You need to tell someone, and soon, too."

"Oh...I, well...It's all so...So wrong."

"Wrong? You wouldn't have fallen in love with Yves if you really loved the man you say you're going to marry. There's something wrong, all right, and it's not what you feel for Yves. It's about what you feel for your supposed fiancé."

"Keith said things. He did things. When I think about it, he's always been that way and thought those things. He told me about men like Yves. That they're womanizers. That's where Yves is now. He went with the director of the movie, and with Keith and

Douglas. They went fishing on Bernard's yacht, then after they come back, Yves is going into town to have dinner with a young woman and her family, and that's why he isn't coming here. And he already knew that yesterday. Oh, I feel so stupid and embarrassed. Well, at least I didn't show my feelings to him because he would've loved that, I'll bet. Another fan throwing herself at him," said Melanie, wiping at her tears.

"Uh-uh, I didn't sense that Yves is that type of guy, and I don't trust what...Is it Keith? What *he* told you, either. I have a gut instinct about this. Did you see Yves go off with your whatever fiancé and the others?"

"No, but I'm sure he did," replied Melanie, sniffling.

"So, there you are. How do you know, other than Keith telling you, that Yves is really having dinner with this other woman?"

"Because Keith said that's what Yves told him."

"Hmmm, I see. Let's get the kids and take a long walk, and have a long talk. Okay, honey?" said Joan as she smiled.

"Yeah, sure. Sorry I cried like that, but I just felt so confused."

"Don't be silly. You have every right to be upset and to cry.

Tracy! Kevin! C'mon! We're going for a walk! Just us, Scott!"

"Of course! Bye, ladies!" shouted Scott, grinning.

Kevin and Tracy ran to them, then they began walking through the trees toward the other side of the island. Joan listened and tried to soothe her, but she felt sure that Melanie was mistaken about Yves because he and Melanie obviously loved each other so much.

* * * * * * * ❧❀❧ * * * * * *

Scott waved at a large yacht as it came into view near the island, and when it was directly across from the dock, he watched a small boat being lowered into the water.

He wondered who was being brought ashore, then as the small boat neared, he grinned when he saw Yves. Scott walked over to the dock to meet him, and he chuckled when he saw that Yves had also brought many shopping bags with him.

Scott kept reaching down from the dock while Yves was handing him five heavy, large, woven-straw shopping bags, filled with gift-wrapped packages and bottles of wine and liquor.

"Welcome ashore!" exclaimed Scott as the rowboat left.

"Merci! Thank you. I am sorry that Melanie won't be coming

because she is on a fishing trip with her fiancé."

"Oh? Her fiancé, huh? I didn't know she was getting married."

"Yes, she is in love with him, and they will be married soon, so, she cannot leave her fiancé to come to dinner. He is a very lucky man, isn't he? Melanie's very nice. And she's beautiful. So very beautiful. It wouldn't be right for her to come to dinner with me. And of course, you and Joan. You understand?"

"Of course," replied Scott, suppressing a chuckle.

"Where is Joan and the children?"

"Gone for a walk. How about a drink?"

"Yes, I would like that. Hmmm, did you like Melanie?"

"I sure did. I'm disappointed that she couldn't come with you."

"Oui, I am too, but she is in love with another man, and that is why she couldn't come here."

"Yeah, so you keep saying. She's in love. How about you?"

"Oh, I am waiting. Perhaps someday," replied Yves.

"You know, I had the impression you were in love with Melanie, and that she was in love with *you*."

"Oh, no. We only met two days ago, I think. I noticed her when she came here. No, I have heard of what they call love when two people first see each other, but that is only in movies. Love takes much time. Perhaps weeks. Months. Years."

"Oh, so you're an expert on love, are you? Well, they say the French are like that. They love love, so, I suppose they know more about it, right? Rum and Coke?"

"Pardon?"

"Would you like a rum and Coke?" asked Scott.

"Ah! Yes, please."

"I'll put what needs to be put in the icebox and the rest I'll put in the pantry along with the gifts you brought. Save it as a surprise. This was really great of you to do this, man. We never expected this, at all. We just wanted to enjoy Melanie's and your company for dinner," said Scott, smiling.

"You were so kind to us yesterday. You are very nice people."

Scott was having a great time. He knew that Yves was trying his best to smile while feeling very disappointed because he thought that Melanie was with her fiancé.

He decided to urge Yves to go for a walk with him, but in a

different direction than Joan and Melanie had taken. When Yves said that he'd enjoy a stroll along the beach with him, then Scott grinned while thinking about what a wonderful surprise it was going to be for both Yves and Melanie when they eventually found out that they were on the island together.

They had walked for about ten minutes, when Scott suggested they undress down to their underwear and go for a swim. Yves laughed and agreed, and then they ran into the water.

After wading back out of the water, they sat on the shore, and then Scott smiled while listening to Yves talking about Melanie, then twenty minutes later, Scott stood up.

"I'm really enjoying having a conversation with another guy for a change," said Scott. "I'll run back and get us both another cold drink, okay? You wait here, and I'll be right back in a few minutes. Okay?"

"Oui, okay. I will swim while you are gone."

"Good! I'll be right back!"

"I feel like having a drink. How about you?" asked Joan.

"I'd love one," replied Melanie, smiling.

"Fine. Let's head back, then. Kevin! Tracy! Come on now!"

"They must love it here," said Melanie.

"Well, sometimes they get bored, then we take them into town for the day. There's a children's amusement park there, with a few rides, clowns, and things, then they're asleep halfway back here, so, we carry them to their beds because they're so tuckered out."

"You're so lucky to have such wonderful and healthy children like Tracy and Kevin. I can't wait to have some of my own. Keith wants a boy first, of course."

"Oh, yes, *Keith*. I'll bet he'll be disappointed when a prize fish slips off his line."

"I don't know what they'll do with the fish they catch. I suppose the hotel serves them for dinner. Dinner! Oh, no! I forgot to leave a note telling them where I'd be!" cried Melanie.

"Well, that's because you had so much on your mind. You told me you bought the steaks and wine from the hotel, so, I'm sure they'll tell your friends that."

"Oh, that's right. I just told the hotel manager that I'd been invited for dinner, but Keith'll understand. He wanted to spend time alone away from me, so, he'll understand that I want to spend some time alone, too. Besides, he's having such a good time with the director and his actress, Brigitte. And our friends, Douglas and Brianna, too. Yes, I'm sure it'll be all right. You know, about not leaving them a note."

They smiled when they saw Scott running toward them, then he asked Melanie if she would excuse them so that he and Joan could talk in private about something slightly personal.

Melanie sat on a dune, and talked with the children as she waited for Joan and Scott to finish their conversation.

"Another guest arrived," said Scott with a crooked smile.

"Oh, yes, I thought so. Where is he?" asked Joan.

"I took him for a walk along the beach, and then I told him I was coming back to get us another drink."

"I see. Then somehow we've got to get Melanie to deliver his drink. How's Yves holding up?" Joan asked him.

"He's so depressed. Trying not to show it, though."

"You think *he's* depressed? Wait'll Melanie's fiancé finds out he's not getting married. But somehow I think he's too busy enjoying the company of a certain actress. I also think he's not only a bit of a jerk, but he's losing out by not being smart enough to know he's let a wonderful girl slip through his fingers."

"How's Melanie doing?"

"She's sad. Upset. Confused, and so in love with Yves. She still thinks she's getting married. Well, she is, but not to Keith. Poor Melanie," said Joan, smiling. "She doesn't realize how happy she's going to be in...Oh, say, ten or fifteen minutes."

"Well, let's get the show on the road," said Scott, grinning.

"This is going to be a dinner to remember."

"By the way, Yves also brought bags of food and wine, and gifts for everyone. We could invite fifteen people for dinner, but I think it'll be just you, me, and the kids who'll be eating because Melanie and Yves'll be staring at each other all through dinner. Probably won't even know we're there," said Scott, laughing.

"Yeah, ain't love grand? We were like them when we first met, then got married."

"We're *still* like them, most of the time. I'm so lucky to have you as my wife," said Scott. "My best friend, and my lover, too."

"Me too, handsome," said Joan, kissing him.

They walked back to Melanie, smiling and holding hands, then Joan told her: "Looks like we're having another guest for dinner. He's a good friend of ours."

"Oh, you must be quite pleased that he dropped by. Well, you sure don't have to worry about not having enough for dinner because I've brought plenty of food with me. Wine, cheese, all sorts of things," Melanie said as she smiled.

"We don't stand on formality here, as you know. Scott was going to take him a fresh drink, but I need him to help me sort out what we're having for dinner. Would you mind taking his drink to him and introducing yourselves? Please?" asked Joan, smiling.

"Of course, I'll do that," replied Melanie.

"Thanks, hon," said Joan.

Melanie was feeling a little better after talking with Joan and the children, but she hoped that she could keep smiling until she left to go back to the hotel, because she didn't want to dampen their spirits.

She kept visualizing Keith and Douglas gawking at Brigitte, and then she visualized Yves smiling at her as she looked into his wonderful, exciting blue eyes.

Melanie knew that she had to push Yves out of her mind and act nonchalant when she saw him at the hotel if he had the young woman from town with him. She felt sure that she'd forget about Yves after she married Keith, and then returned home.

"Here y'go," said Scott, handing Melanie the cold drinks. "One rum and Coke, and one vodka and pineapple juice. We make that juice ourselves, you know, and we have three coolers. One just for ice. They drop it off once a week."

"Oh, that's great. I wondered where you were getting all the ice from. These napkins should keep the drinks cool, and I'll walk fast to make sure the ice doesn't melt too much. Okay, Joan, I'll be back soon to help you with dinner," Melanie said as she began walking away to the door of the cabin.

"Don't even think about it. It's hours away yet, and besides, even then, Scott'll take care of most of the dinner. He's a fantastic cook, too, and that's the only reason I married him."

"And because he's handsome and a wonderful father."

"Yeah, those other great attributes of his sure add to the total package," said Joan, then she laughed.

"Oh! I almost forgot. What's your friend's name?"

"Name? Oh, right. It's Sam," Scott told her.

"All right. Bye," said Melanie before she left the cabin.

"You kids stay here. I want you to wash up before dinner."

"Aw, mom!" cried Kevin and Tracy in unison.

"Uh-uh-uh! I want you to look nice for dinner. Now get to it."

"Okay! Bye!" cried Kevin as he and Tracy ran to the bathroom.

After he'd swam in the ocean again, Yves had written Melanie's name several times in the sand with a stick, and he sat looking at the name as he thought about her on Bernard's yacht, laughing and talking with Keith.

He sighed, then stood up and began getting dressed after he'd decided to walk back to the cabin because he felt that having the children around him would cheer him up.

Melanie walked along the beach, imagining Yves smiling on his way to have dinner with the young woman in town, and she felt annoyed with herself for feeling the way she did about him.

She saw somebody walking along the other side of the trees around the curve in the beach, so, she took a few deep breaths, and forced a smile as she walked toward whom she thought was Joan and Scott's friend, Sam.

Yves rounded the corner of the beach, and then his heart leapt at the same time he stopped walking when he saw Melanie. She gasped when she saw him, then she burst into tears, turned around, and began hurrying back toward the cabin.

"Melanie! Stop!...Melanie!"

He started running toward her, and Melanie wished that she could stop crying as she walked as fast as she could, then she began running.

Yves was gaining on her as he kept shouting at to her to stop, then he reached out and grabbed her arm.

"Melanie! You are here!"

"Yes, of course I am! I told you yesterday that I'd be here."

"You have been crying. Are you all right? Did you have an argument with your fiancé? Is he here?"

"He's...I came alone. I thought you had a dinner date this evening. Keith told me you did."

"Oui, I did tell him. You and I planned it yesterday. Here, with Scott and Joan."

"But I thought...Keith said...Oh. You meant with *me*?"

"Oui, of course. Why would I not? We planned to. Oh, Melanie, I thought you went fishing with Bernard. That you and Keith...I thought you were with him."

"No, I promised Joan and Scott. And you, too."

"You kept your promise. You came here. I am so happy. I want to tell you...Melanie. Ah, Melanie."

"Oh, no. You're smiling that smile. Um, I brought you your drink. Here. Oh, I'm sorry. I spilled most of it when I was running away from you."

"Why did you run away from me?"

"I was...You surprised me. I...I didn't know you were here."

"But I told you I would be here. Uh, I must tell you I know I cannot see you after today."

"Oh? Oh, I understand," said Melanie.

"Yes, I feel too much love for you. You're so...Uh, but I know you want to be with him. Not with me. You are only my beautiful dream. I will stay away from you because it would hurt me too much to see you with him."

"It would? Uh, I...feel...Oh, Yves, I feel so confused. I can't be in love with you. We've just met, so, I...Why do I love you?"

"You love me? Oh, my Melanie. I love you so."

He touched her face, then tears blurred her eyes as she stepped closer to him. Yves grasped her waist, pulled her into an embrace, and then they kissed.

Melanie hugged him tightly while knowing it would always be Yves whom she would love and cherish, as he would her.

It was at that point in her life that she would stop seeing that handsome, blond, young man whom had always smiled and waved at her from across a street, or just before he walked out of sight into a crowd or into a store. Melanie would also stop repeatedly drawing and painting his portrait, and never finishing them completely because she hadn't known the color of his eyes.

Perhaps the reason she would stop seeing that young man a short distance away from her, was because that warmth of close friendship and love she had sensed in him, she had now found in Yves, and their love for each other would intensify, and never falter throughout the rest of their lives.

EPILOGUE

Jason walked through the house, looking at all the furniture draped with heavy, cotton sheets while Linda shouted at the children to stay close to the house while playing outside.

Linda and Jason had been asked by his mother to check the home she'd grown up in, to see if there had been a burglary because the house had been empty since the time Jason's grandmother had died.

Two weeks after his grandmother's funeral, Jason's mother had locked the house, then returned home over twenty years ago, and she had recently been thinking of putting the house up for sale, and then sharing the proceeds with her siblings.

Linda began inspecting the downstairs of the house while Jason went upstairs to inspect the rooms on the second floor. He walked along the upstairs hall, opening doors and looking into rooms, then he opened a door to a big room that Jason realized must have been his mother's bedroom because of the easel standing near the large window at one end of the room.

He entered the room, walked over to the many old canvases and portfolios of drawings stacked against the wall near the easel, then he crouched down and began slowly flipping through canvases while feeling both pleasantly surprised and slightly bewildered at seeing the many portraits his mother had painted.

All the portraits were of him from the time he'd been very young to the age he was now. Jason wondered why his mother had obviously spent so much time painting every detail of his features, including his blond, wavy hair, but she hadn't colored in his eyes, which were the only unfinished part of every portrait.

He knew that his grandmother had been a quite talented seamstress, and he picked up an embroidered cushion from the bed his mother had once slept on.

Jason smiled while looking at the beautiful, intricately sewn embroidery on the cushion, which included the swirling, sewn lettering of his mother's name: *"Melanie."*

The End

Destiny At A Party

He hurried into the living room, then almost tripped over a thick cable stretched across the floor. Hearing his approach, she whirled around to face him, then after placing her hands on her hips, and then looking up at the ceiling, she exclaimed: "Benton! I told you I never wanted to see you again! Never! Never, never, *never*! Please! Please! Oh, God!"

"Destiny, please! I flew all the way from Rome to find you! I followed you to Istanbul, but I'd just missed you, then I raced to Paris, and again, I missed you. Next, I tried to catch up with you in Madrid. Still no luck. On and on. Country to country, but each time you'd just left when I reached your latest destination. Three days of trying to find you. Three days. Three days of tears and uncertainty. Thank God I arrived here in Helsinki before you left for New York. If I have to, I'll follow you to the ends of the earth until you give me an answer. I love you, Destiny. I want to run my fingers through your shining hair. I want to gaze into your astounding eyes that are like the portals to heaven. I want to taste your lips that form words of such wonder. Your perfume intoxicates me. I'm going mad just hoping you'll say yes. Just that one word that means more than life to me. It means the promise of eternity in your arms, and you in *my* arms, my goddess of love. The promise of my happiness. Please marry me, darling. Marry me, please. Please. Oh, please."

"But how can I be sure that you're not just after my inheritance? My wealth that is the envy of kings? Nay, emperors. All men find me more beautiful than any woman they've ever seen in their lives. No, I am more than beautiful. I am stunning. Exotic. Sensual. Intelligent. Warm and loving. But sometimes reckless and daring. Yet, I feel that men don't see my perfection. They only look at my bank account. No, Benton. No. No, oh, ohhhhhh."

"Oh, Destiny. I'd gladly kill myself to prove I want only you, my fantasy. Not your money. How can I spend it if I'm dead? Think, Destiny. There are no banks beyond the deep, dark, cold gates of certain death. Now do you believe me? Destiny. Destiny, please. Oh, Destiny. Even your name is more than beautiful."

"Oh, my darling, Benton, I believe you might love me and not my great fortune, so, yes! Yes, yes, yes! I will consider marrying you. I'll think so very hard about it. Then, Benton, my love, if I decide that you are my one true love. That you love me for myself, then I shall marry you. We'll travel the world on our honeymoon. To every one of my palaces. My villas. My mansions. My estates. My favorite resorts. I own all the greatest resorts in the world, but of course you know that, my angel of love. You whom I still doubt. Kiss me, Benton. Kiss me now. My lips await. Oh, Benton. My Benton. My darling, Benton. Benton. Benton. Oh, Benton."

"Darling Destiny. My Destiny. Destiny, you are my destiny. Oh, Destiny. Destiny. Destiny, my only love."

"Cut! Perfect! Brilliant!" shouted the director.

"I *so* fucking hate soaps! Let's grab a coffee," said Chad.

"Oh, but I can't, darling. I've got to be at Julie's in half an hour. Please don't pout, my sweet. Promise me? I'll try to get to Michael's party by four. No promises. No-no! I might be a teensy-tiny bit late. But remember, Aunt Stephanie and I'll be there soon, dear one. She's picking me up in a cab after I get back from Julie's. Oh, I know you'll be anxiously awaiting me. Please don't be too sad or bored at the party till I get there, darling, darling man. Oh, and how is your house guest?" asked Domenic.

"Unbelievable. Six fucking weeks," he replied, scowling.

"Oh! You swore again! Oh, well, men can be so gruff at times. This must be one of those times. I must run. Until later, you handsome, wonderful creature you! Au revoir, darling!"

"Bye, doll."

Nick stood in front of the full-length mirror as he fastened his belt buckle, then he turned left, then right, then after smiling at his reflection, he walked out into the living room, picked up his magazine, and sat down on the couch.

While Chad finished dressing, he thought about Nick, and then he made a mental note to strangle David when he returned from his vacation.

David had phoned long-distance the day after he'd left for a six-week vacation, to tell Chad that a friend he'd grown up with was coming into town, and David had pleaded with Chad to let that friend stay at the apartment because Chad had an extra bedroom since his brother had moved out last year.

That friend had turned out to be Nick whom had arrived yesterday, and now Chad knew that unless he could dump him onto somebody else, then Nick would be at the apartment for six, damned weeks.

When he'd called Michael Namikovski to ask what time he should arrive at the cocktail party, Michael had told him that David had mentioned that a close friend would be coming to the city, and he'd insisted that Chad bring his house guest with him. Now Chad groaned as he thought about Nick accompanying him to Michael's cocktail party.

Chad had groaned even louder after he'd driven out to the airport, and seen Nick for the first time. Nick had been wearing a very tight-fitting, bright green suit, and his mass of red curly hair had been tied back into a long ponytail with wide, waist-length, yellow ribbons.

He'd also had a huge, orange and blue shoulder bag with rhinestone flowers on it, and at his feet were three, large pink suitcases. He'd told Chad, in a falsetto voice, that he'd borrowed the suit from a friend and the suitcases from his sister.

* * * * * * ⟨※⟩ * * * * * *

On the way to the bathroom, Chad looked into the living room and saw Nick seated on the couch, reading a magazine, and then seeing what Nick was wearing, he decided to give him Michael's address and tell him that he'd meet him there.

Chad wondered where Nick had bought the clothes he was wearing to Michael's. Nick had on a very wide-sleeved, blue shirt with many white stars on it, and a white, string tie with a huge rhinestone brooch at the collar.

The rest of Nick's outfit was even more outlandish. Below his six-inch-wide, bright red, glossy leather belt, Nick had on a shin-length skirt with broad white and red stripes, and Chad assumed that the long skirt swelled out like a big umbrella because of at least three crinolines under the skirt.

Nick also had on a white cowboy hat and a pair of white,

fringed cowboy boots with a bright red tassel on each boot to match his belt and the wide headband on his cowboy hat. Chad thought that Nick, whom he estimated to be around sixty or so years old, looked like a demented majorette from a Fourth of July parade, whom had wandered away from the parade back in the 1950s after swallowing a pound of very strong drugs.

Chad turned around and went back to his bedroom before Nick saw him, and then he shouted: "Damn!"

"Break a heel?" Nick yelled from the living room.

"No! I just got an email asking me to send a résumé!"

He walked out into the living room, smiled at Nick, and hoped his lie would work.

"I'm sorry, but it'll take me over half an hour to get the résumé together and ready to send," said Chad. "But hey, I'll give you Michael's address and you go on ahead. He's dying to meet you. You two can chat over a martini or three till I get there. By the way, you look unbelievable."

"Why, how sweet of you to notice! Thank you all, sugar! And I must say you look so divine," said Nick, grinning.

"Thanks. Divine was my favorite movie star, but she's dead now. And I insist on paying for your cab fare, and I won't take no-no-never for an answer, either. Okay?"

"Well, if you absolutely insist," said Nick. "I've never been one to argue with a very handsome man. You did say this was a casual dress affair, didn't you? Otherwise, I'll change into something a bit dressier."

"Something a bit...Oh, no. You look like a casualty...*Casually*! I mean, you're dressed casually enough. When you get to Michael's, please tell him I'll be there as soon as I can."

"Oh, and let's share," said Nick, smiling. "I'll take the flowers and you can bring the wine."

"Perfect. I'll call a cab for you right now."

"Thanks ever so. I'll run and fetch my purse."

Chad phoned for a taxi, then he went over to his computer and pretended he was working until Nick left the apartment.

He'd been able to sublet his apartment only two days after he had placed the ad in the paper, and Chad had planned to leave at the end of the month; three weeks before the new tenants were to move in. But his plans had changed when David had offered to pay him half the rent if he'd let Nick stay with him until he returned from vacation in six weeks.

Chad hadn't liked the idea and he'd only agreed to share his apartment with Nick for six weeks because David had introduced him to an influential casting agent whom had been impressed with Chad's audition, as well as with his résumé.

Now that he was getting a starring role in a big-budget Hollywood movie, Chad would be moving to California to live with a friend until he found his own apartment.

Michael Namikovski had directed him in four, ho-hum television plays, and although Chad wasn't fond of him, Michael was friends with the agent whom had secured Chad's promising Hollywood movie career.

That was the only reason Chad had decided to accept the invitation to Michael's late afternoon cocktail party, during which a light, early dinner would be served.

He'd reluctantly attended a few other cocktail parties at

Michael's, and besides five or six women and sometimes their husbands, Chad had usually been the only other straight person at those parties.

He was so glad that Domenic's aunt, Stephanie Richardson, would be at the party because he liked her very much, and planned to do his best to get her hired by one of the Hollywood studios.

Chad deemed Stephanie to be a quite talented actress, and he'd acted the part of her son in an off-Broadway theater production. While working in many small plays for years; acting, producing and directing, Stephanie had also helped build props, set up lighting, as well as designing and sewing theater costumes.

Six months ago, his father had passed away, leaving Chad and his brother an inheritance of sixty thousand dollars each, so, he'd decided that when he got to California, and while staying with a friend, he would look for a two-bedroom apartment and ask Stephanie to share it with him and hopefully Domenic, as well.

Stephanie made very little money, so, he felt sure that she would accept his offer. Chad thought that with Domenic's beauty and struggling talent, she would be offered work in minor roles in

Hollywood movies. He'd been trying to persuade her to come to California with him, but Domenic felt that her five-year contract to perform as the lead in the soap opera, "Destiny Weeps," could lead to much better roles in a few prime-time television movies.

Chad hated the soap opera they were in now, and he wanted Domenic to find some way to get out of her contract and come to California with him. They'd been in a relationship for six months, and he felt that he was in love with her.

He hoped that sometime during the cocktail party at Michael Namikovski's apartment, Domenic would agree to move to California with him.

Stephanie hummed as she walked slowly from room to room, trying to appear nonchalant while hoping that she could leave soon because she'd promised Michael Namikovski that she wouldn't arrive late for his cocktail party.

For the past three hours, she'd pretended to be watering the flowers, sitting and looking through a magazine, chatting to nobody after she'd dialed random phone numbers, then pressed the disconnect button, and during all that time, she had been keeping an eye on the large cardboard box on the floor.

The cardboard box contained a clear, plastic ball with a toy mouse inside it, another ball that had a bell inside it, and a small burlap pouch of catnip. But the cat still hadn't taken the bait.

She'd felt sure that her boyfriend was a rather pleasant, sane, trustworthy guy, but she'd been so wrong about her evaluation of him because he'd given her a Siamese cat. The cat from hell.

A week earlier, Fred Marks, whom she'd thought she'd formed a long-term, happy, loving relationship with, had phoned to tell her that he would be arriving soon with a gift for her.

After Fred had arrived in her apartment lobby, and announced himself through the intercom, Stephanie had pressed the button to release the lock on the entrance doors, then she'd hurried to tidy her hair and check her makeup.

When she'd opened her apartment door, she had been delighted to see Fred smiling broadly while holding a large, gift-wrapped present.

After handing her the present, Stephanie had been startled

when Fred had quickly told her that he'd decided to end their relationship, so, he'd given her a farewell gift, and then he'd rushed away.

Stephanie had gaped while holding the farewell gift and watching Fred rush through the door to the stairs down to the lobby. She had then suddenly regained her senses when she'd felt a movement inside the gift-wrapped box.

She had then wondered if he'd bought her a puppy, and she'd worried that it was suffocating inside the gift-wrapped box, so, she'd quickly set the box down on the floor, then knelt and started tearing off the gift wrap.

After removing all the giftwrap, she had opened the flaps of the cardboard box, then she'd gasped in shock when a cat had leapt up out of the box, and started racing around the room while screeching and howling.

Stephanie had been so shocked, that she'd remained kneeling by the empty box, watching the crazed cat clawing its way up her living room curtains, then leaping down onto her couch, and then start dragging its front paws back and forth, ripping open the upholstery, as the cat glowered and shrieked at her.

During the next hour, while she'd desperately tried to think of ways to calm her new, feline foe, the cat had caused astounding damage and havoc in her apartment.

Booboo, as Fred had written on the card that Stephanie had found inside the box, was the cat's name. In the following days, that holy terror of fur had torn all the drapery and lamp shades to shreds, leapt up onto the kitchen counter and pushed the toaster and coffee brewer onto the floor, causing them to smash.

The cat had also chewed on everything in the apartment, so, now there were dozens of tooth marks on almost every article of furniture that she owned.

Stephanie had suffered many scratches and bites while stuffing Booboo into a pet carrier so that she could take it to the veterinary clinic to have the cat's teeth examined to see if all the gnawing on her furniture was caused by cavities.

The vet, however, had assured her that Booboo was just fine and dandy, although a bit rambunctious. A bit? Her apartment looked like a war zone.

If the cat would walk into the cardboard box to ravage a toy, then Stephanie could rush over to the box, quickly close the flaps, tape them closed, grab her purse, and then leave for Michael's late afternoon cocktail party, after she'd paid a quick visit to Fred's new girlfriend's home.

Stephanie winced while recalling that terrifying incident, less then a week after the cat had been forced upon her, when she'd had to spend two hours at the hospital emergency department.

Because of that hospital visit, she'd had to cancel an audition for Desmond Del La Dumont, the effeminate, overly dramatic, dizzy director, whom God knows how, had recently gotten financial backing for a could-be, almost promising play.

Stephanie had only offered to audition for Desmond because of the expense of replacing items that Booboo had destroyed.

She was supposed to have arrived at the theatre at ten in the morning on the day of that audition, so, Stephanie had arisen, set out the clothes she planned to wear, and then she'd run a bath.

She had walked back into the bathroom, shut of the taps, then removed her robe. While she'd been doing that, Booboo had been circling her feet, growling and chewing on her ankles, which she'd wrapped with thick towels.

She recalled how she'd tried not to glare at the cat that seemed to know everything she was thinking about doing next, so, as Stephanie bathed, she had forced a smile at Booboo, sitting on top the heating rad near the bathroom sink.

She had stepped out of the tub, then after drying off, she had leaned over the sink, and started brushing her teeth. It was then that Booboo had decided to frolic.

Booboo had leapt off the heating rad, and clutched onto her bare right shoulder before quickly scrambling over to the middle of her back, just below Stephanie's neck. Then, with all of its claws fully extended, Booboo had slid all the way down her bare back, and then dropped to the floor, and started screeching while jumping up and clinging to the middle of the shower curtain.

Her first reaction to the cat's claws digging into her back, then sliding down it, had been to suck in her breath very fast through her teeth before gasping out a long, loud groan of pain.

She'd winced and clutched the toothbrush so tightly that it had broken in half, and the jagged ends of it had cut into the palm of her hand. When Stephanie had been able to catch her breath, she'd screamed from the excruciating pain.

After staggering to her bedroom, she'd carefully put on an old blouse and a loose-fitting cardigan sweater before wrapping a lightweight bath towel around her waist, then after pinning it together, she'd put on a pair of panties.

Stephanie had been weeping and moaning in the cab on the way to the hospital, and after her wounds had been dressed, she'd been given a sedative, and then she'd hailed another cab, and the driver had wakened her when she had arrived back home.

For over a week, she'd slept at one-hour intervals while groaning from the painful scratches on her back and buttocks, and trying to fall back asleep while hoping she wouldn't roll over onto her back again.

Now she was waiting and hoping that Booboo would venture into the cardboard box. Booboo leapt down from the dining room table, sauntered over to the box, sat down, looked inside it, and then at Stephanie who smiled and cooed at the criminal genius. She picked up a magazine and pretended to be looking through it, however, her gaze was ever so slightly lifted above the magazine at Booboo.

The cat very slowly licked its paws, yawned, then after staring at the cardboard box for a few moments, it darted into the box, and then Stephanie bolted out of the armchair, over to the box, and quickly closed the flaps.

She listened to the screeching inside the box as the cat slammed its body around the inside walls and clawed at them. Stephanie held the flaps of the box tightly closed with one hand as she reached for the tape with her other hand, then she felt victorious as she held the roll of duct tape.

After securely taping the flaps of the box that she'd poked holes in to allow the monster to breathe, her mission was accomplished.

Stephanie then hurried to the bedroom, opened a dresser drawer, and took out the many packages of gift wrap, ribbons and bows that she'd bought a few days ago.

Fifteen minutes later, the gift-wrapped box with the small holes in it, looked rather pretty, although it was rocking in various directions and loud growls, meows and hisses could be heard from inside it.

Stephanie called for a taxi, then after she hung up the phone, she picked up the small piece of paper with the phone number written on it.

• • • • • • • ⁕⁕⁕ • • • • • • •

She knew that Fred had left the city that day to cheat on his latest girlfriend for the weekend, and Stephanie felt sure that he was enjoying the weekend even more because he'd given her Booboo the cat before he'd left the city.

She wondered how long it had taken him to find such a vicious ball of fur with razors for teeth and claws. She also wondered if the cat had been used as a deadly security device at an industrial plant, instead of using several, hefty guard dogs.

She'd never met Fred's new girlfriend, Nadine, which was to Stephanie's advantage because she planned to drop off the cat at Nadine's apartment on her way to Michael's late afternoon cocktail party. She began making the phone call while desperately hoping that Nadine was home.

"Hello?"

"Hello. My name is Lorna Marks. I'm Fred Mark's sister. May I please speak with Nadine Morrison?" asked Stephanie.

"This is she. How nice of you to call. Fred's told me so much about you."

"And he's told me so much about *you*, too. The reason I'm calling is, I'll bet you didn't know how forgetful Fred is. Once he has something on his mind, he just forgets about everything else. For instance, earlier today when he was at my place, he called our mother to tell her that he was on his way, then he just hung up the phone, and rushed out the door, without even thinking of saying goodbye to me. But as I just told you, that's so usual for Fred to do that, and everyone I know is used to that cute habit of his. It wasn't until five minutes after he left that I noticed he'd forgotten the gift he had for you. He'd planned to drop it off at your place on the way out of the city, but as usual, all Fred was thinking about was getting on the road and heading home. What a guy."

"He bought me a gift? How sweet of him," said Nadine.

"Yes, wasn't it? Let's just say it's something perishable, so, I thought I'd better deliver it for him. I'm on my way out to a late afternoon party, and I'll come by your place. I'm sorry I won't be able to stay for a chat because I'm in such a hurry to get to the party. I was supposed to be there over an hour ago, but I was searching for your phone number. Thank goodness I finally found it in my purse. I'll just drop off his wonderful gift to you, then run back to the cab. Perhaps we can get together soon for a coffee."

"I'd love that," said Nadine. "The gift is perishable, huh? Then it must be flowers, right?"

"Oh, I won't spoil his surprise. Fred went to so much trouble getting it. I just know he went to all that bother because he wanted to make sure you'd absolutely adore it."

"Hmmm, I wonder what it could be? Some sort of food? No, don't tell me. I just love surprises," said Nadine. "Oh, by the way, Lorna, would you please give me your parents' phone number so I can call and thank Fred for the gift?"

"Why, I thought he'd told you. Oh, there he goes again. So

forgetful," said Stephanie. "Fred was going to pick up our parents as soon as he arrived, and then they were going to our aunt and uncle's in Elmsville for the weekend. They just moved into their new home, so, they haven't given me their new phone number yet. But Fred said he'd call me tomorrow, so, when he does that, then I'll call you and give you their new number. How's that?"

"Thank you so much, Lorna. You know, I was just talking to my mother about him, and I..."

"Oh, no! There's the cab, now! I'm so sorry, Nadine, but I have to rush. I'll be at your place in hopefully less than fifteen minutes. Okay?"

"Oh, of course. I completely understand. Oh, I'm so excited about the gift! Bye for now, Lorna!"

"Bye-bye," said Stephanie, then she smiled while looking at the now unmoving, quiet box as she put on her gardening gloves.

Before Fred had shown his true colors, several of her friends had told her that they'd often seen him in fine restaurants with a pretty woman whom was approximately in her mid-thirties, however, Stephanie had been sure that Nadine was a client of his. But when she learned that he'd been seen in Nadine's company on several more occasions, Stephanie had felt that perhaps Nadine might be more than just one of Fred's clients.

One day, she had just walked into a restaurant with a friend, when she saw Fred kissing Nadine for a very long time in a secluded booth, so, the following day, Stephanie confronted him.

Fred had told her that Nadine had forced her affections on him, then after he and Stephanie had argued on the phone, Fred told her that he was very busy that week, but to prove how much he loved her, he wanted to drop by her apartment with a gift that he knew she would cherish.

That gift had been Booboo, and although Stephanie had been going through absolute hell because of that furred horror with razor-sharp teeth and claws, she felt so thankful that she'd been able to find out what Nadine's phone number and address were.

After placing the box on the back seat of the taxi, she took off her gardening gloves while hurrying back to her apartment to get the other two items for Nadine.

Stephanie then leaned back in the seat of the taxi and smirked. She didn't feel the least bit guilty about what she was doing because, after all, what would Nadine think if she happened to find out that Fred had given a gift to an ex-girlfriend?

Stephanie felt that she was doing her a favor because once Nadine discovered what Fred's gift was, she'd dump him, and be saved from a warped relationship with a demented Casanova.

When the cab pulled up in front of Nadine's apartment building, Stephanie asked the driver to carry the other two articles while accompanying her to Nadine's apartment, then she picked up the box while hoping that the cat would remain silent and motionless until a few minutes after she delivered it to Nadine.

She felt so pleased that Nadine lived on the second floor of the apartment building, then after arriving at the door to Nadine's apartment, Stephanie thanked the cab driver for helping her carry the other items for her, and then she told him that she'd meet him back at his cab in about two minutes.

When the cab driver began walking back down the stairs to the lobby, Stephanie pressed the doorbell while praying that the cat wouldn't move, meow, growl, or screech inside the box. The door opened, then Stephanie smiled and said: "Nadine? I'm Lorna. Sorry I'm in such a rush that I haven't time to chat with you."

"Oh, hello. It's so nice to meet you."

"This big gift is a bit heavy, so, I'll just set it down here on the floor, all right? Oh, and this bag with the bow on it is supposed to be opened after you open this larger gift. And this...hmmm. Well, I have no idea why he'd buy you this empty plastic box. It's a bit shallow and it looks sort of like something you'd either do dishes in, or perhaps soak small, delicate clothing in," said Stephanie.

"Oh, I know why he probably got me that. He saw a few pairs of my nylons in the bathroom sink one morning, so, I guess he bought me this plastic basin to soak them in."

"Of course. Well, I wish I didn't have to dash. How about I call you tomorrow and we set up a date for lunch soon?"

"I'd love that, Lorna," said Nadine, smiling. "These gifts are wrapped so beautifully. I'll bet you wrapped these for him."

"You guessed right. Fred's always relied on my good taste because God knows he's recently lost all of his. Now, don't forget to open the big box first, okay?"

"Big box first. Right. Got it. And thank you so much again. Enjoy your party, Lorna."

"Oh, I'm sure I will, *now*. Bye-bye!"

She hurried away from Nadine, down the stairs, into the cab, told the driver she was late for a cocktail party, so, please chance a speeding ticket, and then Stephanie relaxed when they'd driven out of sight of Nadine's apartment building.

The big, white garbage bag with the bow on it that she'd told Nadine to open after unwrapping the biggest box, contained a small supply of cat food, and half a bag of kitty litter.

The shallow, plastic container that Nadine had surmised was to soak her lingerie or nylons in, was really Booboo's freshly scrubbed kitty litter box.

Now all Stephanie had to contend with was Michael and her dizzy niece, Domenic Delaney. She found her niece to be incredibly boring and quite annoyingly dramatic, however, Stephanie had promised her sister that she'd pay some amount of attention to Domenic.

"Twenty-forty-seven, East Holloway next, right?"

"Yes, please," said Stephanie. "We're picking up my niece, so, I'll pay you the fare and a tip beforehand. That way, you can ignore the tip from her."

"Okay by me, lady," said the cab driver.

Stephanie calculated the fare so far, and the approximate total by the time they reached Michael's apartment building, then after adding a few extra dollars, plus a very good tip, she paid the cabbie in advance, and then heaved a huge sigh when she thought about having to tolerate her niece again.

Stephanie liked and admired Chad, so, she felt quite sorry for him for being so terribly misguided to even think there was an iota of true emotion in her niece.

She'd been close friends with Chad long before he'd met Domenic, and Stephanie had always wondered what in hell he saw in her niece.

She thought about that for a moment, then felt sure that Chad couldn't see anything in her niece because the only things inside

Domenic were a cold breeze of vanity, a tiny brain, and absolutely no trace of talent or taste, so, she wondered how Domenic had been able to even think about looking in Chad's direction.

She couldn't decide which was worse: the horrible experience she'd had with Booboo, or the hell she knew she'd be going through after just five minutes with Domenic.

Stephanie had only accepted the invitation to Michael's cocktail party because Chad had told her that he hoped to see her there, so, knowing that he'd be at the party was at least some relief to the usual parties Michael hosted.

She grimaced as she thought about his parties as being fifth-rate horror shows without the blood because she felt sure most of Michael's odd cronies didn't have any blood left in their veins.

· · · · · · · ❧✳❧ · · · · · ·

The taxi pulled up in front of Domenic's apartment building, and Stephanie forced a smile when she saw her niece hurrying out of the lobby, and then toward the cab.

"Steph! Darling! You look just too, too!" cried Domenic.

"Thanks."

Domenic got into the back seat of the cab, then groaned before saying: "You have no idea what hell I go through for my fans, no matter where I go, and no matter what time of day or night. But as you know, I'm almost as devoted to my sea of avid fans as they are to me, so, I suffer through, carrying reams of 8 x 10 glossies to hand out for them to cherish. Most of the photos are already signed because I'm often in too much of a rush to sign them while crowds of my fans are begging for autographs."

"You're always prepared," said Stephanie.

"Yes, a true star must be prepared at all times. Excuse me for a moment, please. Cabbie?"

"Yeah?"

"Are you married?" Domenic asked him.

"Yeah."

"Kiddies?"

"Yeah, we have two."

"Do you or you wife have a parent, or a sister, or a brother living with you?"

"*What*? This is a survey?" asked the cab driver, frowning.

"Oh, no, not at all. Mere preparation on my part. I need to know how many autographed keepsakes of me you'd need to take home to your family. Now let's see. You and your wife, the two kiddies, and...Anyone else?"

"Keepsakes?" he asked.

"Yes! Photos of me! I, Domenic Delaney!"

"Huh?"

"Oh, I quite understand that you wouldn't recognize me because you're in your cab while my show is on, but you can tell your family that you had *the* Destiny Blisslove of Destiny Weeps in your cab on this day. Yes, I'm the star of Destiny Weeps, and yes, I play the brilliant and astoundingly beautiful Destiny, so, before we part company, I shall give you photos of me for you and your family. And instead of a tip, I'll let you have two extra, autographed photos of me."

"Y'gotta be joking," said the cab driver.

"Exciting and difficult to believe, isn't it? But yes, I'll be giving you large photos of me. Now back to you, Steph. What do you think of this dress?"

"Interesting," she replied. "You do have a flair for mixing the oddest colors with the oddest colors."

"Oh, thank you, darling! I knew you'd absolutely adore it! And my hair?" asked Domenic.

"Unusual to say the least."

"You're just too kind, darling."

"I've been accused of that," said Stephanie.

"I won't take off these sunglasses until I'm out of the public eye because I simply can't take the chance of being crushed by a mob of adoring, but overly excited fans, and thereby delaying the production of another fine episode of Destiny Weeps. Ah, fame. It has such drawbacks. Oh, if only my audience knew how devoted I must always be at all times, and the tremendous strain of it all. But then I, as the great, desirable, loving Destiny Blisslove, have made a total commitment to my public, and too, as Domenic Delaney, I carry her legend with me long after the cameras stop rolling for the day. Sunup to sundown. From the first light on the horizon to the last moment of moonlight I see before I close my eyes to dream about another new day. Yes, another day of giving my all to the world. To go forth into the arms and hearts of an entire world. To lighten hearts and give the hope of true romance. To be the fulfillment of all the desires of all men who seek the perfect, ideal woman. To blow a kiss that ignites lust in all..."

Domenic blabbed on as the cab driver and Stephanie winced all the way to their destination, and before she got out of the cab, Domenic gave the bored driver eight autographed photographs while he felt so thankful that Stephanie had already paid the fare, and given him a quite generous tip before he'd driven to Domenic's apartment building.

Nick stepped out of the cab, then looked at the old, three-storey apartment building, and he thought it was enchanting. After he'd buzzed and announced his arrival, he loved the old elevator with the ornate gold mirror on the wall, and he admired what was left of the oriental carpet on the floor of the elevator.

Nick then used the little ceramic head of a clown that hung from a rhinestone chain to tap on the brass plate attached to Michael's door, and when it opened, he was astonished by how sophisticated his host looked. Michael's hair was slicked back, except for a cleverly cut bang that hung almost over his left eye, and his mustache swept up into a large curl at each end.

A very long, white silk scarf with a floral pattern was tossed recklessly around his neck and it draped over the arm he'd raised high in the air, at the end of which Michael was holding a mauve cigarette with a gold filter tip.

His floor-length, purple and green Chinese robe was tied at his very large waist with a silver brocade sash.

"How doooooo you do, Nick. Or may I call you, Nicky?"

"Nicky, please. Enchanté, Mr. Maneshevitz."

"It's *Namikovski*, but please call me Michael. Welcome to my humble abode."

"Uh! Oh, my! Fabulous vestibule! Such taste! Impeccable!"

"Thanks ever so," said Michael, smiling. "You have no idea how many cardboard egg cartons I had to spray gold and marbleize with blue and red paint to cover the ceiling and walls."

"Well, it was certainly worth the effort. So theatrical. Oh, my! And I love the flock of pink geese on this wall, and oh, these dolls on the table are darling," said Nick, grinning.

"How so terribly generous of you. I just can't thank you enough. I must say your ensemble is simply stunning, my dear. I find western attire so *raunchy*."

"I *have* been told I have a bit of a flair. Oh, here. These flowers are for you," said Nick, smiling broadly.

"Oh, oh, how wonderful. Thanks so, so much. I just adore roses. Mmmm, they smell so sweet."

"They're mums."

"Mums? Even better. I used to have a whole collection of dried ones pressed in my books. At least, I think they were called mums. Hmmm, or were they autumn leaves? Petunias? Daffodils? Oh, well, they're all the same. Please do follow me and I'll introduce you to the other guests. Everyone! I wish to introduce you to my next, charming guest! This is..."

Michael stood close to the entrance of the kitchen as he bathed in the compliments from his two middle-aged women neighbors, Margaret and Connie, whom he deemed to be rather conservative, so, he hoped that none of his guests would light up a joint sometime during the party.

He wondered if Margaret and Connie had a slight inkling that he was gay, besides being a renowned director. He'd often toyed with the idea of inviting them to one of his more formal parties, though Michael wasn't sure if Connie and Margaret were sophisticated enough, because during those types of parties, many of his guests had been known to snort cocaine during dessert.

Margaret and Connie had arrived in casual attire, and Michael admired Connie's denim overalls and her big, scuffed-up construction boots.

He'd never seen her wearing a tank top before and he found all the tattoos on her large arms rather fascinating. Connie's roommate and very close friend, Margaret, was wearing the hefty, many-chained, black leather jacket that Michael had seen Connie wearing quite often, so, he presumed that because they were almost the same size, they often wore each other's clothes.

Connie and Margaret weighed close to three hundred pounds each, so, it wasn't only Connie's quite big, thick mustache that drew attention from the more fashionably thin guests.

Michael heard the ding of his microwave, signaling another marvel was about to delight his guests, so, he rushed into the kitchen to remove the tray of hors d'oeuvres from the microwave.

He proudly admired the tray of bubbling hors d'oeuvres as he lifted them off the plastic tray with a plastic spatula and onto a big paper plate. Many of his guests had raved about the first batch, and now this batch looked even better.

He'd put a tiny slice of ham on each biscuit, added a tetch of blueberry jam, a dab each of ketchup and mustard, half an olive, an anchovy fillet, then for the crowning touch, he'd laid tiny slices of processed cheese over them.

Now that he'd microwaved this next batch of hors d'oeuvres until they were almost ready, he used toothpicks to stick half a marshmallow on top of each one, then he put the paper plate into the microwave for ten more seconds.

Michael then carried the tray of hors d'oeuvres to the living room and began serving his excited guests.

· · · · · · · ❧✳☙ · · · · · ·

It was now almost four in the afternoon, and as Michael squeezed through guests on his way back to the kitchen with the empty hors d'oeuvres tray, he realized it would soon be time to serve the light dinner he'd prepared to wow his guests.

He thanked his lucky stars that he hadn't forgotten to put six pounds of ground beef in the oven at a low temperature before going to bed the night before, because when he'd taken the ground beef out of the oven at noon, it had been cooked to perfection.

He'd then fried the diced liver and kidneys together, folded them into the cooked ground beef, then dumped it all into the big roasting pan.

After the previously very well-cooked meat had been cooked yet again for another fifteen minutes, he'd added four cans of green pea soup, precisely one and a half cups of salt, two large jars of pickled herring, and three cups of molasses, then voila! Another Namikovski specialty was waiting in the wings. Well, actually, in the oven, and Michael knew that his delightful concoction would be ready to serve in just over an hour.

He'd also prepared a few big bowls of coleslaw, the day

before, and Margaret and Connie had been kind enough to keep those bowls in their fridge until today. Michael pried off the lids of the plastic containers and plopped out the coleslaw onto platters, then he placed sprigs of parsley around the edges.

On the bottom shelf of the oven, he placed the aluminum tray heavily laden with parboiled carrots, onions, yams and spaghetti squash after he'd liberally sprinkled the vegetables with garlic salt, pepper, thyme, three handfuls of cloves, and a handful each of ground nutmeg, raisins and parmesan cheese.

He sighed and wiped his forehead with a tea towel while feeling pleased that dinner was well on its way to being ready at five o'clock on the dot.

Michael shuffled through the crowded room when he heard the buzzing of the intercom, then after finding out whom had rung the intercom button, he bellowed out a few lines of an operatic aria, and then rushed away to quickly tidy his mustache.

When he came out of the bathroom, many guests were staring at the entrance door, wondering whom this next, perhaps famous guest would be, then Michael held the doorknob as he faced his guests, threw back his head, and then announced: "Everyone! Desmond Del La Dumont has arrived!"

Murmurs of who the hell is he? And aw, hell no, not that old, pretentious fart, swept through the living room until the din calmed down to confused chatter again. Michael held the door ajar until he heard the elevator door open.

"Della!" exclaimed Michael, throwing open the door.

"Yes, I am here. Have I been announced?"

"Most certainly. You look fabulous."

"Of course I do. How are you, Mickey?"

"Alive and free and gloriously, madly happy!"

"Remarkable. But parties always lift your spirits. I'm ready to make my entrance."

"I'll let everyone know how lucky there are, now that you're here," said Michael. "Everyone! He's here! Everyone? I said, he's here! The famous Desmond Del La Dumont is here! Thanks! You, too! Hello? Most of the dizzy fucks are high, darling. They didn't hear me announce you. May I take your wrap?"

"No, thank you. I'll carry it with me in case I have an ever so slight perspiration problem. Not one person has looked at me. You know, Mickey, it never ceases to astound me how people have no idea how to react to a famous star such as I. They just can't seem able to put into words their praise, and so, not to appear idiotic, they pretend to ignore me. Ticket buyers!"

"Oh, don't I know," said Michael. "Such provincials. I'll fetch you you're favorite cocktail, and if I recall correctly, it's called, 'Double Trouble.' White wine and root beer served at room temperature in a martini glass. Am I right?"

"Yes, perfect. And with a twist of orange because, as you know, lemon is so com-ohhhhhnnn," said Desmond, sneering.

"Oh, Nicky! Come quick! Della, you'll adore meeting Nicky. He's a friend of David's, and he's dressed tres chic casual. Nicky, may I present a dear friend and so talented and world-famous director, Desmond Del La Dumont," said Michael, grinning.

"Oh, really? A truly and so real world-famous director? Oh, Mr. Dumont! Enchanté!" cried Nick.

"My-my and oo-oo so much. I do adore your ensemble, my

dear. Such taste. The pleasure is more than mine. Or should I say, howdy pardner?" asked Desmond, winking at him.

"Oh, you *rascal!* Thanks ever so much for your brilliant wit and your compliments," said Nick.

Michael felt so pleased that Desmond had followed the dress code by arriving in casual attire. He had on a simple chartreuse tube top over a pink and blue checkered sweatshirt, and below his gold chain belt with the large multicolored stones on it, he'd chosen to wear a pair of white culottes. A pair of red sneakers and argyle ankle socks set off the casual effect, admirably.

Michael found Desmond's floor-length denim cape so fascinating because of its yellow ostrich feather trim, and Desmond had lifted most of his cape and draped it over one arm, giving him that assured and noble look of a classic Roman senator.

"Those two rather masculine gentlemen across the room look somewhat intriguing," said Desmond. "Are they stuntmen, or do they build theater props and such?"

"What two men do you mean?" asked Michael.

"The ones standing over there by the oleander."

"Oh, they're not theater people like us, darling. They're my next-door neighbors, Connie and Margaret. This is the first time I've invited them to one of my more sophisticated parties. I wasn't sure how they'd react at seeing a few gay people because they're very naive ladies, but I'm sure they wouldn't know what a gay person even is, anyway."

"Those men are ladies?" asked Desmond. "Hmmm, well, I suppose the overalls on one, and the leather jacket on the other, make them appear a bit butch. That big mustache and many tattoos on the one wearing the overalls helps to give that impression."

"You know how feminists are," said Michael. "They always feel so inferior to men, so, they try so hard to look and talk like men. I'm sure both Margaret and Connie are deeply impressed by my party because they haven't been around many theatre people before. They're more into what they call contact sports. Connie plays football and Margaret plays hockey."

"I detest sports of any type," said Desmond. "The only thing I like about sports are the locker rooms and showers, although I haven't been invited into either of those. I've still got a lot of catching up to do before I get invited to jock parties because I was a late arrival into the gay world. I didn't find the inner doorknob of the closet door until I was about ten years old. Perhaps a tiny bit younger than that. Oh, isn't that Cynthia San Sims over there?"

"Why, yes it is," replied Michael. "You have such a keen eye. She's hardly recognizable after her marvelous chin implant. It gives her that extended Stan Laurel look, don't you think?"

"Yes, I do. She has a more determined look about her now. That might get her more than walk-ons, but after forty years in theatre, and still unable to remember more than ten lines, I highly doubt it," said Desmond. "But I find that new chin of hers rather interesting. Hmmm, yes, I'll keep her in mind for a play I'm considering to direct about love between a lesbian platypus and a bisexual spaniel. Very few speaking parts other than the two leads, but it should be a sellout because of the sex and nudity. And of course, bestiality *is* a touchy subject, as usual."

"Oh, it sounds so risqué, darling. Only you could have the courage to cross swords with both the law *and* the critics, and that's why I admire you so," said Michael.

"Be that as it may, I've been here for almost ten minutes, and I still haven't been asked for *one* autograph. Such cretins. Mickey, darling, you simply must invite..."

"Oh! The buzzer! Excuse me, Della, while I buzz in a guest. You mingle and dazzle and I'll be right back."

Michael's heart was beating a little faster as he buzzed in Zack, then just over a minute later, he bit down on his lower lip when he saw him getting off the elevator.

He'd asked Zack to bring a friend, but he'd never in his wildest dreams imagined that he'd bring Hank Harrison with him. Now Desmond would be outshone by him because Hank directed more successful plays than Desmond, and he also directed very popular porno films, therefore, Hank made much more money than Desmond, and he was far younger than him to boot.

He felt relieved to see that Hank was dressed casually in a T-shirt and jeans, and Michael noticed that besides the big, black leather boots that Zack had on, he seemed to be wearing light brown leather pants beneath his shin-length, tan raincoat.

"Sounds like quite a crowd in there," said Hank.

"Half of my guests couldn't make it," lied Michael.

"Aw, that's tragic, man. Same as usual, huh? I've never been to one of your parties before, but I've heard. Sorry, but we won't be staying for dinner. I know how you cook. So much effort and all that. But anyway, we can't stay long because something came up, if you know what I mean, so, I've got to shoot a film, very soon."

"With Zack in it?" asked Michael, wide-eyed.

"No," replied Hank. "The guys are a couple of bodybuilder students, working their way through college. They haven't met. Just got off on each other's photos, so, it'll be a hot shoot. Hmmm, I see that Lady Dumont is here."

"Yes, he is," said Michael. "He's a tiny bit peeved that you snatched two of his up-and-coming stars, so to speak, and it's not the first time. Rather naughty of you."

"Hey, their choice, man. They wanted fame. Look at this crowd. Amazing. Attention Goodwill shoppers! Looks like they shopped at Goodwill when they were totally wasted on really bad drugs. Fuck. C'mon, Zack."

"Oh, just a sec. Better take off my coat."

After Zack had unbuttoned his long, tan-colored raincoat, Michael gasped when he saw that under it, he only had on rather revealing, snug-fitting, light brown leather chaps, and a studded, black leather jock strap.

Michael gaped at the tattoos on Zack's heavily muscled body, and then he salivated when he saw the tattoo of a flaming chili pepper on his left buttock as Zack walked away to the living room with Hank.

Domenic saw Zack and Hank across the room, and she gawked at Zack's outfit. She was still staring at him when Stephanie made her way over to her.

"Quite a hunk, isn't he?" remarked Stephanie, smiling.

"My God! He's almost nude," said Domenic. "Is that his lover with him?"

Stephanie immediately decided to pretend that Zack wasn't one of her closest friends so that she could hopefully avoid introducing Domenic to him, because it would make Zack's afternoon worse than it already was by being here at Michael's.

"Steph?"

"Yes?"

"I just asked you about that...That almost nude young man over there with all the huge muscles," said Domenic.

"Have you lost interest in Chad?"

"No, and I'm not the least bit interested in that man over there. I just wanted to know if that's his male lover with him."

"Hmmm, well, I'm not sure if that's his male lover, but I do know Hank Harrison, so, I presume that he's one of his actors. Most likely one of his lead actors because of all he's got going for him. Hank does gay porno flicks."

"Oh? It looks like that almost nude muscleman he's with just finished making a porno sex movie, or is about to start one, because he looks almost erect with anticipation," said Domenic.

"No, he's just gifted, dear. As an actor, too. By the way, Chad's a close friend of Hank's, but how close I really don't know. Although I do know that many young actors have made a few extra bucks performing in one of Hank's gay porno films till they were able to get legit work. Maybe Chad did that, too."

"Chad?" asked Domenic, wide-eyed. "Oh, I can't believe *that*.

Not my Chad. He's so good in...I mean, he told me that he's mad about me. That he adores me. That he wants me. That he desires me. That he respects me. That he likes my hair. That he..."

"Well," interjected Stephanie, "I know of many actors who are as straight as an arrow, but they get lead in their pencil whenever they've been asked to do a film or two for Hank. They need the money till they get legit work, and Chad *is* gorgeous and he *does* know Hank very well, so, there's a chance he might've appeared in one of his porno films. But so what? It's just sex. It doesn't mean anything now that Chad's got a very promising career. Guys I've known who've done gay porno films for Hank are now happily married. Kids and all."

Stephanie knew that Chad had never performed in one of Hank's gay porno movies, but she just loved rapping on Domenic's hollow and rudely painted wooden head.

Domenic kept staring at Hank and Zack, then she turned to Stephanie and said: "Hmmm, well, I suppose *some* very masculine men would act in those types of sex movies, but of course, they must be bisexual to even consider taking on the role of a gay man, then do whatever gay men do when they do a porno sex movie. But no, I just know that my darling, macho Chad isn't the least bit gay or bisexual. No, he absolutely couldn't be. If he were, then I wouldn't want to compete with a man. After all, how could I? A woman, yes, but a man...Well, it's an entirely different sex."

"You've noticed?" asked Stephanie. "Does that mean if he *were* bisexual, you wouldn't see him anymore?"

"Yes, of course I'd stop dating him. I'm not about to get involved in a relationship like that. A homosexual affair of the heart, or whatever body part. If I see Chad do more than just shake that sex actor's hand, then that's it. It's over. Finished completely. Kaput, c'est finis, and other finalities. To hell with him."

"Oh? Maybe you should drop Chad now, if that stud over there already *has* done a porno film with Chad."

"Steph!" cried Domenic. "Now I feel terrible! Well, I'm glad I found out about Chad now before I got too deeply involved with him. I'll wait until he gets here and see how he acts with Hank, and that...That almost nude, big porno stud, then if I see anything too *familiar* between them, then it's goodbye, Chad. And forever, and ever, and ever."

"But I thought you sort of loved Chad. You must admit that even if he *has* dabbled his toe, or whatever other digit, in the male porno industry, at least he doesn't look like that very odd man over there in the Annie Oakley getup, or like Desmond Del La Dumont, or half of the very bad, partial drag at this party."

"That cowgirl outfit *is* out of place, isn't it? I mean, I'd never wear that to a casual party. Especially in the afternoon."

"No? The giddy guy in the cowgirl outfit is Nick, and from what I've heard from the gossip in here, he's staying with Chad for a month or so," said Stephanie, smiling.

"*Him*? With Chad? He never told me that! Well, this certainly changes things. Hmmm, I wonder if he and Chad sleep in the same bed? Do more than just sleep in it? Look at him. He's old enough to be my grandfather. Chad *must* be gay or bisexual, and I bet that's why he didn't tell me he was sharing his apartment with a flaming gay cowboy. Or cowgirl-hopeful. I'm leaving right now."

"No, stay awhile longer."

"Why?"

"Because Hank directs very good and legit plays. Some of the best. I saw him looking at you, so, you might get to meet him. Act in one of his plays and you'll get to know very important people. Any role he'd cast you in, would be much better than what you're doing now," said Stephanie.

"Oh, all right, I'll stay. Damn Chad. I'd better not see him kiss that porno actor. If I do, then I'll stop seeing him outside of work. Him and me. Us. Hollywood. Hah!" exclaimed Domenic.

Nick chatted with guests as he walked slowly around the living room, opening doors and peeking into rooms, and then as he looked across the living room at the clock on the stomach of the three-foot-tall, bright mauve statue of Michelangelo's David, he wondered if he could help Michael in the kitchen.

He weaved his way through the crowded room until he reached the kitchen, then he saw platters of coleslaw on the counter, so, Nick realized that Michael had everything under control.

Nick couldn't resist looking into the oven to see what the main dish looked like, especially because the odors from the oven intoxicated him. After peeking in the oven, he noticed that Michael had absent-mindedly left the oven on at a low temperature, and because it was getting late, Nick turned the oven up as high as it would go to hasten the cooking time. He then decided not to embarrass Michael by telling him that he'd forgotten to set the oven temperature properly.

Five minutes later, Michael's concoction in the oven began bubbling something fierce, then ten minutes after that, the juices started to dry up.

Considering that Michael felt that he didn't have to take his rather bizarre dinner out of the oven for another three-quarters of an hour, it spelled disaster for him, and great relief to any of his guests, however few, with good taste.

· · · · · · • ⊱⋆⊰ • · · · · · ·

"Are you involved in the theatre?" asked Nick.

"Yeah," replied Zack, with his head turned away from him.

"Are you presently in a play?"

"Film."

"Oh, how exciting!" cried Nick. "I'll just bet it's an action movie. You have such brawn and machismo, so, I'll bet you always get the leading lady. *Is* it an action film?"

"Yeah. Porno."

"Porno? Like in pornography?" asked Nick, aghast.

"Yeah, instead of coming *to* work, I come *at* work."

"Oh? How....Uh, interesting. Then that means you'd be nude and the other man would be nude, too, and then you'd both...Oh, my! Be still my heart! You do seem to be well-equipped for your movie roles," said Nick, looking at Zack's leather jockstrap.

"And I only roll with whoever turns me on, big time. I can't get it up for a wimp," said Zack. "Hey, Hank. What time do you have to be at the studio?"

"Oh, I see," said Hank. "Trouble at the O-Gay Corral, huh? Before a lasso gets tossed around you, let's go find somewhere private where we can discuss the studio shoot."

"You mean a studio shoot of another porno movie? How exciting!" cried Nick. "I do hope to see you later, young man. Even more of you in one of your films. You must tell me all the names of the titles because I think you're fabu...Oh...Bye. Hmmm,

I just have to chat with him again later. Hmmm, yes, indeedy-do."

Nick watched Hank and Zack pushing their way through the crowded room, and then he looked around at the other guests nearer to him, and he saw Domenic and Stephanie, therefore, he meandered over to meet them.

"Hello. Fabulous party, isn't it? I'm Nick Forman."

"For men? How appropriate. I'm Stephanie Richardson, and this is my niece, Domenic Delaney."

"No! Really? Domenic Delaney? Not *the* Domenic Delaney of Destiny Weeps?" cried Nick, gawking at her. "Why, I thought you looked familiar! That's my very favorite show! I never miss an episode of it!"

"Thank you, devoted fan. One of so, so many. I was told that you live with Chad Thomas."

"Yes, that's right! Isn't he just too, ever so gorgeous? And I know he's in Destiny Weeps with you, darling, but I'll bet you haven't seen him in just a towel. Scrumptious!"

"Hmmm," murmured Domenic, clenching her teeth.

"Nick, would you excuse us please? I was helping Domenic

with her lines just before you walked over to us. I don't want her

to lose her concentration," said Stephanie.

"Oh, why, I quite understand, and I'll leave immediately.

Imagine! Rehearsing right here! My friends just won't believe me.

I want your autograph, mind. I'll catch you up a little later,

darlings. Ta-ta."

"Farewell, devoted little fan," said Domenic. "Heavens, Steph!

He *does* live with Chad!"

"You didn't believe me?"

"I *couldn't* believe you. I thought by some outside chance, you

were having me on. What does he see in Nick? No, he can't be

involved with him. He can't. Not my Chad. My so handsome, so

masculine, so much of a man, Chad. I'll see how he greets Hank

Harrison and his stud companion before I make up my mind. It

can't be true. It might be true. No, it *can't* be true. Is it? No, it just

can't be true. If it *is* true, then my God! No, I must remain

nonchalant. I am a star. A *great* star. The greatest star, soon. I am

me. I am Domenic Delaney, and as such, I breathe life into

Destiny. Destiny Weeps is the show that brings precious life to audiences with no hope. No talent. No life that matters. Without me, what little life they have would be absolutely meaningless. Yes! I am me. Tis I. Unique. Brilliant. Loving. Beautiful. Talented. I, Domenic Delaney. Soon to be worshiped as a goddess by the entire world. Bringing hope and peace and love to every nation on earth. How could any man in his right mind who has been even *slightly* intimate with me, not want...No, *crave* me, and worship none other than me? Damn that Chad all to hell!"

Nick heard Michael introducing Chad to some guests, so, he fought his way to the kitchen, quickly poured some white wine into a plastic cup and began pushing his way through the crowded living room, then he hurried over to the open apartment door and handed the wine to Chad.

"Chad! You look sensational!" cried Nick. "I just love what you do to a T-shirt! It shows off your adorable pecs! But I love you even better in a towel! Oh, yes!"

"Isn't Chad just so handsome?" remarked Michael.

"Oh, man! Thanks for the wine, Nick," said Chad. "Sorry I'm

late, Michael, but I had work to do. Jeezuz. What the hell is...? Some crowd you have here."

"Alas, only a few showed up," said Michael. "I should have mentioned to you beforehand that Desmond Del La Dumont might drop by, because then you'd have been able to bring your latest résumé with you. But I'm sure he's well aware of your credits and such. Oh, and I'll be serving an early and tasty dinner in...."

"Well, look who's here, already!" exclaimed Chad. "And Hank Harrison, too! Excuse me. I'll go right over. Hank!" He then began struggling through the crowded room toward Zack and Hank.

"Excuse me, coming through," said Chad. "Zack! Hank! Excuse me, please. If you could please just move a little to the...Oops! Sorry. Coming through. Hey, Zack! Hank!"

Hank and Zack were grinning and waving at him from the far end of the crowded room as Chad made his way toward them.

Domenic had heard him shouting and she watched Chad getting closer to them. Her jaw dropped when she saw Zack hug Chad, then kiss his cheek. Domenic was mortified when Chad kissed Zack's cheek, too, while hugging him, then she glared at him as Chad laughed and talked with Zack and Hank.

Stephanie had decided not to tell her niece that Zack was Chad's younger brother because she was enjoying seeing Domenic showing some real emotion toward somebody.

"Well! I'm leaving right now!"

"Domenic! Now hold on," said Stephanie. "Chad and Zack may appear to be close friends, but you don't know exactly how close that friendship is. It might only be sexual or...Ew! How rank! Do you smell something really disgusting? Oh, my God, no! Look at the smoke coming from over there! It's the kitchen!"

"A fire! It's a fire! Oh, all this smoke! We've got to make it to the door!" shouted Domenic.

"Fire!...Help!...Out of my way!" shouted panicking guests.

Chad saw Domenic and Stephanie fighting their way through the screaming guests, so, he tried to push his way toward her through the terrified crowd.

"Domenic!...Domenic! It's me! Chad!"

"Stay away from me!...Shove, Steph! Quick!"

"Wait! Domenic! I'll help you!" shouted Chad. "Move! Let me through! Domenic! Wait!"

"Keep pushing them, Domenic!" exclaimed Stephanie.

"Oh, God! How frightful!" cried Domenic. "A blazing fire in our midst! My career can't end now! No! No! Not when the world desperately needs my talent!"

"We're almost at the door! This smoke is putrid! Blah! It stinks like a burning cat! Litter box, too!" Stephanie shouted. "Hey! Stop shoving me! We'll all going the same way, okay? Ew! What a disgusting stench! Kak! Kak! Huk-ka-kuhkk! My eyes are starting to burn from whatever's burning to death!"

"Hold my hand, Steph! Oh, goody! We made it! Quick!"

"We'll take the stairs! Hurry!" shouted Stephanie.

"Oh, no! Here comes Hank's stud! No! Stop!" cried Domenic.

Zack picked her up with one arm and Stephanie with his other arm, then he started stomping down the stairs with them as Domenic shouted: "Put us down! Let Go! I can walk, damn it! Stop! You heathen brute! You porno man!"

When he reached the ground floor, Zack set them down on

their feet, and grinned at them, then he said: "Gotta take care of the goods. You're Domenic, right? I'm Zack. Nice meeting you."

"I know very well who you are!" she exclaimed.

"Thanks, doll," Stephanie said to him. "What an awful stench that was. I almost choked to death."

"You would've anyway if you had a mouthful of the food. That was Mike's dinner," said Zack. "Really disgusting, huh? I ate here once, and that was enough for me, man. Fucking horrible. Well, I'd better get back up there and see if anyone else needs help. Take care, ladies. Nice seeing you, Steph. Y'look gorgeous as always."

"Thanks again, handsome. By the way, I love your drag. See you soon," she said.

"Wait!" cried Domenic.

"Yeah?" asked Zack.

"I must know. Do you love Chad?"

"Of course I do. Why wouldn't I? And he loves *me*. Okay? Is that all y'wanted to know?"

"Yes! And that's quite enough, thank you!"

"Okay then. Bye!" exclaimed Zack, rushing away.

"Steph! You heard him! He and Chad are lovers! Oh, God! I've been duped! Now I'll cry! I want to cry! I do it so well! Oh, Steph! Chad's gay!"

Stephanie very slightly tried to calm her niece as they sat in the back of a taxi. Domenic was scowling and swearing, and she felt so relieved that they'd been able to hail a cab and get away just as Chad was running out of Michael's apartment building and looking around for her.

"Can you believe it, Steph? Chad's living with that Nick thing and he's in love with that porno star! My God! And he wanted me to go away with him!" exclaimed Domenic. "The four of us would've ended up living together way out in California! Never! Oh, Steph! I like him so much! No! I can't do it! I've got to find a way to stop liking him too much! Oh! This is so awful! I hate him! I must! Oh, love, thy name is sorrow! Great Sorrow! A true tragedy! Oh, how I suffer so! I, the great Domenic! Thank God, I can use this great depth of almost real emotion in some other brilliant performance of Destiny Weeps! Yes! These tears are real! I'm sure they are, Steph! See? At least two tears have fallen!"

"There, there. Try to calm down, dear. If you like him so much, you have to learn to accept certain things, you sad creature. I know of many married couples who are different in that way. You know, the wife or the husband blatantly gay."

"I don't think I could handle that. I've never thought about it. This is just so unexpected. So sudden. So quick. So fast. No, I know I couldn't accept his...His *lifestyle*. His *wanton* lifestyle. No, never. Oh, Steph. I can't see him again."

"Well, I'm afraid you'll have to, kid, because you're working with him for two more weeks."

"Oh, no! You're right! And we have to kiss! Oh! I've got to see if they'll change the script so that he dies tomorrow. And before we kiss. Oh, I feel so used. So embarrassed. So humiliated. So empty. So confused. So heartbroken. So hurt. So angry. So upset. So disappointed. So crushed. So..."

"So Destiny Blisslove, and we all know that's why they cast you in the part," said Stephanie.

"I *am* right for that part, aren't I? I mean, I feel like her. I love like her. I am all the woman that she is. Or the woman I've *made* her to be. Oh, yes, it's true. So true. They knew that only I could be, and was, the great and beautiful Destiny Blisslove. A woman whom all men worship. They *adore*. When I as Destiny weep, all men weep for me and with me. This tragedy that I've now experienced with Chad is beyond grief, but I can use this in my many starring roles. Oh, yes, Steph, I'll carry these tiny pieces of my broken heart with me in the palm of my hand, forever. To display them to audiences everywhere. Domenic Delaney will be even greater than mere Destiny Blisslove. I molded her. Without me, she was only ink. I blew life into her veins."

"Sort of like Dr. Frankenstein, right? I guess it's all over, now. Oh, well. Bye-bye Chad," said Stephanie, suppressing a grin.

"Oh, yes! Goodbye, Chad! Farewell, Chad! Adieu, Chad! Ciao, Chad! Aloha, Chad! Au revoir, Chad! Bon..."

Of course, Stephanie would never tell Domenic the truth about Chad because she felt that her niece was completely undeserving of him. She knew that she was doing him a very big favor by having Domenic dump him.

* * * * * * * ❧❀❧ * * * * * *

Chad learned from other guests that Domenic and Stephanie had left in a cab, so, he stood on the sidewalk, hoping that another taxi would come by soon.

A taxi pulled up to the curb, and then seconds after a very beautiful woman stepped out of it, three of Michael's terrified guests scrambled into the back seat of the cab, then the beautiful woman smiled as she looked at Chad, and said: "Why, Chad. I haven't seen you in at least three years."

"Caroline? Caroline! I didn't recognize you at first! You look sensational! Well, you always did, but wow!"

"I've gone back to my natural color, and this hairstyle's a hell of a lot better than it was."

"What are you doing here?"

"Meeting Hank and Zack. Hank's got some filming to do, so, Zack is taking me to dinner. Where's all the smoke coming from? And that ungodly smell?"

"Aw, Mike's dinner burned. Thank hell."

"I'm surprised you'd come here, because I thought you couldn't stand that untalented old queen," said Caroline.

"Oh, I came here for two reasons. The most important one was because my girlfriend was here."

"Hmmm, oh, yes, Dolores, or something like that. Zack told me that she's some sort of actress."

"Yeah, she is, sort of. We're in a soap together, so, that's how we met."

"I see. Well, you don't seem too enthusiastic about your relationship with her."

"Up till now, I thought I felt more for her, but oh, I don't know. It's just that I thought the two of us would be good together. Like, as a couple in acting, but Domenic isn't very talented, so, it's going to take a lot of effort on my part, finding work for her while at the same time I'll be getting starring roles in movies."

"Oh, Chad. Stop feeling guilty about her lack of talent. By the way, I hear congratulations are in order. Hollywood. Good for you. I knew it was only a matter of time."

"Thanks. Yeah, I'm leaving soon. Just six more weeks. Man, you look so great," he said, grinning.

"Thanks, and I *feel* great, too. We'll be seeing much more of each other because I'm taking up permanent residence in L.A. I'm under contract now, and I'm starring in another movie soon. This time with Alec Baldwin."

"Yeah? Congratulations. That's great. I heard you made it big. Sorry, I haven't seen one of your films yet, but I've been sweating with this really awful soap opera. It's called, 'Destiny Weeps,' and I'm playing the part of a guy who worships Destiny Blisslove, and the script is amazingly bad, but somehow, there's enough TV viewers writing in about how much they love the show, that it's keeping the sponsors somewhat happy for now. It's a wonder that it wasn't cancelled after the first, really awful episode."

"I see. So, now I suppose you're going to tell me about your shower scenes with the leading lady. Wonderful. I've always fantasized about you in the shower," said Caroline.

"Yeah? That makes me feel great. Uh, I've always thought you were the most beautiful woman I'd ever seen, but you were dating Wolfgang Schlintzenhauer."

"Never! I was simply on his arm to make him look straight."

"Oh, really? I sure as hell wish I'd known that at the time."

"So do I. We've both wasted so much time dating the wrong people. So where's what's her name?"

"Who?" asked Chad, frowning.

"Hmmm, Dom Perignon, or whatever."

"Who? Dom Peri...? Oh! Domenic. She left. I think. I'll call her later."

"Well, I'm not going into that reeking building, and have that horrid smoke clinging to my hair and clothes, so, you can tell Zack to get his hot buns down here. Is that handsome lover of his, Hank, still there?"

"I don't know, but I'll run and get Zack for you. God, you're so beautiful! Everything about you. Uh, do you think I could, uh, like, join you and Zack for dinner?" Chad asked her.

"I'd love that. That'd make my whole evening."

"I'm going to kill that brother of mine for not telling me he was having dinner with you. But I guess he's had Hank on his mind, because Zack's been in Chicago for over six months. I'll go get him, and I'll be back as fast as I can!"

Michael wept because his combo cocktail and dinner party had been ruined again, however, he was overjoyed when Nick consented to move in with him the following day.

Domenic broke up with Chad, whom began dating Caroline, then they began living together in L.A., and then they married a month after that. Domenic felt rather sorry for her because Caroline had married Chad, whom Domenic had mistakenly thought was either bisexual or gay.

Chad got Stephanie work in several of his films, so, they all lived happily ever after. Hmmm, actually, I'm not too sure about that because...Well, movie-star marriages seldom last forever. But that's show biz.

The End

A TRYST IN THE FOG

Rachel stopped hurrying past trees and around bushes, and then she quickly turned her head to look back at the trees while listening for the sound of heavy footsteps.

She wiped perspiration from her forehead with the back of her right hand while gathering her ankle-length skirt with her left hand so it wouldn't snag on bushes, then she began hurrying again down the hill toward the boardwalk far below.

A small, dry branch broke when she stepped on it, and that snapping sound caused her to tense up and her heart to beat faster, as she hoped that the sound hadn't brought attention to her.

Rachel kept glancing down at the ground to make sure that she didn't step on another dry branch as she rushed onward while thinking about how very worried Alfred would be, if he knew that she was trying to elude a frightening stranger in the woods.

About half an hour earlier, she had climbed to the top of the hill where she often liked to sit and eat a light lunch while reading a book or letters from cousins, or just admiring the view of the town she lived in.

Before a strange man had begun pursuing her through the woods, Rachel had wished that she'd been sitting beside Alfred at the top of the hill while looking down at the three highest church steeples, the two towers of the town hall, several of the highest stores, and many rooftops of houses in town.

The highest steeple was part of her church, and while Rachel had been sitting at the top of the hill, eating an apple, she had fondly recalled that Sunday almost two months ago, when she'd seen Alfred for the first time, about half an hour after leaving church that day.

She and her best friend, Phoebe, had gone to church with their parents, then after church services, they had received permission to go for a stroll in the big park near the church.

The park had been crowded, but Rachel and Phoebe had noticed a handsome man in his mid-thirties whom they had seen smiling at them each time he'd passed by them.

They'd giggled every time the man had smiled at them, then after church on the following Sunday, they had giggled again each time that same man had smiled at them in the park.

On their third Sunday walk through the park after church, Rachel and Phoebe had been disappointed when they hadn't seen that handsome man.

They were sixteen years old, so, Phoebe and Rachel had found it rather exciting to have had a handsome, older man show more than casual interest in them.

On the following Saturday, they had been in the town's largest department store, when the handsome man appeared beside them while they'd been paying for hankies they'd chosen.

Rachel and Phoebe had blushed when he'd introduced himself as Alfred Wilson, then told them that his father owned the store, and Alfred had volunteered to manage the store on weekends.

Alfred lived in the city of Clarington, which was over twenty miles away, and he had explained that the reason he'd introduced himself to Rachel and Phoebe was because he wanted to know if they enjoyed shopping in his father's store.

It was the dawn of the nineteenth century, but even in such modern times, Phoebe and Rachel had worried about facing social disgrace by acknowledging keen interest in them from a man whom was not much younger than their fathers, unless that man had been properly introduced to them through their parents.

Alfred's explanation for introducing himself to them, however, had allayed Rachel and Phoebe's worries about being seen talking to him. After leaving the department store, Phoebe and Rachel had smiled and often giggled while talking about Alfred, and the possibility that he might be thinking about marrying soon, and he'd taken an interest in one of them for precisely that reason.

Their speculations as to Alfred's possible intentions were often the main topic of their conversation during the following week, and then the next Saturday afternoon, they pretended to be shopping for new blouses in the department store.

Rachel and Phoebe had felt rather pleased when Alfred had taken the time to speak with them for over five minutes before he'd had to rush away to attend to some urgent business.

For the next two Saturday afternoons, Rachel and Phoebe had gone to the department store and pretended to be shopping for various clothing items, and each time, Alfred had smiled and spoken to them for a few minutes.

Early in the evening of the third Saturday, Rachel had walked eight blocks from her home to spend an hour sitting on a bench on one of the big docks to watch fishermen unloading their catch for the day as many seagulls flew closely around them.

About five minutes later, her heart had leapt when she'd seen Alfred walking along the dock toward her as he smiled and waved. He'd then sat beside her on the bench, and they'd talked about the department store, and the view of the ocean.

Rachel's heart had skipped a beat when Alfred had been so bold as to tell her that he found her to be quite beautiful as well as very interesting, and she'd blushed while telling him that she enjoyed his conversation.

He had then told her that he had recently told his father that he refused to court and eventually marry the woman whom his father had selected for him, and that he preferred to marry a much younger woman of his own choosing.

Rachel had been quite excited when Alfred had told her that he wanted to start courting her, however, he worried that if people saw them together, his father would be quite upset until Alfred convinced him that he wanted to eventually marry Rachel.

She had felt flustered at first, then Rachel's blush had deepened when she had agreed to be secretly courted by him, and then she'd almost swooned an hour later, when they had walked behind a boathouse, and he'd taken her in his arms and kissed her.

She had never kissed a man before, so, Rachel had struggled out of his embrace, then after regaining her composure, she had agreed to meet Alfred the following Saturday evening at seven on the pier at the farthest end of the beach.

* * * * * * * ⟶⟡⟵ * * * * * *

The following Saturday evening, Alfred had become much more amorous, and Rachel had been both shocked and quite excited when he'd dared to caress her breasts through the material of her blouse.

He had then held her hand and led her toward a grove a short distance from the pier, then after they were amidst the trees, Alfred had pressed her back against a tree, and then started kissing her passionately.

Rachel's thoughts had whirled while Alfred had been begging her to let him take further liberties with her, and she had protested by telling him that she didn't want to ruin her reputation.

Alfred had then reminded her that he had defied his father by telling him that he wanted to marry her, and then after much more anxious pleading from him, she had let him start undressing her.

Rachel had blushed every time she recalled Alfred making love to her with such fervor while often telling her that he loved her with all his heart, and he hoped they could marry very soon.

Two weeks later, Rachel had panicked when she hadn't menstruated for several days past her usual monthly time. With each passing day, she had felt very worried while anxiously waiting for Saturday evening when she could tell Alfred that she might be pregnant.

On their next Saturday evening tryst, Rachel had wept while telling him that she might be pregnant, and now her parents would be devastated and everyone in town would be shocked.

Alfred, however, had allayed her fears by holding her in his arms while telling her that he'd learned that many young women missed their menstrual cycle after they'd had sexual relations with a man for the first time, but their menstrual cycles had resumed. He had then made Rachel feel overjoyed by telling her that if she were indeed pregnant, he'd marry her immediately.

From then on, Rachel had thought about how astonished her parents would be that she would soon be married, and she'd thought, as well, about styles of wedding dresses, and writing wedding invitations to all her relatives and friends.

She knew that Phoebe was going to love being her maid of honor, so, all Rachel had to do was decide on how many of her other friends she would have as bridesmaids.

She felt sure that even if she wasn't pregnant, Alfred was now thinking that to ensure that her reputation wasn't ruined, he should marry her very soon in case he did get her pregnant sometime during their furtive meetings.

Every day seemed like a week as she waited for her next Saturday evening tryst with Alfred, then they could discuss when he would call at her home to meet her parents, and when he would take her to Clarington to meet his parents.

By Wednesday, Rachel wished that she could tell her parents about her pending marriage, and she also worried that her parents might somehow realize that she was pregnant before Alfred had the chance to meet them, and then ask for her hand in marriage.

Her mother had frowned when Rachel had told her that she didn't feel hungry enough to have lunch, but Rachel couldn't tell her that she felt too excited to eat.

She felt quite restless for the next few hours, and her mother kept asking her why she seemed giddy at times, and anxious at other times, then Rachel felt she had to go for a walk before her mother asked her more questions about her fluctuating moods.

Rachel decided to make a sandwich and take it, as well as an apple and a few unread letters with her to sit at the top of her favorite hill. She'd walked half a block away from home, when she had seen Phoebe smiling and waving at her as she walked toward the front gate of her home.

When they reached each other on the sidewalk, Phoebe had invited her to her aunt's home for a glass of ginger ale, then Rachel had smiled while declining the invitation and explaining that she had decided to sit atop her favorite hill to eat a light lunch and read letters from her cousins.

Phoebe had then pouted while saying that she was leaving for Clarington early that evening with her parents for an overnight visit with her father's parents and she had wanted to spend some time with Rachel before leaving.

Rachel had then promised to spend the following afternoon with her when Phoebe returned to town, then they'd said goodbye to one another after Rachel had wished her a pleasant visit with her grandparents.

* * * * * * *⊱⋆⊰* * * * * *

While she'd sat near the top of the hill eating her sandwich, she'd felt too excited to open and read the letters from her cousins because she kept thinking about seeing Alfred on Saturday evening, when he'd perhaps ask her to marry him. Saturday was only three days away, but the time seemed to be passing much too slowly before she'd be with Alfred again.

Rachel had started eating the apple while looking at the steeple of her church rising above the town as she imagined the bells pealing on her wedding day.

She'd also imagined how pleased her parents would be when she told them that she'd be marrying the son of the man who owned the largest department store in town, as well as three other big department stores in Clarington.

* * * * * * * ⊱❈⊰ * * * * * *

While she had been thinking about her pending wedded bliss, Rachel had noticed mist starting to drift through the trees at the sides of the hill.

That mist had become denser while moving out from the trees, then very slowly spreading out onto the hill, and then moments later, while watching a breeze sweeping away parts of the fog in the trees to her right, she had frowned when she'd seen somebody moving slowly in her direction through the trees.

That person had quickly stepped behind a tree after becoming aware that Rachel was looking directly at him or her, and it was then that Rachel had become scared of that person's intentions.

After she had been able to determine that it was a man lurking in the trees, Rachel had started walking away to the other side of the hill, then she had glanced back, and seen him start moving slowly out from the trees and onto the hill, but she hadn't been able to discern whom he was because of the thickening fog.

Rachel had started hurrying while taking glances behind her, and each time she did, she saw the man following her. Now, with every step she took down the steep incline leading to the boardwalk beside the shore, thick wisps of fog drifted slowly around her, clouding her vision of trees and bushes she passed by.

She worried that if the fog became denser, it would be more difficult to see anyone on the boardwalk, or anyone coming out of the trees and high bushes that lined one side of the boardwalk.

Terrifying, distorted images flashed through her mind like

lightning as she recalled peering through the thickening fog at the large, hulking shape of that man following her across the top of the hill and into the trees.

When she'd broken into a run, she had heard the quickening, heavy footsteps of the man coming through bushes behind her. Each time Rachel had dared to slow her pace to look back, all she'd been able to see were huge bushes shaking while being parted, and the sound of loud grunts, cursing and swearing from the man in pursuit of her.

Sharp branches had scratched her forehead and left cheek when she'd rushed through high bushes, then after she stopped again, and didn't hear any sounds behind her, Rachel hoped that the man had decided to stop following her.

The fog had become much denser, and she realized that she wouldn't be able to see the ocean off to the left of the boardwalk when she reached it.

Rachel felt greatly relieved knowing that once she was on the old boardwalk beside the ocean, her footsteps would often be muffled by sand covering most of the old wooden boards.

Just over a minute later, she reached the boardwalk, and as she began hurrying along it, she continued to take quick glances behind her to see if the man was still pursuing her.

Her heart leapt each time thick billows of fog drifted around her and she couldn't see herself nor the man who might now be close enough to reach out and grab onto her.

A sudden gust cleared a slight amount of the fog around her, then Rachel panicked when she saw a form that resembled a pale gray, wavering shadow of a man standing a short distance away from her.

She didn't dare run into the fog-smothered trees beside the boardwalk, nor could she chance running back along the boardwalk because of the man pursuing her.

Rachel then hoped that the figure in the fog ahead of her might be a friendly man out for a stroll, therefore, she continued walking slowly toward the dark figure in the fog while hoping it wasn't the man whom had been pursuing her.

* * * * * * * ❧❀☙ * * * * * *

She hadn't known that the weather would change so rapidly, causing a dense fog so that she could only hear the huge swells sweeping up onto the shore from the now invisible ocean.

Rachel opened her handbag, slipped her hand inside it, and gripped the letter opener she'd brought to open the letters from her cousins. The letter opener had always fascinated her because the blade wavered up to the handle, which had a carved brass serpent coiling around it.

Rachel hoped that if she threatened the man in pursuit of her with the letter opener, he would turn around and run away somewhere in the fog.

The dark gray form standing ahead of her in the fog hadn't moved while she'd been slowly walking toward it, but she was ready to turn around and run back along the boardwalk if that dark form turned out to be the frightening man.

Rachel took a long, deep breath, then straightened her shoulders, and started to hum while hoping that her humming would cause whoever it was ahead of her to call out a friendly greeting to her.

The dampness of the fog combined with the perspiration on her face caused a shiver to run through her, and the handkerchief Rachel gripped in her hand was quite damp from constantly wiping her face.

She whimpered while tears trickled down her cheeks when she saw that the dark figure ahead of her was only a narrow, dark boat leaning upright against the low retaining wall.

After hurrying past the boat, sheets of fog wafted in front of her at times, so, Rachel kept lightly brushing her hand along the low, cement wall to make sure that she was still on the boardwalk.

She panicked when her ankle wobbled after she had stepped on a loose board, and then she'd quickly clamped her hand over her mouth to stifle a cry of surprise.

She felt so thankful that she hadn't twisted her ankle because that would have hampered her ability to keep hurrying away from the man who might now be close behind her.

She kept stopping to listen for the sound of footsteps behind her, then hearing heavy breathing and hurrying footsteps coming in her direction along the boardwalk, Rachel walked faster. She thought that if she began running, then the man following her would hear the sound of her rapid footsteps, and then he might also break into a run.

A mass of thick fog drifted around her, making it impossible for Rachel to discern anything, then a gust of wind thinned parts of the fog, and as she glanced down to make sure she didn't step into a deep rut, her heart leapt when she saw a dark form very close to her right.

When she stopped walking, the dark form stopped walking. Rachel then took two steps forward, and the dark figure took two steps forward, as well. Her thoughts whirled as she clamped her right hand over her mouth to stifle a scream.

She stifled another scream when a gust of wind struck her from behind, and the dampness of it chilled the perspiration on the back of her neck, sending shivers up and down her spine.

That recent gust had cleared some of the air around her, and Rachel saw that what she'd thought had been her pursuer off to one side of her, and copying her steps, had in reality only been her shadow reflected in a long, wide puddle on the sand where a portion of the boardwalk had been removed.

Parts of the boardwalk lowered in many places, and she recalled how sometimes she'd had to skirt large puddles created by high tides bringing water up through openings in the cement, retaining wall.

Rachel stumbled over more loose, uneven boards while recalling that the town officials had been promising for years to repair the boardwalk before the turn of the century, but now it was 1807, and work on the boardwalk still hadn't begun.

She touched the retaining wall, while thinking about the openings in it to access the beach. Although she worried about walking too close to the ocean, and possibly being dragged out by the undertow, Rachel felt that she had to begin walking on the beach to avoid the man on the boardwalk.

Rachel also knew that if she went through one of those openings to get down onto the beach, the low, concrete retaining wall would then be higher than her shoulders.

She stepped through an opening, and down onto the beach, then she leaned back against the retaining wall while listening for footsteps on the boardwalk.

Rachel hoped that the man would keep pursuing her along the boardwalk while not knowing that she was now on the beach, then moments later, she tensed up when she heard his footsteps come to a stop near the opening of the retaining wall she'd come through.

She held her breath as her heart pounded while she hoped that that the man wouldn't be able to see her through the fog if he looked over the retaining wall.

After hearing his footsteps resume along the boardwalk, Rachel moved away from the retaining wall and began struggling along the sandy beach, stumbling occasionally when the heels of her shoes sank into the sand, causing her to almost lose her balance.

Another dark shape in front of her made her heart leap again, and she stopped, peering ahead of her, with her hand inside her purse, gripping the letter opener. When she heard the man stop on the boardwalk again, Rachel tried to control her breathing, fearing that the sound of it would attract his attention.

The waves washing up on the shore made it difficult to hear any other sounds near her, and then Rachel panicked and she tried not to scream when she saw a dark figure standing near her.

She began backing away from the dark figure, then a gust of wind swirled and cleared the fog in front of her, and then she felt immensely relieved when she saw that the dark shape was only a post with a sign on it.

She hadn't heard footsteps on the boardwalk for over a minute, therefore, she thought that the man had had given up trying to find her in the fog. Rachel walked close to the retaining wall while praying that there would soon be another opening in the wall.

She heaved a big sigh when she felt another opening in the cement wall, then she made her way back up onto the boardwalk, and began hurrying along it while hoping that the man had given up his pursuit of her and he'd returned to town.

She dared to stop for a moment to catch her breath and listen for footsteps, then she sucked in her breath when she heard faint footsteps again on the boardwalk.

Whenever she couldn't hear the footsteps because the man was walking over sand covering portions of the old boards, Rachel felt scared as she wondered how much closer he was to her. As she rushed along the boardwalk while hoping that the fog would soon dissipate, she slammed into a post, and that sudden impact caused her mind to reel in terror.

The impact also caused her knees to buckle and she toppled sideways down onto the boardwalk, then she moaned in pain, as she got up onto her hands and knees.

Rachel dipped her hand into a puddle and splashed water onto her perspiring face, then she winced in pain from the scratches she'd gotten while struggling through high bushes on her way down to the boardwalk.

She stood up, trembling and taking deep breaths, then her heart leapt when she heard the man's footsteps again, then she started edging along the low retaining wall while hoping that the man couldn't see her through the fog.

Moments later, she felt relieved when she couldn't hear his footsteps, and then she felt certain that he had stopped trying to find her in the fog.

Rachel stayed close to the retaining wall as walked quickly along the boardwalk toward town. A few minutes later, the fog began clearing in some areas around her, and she desperately hoped that the fog would soon drift completely away.

She could now vaguely see the trees a short distance away from the other side of the boardwalk, and the waves rolling up onto the shore, however, she still wasn't able to discern much of the area ahead or behind her.

She hadn't heard footsteps behind her for almost five minutes, so, Rachel hoped that she was now safe, unless the man was following her by walking through the trees near the boardwalk.

She stopped walking again when she saw another dark shape far ahead of her, but this time, she could discern that it was really moving in her direction, then hearing casual whistling, she realized it must be either a fisherman on his way home from work, or some other harmless person strolling along the boardwalk.

Rachel clutched her purse tightly to her bosom, with her left hand, then she heaved a big sigh, brushed back her hair and smoothed out her dress before she resumed walking along the boardwalk toward whom she hoped was a fisherman.

Moments later, she began smiling when she felt sure that she recognized the gait of the person now closing the distance between them, so, she quickened her pace as she wiped tears off her cheeks and lifted strands of her damp hair away from her face.

"Rachel? Is that you?"

"Alfred! Oh, Alfred!" she cried while running toward him.

She reached him, and then after throwing her arms around him, Alfred embraced her.

"You're winded and trembling," he said. "Hmmm, this fog is rather unexpected, so, I imagine you became frightened when you lost your way."

"Oh, thank heavens you're here! A man came after me! I ran and ran, then I finally outdistanced him, thankfully! But it was so frightening! He seemed so angry because I often heard him cursing loudly while trudging though bushes and trees!"

"By Jove! That's outrageous! Are you all right? Aw, your face is scratched, and you've torn a small part of your dress! Oh,

Rachel! My poor darling!"

"Now that you're here, I'm certain that the man has ceased his pursuit of me!"

"Phoebe told me that you were going up the hill to read a few letters, so, if I hadn't chanced upon her, I wouldn't have known where you were. I thought that because of this fog, you might have decided to return to town by way of the boardwalk, and thank heavens you did decide on this route because I wouldn't have found you before he did. Did you recognize the ruffian?"

"No, and I dared not look too long at him. Had I stopped to try determining whom it was, then he would have taken that advantage to gain on me."

"Here, sit down on this bench. Your hands are trembling, but rest assured, he'll not attempt to trouble you further with me here beside you. There, there, my darling. Try to catch your breath. Such a frightful ordeal you've had."

"Oh, it *was* so frightful, and all I could see in this thick fog, was the vague shape of someone walking toward me, and I was terrified that it could be the man who had been following me! Oh,

Alfred! Thank God it was you! But what brought you here at this time? This is Wednesday, and you're never usually in town except on weekends to tend your father's store."

"He asked me to come to town today because father wanted me to oversee the new shipment of clothing for the sale we're having at the end of this month. That task was taken care of within an hour, and then I decided that perchance I might meet up with you in the park near your church. I was on my way there, hoping we could speak without bringing too much attention to ourselves, when I saw your friend, Phoebe, and I was quite delighted when she told me where you were. I tethered my carriage at the end of the street closest to the hill that I knew you'd climbed, then I...Oh, what was I thinking? My flask!"

Alfred reached into the inside pocket of his suit jacket, and took out his flask of brandy.

"Here, sip a tad of this brandy. That's it. Now I'll put a bit on my handkerchief to daub your scratches. There we are. Now, this may sting slightly."

"Ew! No, it's all right," said Rachel while wincing.

"Thank heavens these are only superficial scratches."

"Oh, Alfred! I just thought! Was Phoebe greatly surprised when you asked after me?"

"Not at all. I stopped my carriage in the street to greet her, then after I inquired as to her mother's health, I asked if you were well, too, and she told me you *were*, and that you'd climbed the hill that you often do. I then told her that I hoped to see both you and her in my store again sometime soon."

"Oh, thank goodness you told her that, and then you came looking for me!" exclaimed Rachel.

"I've been so worried since you told me that you could be with child, and I thought it best to see you today to reassure you that you needn't feel distraught. Do you still think there is the possibility that you could be with child?"

"I'll know for certain soon, and if I am, then we'll have to announce our marital intent immediately."

"I'm afraid marriage isn't possible, Rachel."

"Why ever not? We love each other."

"If only we had met under more opportune circumstances,

but fate has an uncanny way of wielding the unexpected. I was
blinded by your beauty, which caused my ensuing reckless folly to
result in dire consequences. I tried so often to muster the courage
to tell you, however, each time I was about to, my desire for you
swept away all sense of propriety. The truth I previously and
selfishly failed to disclose to you has now been thrust upon me as
an immediate duty. Rachel, I cannot marry you because I have a
wife and two children."

"You never told me that before! You told me that you loved me,
and that you wanted to marry me! That's why I let you make love
to me! Oh, Alfred! What will I do if I *am* with child?"

"I'm afraid it would prove disastrous not only to my wife and
family, but to all my friends, as well."

"But it would be your child! Yours and mine! What will people
say when they know of this?"

"I cannot let that happen, Rachel. I knew you would feel this
way, and now you could destroy my life."

"*Your* life? Have you not considered *mine*?"

"Yes, I have, which is why I came to town today to look for

you. I was fortunate to have met Phoebe this afternoon, and she told me you often enjoyed the view from the hill nearest your home. Now you know that it was I following you all this time."

"You may have thought that was amusing, but I was terrified because I thought it was a dangerous stranger following me."

"Hmmm, this fog is so thick and the town is far enough away that not a soul can see or hear us. You gave me quite a chase, Rachel. I thought I had lost you, but you walked right into my arms. Now our chance meeting will settle both of our problems. Tomorrow, when they find your body on the shore, people will simply assume that a sudden, strong breeze pulled your parasol from your hand, and when you waded into the water in a foolish attempt to retrieve it, the strong undercurrent swept you out into the ocean. If an examination of your body determines that you were strangled, instead, then I would have no need to worry. After all, you and I have never been seen together, therefore, how could I possibly be suspected of murdering you, my sweet, gentle, little Rachel? Your neck is so lovely and delicate. So easy to put one's hands around. Hmmm, yes. So easy."

"Oh, you're just trying to frighten me. Tell me you didn't mean what you just said. Alfred? What are you looking at? Do you see somebody on the beach?"

"No, the fog is too dense to see anyone on the beach. I was trying to see how high the waves are. Hear them? They make such a tremendous sound. Hmmm, being in this dense fog almost feels as if we were lost in the clouds. The fog's moisture feels so refreshing on my face that it almost quells the rage inside me."

"You sound so strange. So...Alfred?"

He turned his head to look at her, then he bared his clenched teeth while raising his hands toward her neck.

"No! You can't mean this! Oh, please, no! Alfred! No, please don't! No! No! Aaaaaaaa!"

An occasional breeze whisked parts of the thick fog away for a few moments to reveal a dark figure rushing along the boardwalk, then through the deserted streets of town.

The door of a house opened, and the dark figure stepped quickly inside without having been seen by anyone.

"Oh, there you are! I was worried that you'd lose your way in this thick fog! You look rather flushed! I hope you weren't hurrying home because you might have bumped into something and hurt yourself! Oh, and you've torn a bit of your clothing, and how did you get those scratches on your face? For goodness sakes, slow down or else you'll trip on your way up the stairs! You're always in such a rush! Oh, and dinner will be ready in less than an hour! I said...hmmm....Did you hear me up there, dear?"

"Yes, I heard you, mother!" Rachel shouted down to her.

"Wash your face, then put some of that medicated lotion on those scratches, dear! You don't want to get an infection! Mr. Halston died from an infected scratch, remember? Rachel?"

"Yes, I remember! I'll use the lotion! I don't want to die!"

"Heaven forbid, I should hope not! Oh, and bring your dress with you when you come back downstairs, all right? Just leave it in the sewing room and I'll mend it later! Enjoy your bath, dear!"

"I will, thank you!"

Rachel hurried to her bedroom while feeling relieved that her mother hadn't noticed that she'd been crying. She entered her bedroom, closed the door, then after heaving a long, shaky sigh, she dropped her handbag onto the seat of an upholstered chair.

Rachel undressed before she picked up her handbag, took out the bloody letter opener, and she felt immensely relieved for having taken the old handbag with her that day.

Her mother thought she had thrown that handbag away last year, but Rachel had found it at the back of her closet, earlier that day. Now she could dispose of the old handbag by burning it in the furnace, along with Alfred's billfold and her bloodstained, old blouse that her mother had been telling her for weeks to discard.

Several days later, Rachel felt greatly relieved when she began to menstruate, and it was then that she realized it happened later than usual sometimes.

She often tensed up and shuddered whenever she thought about her terrifying flight through the fog while trying to elude the man in pursuit of her, and then about how shocked she'd been when she'd found out that the man had been Alfred.

He'd been much larger than her, and very strong, so, Rachel

had felt so scared when he'd started strangling her while she'd been pounding his shoulder with her left fist at the same time she'd been trying to open her handbag with her right hand.

After she had taken the letter opener out of her handbag, then stabbed the side of his neck, it had taken her almost five minutes to stop shaking, and then regain her composure.

Rachel had then reached inside Alfred's suit jacket and removed his billfold, therefore, people would assume that he'd fallen victim to a ruthless, murdering thief.

She had once felt that her trysts with Alfred were similar to the tale of Romeo and Juliet. In this version of that tale, however, Juliet didn't die, nor had she any intention of committing suicide.

Rachel often wept while grieving over the loss of Alfred, for her destroyed wedding plans, and from the terror of almost being murdered by him.

The End

COMIC BOOK ROMANCE

Two zephyrs held hands as they whooshed over the rooftops, leapt off, then passing Lina as she stood on the balcony, they giggled while playfully lifting and fluffing her hair.

She had smiled when she'd felt their cooling kiss upon her warm face, and she sighed as she drank coffee and occasionally waved at the young man on the balcony across the lane.

It must have been a pair of zephyrs and not just one little breeze that had just swept by her. Lina felt certain of that because it seemed that most things and people were paired, whereas she was single. Too single for her mother's liking.

She smiled and waved again at the young man who looked terrified as he stood on the balcony, with his back pressed against the outside wall of the apartment building while Mario Mangello was inside the apartment, looking through closets to see if his wife, Carmella, had a lover hiding in one of them.

The young man was wearing only a tank top, and holding his hands in front of him while he stared at Lina and wondered if she would call out to Mario to tell him that a guy was on his balcony. Lina smiled and waved at him again before she went back inside for more coffee.

"Lina? While you're shopping, don't forget to pick up a box of tea. I'm down to my last tea bag," said Anna.

"So what? You've had that last tea bag for years because you never drink tea," she said to her mother.

"Then why have I only got one tea bag left?"

"All right, what kind do you want, then?"

"Lipton's. No, Red Rose. Tetley's? Hmmm, maybe I should try one of those flavored teas. Or are they spiced teas? Hmmm, yes, I think something zesty or spicy would be nice, dear."

"I'll see what they have," said Lina.

"Then there are teas to relax you, so, I suppose some teas make you all on edge, so, would you look for one of those types?"

"Yes, mother."

Lina felt sure that there were only two brands of tea at the corner store, therefore, she'd have to stop by the pharmacy to see if they sold a tea to soothe ruffled nerves.

"You know, after thinking about it, I wonder what flavor that relaxed tea will be? What do you think?"

"Oh, probably something minty," replied Lina.

"I like mint because it's so refreshing, so, I'll like that tea. Hmmm, no, on second thought, that tea'd make me drowsy all day, and I nap enough as it is, so, maybe you should get me some sort of tea that's a pick-me-up. Ohhhh, it's so hard to decide!"

"Red Rose or Tetley's, mother. That's all they carry, I think, but if they happen to have something like lemon, or some other flavor, then I'll get you that."

"I was in Gina's kitchen just yesterday, looking for the sugar to refill the bowl for her, and I looked in one of the cupboards, and I saw she had a flavored tea. Hmmm, what was it now? Hmmm, orange something. I think it was a Chinese orange. Oh, yes, now I remember! It was called orange Peking," said Anna.

"Hmmm, are you sure it wasn't orange *pekoe*?"

"That's it! Orange pekoe!"

"That's the type of tea you have now."

"Oh? It doesn't have much of an orange flavor, dear."

"Right. So, I'll buy whatever they have that's flavored. They probably only have a lemon-flavored tea, though," said Lina.

"Oh, and don't buy any of their toilet paper because I get it at Price Mart for half the price."

"Right. No toilet paper. While I'm there, I'll also pick up a copy of the Enquirer. Okay?"

"Oh, please! It's the only paper that tells you all the news before it happens, and they know about Hollywood divorces before any of the regular newspapers do. And they're almost always right."

"Right. So right. Okay, after I finish this coffee, I'll be going to the store, so, look over that grocery list and see if there's something you might've forgotten to ask me to put on it."

"Hmmm, seems like everything I want is here on your list, and I suppose you didn't put the Enquirer on it because you won't forget to pick it up. Hmmm, yes, I think that's everything. Oh, you don't have any fruit written down, dear."

"I'll just pick up whatever's fresh."

"But they *always* have a nice selection of fresh fruit. See if they have any cherries because I love cherries. Well, no, strawberries because I can do more with *them*," said Anna.

"Are you sure? Because we've got so much fruit as it is, but okay, I'll get a carton of strawberries."

"Strawberries. So nice with so much. Strawberries on ice cream, and strawberries on cereal, and you can squash them to make a lovely strawberry jam for your toast. So versatile."

"Versatile? Okay, then. Bye, mother."

"Bye."

Lina left the apartment, and she was going to take the stairs down from the third floor, but Mrs. Henshaw was holding the elevator door open with her walker and beckoning her, so, she hurried over to the elevator, and stepped into it.

"Thanks. I was going to walk down," said Lina.

"*Walk* down? Young people are always throwing that in my face. What floor do you want, dear?" asked Mrs. Henshaw.

"The ground floor, please. I didn't mean to imply that you..."

"No, it's all right. I understand, perfectly, dear. Besides, the damage is done now. Of course, *I* understand, but young people like you, oh, no, they can never understand how I suffer so much. Sometimes I feel so..."

"Please! Hold the elevator!"

"Oh, it's Mrs. Jelnik," said Mrs. Henshaw.

Lina held the elevator door open for Mrs. Jelnik, who was grimacing as she moved very slowly toward them with her walker.

"You'd better hurry, dear! I don't mind how long it takes you to get here, but you know how impatient young people like Lina are! Can you go any faster? You poor thing! Lina, would you mind helping her walk, please? That's if you're not too, too impatient."

"Certainly. I'm not in any hurry, really," said Lina, smiling.

She went over to Mrs. Jelnik, who told her that she didn't need any help, then Lina walked beside her, and then they got on the elevator with Mrs. Henshaw.

"Going up or going down?" asked Mrs. Jelnik.

"This is the top floor, so, obviously we're going down, dear. Isn't that right, Lina," said Mrs. Henshaw.

"Yes, we are."

"Well, I suppose if you're going down *now*, then I'll come down right now with you. Unless you were waiting for somebody else, and if you *are*, then I suppose I'll just have to wait with you, although my legs are in so much pain," said Mrs. Jelnik.

Lina was about to press the button, when another elderly woman neighbor hailed them.

"Who's that? Doris? Are you coming, too, dear? My, this certainly is a busy time of day. Do you need any help? If you do, we might be able to talk Lina into helping you, dear! But then you know how young people are! Well, Lina?" asked Mrs. Henshaw.

"Certainly I'll help," Lina said as she stepped off the elevator.

"Please! I don't need any help! I'm *not* a cripple! God knows I almost am, though, with these legs of mine. Oh-o-o-o, nnnfff! Oh, God! The pain! My poor legs!"

"There won't be enough room on the elevator with all the walkers, so, I'll take the stairs down," said Lina, smiling.

"But we were depending on you to help us place the walkers on the elevator for us, in a way that we could get off again. Oh, never mind. I understand. Young, healthy legs, and all, and I imagine you're in too much of a hurry to help those less fortunate than yourself. I wish I didn't have to rely on elevators, but with these legs of mine, well, it isn't pleasant. But then of course, if you can't or *won't* help," said Mrs. Henshaw.

"Oh, of course, I'll help you," Lina told her.

She looked at the walkers, then around at the floor of the elevator that had been designed to hold no more than five, slender people, and then Lina hoped that the elderly ladies would agree with her plan.

"Now, you step back over this way, Mrs. Henshaw, and Mrs. Jelnik, if you move a bit more to your right. Hmmm, just a bit more. Yes, that's it. Now if Mrs. Langsford's walker was put here, well, she'd have to move over here just a...Hmmm, you'll have to let me move your walker for you," Lina told Mrs. Langsford.

"I'm *trying*. You young people just don't understand it's so difficult for me to stand on my own. Uh! Oh, God. Oh-o-o."

"Oh, but I *do* understand. You can hold onto Mrs. Henshaw's walker while I'm positioning *your* walker. All right? It's so hard to turn these things to fit like...No, like this. Well, I'll try putting it *this* way. This elevator is so small," said Lina.

"Are you implying that I'm overweight?""

"No, not at all, Mrs. Langsford," replied Lina. "It's just that this elevator *is* a bit small."

"Well, it's not my fault! I gained all this weight after I had my sixth heart attack and my tenth stroke! Of all the nerve! Young people have no idea!"

"Please! I didn't mean that! I'm sorry you took it that way!"

"You'd think with *your* legs, you wouldn't have to use the elevator. If I were lucky enough to be *your* age, I'd be running up and down the stairs," said Mrs. Jelnik.

"Sad how lazy young people are today," Mrs. Henshaw said.

"Simply awful," added Mrs. Langsford.

"But I was going to take the stairs before you asked me to..."

"Too late for apologies, Lina. I mean, after all, the damage is down, now," said Mrs. Henshaw.

"No, you don't understand. I meant that I..." Lina started to say.

"Well, with you on the elevator with us, Lina, it's apparent that there isn't enough room for me. Oh, well, I'll just have to accept that, and I'll have to use the stairs, and oh, I can just imagine the pain of it all. Oh, God help me!" groaned Mrs. Jelnik.

"Oh, you poor, suffering soul. Well, if you're taking the stairs, Cora, then so am I," huffed Mrs. Henshaw.

"No! Please don't do that! I was going to walk down, but when you held the door open for me, I got on," Lina told her.

"Don't you think it's just a little too late for apologies now? The damage has been done, so, we'll take the stairs, thank you, and God knows how we'll manage, but we'll do it somehow. Come on, Cora, let's face the hell we've been pushed into because *somebody* younger than us feels that she needs the elevator more than we do. We'll brave those stairs, and whichever one of us makes it down, can call an ambulance for the other. Who knows, though? Maybe *neither* of us'll make it," said Mrs. Henshaw.

"But that's not necessary!" exclaimed Lina as she quickly stepped off the elevator, then Mrs. Henshaw and Mrs. Jelnik began struggling off it with their walkers as they frowned and groaned.

"No, please stay on the elevator," Lina urged them.

"At least it was nice of Lina to get off the elevator to give us room to get off it, so, there must be *some* trace of generosity in her. Well, now you can get back on it, Lina, and I certainly hope you think there's enough room for you, now. Well, off we go to try our luck on the stairs, but I'm so terrified," said Mrs. Henshaw.

"Please don't! You might fall on the stairs!" cried Lina.

"Well, you should've thought of that before you made us walk all the way down those steep stairs."

"Young people, huh? Awful. Just awful," said Mrs. Langsford.

"But I certainly didn't want you to have to use the stairs. You misunderstood me," said Lina.

"Oh, of course, I'm sure we did, young lady. Oh-o-o-o, my legs! Oh, God! Ew! I wish I had my walker, but how can I possibly take *that* downstairs while I'm holding onto the banister? Uh! Uh! Oh-o-o!" cried Mrs. Jelnik.

"Not to worry, dear. I can struggle down two steps, then you can pass me our walkers, one at a time, then I'll struggle down two more steps, and then you can hand me the walkers again, and so on 'til we get all the way down to the lobby," said Mrs. Henshaw.

"*If* we *can* make it all the way down without falling and

breaking our necks. But yes, you're right. Passing the walkers down to you every two steps sounds like it should work. Okay, Margaret, you try going down the first two steps."

"Lina? Don't just stand there! Are you getting on the elevator with me, or not? I haven't got all day! I have a doctor's appointment! You've already ruined *their* day, so, please don't ruin the rest *my* day! Italians! So insensitive!" yelled Mrs. Langsford.

"But I..." Lina was about to say.

"Well, don't keep the poor woman waiting, Lina! I mean, my God! Try to show *some* sensitivity!" exclaimed Mrs. Henshaw.

"Um, I...Right. I'm coming, Mrs. Langsford," said Lina.

She pressed the button for the ground floor, then Lina smiled at Mrs. Langsford, who was pouting and moaning.

"This elevator is quite slow, isn't it?" Lina remarked, but Mrs. Langsford just replied with a long groan.

"It's a nice day, isn't it? You know, I hadn't planned to use the elevator, but when I left the apartment, Mrs. Henshaw was holding the elevator door for me, so, that's why I decided to take the elevator down to the lobby, instead of the stairs. I had no intention of them having to use the stairs."

"Hmmmm," murmured Mrs. Langsford, glaring at her.

"So, you told me that you have a doctor's appointment. Not many doctors work on Saturdays, unless they work in a hospital."

"Oh, so now I'm a liar as well as a fat cripple, am I?"

"No! I meant that most doctors' offices are..."

"We're at the ground floor, now, but I don't suppose there's any chance you'd help me off with my walker. Oh, well, there's no use asking young people today for *anything*."

"Here, let me help you," said Lina.

"Damn! I forgot my purse! Now I'll have to go all the way back up to my apartment! Uhnn-nff! Oh-o-o, the pain."

"I can go up with you and if you give me your keys and tell me where your purse is, I'll run in and get it for you, so, you won't miss your doctor's appointment. Okay?"

"My appointment's not for another three hours, so, why are you trying to rush me? I'm old, and if you haven't noticed, I use a walker. Young people are always in such a hurry. Just awful. Oh, I just remembered I took what I might need out of my purse and put it all in the pockets of this linen jacket. Thank God. Now I can get on my way out."

"I see. Well, all right then. Have a nice day, Mrs. Langsford."

"I *had* hoped for that, but then there *you* were. Push, push, push. Ohhhh, mmfff! How I suffer so."

Lina walked over to the staircase to listen for the other two, elderly women, then not hearing anything, and becoming worried, she walked up one floor, and then called out to them.

She became very worried, so, she hurried up to the second floor, then to the third, but they weren't there, either. Lina sighed and walked back downstairs, and when she was half a block away from her apartment building, she saw Mrs. Henshaw and Mrs. Jelnik hurrying to catch a bus, without their walkers.

She was nearing the grocery store, when a colorful beach ball bounced across the street while four small boys shouted to her, asking her to get the ball for them, so, Lina chased after the ball, then tossed it back across the street to them.

Mrs. Tomasso began shouting at her from the second-floor window of her apartment, telling Lina that her daughter had just dropped the ball from the window and that Lina had no right to give that ball to those boys.

The boys ran away with the ball, laughing, as Lina tried to apologize and tell Mrs. Tomasso that she hadn't known that the ball belonged to her daughter, but the window was slammed shut before Lina could finish explaining.

She heard laughter behind her, then turning around, she saw seventeen-year-old Rita Colbrinni wearing a red, sparkling shawl, sitting at a small card table outside the corner store, and holding a deck of tarot cards.

"Wanna know what the *rest* of your day's gonna be like?"

"It can't get any worse, believe me," replied Lina.

"C'mon, let me play three cards and tell you," said Rita.

"I don't believe in tarot cards, and neither do you."

"Sure I do, when I'm wearing my magic shawl. Oh, c'mon."

"Two cards, and that's all," said Lina, smiling.

"Great."

Rita shuffled the cards, then after she fanned out the deck on the table, she picked up a card.

"Hmmm, this card tells me you're going somewhere."

"Right. Into the store," said Lina.

"Aha! You see? I was right. Hmmm, now this one tells me...It says...Just a sec, it's coming to me. Ah, yes. Yes. Hmmm, uh-huh, hmmm, very nice. Lucky you," Rita told her with a crooked smile.

"What?" asked Lina. "This is so silly."

"Shhhhh. Aha! I've got it! I see that you're going to meet a tall, dark man. Ahhhh, and he's a handsome man, too. Hmmm, yes, and...Ahhh, yes! He's Italian!"

"Everybody in this neighborhood is *Italian*. Well, there are a few old ladies in my apartment building who aren't," said Lina.

"Hmmm, I see that he's a plumber. No, not a plumber! Hmmm, it's coming to me. Ahhhh, yes! He's a factory worker! No, even better, a factory *supervisor*. Yes, that's it!"

"Uh-huh, sure. Bye, Rita. Thanks for the fortune."

"No, wait a sec! Don't you wanna know how many children that you and that tall, handsome man are going to have?"

"No thanks, because with my luck, I just know that they'll all be from his ex-wife."

"Yeah, well, maybe. Okay, bye."

"Bye," said Lina, smiling as she pushed the store door open.

She entered the store, picked up the few items her mother had wanted, then after Lina stopped her shopping cart by the magazine section, she put a copy of the latest Enquirer into the cart, and then she began glancing through other magazines.

Danny D'Amato, the son of the grocery store owners, saw Lina looking through a magazine, so, he feigned a scowl at her.

"Ay! Y'think this is a library?" Danny asked her.

"Yeah, for underaged kids who look at all the boob mags."

"Like hell they do. The real adult ones are in plastic."

"Just as plastic as the women in them," said Lina.

"So? Are y'going to buy one, or read 'em all?"

"Don't you have something resembling a life form to get on with, instead of annoying me?"

"Aw, go to hell! Hey, I'm off in half an hour. Wanna have a coffee with me?" asked Danny.

"You'd be disappointed having coffee with me because I've got more than air in my head."

"So, who looks inside the head?"

"Right," she replied as she smirked while wheeling her cart over to the checkout counter.

Danny suppressed a grin as Lina began placing items on the counter, then he said: "Oh, the Enquirer. My mom reads that. Kinky stuff like aliens getting women pregnant, or tamer stuff like movie stars on heavy drugs at an orgy. Oh, these strawberries are a great buy, aren't they? Tea? Maybe I should've asked you if you wanted to have a cup of tea with me, instead of a coffee. Love to see inside *your* cupboard, Lina."

"You want to go through my purse, too?"

"I'd love to go through *all* your personal things," said Danny.

"Right. How's your mother?"

"Same. Wants me to get married, yesterday."

"To which mother of your children?" Lina asked him.

"Uh-uh-uh! Those are all lies. You know, if you did *all* your grocery shopping here, I'd carry them home for you."

"Thanks, but I don't have a leash to put on you. Besides, dogs aren't allowed in our building."

"Awww, you play so hard to get," said Danny, smiling.

"Well, *somebody* has to in this neighborhood. Why, Danny! I didn't know you could count change! Oh, I see now. The cash register automatically indicates how much change to give back. Gee, for a moment there, I thought you'd impressed me."

"You're a rotten woman, Lina. I could change all that if you let me take you out some night. All you need is to go out on a date with me just once, and then you'd see how much of a sweet guy I really am."

"That's okay because I get daily reports on *your* sweetness from *so* many people."

"Yeah? So, how about that coffee, then? Or tea?"

"No thanks. I don't have time to bleach my hair and get breast implants just to have a cup of coffee with you, and then I might want to talk to you, too, and about more than the latest color of my nail polish."

"What's there to talk about? Other than you and me?"

"Right. Bye now. Oh, look! There's one of your girlfriends holding a can of soup and staring at it. You'd better rush over there and tell her what it is and how to open it because I'm sure that anything that's not shaped like a pizza box is confusing for her. Say hello to your mother for me."

"Ciao, gorgeous! Hey! And if you change your mind about having a coffee with me, then let me know!"

"Right!" replied Lina, smirking.

Lina certainly didn't want anything to do with Danny D'Amato because she'd seen him with so many young women in the neighborhood, and she'd had enough bad relationships, already.

She began to recall the first time she'd thought she had met the right man. His name had been Carl Dawson and she'd met him while she had been studying nursing.

Lina had attended a party at a large rooming house close to the campus when she'd seen Carl talking with some friends, but she hadn't met him that night, although he had smiled at her several times before he left twenty minutes after she'd arrived.

Two days later, she had been sitting on a park bench, reading a book, and Carl had sat down next to her. He'd introduced himself, then asked her if she'd like to have a coffee with him, and that had been the beginning of their very brief relationship.

A month later, after a wonderful time together, Carl had wanted to make love to her, but he'd put his request to her in a rather subtle way.

He'd told her that he wanted to spend some time completely alone with her, however, he had said that he shared a very small apartment with three other young men, and because Lina lived at home with her mother, Carl had suggested that they rent a motel room to get a little closer.

Lina had felt that becoming intimate with him in a motel room seemed a bit sordid, and she'd asked him if he understood how she felt about that. He'd then told her that he loved her, and wanted to marry her very soon because he couldn't stand waiting to make love to her, then he pleaded with her to reconsider by coming to an expensive hotel with him the following week.

Lina, after careful consideration, and knowing how much he

loved her and wanted to marry her, had decided to throw her inhibitions away and go to bed with him, and she'd planned to tell him that when he came back to the city after visiting his parents, which is where he'd said he went every weekend.

Her best friend, Belinda, had asked her who this mysterious man was that Lina had been sort of surreptitiously dating for about a month, and Lina had told her that she wasn't secretly dating him, but that they always met at a bistro or local nightclub.

Lina had then told her that she'd introduce Carl to her sometime during the next week because he always went away on the weekends to visit his parents.

Belinda had urged her to come with her to a small party that Saturday night if Carl was going to be away. After much prodding, Lina accepted Belinda's invitation, and when they arrived at the home of Belinda's friends, the host greeted them at the door, and then led them to the living room while saying that he wanted them to meet his two best friends.

The host introduced them to Carl and his very pregnant wife, which had shocked and angered Lina, especially when she'd almost made love with him. So, it was goodbye to Carl.

Tony was next. He'd told Lina that he adored her, but two weeks later, she learned that he had two other girlfriends whom he also adored just as much as her, and one of his other girlfriend's was pregnant with his baby. Goodbye, Tony.

After three years of similar experiences, Lina wondered if she'd ever meet a man who wasn't either married, or had another girlfriend. Being a nurse at the local hospital hampered her social life because she often worked early morning or late night shifts, and all the male medical staff were married.

She was beginning to think she'd never be married now that she was almost twenty-six years old, and all the girls she knew, or had gone to school with, were married.

Her mother was constantly trying to set her up with men whom Lina found very undesirable because of their personalities and the fact that many of them were recently divorced.

She set the grocery bags down on the kitchen counter and began helping her mother put the groceries away.

"Here. I bought this package of tea because it has assorted flavors. Would you like me to make a cup for us?" asked Lina.

"Oh, no thanks, dear. I don't like tea that much. Didn't they have any *real* tea?"

"This *is* real tea, but the only difference is that it's flavored, and you told me you wanted a box of flavored tea."

"Oh? Hmmm, I must've been talking about something else that was flavored, and you thought I meant the tea. But it's all right, dear, I'll pick up some real tea when I go shopping next week. Hmmm, and I was so sure that the store carried *real* tea. Oh, well."

"Mother, I told you that they had real, or regular tea at the store, but you...Never mind."

"Oh, by the way, dear, speaking of shopping, that nice man who delivers the groceries sometimes, asked about you again, the last time he was here. He's always asking about you."

"Right," said Lina.

"Well, I was thinking that the next time he delivers the groceries, you could ask him if he'd like to have a cup of coffee before he goes back to the store. Wouldn't that be nice?"

"Oh, I don't think his wife would like that."

"He's married? Are you sure? He told me he wasn't."

"I thought so, and I'll bet he'd have told me the same thing. Here's your strawberries. They look delicious, don't they?"

"Strawberries? Didn't they have any cherries? Oh, well, these'll do, I suppose, but I don't understand why they wouldn't have any cherries because they carry so many other fruits. They also carry other things that the larger stores don't carry. Fresher produce, too. All the stores are carrying cherries, so, I don't know why *they're* not. Oh, well, as I said, the strawberries will do, dear."

"You told me you wanted strawberries," said Lina.

"Cherries, strawberries. They sound so much alike, and that's why you didn't hear me right. But the next time I see Mrs. D'Amato, I'll ask her why she doesn't carry cherries. Or did they have some?"

"Yes, they did, but...Hmmm."

"That's all right, dear. We all forget things. Oh, was Danny working at the store today?" asked Anna.

"Uh-huh."

"Did he ask you for a date again?"

"He did. I qualify. I'm female. I told him no. Period. The end."

"He's such a handsome young man. Why, he's the handsomest young man I've seen in the neighborhood for years and years. I don't think I remember seeing anyone as handsome as him, even when I was a little girl. I watched Danny grow up, and I just knew because he was such a good-looking boy that he'd turn out to be a very handsome man. He doesn't have to work in the store, but there he is, almost every Saturday," said Anna.

"That's because they own the whole block and he lives in the same building the store is in, and Danny likes working at the store on Saturdays because he gets to check out the women while he's checking out their groceries."

"Do you remember when you were a little girl and you used to play a store owner? You had that card table set up with a tablecloth over it, and all the children would pretend to be buying their toys from you, then you'd argue about prices. It was just so cute, and Danny and you were just like brother and sister back then."

"And as we got older, he wanted to explore incest with me."

"He loved to play games, and Danny was always the smartest boy in school, too. Oh, and always the most popular boy because he always had so many friends."

"Right. Hoods. You forgot to mention they were always the toughest guys in the neighborhood, too."

"Oh, now, Lina, he was never really a *bad* boy. Danny's always been very polite to me and everybody else. And such personality! Always smiling and joking. Brains, looks, personality, and ever since he was in his teens, he's asked you for a date and you'd never go out with him. I don't know why, dear, because you told me he's the nicest boy you've ever known," said Anna, smiling.

"Oh, sure, he has all those traits, and yes, he *is* the nicest guy I've ever known, but regardless of his great looks, brains and wonderful personality, he's always been girl-crazy. Danny's only interested in dating a girl once, and then it's on to the next one."

"Oh, really? Then why has he only been interested in you for all these years?"

"Two reasons. One, we've always been best friends, and two, I'm the only woman he hasn't checked off his score card. I'm not one of his bimbos, so, there's no way I'd ever date him, but he never gives up, and he's constantly trying to rile me, too. You wouldn't believe the lines he hands me, but I know exactly what he wants. Danny's not interested in me for anything other than one date. I know that. Oh, he irritates me so much that sometimes I'd like to throttle him because I keep telling him no, and he keeps asking and asking."

"He's so polite every time he drops by, and when he calls here on the phone almost every day, asking to speak to you, and every time I go into their store when he's there, he asks me how you are, so, I just know he's still interested in you, dear."

"I told you why. I'm female, and that's the only reason."

"But you're a very *pretty* female and I'm sure that's just one of the reasons why he calls here so often, asking for you."

"I know that, mother. He just won't give up, but Danny's the last man in the world I'd ever date. He's got everything I'd ever want in a man, but fidelity. So, uh-uh. Date him? Never."

"If you married him, you'd never have to work again. His father owns over a dozen markets, and bigger ones than that store, too, and he also owns several other businesses, too. They're such wonderful people, and that's why the D'Amatos are so well-loved in this neighborhood. Danny will be taking over his father's businesses when he retires, and that could be sooner than you think because Mr. D'Amato might retire very early with all *his* money, and having Danny for a son. He's a very good catch, dear."

"The *catch* is Danny's many, many girlfriends come with him."

"Oh, now, Lina, he may seem to have a roving eye, but that's because he's single. Danny's just looking around to see which girl suits him best."

"Right. Looking around forever. I'm going to run a bath."

"Oh, that's right! You're not working this weekend. Are you going to a dance, dear?"

"They have raves now, mother. A rave is where fifty thousand young people squeeze into a small, tight space, and shuffle their feet to deafening music while they're looking for their dates who are lost in the crowd somewhere. Too intimate for me."

"Well, if there's so many people at those dances, there's a good chance you'd meet a nice, single young man."

"Right. I'm meeting Belinda, instead, and we're having dinner together as I told you before, and then after that, we're going over to those friends...Hmmm, well, acquaintances, really. Those *people* I told you about who are part of our book club. We'll be discussing books, not who is dating whom."

"You and Belinda should go to a nightclub sometime, if you don't want to go dancing and raving, dear," said Anna.

"Men think that two women alone in a nightclub are there to meet men for an hour or less, and maybe a price. Anyway, we're going to the book club meeting."

"That's nice, dear. Will there be any young, single men there?"

"Uh-huh. Very single, but not interested in dating women."

"Oh? There's so many shy men these days. Just like Danny. He's always asking about you, but now, after you've turned him down so many times, I'll bet he's too shy to ask you for a date."

"More sly than shy. I have to get ready to go out, so, I'll be in the tub if you're looking for me. Bye," said Lina.

"All right, dear. Enjoy your bath."

* * * * * * ❈ * * * * * *

Lina laid back in the bathtub, and sighed. She felt sure that she'd never be able to convince her mother that Danny was interested in so many women, and that he was no different from most of the other men that her mother tried to set her up with.

She began hoping that a single, trustworthy, young man would be at the small book club meeting, and be interested in joining their club, then perhaps he'd eventually be interested in her, too.

Lina thought that if a young man like that wanted to spend his Saturday nights at a book club meeting, instead of some wild party, then there was the outside chance that he wouldn't be the type of guy who would cheat on his girlfriend.

"Lina? Telephone!" cried Anna, opening the bathroom door.

"Please take a message. Who is..." she started to say.

"It's Danny. I didn't know you'd asked him to start calling you again. It's been almost two weeks since the last time he called. This is wonderful! I'm just as excited as you!"

"Danny? Damn! And I never asked him to call me the last hundred times! Gawwwwd! Tell him I'm busy! Please!"

"He wants to know if you're still having coffee with him."

"I didn't tell him I was having coffee with him! He asked me, and I told him no!"

"You did? Oh, I see. Well, I'll tell him that, dear."

"Thank you. Danny D'Amato. Gawwwd!"

She dunked her head underwater, and wondered just how bad her day was going to get because so far, she'd upset three old ladies at the elevator, unintentionally stolen a ball from a little girl, crossed swords with Danny, and for sure the next time she went to the store, she was going to ask her mother to write down exactly what she wanted, so that there'd be no confusion.

"Lina?" asked Anna, opening the bathroom door again.

"Yes?"

"Danny wants to know if the reason you don't want to have coffee with him is because he should've asked you to have a cup of tea with him, instead."

"Gawwwd! He saw the tea bags and he...No, mother. Please tell him I don't want to have coffee *or* tea with him. Okay?"

"Oh, all right, dear, I'll tell him that."

"Thank you. Why does he constantly ask me, anyway? I'm no

Sally Silicone. But day after day, year after year. Gawwwd!"

Lina began thinking about the type of woman Danny would eventually marry. She felt sure that the woman would have to have the I.Q. of a tomato, and she'd also have to have a figure like two tomatoes on a thin stalk of celery.

Lina had made up her mind long ago, that there was no way she was going to be another notch on Danny's conquest stick.

"Lina?" asked Anna, peeking into the bathroom.

"Tell me he's not still on the phone. Please."

"Well, he wants to know if you want to go for a milkshake, or something like that, instead of coffee or tea."

"A milkshake? Gawwwd! No, I don't. Not a milkshake, or a Coke, or an ice cream soda. Not even a sundae, okay? Tell him I'm going to take a long, long bath, and then after that, I'm going to be taking a long, long time dressing, so, by the time I'll be ready to go out, I definitely won't have time for any of the things he suggested. Milkshakes and whatever. Please tell him that, and then hang up the phone. Thanks."

"All right, dear. I'll tell him. No milkshakes or soft drinks."

Lina heaved a big sigh, then she stood up, turned on the shower to shampoo her hair, and hoped the water gushing over her head would clear her thoughts of all the aggravation she'd had that day.

"Lina?"

"Just a minute! I'll turn off the shower! There. *Now* what?"

"Danny said..."

"What? He's still on the phone?"

"Yes, dear. He wants to know if you want a cocktail, instead."

"A cock...Hmmm, I can imagine what *that* word means to him. No, no cocktail. No anything, ever. Never. You know I'm going to dinner with Belinda, and after that, we're...Tell him I've made other arrangements. Possibly for the rest of my life."

"Oh? I'll tell him that, dear," said Anna.

"Then hang up the phone and have our number changed."

"Oh? Have we been getting obscene phone calls? Thank goodness I didn't hear any of them. I hope they stop calling because I'd have to call so many people to give them our new number. Oh, and don't use your hairdryer while you're still in the tub, dear."

"No, I won't. Not yet, anyway. *Now* I'll finish my shower."

She resumed showering, then less than a minute later, Anna opened the bathroom door again.

"Lina?"

"No. No, it can't be. It can't. Yes, what is it *this* time?"

"Mr. and Mrs. D'Amato are going out for dinner, too, and Danny doesn't feel like cooking. Italian men have a real knack for cooking, don't they? Your father was a marvelous cook. Well, Danny wants to know if he can join you and Belinda for dinner."

"Oh, no! Tell Danny that we booked a very tiny table and the rest of the restaurant is booked solid. You can also tell him that I've made dinner reservations for the next ten years. Please? Thank you."

"Oh? I'm glad to hear you're planning ahead like that, dear. It's nice to know you'll be going out more, but poor Danny. I just know that he'll be so awfully disappointed that he can't have dinner with you and Belinda."

"I'm sure he'll be awfully disappointed for just a few seconds after he hangs up whatever girlfriend's phone he's calling from."

"Poor Danny. All alone for dinner tonight. I know! I can invite him *here* for dinner. I can run over to Guido's and buy...Hmmm, veal? It's been over a month since I cooked dinner for him. He's always had such a good appetite, hasn't he? Oh, do you remember which of my veal recipes he likes best?"

"No, I don't, but I have a feeling he likes...Never mind. I'll bet he'll be invited elsewhere, and very fast, too."

"Oh? But then, you never know, dear. Sad that he's left alone like that because he's such a nice boy, and single, too."

"Mother? The phone? He's waiting. Bye. Gawwwwd!"

Lina finished dressing, and she smiled while thinking about her mother telling her that just as she was inviting Danny to dinner, he'd said that a friend of his had dropped by at that very moment and asked him to come to his home for dinner, which Lina knew was a lie.

She began thinking about dinner, and she wondered if there was a chance that a handsome, single, never-married waiter might bring a bottle of wine to their table because he found her attractive.

It would be even nicer if he told them that he'd pay for the dinner. If that didn't happen, then there was that other possibility that she'd hoped for, which was that a nice, single, young man might appear at the book club meeting that night.

She picked up her handbag, looked in the mirror, smiled, and walked out of the bedroom.

"Lina? Oh, you look so nice."

"I'm leaving now. Did you want to ask me something?"

"Yes, I did, dear. Do you know if Danny likes that funny tea you bought?"

"I'm sure he likes funny tobacco, but I don't know about tea."

"Well, I just thought he might've liked it because that package of tea you bought for some odd reason will just sit in the cupboard for heaven knows how long if neither of us likes it."

"Oh, I'm sure that if one of us takes the tea back, they'll give us a refund. They always do," said Lina, smiling.

"Well, I just thought I might brew him a cup of it when he comes over later, after he has dinner."

"What? He's really coming over here?"

"Yes. Well, he said he'd try to make it for dessert and coffee, but he wasn't too definite."

"Right. Don't make tea *or* coffee because I'm sure Danny won't be dropping by for dessert. All right, I'm on my way. Bye."

"Have a nice time, dear. You're so beautiful, and so single, too. Oh, well, one day soon," Anna said, then she heaved a sigh.

"Yes, soon. If soons are measured in decades," said Lina.

"You know, dear, that with women's liberation, women are asking men for dates now, so, you should try to think more liberal, too. I'm sure many men like a woman who's more liberal."

"Yes, that's true. Men have always wanted women to be more liberal in certain ways."

"Oh? If I'd known that before, I would've asked your father for a date long before he asked me," said Anna.

"Right. I'll be home around eleven. This is the first time in a very long time you've been alone on a Saturday night."

"Yes, well, now I'll know how *you* feel. Bye, dear."

"Hmmm, bye, mother. Enjoy your television show, or whatever else you've planned to do this evening."

Belinda saw the frown on Lina's face when they met outside the restaurant, and she hoped that Anna was feeling all right.

"You look slightly tense, Lina. Is everything all right?"

"*Now* it is. Once I have a martini, it'll be even better. What a day this has been! One very annoying thing after another, and one *especially* annoying thing. C'mon. Let's go in."

All the waiters were men in their late sixties, so, Lina ordered a martini and hoped things would improve after dinner. She smiled when the martini arrived, then she sipped on it, and sighed.

"I really need this. I swear to God if I'm ever asked to take the elevator in my building again, I'll plead no thanks, and then run for the stairs because I had a fiasco with three elderly women and their walkers. Gawwwd! They use those walkers as props to lure young people to guilt, and they made me feel so guilty about...Oh, it's too long a story. Forget it," said Lina.

"I know what you mean, because my grandmother uses a walker whenever she wants attention, but there's nothing wrong with her legs when she really wants to go somewhere in a hurry. But there are elderly people who really *do* need walkers."

"Oh, and then there was the store! Danny D'Amato. You won't believe this, but he actually called me again for I'm sure the umpteenth time this month, and this time he asked me if I wanted to have coffee with him. I'd already told him I didn't want to, when he asked me at the store."

"Danny called you? But I thought you'd told him never to call you again."

"I did. But he just keeps calling."

"Then why not just change your phone number, and make sure the new one's unlisted?"

"Because his parents are two of my mother's closest friends, so, even if she agreed to me getting an unlisted number, I know she'd give it them so they can call her, then it'd only be hours before Danny would find out what the new phone number is."

"I see. Well, if you really want to avoid him *that* much, then surely you can think of some way to do it."

"I don't want to avoid him *completely*. Besides, my mother is like a second mother to him. I just wish he'd get it through his head that I won't go out on a date with him because I know he just wants to add me to his mile-long list of conquests, but he's so damned persistent, and ohhh so annoying at times. Like when I began getting ready to have dinner with you here. I got into the bathtub, and then less than a minute later, he called again. He asked my mother to ask me if I wanted to have a coffee with him, and when I told her to tell him no, then he asked her to ask me if I'd rather have a cup of tea with him, instead, and when I said no to that, too, he asked...Well, it was one thing after another, and each time, I said no. Gawwwd! He even wanted to join us for dinner. Can you imagine?"

"Well, *I* wouldn't have minded. He's sensational-looking."

"Yes, he certainly is, and he knows that all too well. But *you*? You know he only likes airheads."

"Yes, but wow, I wouldn't mind acting like an airhead for just one evening with him. But no, you're right. I'm sure that he'd forget about me after he got what he wanted. Of course, I'm not saying I'd ever let him *get* what he wanted. No, I'm looking for a man to marry me, and as you said, Danny's not planning to settle down for years, yet."

"If ever. Hmmm, I'm going to order the lemon chicken."

"I'll have the prime rib," said Belinda. "I'll ask for a small portion. Red or white wine?"

"Well, you're having the prime rib, so, hmmmm, let's order glasses instead of a carafe. That way you can have red and I'll have white. Oh, this is so relaxing. I was so tense before I got here. Mmmm, this martini tastes great, so, I might order another one. I brought a bottle of white wine to take to the meeting, so, I'll ask the waiter to put it in the fridge for me to keep it cool."

"That's a good idea. I brought red wine to drink while listening to what everyone else read this week. If it gets even *more* boring, I'll grab whatever booze the others brought, and get sloshed."

"It'd be great if somebody new came to Janet's tonight. Male. And single. And trustworthy," said Lina.

"I'll drink to that! Never say die! Hope springs eternal! Ay!"

"If there *are* any single men our age left. Mother's still scouring the world, looking for one for me. Gawwwd!"

* * * * * * ❈ * * * * *

The dinner relaxed Lina even more, and she dismissed her plan to send cards of apology to Mrs. Henshaw and the other women, because she realized that they'd take *that* the wrong way, as well.

They hailed a cab, and arrived for the book club meeting, then Lina suddenly recalled that she'd left the bottle of wine that she had meant to bring with her, at the restaurant.

"I was bringing a very nice bottle of white wine, but I gave it to the waiter to put in the fridge at the restaurant, and then I forgot all about it. I'm so sorry," said Lina.

"Oh, really? Well, not to worry because we have white wine, but of course, you knew that," Janet said as she frowned.

"It's only seven or eight blocks from here to my home, so, I can rush back and get another one. I'm sure it'd only take me fifteen or twenty minutes."

"No-no! Don't be silly! Besides, not many people turned up, anyway, so, I'm sure we can make do with much less wine, somehow, Lina. Oh, and Donald told me there's a new young man coming, as well. He called us...Hmmm, when *was* that? Anyway, he's very interested in joining our little book club," said Janet.

"I see. Well, I hope he doesn't forget to bring *his* wine."

"Here. I brought a bottle of Beaujolais," said Belinda.

"Oh, thanks, Belinda. Thank God you thought of red, otherwise, you might've left a bottle of white wine in the fridge at the restaurant just like Lina supposedly did with her bottle of white wine. You ladies go on through to the living room while I get a glass of wine for you. Left it at the restaurant. The waiter put in the fridge. Uh-huh, yes, I'm sure that's what happened. Oh, well, like I just said, we'll make do, somehow. Now don't you worry, Lina, because I'm sure we have enough white wine for you, Donald and I, instead of just Donald and I. Bye-bye. I'll be right in."

"Oh, um, Janet? Forget the white wine bec...Damn. She's gone. I feel so embarrassed," Lina said as she frowned.

"Basta. How do you spell bitch in *her* style of English? C'mon. Let's go sprawl out in the living room because I've just got to see if Blair's in drag again, tonight. Something librarianish, I'll bet, if he *is* in drag," said Belinda.

"He's in drag most of the time. Janet said a young man's coming, so, I hope he's single. And straight. But with my odds...Oh, hi, Donald. David. Blair? It *is* you, and you look almost identical to my neighbor, Mrs. Henshaw," said Lina.

"Thank you, darling, and you, as always, look like a fabulously beautiful movie star. And Belinda, you look...Well, lovely."

"Thanks. Lovely's good. It must be difficult for you to find such nice outfits, Blair. I know that because my mother is only about eighty-five pounds less than you, so, she's always had a problem finding something large enough to fit *her*, too, which is why she has to make a lot of her own clothes. Yards and yards of material, just like whatever that is you're sort of wearing, so, you must be a whiz with a needle and thread. I admire talent, and that thing you're wearing looks...Well, *lovely* on you."

"Your nails suddenly look longer, darling," said Blair, smiling.

"They retract after a glass or two of wine. *Maybe*. You know, Blair, I've met many gay people, and they're so nice. It's interesting how very much different they are from you. So, Donald, how are *you*?" asked Belinda.

"Fine, fine. Just fine, thank you. Very fine. Robust, Janet always says."

"Very fine and robust. How nice for you. How did you enjoy whatever it was? What book *was* it we were reading? Do you recall, Lina? I skimmed through it. Nice nap immediately after."

"Oh, it was...Um, it was..." stammered Lina.

"Here we are!" exclaimed Janet, entering the room. "Beaujolais for Belinda, and a glass of *our* white wine for Lina. She *said* she forgot *her* wine. Some story about a fridge and a restaurant. So hilarious. Well? Shall we chat?"

"Oh...my...*God*. B–i–t–c–h," Lina whispered to Belinda.

"You spelled it sohhhhhh correctly," Belinda whispered.

They discussed the book they'd all read during the past week, and Lina kept looking at her wristwatch and wondering if the young man who wanted to join the sort of friendly, little book club had changed his mind.

She still hoped he would be somewhat interesting and somewhat attractive because she was getting to the point of desperation to meet a young man who might have something in common with her.

Lina realized that the book club wasn't too interesting, but it was a way of telling her mother that she was socializing on Saturday nights because bars were definitely out, and she didn't like going somewhere alone to dance.

Lina felt grateful that Belinda had decided to join the book club, even though she disliked most of the books they chose to read. Then again, with Belinda there, the young man might be more interested in her because Belinda was quite attractive.

Lina almost spilled her wine when the doorbell rang, then she tried to look nonchalant as she heard Janet talking to the young man at the door.

She heard Janet laughing and talking as she walked toward the living room, so, Lina put on her best smile for the young man, then she gasped as she saw Danny D'Amato, grinning and carrying a big pile of comic books.

"Everyone? This is Danny D'Amato. Danny, this is my husband, Donald. That's Blair sitting over there in the dress, and that's his roommate, David. The nice, pretty girl is Belinda, and then...Well, then the Sophia Loren-looking one sitting beside

Belinda, goes by the name of Lina, and she..."

"Gawwwd! Danny, what the *hell* are you..." Lina started to say.

"Hi, Lina! I brought some books for the meeting! They're my nephew's! Great, huh?" exclaimed Danny.

"You two know each other?" asked Janet, wide-eyed.

"You bet we do. Lina and I grew up together, and she's always had a crush on me. Right, Lina?" said Danny, grinning.

"Danny! *You...Me?* A crush? A *crush*?" cried Lina.

"Well, okay, it's not exactly a crush, I guess, right? But we're practically engaged."

"*Engaged*? No way in hell are we engaged!"

"Danny called me around dinnertime. Said he loved books. Are they some sort of adult fiction comics?" Donald asked him.

"I forgot to look at 'em all. Sorry, man. I was in a hurry to get here, but I really think you'll like 'em, though. Hey, and Lina? Your mom gave me their phone number because you forgot. That's because you were in such a big hurry to get to the restaurant. So, what do we do? Trade comic books? Take a look at these. You like this one?" asked Danny, then he winked at Lina.

Danny started passing around comic books as he smiled at Lina whom was furious with him.

"Lina, you didn't tell me your fiancé was coming. You *did* say you're engaged, didn't you?" Janet asked Danny.

"Practically," he replied, grinning.

"Danny! No, we're not, Janet! We're not even *close* to engaged! Gawwwd! I'm being stalked!" cried Lina.

"Hey, I said *practically*, so, chill out. Man! She gets like that sometimes. Hot-blooded. Great, huh, guys?"

"Oh, I understand. We all do. You know, I was a bit nervous before *my* wedding, too," said Janet.

"Lina? You never told me this. I thought you said you'd *never* date Danny, and all this time you *were*. Well, then I suppose congratulations are in order. And you told me that he loves wild women. You vixen!" exclaimed Belinda, smiling.

"That's it! Danny, you crazy son of a ...! First the telephone, and now this? Gawwd!" Lina shouted at him. "I'm leaving! Stay, Danny! Sit! Heel! Goodnight, everyone! Gawwd! Danny, I'm going to kill you! Goodbye!"

"Oops!" exclaimed Danny. "Guess she had bad service at the restaurant. If everything's not just right, Lina gets into a real snit. Great, huh? Hey, just a sec, Lina! I'll walk you home! I dropped off dessert at your mom's! Lina? Women, huh? She can't wait for us to get home and get it on. Well, I'd better run and catch up with her. Nice meeting you all. G'night! Hey, Lina? Honey? Wait up! Stop running!"

"He's absolutely gorgeous! Now *that*'s a man!" cried Blair.

"My God," said Janet. "You'd think they'd have *some* reserve. They're so highly aroused with each other, so, it's no wonder Lina left that bottle of white wine at home."

"Restaurant. I'm a witness," said Belinda. "Well, I think I'll be on my way, too. Oh, Danny forgot his comic books. If I give you his address, would you mind dropping them off, Donald?"

"I will!" exclaimed Blair.

"Thank you, Blair. I was going to mention that a nose job would improve your appearance, immensely, and I'm sure Danny'll give you a quick one. Goodnight. Oh, and I've decided to quit this book thing. Hmmm, not just a nose job, Blair. Chin, for sure. Maybe the cheeks, too. Oh, well, I'm sure Danny'll know best. Here's his address. Bye," said Belinda, hurrying away.

Lina strutted down the street, fuming. Her spirits lifted when she saw a couple getting out of a cab, so, she hurried toward it, got into it, and heaved a huge sigh.

She then heard shouting, and then looking out the rear window, she saw Danny running toward the taxi. Lina told the driver to burn rubber and that she'd tip him heavily if he did.

Seven blocks later, she slapped a twenty in the driver's hand, jumped out of the cab, and hurried toward her apartment building. She saw Mrs. Henshaw, Mrs. Jelnik and Mrs. Langsford milling around the elevator with their walkers, so, she rushed past them, and hurried up the stairs.

Lina swore when she dropped her keys, then she fumbled with the lock, opened the door, closed it, leaned back against it, and closed her eyes as she sighed.

She opened her eyes again, and walked into the living room,

then gasped when she saw at least two dozen, big vases of long-stemmed red roses in the living room.

"What the *hell* is all *this*?" cried Lina.

"Roses, dear! They're for you, and they're from Danny! Oh, and there's orchids, too! Mr. and Mrs. D'Amato are coming over with bottles of champagne, soon. Lina, why didn't you tell me you were...How did Danny put it now? Hmmm, almost engaged?"

"*Practically* engaged," said Lina through clenched teeth.

"Yes! That's it! He said something about you needing a push. I had no idea you two were seeing each other secretly. Oh, it's just so Romeo and Juliet! But I don't know why you never told me, dear, because I've told you so often that I approved of him, so, you two could've dated openly. Oh, yes! Marriage, at last!"

"Mother! I am *not* going to marry Danny! Never!"

"Common-law? Well, I know that many young people do that these days, but I wanted to see you in a wonderful, white wedding dress because you'd make a beautiful bride, dear. I hope you change your mind about the common-law idea. Oh, and Danny brought dessert, too, just like he said he would. It was so busy here, earlier, because of all the men bringing in all the roses and orchids, and in such lovely vases, too."

"This day is like a nightmare! It's *got* to be a nightmare! It *can't* be real! I'm dreaming!" cried Lina.

"I've been dreaming of this day, too, dear, and now it's arrived. But where's Danny? I'll bet you were in such a hurry to get back home and see all the flowers that Danny couldn't catch up with you, so, I guess he'll be here any minute now. I'll put the coffee on now, and...Oh, unless you'd rather have champagne. It should be here soon. Imagine! You and Danny D'Amato! Oh, I'm so pleased! Of course, I always knew you two would marry someday, and everybody in the neighborhood knew that, too. Best friends since childhood, and now soon to be husband and wife. My! I'm almost shocked, if I hadn't expected it all along. But that doesn't mean that I'm not shocked, because you kept telling me you weren't interested in him. I don't know why you've kept him waiting so long, dear."

"Gawwwd! I'm going to my room! If he comes here, tell him I'm out! Please! I wish I had a lock on my bedroom door!"

"Don't you think you should wait 'til after you're married?"

"Mother! Gawwwd! Damn that Danny!"

"Wait! Lina?...Hmmm, what will the neighbors think? Right here in my home, and in her bedroom, too. Shocking."

Lina slammed her bedroom door shut, and then she wondered if she should try leaping from her balcony to the next door neighbor's balcony.

She recalled her mother telling her that Mr. and Mrs. D'Amato was arriving soon with bottles of champagne, so, what had Danny told his parents? She hoped that her mother had understood her when she'd told her to tell Danny she was out, and that meant out of the apartment, and not just out of the living room.

She gasped when she heard her mother and Danny talking, then within seconds, he was knocking on Lina's bedroom door.

"Lina? Are you changing, honey? You didn't have to do that because you looked really great in the dress you had on!"

"Go away!"

"Aw, don't worry! I won't open the door! But I bet y'look great in your undies!"

"Danny! You're insane! I hate you!"

"Gee, I'm sorry, honey, but when I couldn't find a book, I grabbed my nephew's comic books! How was I to know? Didn't anyone else bring comic books?"

"Gawwwd! Why the hell did you bring comic books? You *never* read comic books! You like war novels, or sports novels, or biographies, or the latest bestseller, or...Damn it! You know what I mean! Why the hell didn't you bring one of those?"

"I lent all of my books out! Like, I'd already read 'em, right? Does this mean that you're mad at me?"

"Mad? *Mad*? I'm livid!" yelled Lina.

"Wow! The comic books weren't *that* bad! There were a couple of great Spider-Man ones! Superman! Batman! And, like, you didn't even look at 'em, honey, so, how would you know if they were bad comic books or not? Damn! I forgot 'em there! Now my nephew's gonna kick my shins black and blue 'til I go get those comic books back for him! Hey, Lina? I love you, honey!"

"Well, I *hate you*! Why the hell are we shouting?"

"Because the door's closed!"

"I can hear you fine without yelling! Gawwwwd!"

"Okay. Hello-o-o-o-o-o-o-o in there, hot stuff. That better?"

"Much. I told you I'd never date you, didn't I? And I keep telling you that, don't I? Yesterday. Weeks. Months. Hell, for years I've told you no to even a cup of coffee because you run around with every pretty girl you see."

"Have to. Can't get a date with the most beautiful one. You."

"I know *your* type. Boy, what a line!"

"Aw, Lina, I've always wanted a date with you, so, I figured the best way, knowing how you don't trust me, was to marry you. Honey? Will you marry me? Please? I'm going crazy without you. You keep saying no. I don't want some bimbo. I want *you*. You're smart. Sweet. And you're so hot-looking. I mean, beautiful. *Really* beautiful. Really! Lina? I said I was sorry about the comic books. We both like the same books. We've grown up together, so, we know each other very well, and hey, your mom likes me, Lina. And my parents *love you*. They want me to marry you, and I told 'em I've been trying for so long, but you just keep saying no. I love you, honey. Lina? Don't y'love me just a little, tiny bit? I could live with that. Lina? Aw, c'mon, man! Marry me! Please!"

"If I marry you, will you leave me alone?"

"Yeah, you bet! Scout's honor!"

"Gawwwwd! Okay, then I'll marry you! Damn you, Danny!"

"Hey, Mrs. Tantorini! I'm marrying your daughter! Wow!"

"Lina? I'm so happy, dear! Open the door!" cried Anna.

"Yeah, c'mon, man!" yelled Danny.

"Just a minute. I've got to blow my nose," said Lina.

"She's bawling! She loves me! You liar, Lina! I knew you really loved me! Why did y'make me suffer for so long? You *knew* I loved you! Y'coming out here?"

Lina blew her nose, took another tissue and dabbed at her eyes, then she swore. She'd done her best not to get involved with Danny, and now she realized she loved him, and too much.

Her heart was beating fast as she opened the door, then Danny opened his arms, and she rushed into them.

"Should I put the coffee on, or...Oh, there's the door! Must be Mr. and Mrs. D'Amato and the champagne. Would you two like a glass, or are you going to do a common-law?" asked Anna.

"Mmmmmm," they said through a kiss.

"I see," said Anna. "I wish you'd reconsider about the white wedding dress, dear, because as I told you before, you'd make a beautiful bride. Oh, well, then, I'll go see who's at the door. Thank God, you're not single anymore!"

"Mother? White wedding dress," said Lina, in between kisses.

"*More* waiting! Ay!" exclaimed Danny.

The End

Spring Love Lasts Forever

Camilla walked along the top of the hill, then stopped for a few moments to look down at the landscape flaunting the recent season's fashions. Trees and bushes were dressed in lovely shades of green, the orchards in white and delicate pinks, and all the gardens in arrays of many different, marvelous colors.

Each time a slightly warmer breeze swept up from the valley below it brought with it the wonderful aroma from slowly swaying daffodils and tulips.

She walked onward to the high boulders that overlooked the lake, then Camilla sat down and looked out beyond the lake at the breathtaking view of lush forests spreading to the horizon. Brock would be joining her soon. They'd made a promise to sit there together and share the wonder.

She then began to recall the conversation she'd had with her adopted mother before Camilla had left home to walk to her favorite place.

"Nobody came to visit," said Kathleen. "Well, I suppose I should've expected that. I'm so happy that you'll always have Brock to keep you company every day."

"Yes, so am I," replied Camilla, as she sat in a chair beside Kathleen's bed. "Oh, before you have your nap, would you like me to close the rest of the curtains?"

"No, thanks, dear. You're always doing you best to please me and everyone else, and that's just one of the reasons that your great grandmother loved you so much. Your grandmother, too, and you know that I love you."

"Yes, I know, and Brock loves me, too."

"Are you going over to his home?" Kathleen asked her.

"No, we're meeting at our favorite place. I don't know how long he'll be, but I know it'll be soon. You look very tired."

"I am. Are you going for your walk, now?"

"No, I'll wait until you fall asleep before I go."

"Thank you, Camilla. Mmmmm, I can hardly keep my eyes open. I've never felt so comfortably tired. After I have my nap, I want you to tell me all about your walk with Brock. Okay?"

"Yes, I'd like that. Your eyes are closed now, so, are you beginning to dream?"

"Mmmm, I'm starting to. Yes, I....Mmmmmm."

"You're almost in a dream. Sleep. Go into your dream. That's it. Sleep, dear one," whispered Camilla while smiling.

She slowly stood up, walked over to Kathleen's bedroom door, then closed it behind her before going back downstairs and out of the house to meet Brock at the top of the high boulders overlooking the lake.

Abigail called the children to the table for lunch, then she sat down with them, and she smiled while Kip and Katrina talked excitedly about the game they'd just finished playing.

Brock entered the house, carrying a small bouquet of spring flowers, then after putting them in the vase on the table, he went over to the stove, picked up the pot and started serving the delicious, thick soup he'd prepared.

"These flowers are lovely, Brock," said Abigail. "It won't be long before vegetables start growing in the garden. It'll be so nice having fresh vegetables soon, instead of the ones we have stored in the cold cellar. I love spring. It brings so much promise of a whole new world, and it seems to scrub everything clean. What kind of soup did you make?"

"Beef vegetable," replied Brock.

"I like chicken soup just as much," said Kip.

"Me too," added Katrina.

"Oh, I know," said Brock, smiling. "Twins always seem to like the same things. I'll make a big pot of chicken soup for your lunch tomorrow and I'll put lots of noodles in it, too."

Brock put the pot back on the stove, then after he put a dozen buttered tea biscuits on a plate, he placed the plate in the middle of the table. When Abigail and the children began eating tea biscuits with their soup, she said to Brock: "Hmmm, I was just thinking about Gordon."

"I suppose that because he left here last week to start building that addition onto Mr. and Mrs. Bradshaw's home, you're wondering how much longer it's going to take him to finish that job and return home," said Brock.

"Yes. Yes, of course. That's what I was wondering. So, um, when Barbara Martin dropped by two weeks ago with her children, we had a very nice chat. I must give her a call and ask her what she's been up to lately," said Abigail, then she turned her attention to Kip and Katrina to say: "As soon as you two finish eating your lunch, I want you to go right upstairs and have a nap."

"Aw, do we have to?" asked Katrina.

"Yes, you do."

"But I wanted to play on the swing after lunch."

"Yeah, and I'm not tired, either," said Kip.

"I have an idea. How about if I have a nap with you?"

"Yeah!" exclaimed Katrina and Kip.

"Okay, but don't expect me to have a nap with you every time I ask *you* to have a nap. Just this once, okay?"

"Okay. Ahhhh-hmmm. I'm getting tired, already," said Kip.

"Now you know why I wanted you and Katrina to have a nap for an hour," said Abigail, smiling.

"I wish I didn't get lotsa poison ivy on me. You got just as much on you, Kip. Next time, we better make sure we don't play anywhere near the stuff, so, we don't have to put the lotion on all the rashes, and have to cover lots of them with bandages. Mom? Will you change my bandages before I have my nap? Please?"

"Mine too, please?" asked Kip.

"Alright," replied Abigail.

"I'll help do that," said Brock.

"You were over at Mrs. Seymour's house, yesterday. How was she? And of course, Camilla?" asked Abigail.

"Just fine," replied Brock. "I'm going to meet Camilla while you and the children are having a nap."

"You told me that you love her. Oh, Brock, are you sure you know what love really is?" Abigail asked him.

"I certainly do, so, I know I really love her and always will. You once told me that love comes in many different ways, and the way I feel for Camilla will last forever."

"At one time, I never thought that you two would ever fall in love. Well, I've always been a romantic, so, I believe and hope that you and Camilla *will* love each other forever."

"Thank you, Abigail. Your love for Gordon and his love for

you is a very good example of what true love is."

"Mom? I don't want anymore soup, so, I wanna go have my nap now," Kip said as he smiled.

"I wanna have my nap now, too," said Katrina.

"Yes, alright. Brock? Would you please help me get the children ready for their nap?" asked Abigail.

"Certainly."

He washed his hands again, then opened the cupboard and got out the medical supplies. Brock cut the bandages away from Katrina and Kip's arms, legs and other parts of their bodies, then he and Abigail daubed medicated lotion on their rashes and sores before they began putting fresh bandages on them.

"I sure wish somebody told us before what poison ivy looked like 'cause then we wouldn't have got it on us," said Kip.

"Yeah, and sometimes it's real itchy and sometimes it hurts in some places. I thought you said that poison ivy was just supposed to be itchy most of the time," said Katrina.

"Yes, I know, but when you scratch itchy areas too much, then sometimes you scrape off some skin, and then those areas get infected, and that's how you get these sores," Abigail told them.

"Daddy said he's going to burn all the poison ivy as soon as he comes back from working on that house."

"Well, I hope he does get rid of all the poison ivy around here by burning it all away. All of it. I wish he could've done that a long time ago. That poison ivy is everywhere," said Abigail. "It's like a plague the way it spreads. Hold your arm up, Katrina, so that Brock can wrap the bandage around it. There, that's much better. Now no talking when you go upstairs and get onto my bed. Promise? Just close your eyes and go to sleep."

"We promise," said Katrina and Kip in unison.

"There, all the nice, new bandages are on. Now go right upstairs, and I'll be there in a few minutes. Okay?"

"Okay, mom. C'mon, Katrina. Bye, Brock. Don't forget about making some chicken soup for lunch tomorrow," said Kip.

"Oh, I won't forget," Brock told him. "I'm going to make lots of it. I'll see you after your nap."

After the children went upstairs, Abigail got up from the kitchen table, then walked over to the door, opened it, and stepped out onto the porch. She took a deep breath of cool spring air, then smiled while looking around at the landscape, and then she walked back into the house, and yawned before she told Brock that she was going upstairs to have a nap with Kip and Katrina.

They smiled and talked while Brock accompanied her upstairs to her bedroom, then their smiles broadened when they saw that the twins were holding hands as they slept.

Brock leaned over the bed, then slowly and gently picked up Katrina, then after Abigail got onto her bed, and laid on her back, she raised her right arm, then Brock lowered Katrina onto the bed, and then Abigail put her arm around Katrina who was sound asleep, but she instinctively cuddled up to her mother.

Abigail lifted her left arm, then Brock gently picked up Kip, and laid him close beside her, and after Abigail put her arm around him, Kip also instinctively cuddled up to her.

"It's been a long time since I've held them in my arms while sleeping with them," said Abigail, as she smiled. "It feels so wonderful, and I love them with all my heart."

"They look so cute asleep and cuddled up to you."

"Mmmmmm, yes. Thanks for making that very nice lunch, Brock. The soup was delicious, and the children loved it, too."

"Thanks, I try my best. After you fall asleep, I'm going to meet Camilla at our favorite spot. It's high up on some gigantic boulders near the lake. There are very tall, beautiful pine trees close to the boulders, and we can see for miles and miles. I'm sure it won't be much longer before the ice starts breaking on the lake, then it'll look like there's thousands of white and pale blue jigsaw pieces drifting on the lake while slowly melting away."

"You know, Gordon and I used to walk through that area quite often while we were dating and many times since then. I remember being there very early some mornings and seeing loons on the lake. Their sounds are so haunting. When we were there later in the day, there'd be sailboats slowly skimming along the surface of the lake like a magical breed of swans. Mmmmm, I think I'll dream about that view during my nap. Mmmmmm, I'm so comfortable that it feels like my body is lifting up into soft clouds. Mmmmmm, I love looking at the children while they're sleeping. Ahhh-hmmmm, I'm so tired. Mmmmmmmm, so nice and sleepy."

"The land around us is so beautiful at this time of year because of all the blossoms and flowers. Now the tulips are growing everywhere. Spring flowers are so beautiful with delicate, heady scents. I'm going to pick a bouquet for Camilla."

"Spring," said Abigail, smiling. "I love all the new greens. So bright and cheerful, and all the forsythia bushes with their shining yellow flowers. So many pink and rose blossoms on the trees. The whole world around us wakes up each spring in a symphony of color and sweet bird songs are everywhere. Mmmmm, oh, yes, spring is so lovely. So very lovely. There'll...be...there'll be...lilacs soon. Mauves, pretty blues, pinks...and...some...whites, too. Then...soon, there'll be more flowers...and rich, green grass. It's...so cool...in the summer. I...I love the smell of...freshly mown grass. It's such...such a fresh, clean...smell. I...mmmmm."

"You're touching a dream, Abigail. Feel it on your fingertips? It's there. So soft and so gentle, and with a thrilling promise. There. It's surrounding you now like a loving, very slowly moving mist. You're walking deeper into it. It's like a smile. A kiss. Softly, Abigail. Softly you step. Your dream is lifting you to float away to wonderful lands and promises you prayed for that are coming true. Sleep, Abigail. Dream and dream within dream after dream. Shhhhhh. Softly drifting. Softly, softly. I'm going out to the garden now to gather a bouquet of spring flowers for my Camilla. She is so very beautiful and so wonderful, and I'll love her forever. Sweet dreams, dear Abigail," whispered Brock.

Brock leaned over the bed to kiss Abigail's forehead, then after kissing Katrina's cheek, and then Kip's cheek, he smiled at them for a few minutes before he left her bedroom and went back downstairs, and out of the house.

He began picking spring flowers for Camilla and after making a big bouquet, he began walking to their favorite meeting place. Reaching the top of a hill, Brock stopped, turned around, and blew a kiss to the house where Abigail, Katrina and Kip were napping, then he resumed walking to meet Camilla.

He saw her sitting with her back against the trunk of a tall pine tree, and his smile broadened as he approached her, and then he knelt beside her, and gave Camilla the spring bouquet.

"Oh, they're so lovely. Thank you, Brock."

He then sat, leaning back against the tree, with Camilla in his arms, then he smiled as he asked her: "Are you comfortable?"

"Oh, yes. Mmmmmm, isn't it a beautiful day?"

"As beautiful as you."

"Mmmm, thank you. The first time I saw you, I hoped that a man as handsome as you would want a long-term relationship with me, then the more we spoke, I became even more infatuated with you when I discovered how sincere and wonderful you are. I'm so happy that we'll now be together forever."

"I am, too, sweetheart. I'll always love you, Camilla."

"And I'll always love you, Brock."

Spring turned into summer. Summer into autumn, then winter sprinkled them with snowflakes while Brock and Camilla sat looking out at the beauty before them from season to season.

Every person, animal, fish and bird had died from the nuclear pollution that had drifted throughout the world.

Brock had served Abigail, Katrina and Kip a soup containing a a flavorless, odorless and painless poison before they suffered too much, and Abigail had been so thankful that he had been willing to send them into what she had said would be a beautiful world of everlasting, wonderful dreams.

Camilla had done the same for Kathleen and her family, and now Brock and Camilla, whom nobody had believed could ever fall in love, sat with their arms around each other.

They knew that they loved each other. That somehow it had become possible. Their true love for one another would continue until they slowly deteriorated many years in the future. That future that would be the forever for two androids in love.

The End

#

Like brightly colored wings of fantasy birds, the sailboats swept past canoes and rowboats to sail around more than thirty different sizes of islands in the lake.

Many of the islands were crowded with colorful cabins and on one of the islands, a married couple sat on the sandy shore, waving at water skiers speeding by, and at people in rowboats and canoes.

The elderly couple had pulled their rowboat up onto the shore, spread out a blanket, then after they'd enjoyed their picnic lunch, the husband, Ken, scanned the lake with binoculars.

He passed the binoculars to his wife, Debbie, and she looked through them at the many cottages lining the lake to her far left, then to her far right, and then she began viewing the rising slope of massive boulders that formed a very high ridge.

The highest part of the ridge was directly across from where

Debbie sat, and as she looked at the forest up there, she wondered if there was a road through those trees that led to more cottages somewhere out of sight on the ridge. While training her binoculars on that central area of the high ridge, a sudden flicker of white caught her attention.

Moments later, Debbie could discern that the flicker of white was really the wind blowing the white dress of a young woman whom had walked out of the trees to stand near the edge of the ridge to look out at the lake.

Debbie then presumed there must be a road somewhere through the trees to that central area of the very high ridge, then tilting the binoculars downward, she saw a series of wooden steps leading down to a dock.

The wooden staircase hadn't been immediately noticeable because it was painted almost the same color as the huge boulders that formed the high ridge.

She tilted the binoculars up to look at the young woman again, then Debbie tensed up because she thought that the young woman was standing too close to the edge of the ridge.

"Oh, no. Ken? Here," Debbie said as she handed him the binoculars. "There's a girl at the top of that very high ridge, and I'm sure she's standing too close to the edge of it."

"Where?" he asked, looking through the binoculars.

"Right at the very top. No, look right across the lake at the center area of the top of the ridge. See her?"

"Wait a sec. Oh, yeah, I see her now," said Ken. "No, she's not as close as you thought, hon. From where we are, it only looks like she's standing too close to the edge, but there's long grass or something like that in front of her lower legs, so that means she's gotta be standing back a little ways from the edge."

"Oh, thank God," said Debbie.

"Hmmm, wait'll I focus these a bit more. Yeah, now I see her better. She's quite pretty. Matter of fact, she's beautiful. Yeah, and I'd say she's around sixteen."

"I didn't notice the steps going up there at first."

"There's steps? Oh, yeah, I see them now. They're almost the same color as the rocks of the ridge. What a great view it must be from way up there, huh? Hmmm, I can't see a cottage or a cabin up there. Must be back farther on the ridge. Way up there away from all the dozens and dozens of cottages and cabins down around the lake," said Ken. "Now that's what I call privacy. They must be rich as hell. Oh! She just turned around, and she's starting to walk away from the edge. Ah, there we are. A very nice-looking lad just walked up to her and held her hand. Hmmm, now they've walked out of sight. Guess they're going back to their cottage for a glass of lemonade. Hmmm, there's four, long flights of stairs up from their dock, but I don't see a boat anywhere near the dock. Here, take a look."

Debbie took the binoculars from him, and looked across the lake, then she said: "Oh, yes, so I see. The others have probably taken the boat out for awhile. Their cottage property is so high above the lake. They obviously don't use the cottage during the winter because all those steps up from the dock must get coated with ice and snow. Lovely spot though, isn't it?"

"I bet one of these days, they'll get an offer from a hotel to sell that land," said Ken. "Hmmm, I'd love to see the lake from up there. When I was a kid we'd come up here for six weeks in the summer. We loved camping on these islands."

"You told me this one is called Loon Island. Right?"

"Yep. And there's at least ten other islands named after birds y'see around here. When I came up here, we often rowed our boats over to Redwing Island that's far on the other side of the lake. Way back then, there were hardly any cottages on the road down from the highway, and the ones that *were* on the road were spaced quite far apart. Now, this whole area's built up into a town. Hardly any cottages at all around the lake back then, either, but look around you now," said Ken. "Tons of 'em. I bet all these islands'll be packed with 'em before long."

"Well, I suppose because it's such a beautiful lake, every inch of property around it has been bought up. Such a shame."

"Yep, it sure is. That whole area at the top of the ridge is the only place left where there's no cottages. Way up there with a wonderful view of the lake and islands. I bet they own acres of that forest up there, but down around the lake, most of the trees have been cut down to make way for all the cottages and cabins."

"It must've been so nice around here when you were a boy. Now all the beaches at the end of the road near the docks, are so crowded because of the four, big hotels," said Debbie.

"Yeah, and you used to be able to fish in this lake, too. Now with hundreds of people and all their boats, the lake's mostly all polluted. All built up now. When I was a boy, and if you weren't looking closely when y'were driving along the old highway, you'd miss seeing the road leading down to this lake. But nowadays, there's that big, neon sign letting you know it's here. The road wasn't paved, either, and after you pulled off the highway, and started driving down the road back then, there were only three or four cottages on the way 'til you got to the lake. There were even farms around here, too. Now, there's not a deer, or any other wild animal within maybe a hundred miles of the lake. It's rare to even see a bird around here anymore, either."

"Enough of your nostalgia," said Debbie, smiling. "Let's head back to the hotel for awhile. Okay?"

"Yeah, okay. Y'know, sometime before our vacation's up, I'd like to tie the boat up to that dock at the bottom of that high ridge, then go up those stairs to the top and see what their cottage looks like. I beat it's a beauty."

"I don't think you'd better do that, because they'd probably tell you to get off their property because they've had so many other curious people come up those stairs and invade their privacy."

"Yeah, guess you're right. Okay, let's pack our stuff in the boat, and go back to the hotel," said Ken. "I bet that cottage somewhere up on the high ridge is nicer than our hotel. I hope they realize how lucky they are. Lots of money. Good-looking kids. Best view of almost the whole lake. Yes, sir. She was a very pretty girl. She smiled down here at Loon Island a coupla times. Maybe she was smiling at us."

"Hmmm, I'd better keep an eye on you, or else you might row the boat over there on your own to say hello to that beautiful girl. She had a lovely figure. I'll bet her parents guard her very carefully, so, don't get any ideas, old man."

"Me? No way," said Ken, grinning. "I like slightly mature women like you."

"Slightly mature, eh? Seventy-four is more than slightly

mature. But thank you for the compliment, sweetheart, and you're the perfect age for me," said Debbie, then she kissed his cheek.

As she looked out at the lake while Ken rowed the boat back toward their hotel, time began slipping back to the days when Ken had vacationed at the lake when he'd been a young boy.

With each dip of his oars into the water, cottages lining the lake began to shimmer and disappear.

As they neared the crowded beach where their hotel was located, dozens of laughing children and adults on the crowded beach slowly faded away.

Seconds later, Ken, Debbie, and their rowboat vanished because time had swept back many years to a summer with Luke.

From the day school ended for the summer until the day before it resumed in September, Luke, his two brothers, and their parents stayed at their cottage, which was close to the big lake where Debbie and Ken would spend a vacation many years later.

Back in Luke's time, the cottage he stayed at for the summer was one of only four lining a gravel road leading down to the lake, and if one weren't careful while driving along the 2-lane highway, they could miss seeing the small gravel road because there wasn't a sign indicating that there was a lake at the end of that road.

Luke and his brothers loved spending all day swimming, fishing, and often taking their rowboat out onto the lake to play pirates with other boys in rowboats.

At one end of the lake, there were two roads: one leading to a few cottages scattered around one shore of the lake, and the other small road passed by a large marsh where the boys would catch bullfrogs and turtles.

Behind their cottage was a footpath through the woods to the lake, and a small distance along that footpath, the land began rising as bigger boulders began forming high, rocky hills, which the boys enjoyed climbing, then while standing at the top of a high hill, they could see the back of their cottage.

Eight miles from their cottage, along the main highway, there was the small town where everyone shopped for groceries, summer clothing, shoes, souvenirs, and there was a post office. Whenever Luke and his family were driving either to or from town, and the car had driven up to the top of a high hill, there was a small, unpaved road from the highway through the forest.

When they'd first seen that road that was approximately two miles away from the road leading to their cottage, Luke and his brothers had asked if there were more cottages along that other road, and their parents had told them that it was apparently a private road to a just one cottage at the end of it.

Luke and his brothers had talked about that other road that they knew led to some area of the very high ridge above the lake, and they'd agreed that the cottage at the end of that road must have an amazing view of the lake.

They knew that they could get to about the middle of that road by climbing over all the high boulders leading away from the rear of their cottage, but they'd decided against venturing down to the end of that other road because they had felt sure that the owners of that cottage would be very angry at having trespassers invading their privacy.

· · · · · · · ⚜ · · · · · · ·

Luke and his brothers often climbed tall pine trees that grew near the high boulders behind their cottage, and then they could see a few cottages on two of the many islands in the lake.

The boys would row a boat out to Loon Island, then they'd build a fire, and roast wieners or marshmallows.

One day on Loon Island, Luke saw a big boat docking at the base of a very high ridge, directly across the lake. He watched people carry suitcases and boxes up a series of wooden stairs, then after reaching the top, they walked out of sight, and he felt sure that they owned that cottage he'd been told was situated at the end of the road that was about two miles away from the road his cottage was on.

He thought it would be great to have a cottage so high above the lake because the view would be spectacular. Luke noticed that the land slowly rose for about half a mile until it peaked at the secluded area where he'd seen the people climbing the stairs, then the land sloped again almost a mile farther along the lake.

He decided to take the footpath at the back of his cottage, and see if there was another path somewhere in the forest that led to the high ridge. The following day, he put a couple of apples and two soft drinks in his knapsack, then he went around to the back of the cottage, and started walking along the footpath.

When he got to an area where he surmised the highest point of the ridge to be, he left the footpath and began making his way through bushes and trees.

· · · · · · ● ✤✻✤ ● · · · · · ·

Over half an hour later, after climbing over very high boulders, struggling through brush, and passing tall pine trees, Luke heard people talking, so, he stopped and peered around the trunk of huge pine tree.

He saw two men talking as they sat in lawn chairs, then trying not to make a sound, he walked around more tall bushes, and he was surprised to see a big, two-storey, wooden house, with several big bay windows.

He then realized that he was looking at the cottage that he'd been told was at the end of the private road, and he was impressed by the size of the cottage.

His parents had a three-bedroom cottage, so, Luke felt sure

that there must be at least eight or ten bedrooms in the big cottage he was looking at. He crept through the trees, and when he was able to see the front of the huge cottage, he saw a large, gabled veranda with five big, wicker chairs.

Luke took an apple and a Coke out of his knapsack, then as he munched on the apple, he wondered how often the owners of the huge cottage occupied it during the summer.

The grass of the very big front lawn had been mown recently, so, Luke presumed that the two men he'd seen sitting in deck chairs at the rear of the cottage had most likely mown the lawn sometime that morning.

He began moving out from the trees after deciding to go to the edge of the property and look out at the lake, and then Luke saw Julie. When she had appeared on the veranda, he had felt sure that she was the loveliest girl he'd ever seen.

He watched her go down the veranda steps, and walk slowly to the edge of the property, then he knew that she was enjoying the view of the islands and watercraft in the lake.

He stepped a little farther back into the trees when he saw her turn around and start walking back to the cottage while he wondered what her reaction would have been if she'd seen him standing in the trees not far from the veranda of her cottage.

While she walking nearer to him, Luke was admiring her beautiful, slender figure, and her long, wavy, black hair, and he liked the way her bright yellow and green striped, knee-length dress slightly billowed whenever a breeze swept around her.

When he stepped forward to take a closer look at her, he stepped on a dried branch, and when it snapped, the beautiful girl looked over in his direction.

"Julie! Lunch is ready! Please call your father and uncle in!"

"Okay! Father! Uncle John! Lunch! Booze! Whatever!"

"Julie!"

"Hey! They might want a liquid lunch!"

"Enough of that, young lady! Just go find them and tell them lunch is ready! Thank you!"

"Certainly!" Julie shouted to her mother. "If they haven't heard us shouting, then that means they're asleep! Or they've been eaten by bears! I'll go get them, alright? You know, there really isn't any reason to shout because a whisper carries for miles around here. If they haven't heard us shouting, then they must be miles away. Correct? However, if they've gone for a very long walk, then I'll invite a guest for lunch."

"Oh? Did you see a boat coming near the dock?"

"No," replied Julie. "I meant that I'll invite that boy over there in the bushes to have lunch with us."

Luke felt so embarrassed at being discovered, and he didn't know if he should run away, or stay long enough to apologize for being so close to their enormous cottage.

"Well?" Julie asked him, as she smiled. "Would you like to have lunch with us, or are you one of the forest cannibals?"

"Who? Me?" asked Luke. "Hi. I was just walking by here. I came through the forest."

"And? Lunch or not?" she asked.

"Um, well, sure, okay," he replied, blushing.

"If you're not deaf, then you obviously know my name is Julie, and you've deduced, hopefully, that the woman staring at you is my mother. So, out with it. Tell us your name."

"I'm Luke. Luke Marshall."

"Marshmallow?" asked Julie, with a crooked smile.

"No, *Marshall*. I was going home for lunch, so, uh, well, I..."

"You already said, you'd have lunch with us, so, come on. You may call my mother, Mrs. Fenhurst," she told him as she smiled.

"Hello, Mrs. Fenhurst," said Luke.

"How do you do, Luke? It's so nice to have a guest for lunch."

"Luke, would you come with me, please? You and I can tell my father and uncle that lunch is ready," said Julie.

"Yeah, sure," he said, stepping out from the bushes and trees.

"Gee, no machete," said Julie. "I was hoping you'd add some excitement to our day. Oh, well, you might surprise me, yet. Now let's go find daddy and Uncle John."

"They're at the back of the house. I saw them there before."

"Standing?" she asked him.

"Yes, they were, and talking, too," replied Luke, smiling.

They walked to the back of the house, then as they looked around at the trees, Julie said: "They're not here now, so, I suppose they went for a stroll in the woods. I'll wait here, and you go on ahead because they could be taking a leak."

"Oh. Uh, yeah, maybe they could be doing that. Okay, I'll be right back."

"With them, too, I hope," said Julie, smiling. "Bye."

· · · · · · • • ⟫⟫⟩⟩⟨⟨⟨ • • · · · · · ·

Luke went to the far end of the lawn, then walked into the bushes and trees to begin looking around for the men. He climbed huge boulders and looked down through the trees, then after he'd stood at the top of five other boulders he'd passed on his way through the forest, he saw a movement near a small clearing, so, he scrambled down the boulder and walked toward the clearing.

Suddenly, a huge, dead tree that had only about five very big branches left on it fell over and barely missed the tips of his shoes when it crashed to the ground.

Luke had cried out in both shock and fear as he stood between two of the very big, heavy branches that had narrowly missed hitting his head and shoulders when the tree had fallen.

"Whew! That was close!" exclaimed Thomas.

"Did you see that?" exclaimed Luke, wide-eyed. "It almost fell on top of me!"

"Yes, and you're very lucky that neither of those two massive branches hit your head when that enormous, old dead tree toppled over!" exclaimed John. "It must have been uprooted when it was struck by lightning during that huge thunderstorm we had a few weeks ago, and it just toppled over now!"

"Wow! If I'd taken just half a step more, I would've got hit by this really huge tree! I've seen a lot of big, fallen trees after a really big thunderstorm, but I've never almost been hit by one before! Look at the size of it! It must've stood over sixty feet high! Boy! That sure was scary!"

"Yes, it sure was. We were just as astonished as you were when that enormous tree just suddenly fell over like that. From now on, I'm going to look closely at all the trees I'm walking near when I'm out here. You'd better do the same. John, after lunch we should check to see if there are more trees that have been partly uprooted from being struck by lightning. If there are, then I'll hire some men from town to cut them down before somebody is seriously hurt, or worse, killed. Are you alright, son?"

"Yeah, *now* I am," replied Luke. "Whew! I could've been killed. It sure is a huge tree."

"Sure is. When it hit the ground, it caused such a rumble that I thought there'd been an earthquake. Sometime in the next few days, I'll get out the chainsaw and John and I'll cut up the tree. There'll be enough to keep the fireplace going for quite some time, but it was a heck of an awful way of getting more wood for the woodpile. Your nerves must be shot, and it's a wonder you didn't jump as high as the height that tree once stood because of the shock of almost being hit by it."

"Yeah, I almost *did* jump that high when the tree fell and nearly hit me like that," said Luke. "Oh, are you Mr. Fenhurst?"

"Yes, I am, and this is my brother-in-law, John Lokston."

"Pleased to meet you. My name is Luke Marshall. Julie asked me to tell you that lunch is ready."

"Did you arrive by boat, Luke?" asked Mr. Fenhurst.

"No, sir, I came through the woods way over there, and when Julie saw me, she invited me for lunch. I was on my way to the cottages down on the other side of this high ridge and I was

passing by your place."

"Oh, I see. Well, you run on ahead and tell Sarah and Julie that

we're on our way. Please."

"Sure, okay," said Luke, smiling. "See you there. Bye."

Luke hurried back toward the large cottage while thinking that

he shouldn't be imposing on the Fenhursts by accepting their

invitation for lunch, but he was rather interested in Julie.

After reaching the edge of the forest again, he saw her sitting

on the grass near the front of the cottage, so, he smiled as he ran

over to her.

"Hi! I found them. They're on their way, now. A huge tree fell

over and it almost landed on top of me."

"Oh, no! That must've been so scary!" exclaimed Julie. "I'm

glad you weren't hurt!"

"So am I. That tree was so big that it would've flattened me.

Lots of those huge trees are knocked over by lightning. Sometimes

there's really big thunderstorms around here."

"I know. Last summer we had one and I thought it was going

to blow some of the cottages into the lake," said Julie. "The roots of those tall pines are so huge, aren't they? I like climbing up the roots or walking along the fallen tree trunks, but they can be slippery when they're damp because of the moss that starts growing on them after there's been many rainfalls."

"I like doing that, too. Like, climbing up all those really big roots of pine trees that've been knocked over by a lightning bolt. Uh, I saw you when you arrived here. Well, not *you*. It must've been your parents and your uncle," said Luke. "I saw them carrying suitcases and other things up from the boat. Are you going to be staying for awhile?"

"Our plans aren't definite. Do you know how long you'll be here at the lake?"

"Yeah. We always come up here for the whole summer. My dad comes up every weekend, then when he gets his holidays, he's here for three weeks. We come back up again for Thanksgiving, too, because my dad gets a two-week holiday at that time."

"That's very nice," said Julie. "Not many people can come up here for that long. Have you any brothers and sisters?"

"Well, yeah, in a way. I was adopted when I was ten because my parents died in a car accident when I was four years old, and they didn't have any relatives. At least, I'm sure they didn't or else I would've been taken in by them. When I started getting older at the orphanage, I began worrying that I'd never get lucky enough to get adopted. Like, not many people want a kid after he's older than four or five years old. My new parents already had a son and his name is Glen. He's a year older than me. My younger brother, Ross, is almost seven, and I'll be seventeen in October."

"You're adopted? Of course, *that's* why," said Julie.

"Why what?" asked Luke.

"Oh, nothing, really. I just wondered why you were alone when you came here. I thought that because you weren't with one of your brothers, that you weren't accepted by your new family."

"Well, not really. We play together a lot. My brothers and me, I mean, but because Ross is a lot younger than me, he has friends his age who he plays with most of the time," said Luke.

"And you and Glen? Are you friends?"

"Sometimes. Well, he doesn't really want to be my friend, but

I've always tried to be *his* friend, or one of them. Sometimes he can be mean by telling me that if I hadn't been adopted by his parents, that I'd be in reform school by now because he says orphans always turn out to be in big trouble with the police. Glen also keeps telling me that because I'm adopted I won't inherit anything from his parents, but I don't care if I don't. I'm just glad I've got a home."

"I see," said Julie. "Do your adoptive parents treat you the same way as their sons do?"

"Sure, most of the time, but I know that's because they feel more for Glen and Ross because I'm not their own. They got me because they wanted a brother for Glen, and because their mother didn't think she could have another baby after Glen was born, and then she found out she was four months pregnant with Ross after they'd adopted me."

"That was a wonderful surprise for them," said Julie.

"Yeah, it was. After Ross was born, I got the feeling that they wished they'd waited a little longer before they adopted me. They try not to show it, but I can tell they like Glen and Ross more than me because of the way they spend more time with them, and talk to them more. That's okay, though, because I understand that they'd show more attention to their own sons. I mean, they're a *real* family, right? And I'm just a...hmmm," said Luke, then he paused and said, "I guess things'd be different if my parents hadn't died because I, uh, I know I would've been really happy if they'd...Um, so, how old are you?"

"I'll be seventeen next January," she replied.

"Oh. You're, um, like the rest of your family. Like, they're all really nice-looking. Your mother's beautiful and your dad's handsome. So's your uncle," said Luke.

"Oh, really? So, what you're saying is, that you think I'm nice-looking, too."

"Well, yeah, sure. The rest of your family is."

"Thanks. Your parents must have been just as attractive as you find mine to be because you're rather nice-looking, yourself. I would've said you were rather handsome, but I wouldn't want to make you too vain," said Julie, smiling.

"Uh, handsome? Really? Well, I, um, I....So, this is really a great place. I didn't know there was a huge house here. You've got a fantastic view of the lake from here. You can see for miles. I go to one of the islands, sometimes, and then we make a bonfire and have hot dogs, or we toast marshmallows."

"That sounds like lots of fun. I felt marooned here because there were no other people my age until you finally appeared."

"Yeah, being way up here, you don't get anyone climbing up all those steps to see what's up here, or who's up here. Hey, I've got a rowboat. Tomorrow, we're going over to Loon Island. That's the one right across from you. You wanna come with us? I can meet you down at your dock."

"Okay, I'd like that. I'm sure my parents will let me come with you. What time?" asked Julie.

"I guess around, oh...How about noon?"

"Fine by me. I'll bring some sandwiches and a couple of dozen cookies. I bake cookies to keep me from getting bored. Chocolate chip. Peanut butter. With nuts and without, and I make lemon sugar snaps, too."

"Yeah? That sounds great," said Luke, smiling. "But you don't have to bring sandwiches because I'll bring enough wieners and buns for you."

"I'll *still* bring sandwiches because you and your brothers and friends might like some. I'll make up half of the sandwiches with tuna salad, and half of them with egg salad, and I'm sure you'll like them."

"Yeah, I would. That's really nice of you. We can go swimming and...Oh, there's your dad and your uncle."

"Time for lunch. C'mon," said Julie. "During lunch, we'll talk about our picnic tomorrow. You almost didn't make it for lunch because that really big tree almost fell on top of you."

"Yeah, that was pretty scary," said Luke. "Thanks for inviting me for lunch. Um, guess I'd better wash my hands first."

"The bathroom's upstairs. It's the third door on your left, down the hall."

Luke liked the interior of the house. The furniture was an eclectic mix of modern and antique, and the staircase had an ornately carved banister with beautifully shaped white spindles.

The hallway leading to the bathroom was covered with a thick, oriental carpet, and gilt-framed paintings hung on the walls. He entered the bathroom and admired the cedar panelling on the walls and ceilings, and the bathtub that was very big, with brass feet that were shaped like fish.

Luke washed his face and hands, combed his hair, then after walking back along the hall to the staircase, he saw Julie waiting for him at the foot of the stairs.

She led him into the dining room and he saw that her parents and uncle were seated at a big table that was covered with a white tablecloth.

There was a large, crystal bowl filled with fruit in the center of the table, and two silver, pheasant candlesticks set at each side of the bowl of fruit. Julie gestured to a chair, and Luke sat in it, then smiled at them.

"Thomas and John told me of that frightful experience you had in the woods. It must have terrified you."

"It sure did, ma'am," said Luke. "The tree was so big, that the ground shook when it landed."

"Oh, yes, I'm sure it must have, and I'm so relieved that you weren't hurt," said Mrs. Fenhurst.

"So were we," said Thomas. "John and I are going to take a walk around the property later this afternoon to make sure there are no more trees ready to fall. If a tree that size hit the house, it would cause quite a bit of damage."

While they were talking, Julie's mother left the dining room to go to the kitchen, then a few minutes later, she returned carrying a silver tray with salad plates on it.

When they'd finished their salads of lettuce, sliced avocados, quartered tomatoes, and finely cut, raw vegetables, Julie's parents got up from the table, picked up the salad plates and took them to the kitchen, then less than a minute later, they brought back plates of food, and Mrs. Fenhurst placed a plate in front of Luke.

Each lunch plate had a slice of ham-and-cheese quiche, portions of coleslaw and potato salad, as well as cantaloupe and two other types of melon cut like flowers.

The food serving wasn't too large, considering the various foods that had been very creatively arranged on the plates, and

Luke felt like he was eating in an expensive restaurant.

They talked about the cottages by the lake, and Julie's parents agreed to Luke's plans with Julie for the following afternoon. Mr. Fenhurst refilled the adults' glasses with white wine from a beautiful crystal decanter, and from another similar decanter, he poured ice-cold ginger ale for Julie and Luke.

After lunch, Julie accompanied them when Thomas took Luke by motorboat to the south end of the lake, close to the road leading to his cottage. Luke thanked them for their hospitality, and told them how much he'd enjoyed the lunch and his visit, then he said goodbye to Julie and her father.

Luke thought about Julie as he walked home, and he felt so lucky to have met her. It had been quite an exciting day for him; meeting Julie and her family and being invited to a wonderful lunch, and that quite scary incident before lunch when a huge tree had almost fallen on top of him.

Luke felt that the most exciting part of the day had been talking with Julie, and she had agreed to come with him to Loon

Island the next day. He hoped that she would enjoy their time together on the island so much that Julie would want to spend every day with him for the rest of the summer.

When he arrived back at his own cottage, he regaled his brothers with his experiences during his visit with Julie.

"And she's coming with us tomorrow," said Luke, grinning.

"She's that gorgeous, is she?" asked Glen.

"Oh, yeah, really. So beautiful, and she's so nice, too."

"Hmmm, things are looking up for me," said Glen.

"No way, man," said Luke, smiling. "I saw her first."

"She might be interested in a *real* man," said Glen.

"Hah! Don't even try, jerk. She's a very nice girl. She doesn't need a guy like you coming on to her," said Luke, smirking.

"Oh, yeah? Girls like what they call cute guys like me."

"I've had lots of girls call me cute, too. In fact, Julie said I was rather nice-looking."

Yeah? Then she must've had on very, very dark sunglasses all the time she talked to you," said Glen as he smirked.

"If that girl likes playing with cute guys, I bet she'll wanna play with me, too. Mom says I'm cute, and I never heard her call you guys cute," said Ross.

"Get real," said Luke, smiling. "She doesn't rob cradles, squirt, and don't gawk at her. You, too, Mr. Glen Bigshot."

"Hey, it's open season on girls all summer," said Glen.

"Stick to the dummies y'got now. Hey, how many guys and girls are coming tomorrow, anyway?" Luke asked Glen.

"Well, there'll be Tony and Carol, and Jimmy, and you with Ross in tow, and Julie and I, so, that'll make seven all together."

"Julie and *you*? Only in your dreams," said Luke.

"You said they were rich, right? So, think about it. This family might not be as rich as hers, but we're not really poor. And your parents left you nothing, so, what would you have in common with a girl like Julie?" asked Glen. "Nothing, right? It takes more than personality and good-looks to impress a girl."

"Well, I know they're not snobs because they invited me to have lunch with them, and they were really nice to me, too."

"Of course they were," said Glen. "That's what people call the fine manners of the upper class. *Class*. Something you don't have. They were being polite, and so was Julie, but wait'll she meets *me*, then she'll be even *more* polite."

"Yeah, right, as if she'd be impressed with you. Her parents have probably got more money than you could imagine, so, because of the money *this* family has, that'd put you on the same social level as me," Luke told him, with a smirk.

"Oh, yeah? Just wait and see. Girls like her can recognize how different you are from me," said Glen.

"Yeah, real different!" cried Ross, laughing. "You've got a real big nose and you're not as good-looking as Luke!"

"Hey you! Whose side are you on, anyway? Your nose is gonna be just as big as mine when you're the same age as me, twerp! Say you're sorry or we won't take you with us tomorrow, and I mean that," said Glen.

"I don't care," said Ross. "I'll ask somebody else to take me over to the island, and lotsa guys'd take me there. So there! Bye! I'm going to play with Gordie and Terry!"

"Good! And don't come back for five hours! Brat! I sure hope I never have kids like him," Glen said to Luke. "Hmmm, yeah, I can't wait 'til tomorrow when I meet Julie."

"Maybe I shouldn't've invited her," said Luke. "Well, even if it turns out that Julie *does* like you more than me, I'd still like to be friends with her."

"She won't have time to be friends with you because she'll be with *me* all the time. Most girls don't want to date guys who are orphans because they can't meet that guy's parents to find out if there's something weird about them *and* the orphan.

"I'm not really an orphan anymore. I'm adopted."

"That doesn't count because you're not related to us. Hey, that doesn't mean I don't like you, okay?" said Glen. "I'm just telling you how girls feel about guys with no real parents."

Luke felt sure that Julie liked him, regardless of what Glen had told him, and he thought about her until he fell asleep. He began dreaming about her very big cottage high above the lake, and beautiful Julie's lovely smile while she'd been talking with him.

He had been going to the island with his friends several times a week, and because they always had so much fun there, he felt sure that Julie would have a wonderful time there, too.

Two weeks earlier, his brothers and friends had left for Loon Island without him, so, Luke had walked along the shore until he'd been as close to the island as he could get, then he'd started swimming across the lake to the island.

He had thought that the island was closer to the mainland, but the longer he swam, he realized it was much farther away. Instead of panicking, he'd floated on his back for awhile to rest, and then he had slowly started swimming again, but he had become a bit worried when he had started to feel tired.

He'd swam just over halfway to the island, when he'd felt a cramp in his left leg, and because it had become so stiff that he hadn't been able to move it, he'd started to sink beneath the surface. But after he'd sank a small distance below the surface, he had rubbed his leg vigorously until he'd eased the cramp in it.

Luke had then quickly swam up to the surface, and then floated on his back until he'd felt strong enough to resume swimming to the island. He had felt elated when he'd seen that he was nearing a part of the island that was far from where Glen, Ross, and his friends were, then after he scrambled ashore, he laughed, then began walking through the trees to the other end of the island.

His friends and his brothers had been surprised to see him, and they'd asked him how he had come to the island, and when Luke proudly told them, they had been astonished.

Luke, however, had decided never to try swimming that distance again because he'd become scared when he had developed a severe cramp in his left leg.

When his adoptive parents had learned that he'd swam all the way to the island, they had scolded him and made him promise that he'd never try doing that again.

Even though he'd been scolded, Luke had still felt very pleased that all his friends thought he was quite daring for having swum from the mainland all the way to Loon Island.

Luke and his brothers packed their knapsacks, then after Glen told him that he'd pick up Julie at her dock, Luke told him that he'd meet him on Loon Island because he'd get a ride in one of their friends' boats.

"You go on ahead, okay?" Luke told him. "Julie likes to read, so, I'm going to look for a good book to lend her."

"Okay, but if you're not down at the lake in fifteen minutes, then Larry and his brother'll leave without you," said Glen.

"So, I'll swim over there if I can't get a ride."

"Yeah, right," said Glen. "The last time you did that, you got a cramp in your leg, so, this time you might get a cramp in *both* of your legs, then drown. Even if you didn't drown, you'd be in deep shit for months because you promised you'd never try swimming all the way over there again. Hey, that's a great idea! Yeah, swim to Loon Island again, and then you won't be allowed to go near the lake for the rest of the summer, and that'd leave me with Julie."

"Okay, I *won't* swim over there, and I won't be late getting down to the lake, so, tell the guys to wait for me," said Luke.

"I might. Okay, I'm going. See you later, goof."

"Yeah, see you later."

* * * * * * * ❖ * * * * * *

Luke had planned to take the same route he had taken before to Julie's cottage because he'd get there before Glen arrived with the boat to pick her up at the dock below the very high ridge.

He knew that Glen was going to try his best to impress Julie, but Luke felt sure that she'd be more impressed when he told her that Glen was the worst swimmer of everyone they knew, then he would tell her how he'd swam all the way across to Loon Island two weeks ago.

Luke waited until he saw Glen going around the curve in the road, then he grabbed his knapsack and smiled as he left to go through the forest to Julie's cottage.

He left the footpath at the same spot as he had the day before, then he began making his way through large bushes until he reached an area where there were mostly trees.

Luke hoped that he wouldn't arrive at Julie's after Glen because then he wouldn't have any way of getting to the island to join them.

Plodding along, climbing over huge boulders, sliding down hills, and then climbing over other ones, he felt sure that he'd been walking for over half an hour through the dense forest, and he was

becoming more anxious about getting to Julie before Glen did.

He recognized many of the boulders he'd seen the day before,

and while climbing them, he knew that he was close to Julie's

cottage because he saw the spot where the huge pine tree had

toppled over and almost struck him.

When he eventually reached that area, and he didn't see the

fallen tree, Luke realized that Mr. Fenhurst and his brother-in-law,

John, had already sawed and chopped the tree into pieces for the

woodpile, so, all that was left was the memory of how close he'd

come to being killed.

Luke began running, then five minutes later, he rushed through

the bushes and out onto the lawn near the front of Julie's cottage,

then he knocked on the front door, and when her mother answered

the door, he smiled as he said hello to her.

"Why, hello, Luke. I'm so glad to see you again."

"Um, is Julie home?"

"No, I'm afraid she's not, dear," replied Sarah, smiling.

"Awwww, no. That means that Glen *did* get here before me. Darn. I guess I'd better just go home, then," said Luke, frowning.

"Why don't you stay for lunch with us? We'd love to have you. Please? I won't take no for an answer, and Julie will be back by the time we finish our lunch."

"Well, I....hmmm, okay. Thank you, ma'am. Um, I'm just going to look over at the island for awhile first, okay? I want to see if I can see them over there."

"Certainly. We're not in any hurry."

"Great! I'll be back in five minutes! Bye!" cried Luke.

He cupped his right hand above his eyes while looking across the lake at Loon Island, and he could see smoke rising above the trees and small figures moving around near the bonfire.

Luke had been very disappointed at not getting to Julie's in time to go with her and Glen to the island, but he'd smiled after realizing that when she returned, he could spend almost half an hour with her before he had to return home because he was going into town with his parents and brothers to do some shopping.

He turned away from the edge of the high ridge, and began walking back to the big cottage, and he saw that the front door was almost wide open, so, he entered the cottage.

When he walked into the living room, he saw Mr. Fenhurst and Julie's uncle, John, reading books, and then after he greeted them, they asked him to sit down.

Sarah was smiling as she entered the room, and handed him a glass of cold lemonade, and then she returned to the kitchen.

"Lemonade, eh? Well, when you finish that, we'll have a cocktail together," said Mr. Fenhurst, smiling. "After all, you're almost old enough now to have something a bit stronger."

"Yeah? Thanks sir. Well, I've had a few drinks at a friend's before, a few times," Luke told him. "But I'd get grounded for twenty years if anybody knew about it."

"I thought so," said Julie's father. "In that case, I won't tell anyone if you have wine with us at lunch. Besides, our Julie drinks wine, too, sometimes."

"Oh? Then I'll have some wine with lunch, too."

"That's the spirit," said Thomas, as he smiled.

"I was supposed to go with all the other guys to Loon Island, but I didn't get here in time to go over there in the boat with my brother and Julie. I don't mind, though, because I'll be having a much better lunch than them," said Luke, smiling.

"Now that's the way to think," said John, grinning.

He felt much more relaxed than he'd thought he would've been with her family, and when Luke had finished drinking his lemonade, Mr. Fenhurst prepared martinis.

Luke took a drink of the vodka martini, and he was surprised by how smooth the ice cold drink tasted. Mrs. Fenhurst then entered the room to announce that lunch would be served in ten minutes, so, Luke asked to use their bathroom to freshen up before they dined.

When he looked up into the mirror above the bathroom sink, after he'd washed his hands, Luke felt so relieved that he'd shaved before he had left home.

He felt rather proud that his beard had started to grow recently, then after he'd dried his hands and face, he grinned into the mirror before leaving the bathroom to go back downstairs for lunch.

Seeing the bay window at the end of the upstairs hall, he went to look out of it because being on the second floor he hoped that he'd be able to see part of the island where Julie, his brothers, and their friends were.

Luke could only see the tops of the trees on the island, so, he decided that after lunch, he'd go to the edge of the property for a better view of Loon Island.

He began thinking about Julie again, and he realized he liked her even more than he had before, then he felt a rush of tingling sensations and a sudden, strong love for her, and that made Luke even more annoyed that Glen had said that he might make a pass at her. He then felt confident that Julie would like him more than she would Glen, then Luke whistled as he went downstairs, and then he smiled as he sat down at the dining room table.

"You seem much cheerier, Luke," said Mrs. Fenhurst.

"Yeah, I *am* feeling a lot better than I was when I first got here," he told her, as he smiled. "I suppose it's because I'm hungry and looking forward to a very nice lunch."

"Where's John?" she asked her husband.

"He left his cigarette case on the patio table at the back of the house, so, he'll be back soon, unless a big tree falls on him."

"That's not at all amusing," said Sarah. "It was quite a frightful experience for Luke. Awfully frightening. Thomas, would you pour us a glass of wine, please?"

"Certainly, dear. Mmmmm, you've prepared salmon for lunch. My favorite," said Thomas.

Luke found the lunch to be as delicious as the one he'd enjoyed with them the day before, although he was missing Julie more as the time passed.

Immediately after lunch, Luke excused himself from the table and hurried outside to wait for her down by the dock. He was just about to go down the flights of stairs to the dock, when he saw Julie walking up, then his heart leapt when she smiled at him.

"There you are. You look prettier than ever," said Luke.

"I do? Thanks very much."

"By the way, you missed a great lunch. Let's sit near the edge of the ridge and look out over the lake for awhile."

"I'd love that," said Julie, holding out her hand to him.

They sat on the grass near the edge of the high ridge while they watched sailboats out on the lake. Luke was feeling both nervous and rather excited as he occasionally glanced at her, and thought about how very beautiful she was.

"Uh, maybe it's because of the sunlight at this time of the day, but you look even prettier."

"Why, thank you, Luke," said Julie, smiling. "I think you're quite handsome, and I wondered how long it would be before you noticed me."

"I thought you were really beautiful the first time I saw you, but I was too shy to tell you that, then."

"You were just in a fog, that's all. Or was it a bush?"

"I was that cannibal of the forest," replied Luke.

"You seemed like such a boy then, hiding in the bushes like that, but now you're much more mature."

"Yeah? Thanks," he said, said grinning.

"How would you like to play a board game with me?"

"That sounds great. What kind of...Oh, no, I forgot. We're all going into town soon to do some shopping. Um, would it be okay

if I come back again, tomorrow?"

"I'd love to see you *every* day, but don't go now. Please."

"Sorry, Julie, but I have to go now or else I'll be late getting

back to my place. I'll come back here tomorrow, okay? I'd better

run. Bye," said Luke, then he started to hurry away.

"Luke! Wait! Stay! Please!" cried Julie.

"I wish I could! I'll be back tomorrow! Honest! Bye!"

* * * * * * • ⟩⟩⟨⟨⟩⟩⟨ • * * * * * *

Luke hated having to leave her because he felt so pleased that

she wanted to spend more time with him, and that Julie had told

him that she'd like to see him every day.

He stopped to look back and smile while waving at her before

he reached the back of her cottage, then he smiled and waved at

her again before he began hurrying into the forest.

Luke could see part of the clearing in the forest not too far

ahead, and he knew that he could make better time by running

across it. He pushed his way through more bushes, then after

reaching the edge of the clearing, he stopped and gaped in

astonishment when he saw Julie and her family seated on the grass, and she waved to him as he walked slowly toward them.

"How did you get here before me? Is there a shortcut?"

"No, there's not," Julie told him.

"But how?" asked Luke, bewildered.

"Think, Luke," said Mrs. Fenhurst. "Think very hard."

"You mean there's a path that comes around to here?"

"No. Think harder. Remember the lake and Loon Island."

"What's Loon Island got to do with it?" Luke asked her.

"You were swimming to it, remember?"

"Yeah, I sure remember that because I almost drowned halfway over to the island," he said.

"You did?" asked Sarah, wide-eyed. "Another frightful experience. First, almost drowning while swimming to Loon Island, and then that enormous tree falling over and almost hitting you. Come sit with me for a moment. Would you please, dear?"

"Well, okay," said Luke. "But then I've got to get on home because I'm supposed to go into town."

He sat close beside her, then Sarah put her arms around him

and hugged him, and then Luke felt so relaxed and pleasantly comfortable in her embrace.

"Luke, dear, we'd love to have you stay with us and be a part of our family," said Sarah. "Julie feels very strongly for you, and I can tell that you feel the same way about her, so, I know you both would be very happy together. Would you like that?"

"Oh, yeah, I'd love that. Really," he replied. "But I've already been adopted by a family."

"I know all about your family," said Sarah. "Luke. You didn't make it to Loon Island, dear."

"I know. I thought I could get here in time, then when I got here, Glen and Julie had already gone over there."

"No, Luke. You didn't make it to the island when you tried to swim there," Sarah told him.

"I...I didn't? But if I didn't, then..."

"Yes, Luke," said Julie. "We thought that if that huge tree fell almost on top of you, that it'd make you think about life and death. That you'd remember you weren't able to reach Loon Island."

"No, I really did do that because I talked to my brothers and my parents ever since I swam over to Loon Island!"

"You only thought them, Luke. You thought them while we waited for you to realize what had really happened to you."

"I only thought about them all this time? I was sure I really talked to them. We even planned to meet at the island, and Glen was coming here in the boat to take Julie over there. It all seemed so real. I just can't be dead because I don't feel like I am, but there's something...Well, something *different*. I feel like I'm...Oh, I...Awww, no. Oh, Julie," said Luke, as he started to cry.

"Luke. Hold my hand," Julie said as she smiled.

He slowly raised his hand, and Julie held it, then after Sarah released him from her embrace, Luke stood up, and then Julie told him to close his eyes for a moment. He closed his eyes, then a moment later, after opening them again, he was so surprised to find himself standing at the edge of the high ridge, looking out over the lake as he held Julie's hand.

He turned to face her and she stood up on her toes to kiss him, then Luke felt a rush of tremendous love for her and a great peace within himself, and he had never felt so happy before in all his life.

Luke felt their bodies rising, then they were flying above the islands, swooping and soaring, then flying slowly around more islands as they laughed and sometimes kissed.

He now knew that he'd love Julie forever, and then while clinging tightly to him, she whispered in Luke's ear that she would love *him* forever, too.

The End

Johnny had taken a plane sixty-five miles from the city to a smaller city, then rented a car that had started having engine problems as he'd neared a small town ten miles from his intended destination, so, he'd hired a taxi to take him the rest of the way.

Now, as he sat in the back seat, holding gifts while the cab sped along the two-lane rural highway, Johnny wondered what sort of questions he'd be asked by Amanda's parents.

He'd met her six months before through René, a young man he worked with, then every time he had invited René and his girlfriend to his apartment, they'd brought Amanda with them, and she'd always brought a book with her, which she would say was one of her most treasured books that she wanted to lend to him.

Johnny hadn't liked any of the books Amanda had brought with her, but he'd never wanted to hurt her feelings, so, he had always skimmed through a book, then told her that he had liked reading it.

He'd then started seeing her at the small grocery store two blocks from his apartment, even though there were two supermarkets close to where Amanda lived.

She had then started phoning him every few days to say that she'd been visiting a friend who lived almost next door to him, and would it be all right if she dropped by Johnny's apartment to pick up the book she'd recently lent him, and then lend him another book that she just happened to have with her.

Two months before Johnny had been introduced to Amanda, his six-month relationship with Loreen had ended, and then almost all of his friends had wanted to introduce him to other young women whom they'd felt would be perfect for him.

He'd decided not to start dating any young woman on a regular basis until he'd come to terms with the surprisingly sudden and somewhat rather rude rejection he'd received from Loreen when she had told him that she'd fallen in love for the first time in her life with a man whom she'd recently met.

Johnny felt that he should have known that Loreen would fall in love with somebody else, because she had led such a busy social life that they'd only dated once a week, and she'd never wanted to become more intimate than just kissing him hello and goodbye.

After he'd been introduced to Amanda, she had continually found excuses to either run into him where he shopped, or to drop by unexpectedly at his apartment.

. . . . ⚜ . . . .

One Saturday around two in the afternoon, he'd been at the checkout counter in his local grocery store, when someone tapped his shoulder. Johnny had looked back, and seen Amanda standing close behind him, and she'd had a package of chewing gum and an apple in a shopping cart.

"Hi, Johnny! I was on my way to visit you when I saw you come into this store, so, I thought I'd pick up a few things, too, while I was in the neighborhood."

"Oh? I didn't notice you while I was shopping."

"You didn't? Well, that's because you were so deep in thought when you were selecting the grapes, and I didn't want to disturb you. Oh, you're buying mangos! And look! Pineapple, apples, and those blueberries and strawberries look so wonderful, and isn't it a coincidence? Those are all *my* favorites, too. By the way, did you finish reading that book I lent you?"

"Yes, I did," he replied. "It was nice."

"Really? I'm so glad you liked it. It seems we like so many of the same things. Well, it's a good thing I ran into you here in the store, because I have another book for you to read, and it's another romance. Girl gets boy again. Oh, do I ever need a coffee! You make such marvelous coffee, so, I always look forward to having a cup or two of it, and right now it'd be a lifesaver."

"Um, well, sure. Now that you're here, we can walk back to my place and I'll make some for you," said Johnny.

"You will? Oh, you're so sweet to invite me to have coffee with you! I'll help carry your shopping bags."

They'd walked back to his apartment, then after Johnny had put away the groceries, and made coffee, they'd sat in the living room, discussing the book that Johnny had hated, but he hadn't wanted to hurt her feelings by telling her that.

Amanda had told him that he simply must let her return the favor of being invited into his apartment for coffee, by inviting him to have a cup of coffee with her and a few friends at a cafe. While he'd been trying to make excuses, Amanda had pouted, so, he'd agreed to meet her at the cafe early that evening.

Johnny met her at the cafe, then listened to her friends speaking French, and after an hour and a half, he wished that he could speak French, too, so that he could join in on their conversation.

When he was alone with her later that night, Amanda had told him that she came from the same region as her friends, and that because everyone was French there, they didn't have much opportunity to speak their language here in the city, except when they socialized two or three times a week.

She was always so eager to please him, so, Johnny kept accepting Amanda's invitations to have coffee with her friends because she'd become so unhappy if he wouldn't.

She'd been phoning him almost every day, and they were seeing each other two evenings per week when they met with her friends at their favorite cafe, so, eventually, Amanda began referring to Johnny as her boyfriend.

He wasn't enthralled with Amanda telling her friends that they were an item, however, because almost every time he turned around she was there, Johnny reluctantly began asking her to accompany him to the theatre and other places he frequented.

"You know, in all the time we've known each other, you've never talked about your family, school, or for that matter, any..."

"But why should I? This is *now*, Johnny. What I did at school is in the past, and I never dwell on the past, especially when the present is so exciting. Meeting people, and of course, *you* because I find you so interesting, and talking about my family isn't. I mean, what's there to know besides the fact that I have parents and...Well, I was so sorry to hear about your parents passing on. So sad. I know! Why don't we talk about that book I lent you, and then we'll go have a coffee with my friends? I know you really love them. Can we? I really want to. Please?"

"Sure," Johnny replied. "It's just that I feel out of place because I don't speak French, and you and your friends speak it all the time we're together."

"Oh, that's not really true," she said. "Why, I've talked to you sometimes when we're with them, and Andre and Louise adore you, and they think we make a perfect couple."

"But they hardly know me, and besides, they ignore me when I try to talk to them because I don't speak French, and that's all they prefer to speak, so, I never know what they're saying when they talk about me."

"Why, they're saying wonderful things about you. Really. It's just that it sounds so much better in French because you know how French is such a romantic language," said Amanda, smiling.

"I had a terrible time with French at school, but yeah, it does sound sort of pleasant, so, I'll buy a Berlitz language book and try to learn how to speak French."

"Wonderful! Then we'll have even *more* in common! So, are you ready to go? We're going to have such a good time."

"Uh-huh, I'm ready. Let's go," said Johnny, forcing a smile.

They'd been sort of dating for almost two weeks when Amanda started talking about marriage, and on the rare occasions that they socialized with two or three of her friends who spoke English, Amanda would tell them that she felt sure that Johnny was going to ask her to marry him very soon.

She also told the same thing to her French friends who congratulated Amanda and Johnny, and surprisingly in English, too. Her French friends had then told them that their own love relationships had greatly improved after they'd been married, and it had been a continuing, wonderful experience for them.

Johnny was surprised that her friends only spoke English to him when he seemed dubious about his relationship with Amanda, and when he told her friends that he and Amanda rarely kissed, then her male friends assured him that French women were extremely amorous after they were married.

Amanda was reasonably attractive and so eager to please him in every way she could, therefore, considering what her friends had told him about love and sex occurring after marriage, Johnny had finally proposed to her.

Now, here he stood at the entrance gates to her family home, with a suitcase in each hand and gifts tucked under his arms as he gazed down the long road to the farmhouse. Johnny and Amanda had agreed to spend two weeks here, then he'd meet her family again, six months later, when they were married in the city.

He had a strange foreboding that even worse things were about to happen because of all the small accidents he'd been having since the time he'd become engaged to marry Amanda.

Johnny began recalling that quite embarrassing incident that had occurred when he'd taken her to a seafood restaurant the day after he'd proposed to her. After Johnny ordered lobster bisque for them, he had excused himself to go the restaurant washroom.

He'd had to rush to the washroom to splash cold water on his face because he had felt drowsy from boredom while Amanda had been talking about the recent romance novel she'd read and loved.

On his way back from the washroom, Johnny thought he saw a couple of his friends across the restaurant, and he was about to sit back down at the table with Amanda, when he realized they were indeed his friends, so, he raised his hand to wave at them.

Unfortunately, the waiter just happened to be holding a tray in one hand as he leaned over their table to serve a bowl of lobster bisque to Amanda, and Johnny's quickly rising hand had accidentally poked the waiter's elbow, which caused the waiter's hand to jerk forward, and then almost the entire contents of the bowl splashed onto Amanda's chest.

Johnny, the waiter, and Amanda had gaped at the lobster bisque streaming down the front of her dress and onto her lap, then Johnny had grabbed his napkin and tried to step quickly around the waiter to help sop up the bisque on Amanda.

When Johnny leaned toward her to start sopping up the mess on Amanda, he bumped into the waiter's other elbow, causing the tray to tilt, then the other bowl slipped off the tray and landed on Amanda's chest, splattering more lobster bisque all over her as the bowl slid down onto her lap.

She was shrieking while both Johnny and the waiter were stammering apologies, and all the patrons in the restaurant were gaping at them.

The waiter spun around to rush back to the kitchen to get towels, then he bumped into Johnny who was standing close behind him, then the waiter stumbled back away from him, lost his balance, and then toppled over backward, and Amanda screamed when he fell over the table.

Johnny gaped while watching the table tilting toward Amanda as the waiter struggled to get up off it, then Amanda screamed again when the waiter slid sideways off the table, and onto her lap.

She wailed loudly when the waiter struggled to get off her lap, then her chair toppled over backward, sending both him and Amanda sprawling onto the floor.

The waiter kept slipping on the lobster bisque while trying to get up, and he'd just gotten up onto his hands and knees at the same time that Johnny had bent over to help Amanda to her feet.

Unfortunately, when Johnny grabbed her hand and started pulling her up off the floor, the waiter raised his head, consequently, his forehead collided with Amanda's forehead, and she was knocked unconscious.

The waiter groaned and held his forehead as he swayed to his feet, then a crowd gathered around Johnny, asking him if they should call an ambulance, as Johnny knelt to tug Amanda's skirt back down because it had wriggled up, exposing her panties.

He had tried to pull her up onto a chair, and he'd managed to get her into an almost standing position, when his foot had slipped on some of the spilled lobster bisque, and then as he was losing his balance, he had reached out to grab onto the shoulder of the person nearest to him in an effort to steady himself.

Unfortunately, the person he'd reached out to, had turned around to walk back to his own table, so, Johnny had lost his balance, then still holding Amanda in his arms, they'd both fallen to the floor, then she'd screamed in pain when one of his knees had accidently rammed down onto her left hand.

He had then reached up and gripped onto the edge of the table to struggle up onto his knees, however, his tight grip had pulled the tablecloth off the table, and then both the water and wine glasses, as well as the vase of flowers, and everything else that had been on the table had fallen onto Amanda.

He'd felt so embarrassed when he'd seen her lying on the floor, surrounded by broken glass and dishes, and with her dress soaked with wine, water, and lobster bisque.

Johnny had taken a napkin that another patron seated near their table had handed to him, then after dipping it in that patron's glass of water, he had started patting Amanda's cleavage and arms.

She started to regain consciousness while moaning and asking what had happened, then Amanda began trying to get up onto her hands and knees as she begged Johnny to take her home immediately because she felt quite embarrassed.

Unfortunately again, as she tried to stand, she lowered her right hand to the floor to support herself, and her hand pressed down hard on a broken wine glass.

Luckily, there was a nurse in the restaurant who rushed over to them and attended to the cut in the palm of Amanda's hand while advising them to go to a hospital immediately.

Johnny had felt terrible about that restaurant incident as he'd waited in the emergency room at the hospital while a proper bandage was applied to Amanda's right hand, and he had then kept apologizing to her all the way to her home, and while saying goodnight to her at her door.

Lobster bisque, wine, and water had matted down Amanda's hair, soaked her torn dress, and splattered over her most expensive shoes, which were now definitely ruined. Amanda, however, had forced a smile while leaning back away from the open door after kissing Johnny's cheek and telling him not to worry, then he'd advised her to go straight to bed as he closed the door to hurry back to the waiting cab.

Unfortunately again, another accident occurred when he'd pulled the door shut while Amanda still had her bandaged right hand touching the doorjamb.

She'd screamed from the pain when the door had slammed against her hand, then after a few moments, when she had stopped sobbing and had caught her breath, she'd said it was her fault for not taking her hand away from the door before it closed, and then she had thanked Johnny again for a lovely evening.

Other embarrassing accidents happened when they were together, such as spilling his full cup of coffee on her when he'd stood up quickly for some seemingly good reason at the time.

On a few other occasions, he'd suddenly stumbled over his chair while carrying a plate of food, which had accidentally fallen all over Amanda.

She had always smiled after being wiped almost clean with

napkins, and Amanda would assure him that she was having a delightful time, even though since the time he'd proposed to her, Johnny had accidentally stained most of her clothes with sauces, beverages and food.

Amanda even laughed off the accident that had happened just as they'd been about to go down a staircase at a theater. Johnny had turned to say goodbye to friends, and he'd accidentally bumped his hip into hers, causing Amanda to lose her balance and tumble down to the bottom of the stairs.

Johnny had felt so thankful that there had been thick carpeting on the stairs, and that Amanda hadn't been too badly hurt. He'd carried her to a cab while she had smiled through her tears and told him that she'd loved the theatre performance, although she had sprained her right ankle and left wrist.

He felt a sudden pang of embarrassment as he recalled arriving at Amanda's apartment early one evening to take her to the theatre. She hadn't been ready, so, he'd had to wait in her living room while she hurried to take a bath and get dressed for the theatre.

Amanda was taking her bath when she started screaming from intense pain caused by a kidney stone, so, Johnny rushed to assist her, and as he stood outside the bathroom door, Amanda had been in too much pain to coherently tell him what her problem was.

He'd felt certain that her life was in danger, so, he had opened the door, and seen her weakly trying to struggle out of the bathtub as she screamed and groaned in severe pain.

Johnny had then hurried to the tub, leaned over, and started pulling her up out of the tub while planning to pick her up in his arms, and then carry her out of the bathroom.

Unfortunately, as usual, when he'd lifted her halfway up out of the tub, the bath mat he'd been standing on had slipped backward, causing him to lose his balance and start falling forward.

Both he and Amanda had shouted in shock when he'd fallen into the tub, still holding her in his arms, then Johnny had started slipping and sliding in the tub while trying to get up off her while she was on her back, submerged in the bath water.

When he'd pulled her up to the surface, Amanda had gasped, spluttered, then started wailing and Johnny hadn't been sure if she'd been wailing from whatever was causing her so much pain, or from the shock of being accidently pushed underwater.

Sopping wet, Johnny had climbed back out of the tub, then knelt, and reached out to start pulling her back up out of the tub. He had felt relieved after managing to get her up and over his shoulder, then Johnny began struggling to stand back up.

Unfortunately, his wet shoes slipped on the even wetter, tiled floor, and he started falling over backwards while Amanda had been screaming.

When Johnny landed on his back, Amanda's forehead struck the tiled floor, knocking her unconscious, however, Johnny didn't know that until he'd sat up, turned his head to look at her and ask if the severe pain she was feeling had subsided because she wasn't groaning or weeping anymore.

Johnny had felt awful when he'd realized that Amanda had passed out from the pain, but he hadn't known that she'd struck her head on the floor when he'd fallen over with her in his arms.

He pulled her up into sitting position, then he knelt, hugged her, and then he began grunting while struggling to stand up with her in his arms so that he could carry her to her bedroom.

Amanda was regaining consciousness as Johnny began lifting her up off the floor, and she moaned and asked where she was. He was just about to tell her where she was, when her forehead hit the bottom of the sink, knocking her unconscious again.

Johnny swore when he realized that while he'd been lifting her up off the floor, he should've noticed that her head was too close to the sink.

He then carried her to what he had presumed was her bedroom, laid her on the bed, then he'd picked up the phone, and called for an ambulance while Amanda was starting to moan as she regained consciousness again.

She'd cried out when she had suddenly realized that she was nude, then she'd quickly placed her hands over her bare breasts, then over her pubic area while shouting at Johnny to leave the room. He'd been hurrying out of the room when he'd heard her scream in pain again, and then Amanda had fainted.

Johnny had rushed back to the bed, and then kept his eyes averted from her nudity while he'd placed a pillow over her breasts, then another pillow on her lap.

After phoning for an ambulance, he'd realized that Amanda would feel embarrassed about being seen nude by the ambulance attendants, so, Johnny had sorted through the closets, looking for something to put on her.

He hadn't been in her apartment before, so, it wasn't until he'd taken some dresses out of the closet and looked at them that he realized that he had carried her into her roommate's bedroom, and her roommate was much shorter than Amanda.

He had then rushed to her bedroom, snatched the first thing he'd reached for, and then rushed back to the other bedroom, holding a big, hip-length white cardigan.

He'd spread the sweater coat out beside her on the bed, then put her right arm into a sleeve, and it was then that Johnny had realized that he'd have to sit her up on the bed to get the sweater around her back, so that he could slide her left arm through the other sleeve.

He had started to pull her up into a sitting position when Amanda had begun to moan and open her eyes again, then she'd shrieked when she'd seen him leaning over so close to her, then she had quickly leaned sideways, and because she'd been sitting near the end of the bed, she had toppled off it, and then screamed and fainted after she'd landed on the floor.

Johnny hadn't realized that when she'd fallen off the bed, Amanda had tried to break her fall by holding out her right hand, but that had caused her to break two of her fingers, and the pain had made her scream and faint again.

He had lifted her back up onto the bed, then sat her up, and put her left arm into the sleeve of the cardigan, then hoping to save time when the ambulance arrived, he'd thrown her over his shoulder again, and carried her to the apartment door.

Johnny had carried her out of the apartment, but when he'd reached the elevator, he had found that it had been stopped at the floor above for some reason, so, after continually pressing the button for a few minutes, he'd carried Amanda down the hall to the staircase.

Johnny had held onto the banister with his left hand and started going down the stairs while hoping that Amanda wouldn't slip off his right shoulder before he reached the lobby, three floors below.

He'd walked down one flight of stairs when he'd heard yelling and the rumble of many footsteps behind him. Five boys ranging in age from ten to twelve years old were racing down the stairs, and they didn't have time to stop before they rounded the corner of the landing to continue on down the staircase.

The boys had bumped into him, knocking Johnny back against the wall, and Amanda had slipped off his shoulder and started tumbling down the staircase.

When her body slammed to a stop fifteen steps down on the next landing, the impact had dislocated her shoulder, and broken her left ankle and her right wrist.

Johnny hadn't known that she'd already broken two fingers on her right hand after falling off the bed, nor had he known of the damages Amanda had suffered in the fall down the stairs, until the doctor at the hospital told him.

The boys had helped him lift Amanda back up onto his right shoulder, and then they'd started laughing because the cardigan that Johnny had haphazardly put on her, had shifted up above her waist, then a couple of the boys had squeezed and slapped her exposed buttocks, and then they'd giggled before running down the next flight of stairs.

Johnny had been sweating when he'd reached the main floor, then he had staggered along the hall toward the lobby, carrying Amanda on his shoulder.

A maintenance man had shouted a warning to him, but it had been too late for Johnny to notice the freshly applied liquid wax on the hardwood floors near the lobby, so, he'd slipped and crashed to the floor, landing partly on Amanda.

When part of his body had slammed down on top of her, his weight had broken six of her ribs, however, Johnny hadn't known that until the ambulance had arrived at the hospital, and the doctor had told him the extent of Amanda's damages.

The obese maintenance man whom had poured the wax on the floor had rushed to help Johnny and Amanda, then he'd also slipped and fallen on top of her, breaking her nose and jaw, and fracturing her lower right leg, which Johnny hadn't known until he got her to the hospital and...Well, you know the rest.

By the time the ambulance screeched to a stop in front of the apartment building, many swellings and bruises had started to appear on most of Amanda's body, and as Johnny had sat beside her in the ambulance, holding her hand and watching her lumps rise, the ambulance attendants had asked him if she'd tried to commit suicide by jumping off her balcony.

He'd been rather worried about her when the doctors had told him that Amanda would have to remain in hospital for two weeks, and Johnny had assumed that there had been some sort of complications during surgery to remove the kidney stone.

He'd been having at least four accidents per day since the time he'd proposed to Amanda, and the same bad luck had started happening to her, as well, when they were together, so, because of this latest unfortunate mishap, she couldn't accompany him to her parents' home as they'd planned.

Johnny had kissed her goodbye as she laid in her hospital bed, then turning away from her, he'd bumped into a rather portly nurse, and then after quickly stepping back away from her, he'd lost his balance, and when he'd fallen backward onto Amanda, his left elbow had smashed into her broken nose, and the pain had caused her to scream and pass out.

He recalled how embarrassed he'd felt for being rather clumsy, and how he'd tried in vain to apologize to the shocked nurse who had been covered with what had looked like to him, the contents of a rather foul-smelling bowl of chili.

Johnny hadn't known that when he'd bumped into that nurse, he'd made her spill the bedpan that Amanda had just used for a loose bowel movement.

The finger of fate seemed to be continually poking him very hard in the stomach, and because he now felt quite nervous about meeting Amanda's parents, his face and clothes were becoming soaked with sweat as he began walking down the long road to the big, old farmhouse.

He glanced around at the fields and the hills in the distance while hoping that his streak of bad luck would end soon. He was nearing the large farmhouse that had three other buildings near it, which Johnny presumed were two barns and a garage, when he saw a woman whom he assumed to be Amanda's mother, waving a tea towel at him as she stepped down the porch steps.

When she began walking nearer to him, Johnny forced a nervous smile, then she called out to her husband, who then hurried out of the farmhouse to help him carry in his suitcases.

Amanda had told him that her parents spoke English, but Johnny had never asked her how well they spoke it, and then he felt greatly relieved at finding that they spoke English with hardly a trace of an accent.

"You sit right here, young man, and I'll get you a cold drink because you must be exhausted after carrying those things down the road in all this heat. Would you like a glass of lemonade or something stronger?" asked Amanda's mother.

"Lemonade's just fine, thanks," replied Johnny, smiling.

"I'll be right back. Now I want you to call me Edna, and my husband, Frank, but once you're married to our daughter, we wouldn't mind if you wanted to call us mother and father, or mom and dad, or mommy and daddy, or even mama and papa. Whatever you like is, well, I suppose almost okay with us, although I really don't think we'd like to be called maw and paw. Frank? Lemonade, dear?"

"No, thanks. I'll have a beer. I hate lemonade. It's an old lady's drink, or for sissies, or whatever."

"Fine then, dear, beer it is. Oh, take off your jacket, Johnny. Why, you're almost completely soaked with sweat, but in this heat and being *you*, well, what can you expect?" Edna said as she walked away.

He smiled as Amanda's father stared at him, then Johnny tried to think of something to say to him. But each time Johnny made an effort to start a conversation, Frank would either start glancing through a magazine or squint his eyes at something across the room while mumbling something incoherent.

Johnny then decided to wait until Edna returned with the cold drinks before trying to find a pleasant subject they could discuss.

Edna served them their cold drinks, then she and her husband immediately began talking to each other as Johnny sat in an armchair, smiling and nodding his head.

He wished that he knew what Frank and Edna were talking about as they looked at him, but not being able to speak or understand French, he could only guess by their expressions what they were saying about him.

Johnny began drinking his lemonade, smiling at them once in awhile as he looked around their living room, then he wondered if they were disappointed that he couldn't speak French and that was the reason they shook their heads and occasionally frowned as they continued talking and looking at him.

After five minutes, Edna and Frank stopped talking, stared at him for a minute, sighed, then Edna stood up and left the room.

"You plan on learning how to speak French now that you're going to be part of the family?" asked Frank.

"Yes, I'll try my best to learn, and I'm sure that Amanda'll help by speaking French to me until I get the hang of it. I can say please and thank you in French, and a couple of other words, though."

"That's it? Please and thank you? You've got a long way to go. We don't like speaking English that much, ever, but we're doing it for you because you're our guest, and we're trying to be polite. So, you're a city boy, huh?"

"Yes, but my parents had a cottage up near Markston Lake. I spent all my summer vacations there, and a few holiday weekends during the year, so, I suppose I'm not *all* city boy."

"I see. Sort of a wanna-be country boy. Guess there weren't any farms around that area, right?"

"No, it's mostly a resort area," replied Johnny.

"Mostly? What about the rest of the area? Or do you know?"

"Oh, I...Well, permanent residences, I suppose."

"You *suppose*?" asked Frank.

"I mean, yes, they were. And of course, there were small businesses, too. Oh, and there's a hospital far out of one of the towns near us. It's mostly for mental patients."

"Mostly? What about the rest of the patients in it?"

"Well, I suppose there are other patients who have a lingering illness because I was told there were many older people there."

"*How* old?"

"Oh, uh, hmmm, I suppose in their eighties or so. Well, that's only a guess, though," said Johnny.

"So, you don't really know how old, huh? Do you."

"No, I don't. Sorry, sir."

"Do you think *everyone* gets sick when they're old?"

"No, I don't suppose they do."

"Do you think *I'm* sick?" asked Frank while suddenly leaning forward in his armchair.

"Oh, uh, no. Are you? I mean, not that you look that old. Oh, and or sick, either. No, not at all."

"So, I don't look sick? How old do you think I am?"

"Well, I...I'd say...Um, I...Oh, late-sixties?" asked Johnny.

"I'm forty-eight."

"Oh? Oh, I see. Well, um, I never was any good at judging people's ages."

"That's rather obvious. Late-sixties. Hah! What a laugh!"

"Did you tell a joke, dear?" Edna asked Frank as she returned to the living room.

"No, *he* did. It was a city joke. You wouldn't get it."

"No? Oh, I understand, now. Men's jokes. So, Johnny, do you always sweat so much?" she asked him.

"Well, just today it seems, Mrs...Um, Edna. Sure is hot, huh?"

"Yeah, it has been for awhile, and we don't have air conditioning. You have a problem with that?" asked Frank.

"Oh, no, sir," replied Johnny. "It's cooler in here than outside."

Johnny began sweating more as they stared at him, and he smiled while wiping his forehead. Frank and Edna slowly shook their heads as they spoke to each other in French, then a few minutes later, they looked at him.

"It gets hotter in here at night. Sweltering hot. But we've got screens on all the windows to keep the mosquitoes out. Gotta keep 'em open when it's so hot at night," said Frank. "We've also got flush toilets like you have in the city, so, you don't have to worry or complain about being bit on the ass by using an outhouse."

"How nice. No mosquitoes and flush toilets. You live so well here in the country, but then I never thought you didn't just because you're far from a big town or city. So, uh, quite terrible news about Amanda, wasn't it?" Johnny remarked while wiping sweat off his face.

"Kidney stone, among other things. Accidents *they* said. Huh!

And to my sweet daughter," Edna said as she scowled.

"Yes, two weeks in the hospital. Complications," said Johnny.

"Lot of those in city hospitals these days. Too crowded. Too many patients and not enough doctors," said Frank. "She's there in that big hospital, lying in pain with all those real awful injuries. Bandaged from head to toe, and probably moaning and bawling her eyes out from the excruciating pain that not even heavy drugs can help. But no, you *still* decided to come here without her. How nice. Well, I guess after you made *your* plans, you felt that you just couldn't change 'em because you hate hospitals and I bet she told you to go on ahead without her. Right?"

"Yes, but I told her I didn't want to come here without her."

"Why? You think we didn't want to meet you?" asked Frank.

"No, not at all. Really. She, uh, she told me how nice you were. How hospitable, too. That you wanted to meet me before the wedding, so, she insisted that I come here."

"I hope you know you're a very lucky man because our Mandy's a nice, clean girl," said Edna, glaring at him.

"Of course she is. I never doubted that for a moment. Mmmm,

that sure was nice lemonade," said Johnny, feeling very nervous.

"Oh, so now you want *more*, do you?" asked Frank.

"No, I was just complimenting your wife on..."

"Call me Edna, remember? There isn't any more lemonade left, but Frank's having a beer, so, would you like one?"

"Oh, well, I..."

"Better give him one, hon," said Frank. "He's sweating like hell. Jeezuz!"

"Okay, I'll be right back. I guess I better bring you a towel, Johnny. So much sweat."

"Uh, thank you...Edna," said Johnny.

"We're having supper in an hour or so, so, I'll show you where you'll be sleeping. But don't worry, you can get your beer after. Hmmm, on second thought, I'll bring it up to you, and that way you can unpack," said Frank. "You'd better change out of those wet clothes and take a shower, and one of us'll call you when it's time to eat. Guess you need a rest from walking all the way up to the house in this heat, being a city boy and all, so, I'd advise you to wear a T-shirt and a...Do you sort of...Well, *guys* wear jeans?"

"Yes, sir, I brought a pair, knowing I was..."

"Wear those. It gets real hot in here as the sun's going down."

"Yeah, sure. Thanks for the advice," said Johnny.

"If you're not too weak to stand after your strenuous walk up to the house, then I'll show you where you'll be staying for the very short time you're with us."

"Oh, uh, sure, thanks. I'm really not tuckered out, though."

"Y'sure as hell look it, the way you're sweating. Guess you city...Well, *people* aren't used to walking more than a block, without taking your car. I'll walk up the stairs ahead of you, in case you pass out, then fall back on top of me," said Frank.

"You don't have to worry about that, because like I said, I'm not in the least worn out, or tired, or very weak from walking up the road to your home."

"Yeah, well, that's what *you* say, but I know your types, so, I want you behind me when we start going upstairs because if I was behind you on the stairs, and I tried to catch you when you pass out and fall backward, then we'll both go crashing down the stairs. Now take a deep breath, and follow me, okay?"

"Yes, sir, but like I...Um, never mind," said Johnny.

He followed Frank up the stairs while hoping that once Edna and Frank got to know him a bit better, they might overlook what they obviously deemed to be his shortcomings.

"This is your room. Good enough for you?"

"Oh, it's great, thanks," said Johnny. "I'll just unpack and..."

"I'll bring your beer up in a minute."

"That's very kind of you. Thanks."

"Yeah, sure. See you," said Frank as he walked away.

Johnny dropped his suitcases on the floor, then he plopped down on the bed and began wondering how much worse it was going to get during his two-week visit with his future in-laws.

He'd felt rather uncomfortable because he'd been perspiring heavily from the heat, from Frank's questions, and from Edith telling him that she was worried that he might damage her favorite armchair by getting it damp with his sweat.

Compounding all the other factors that had made him perspire heavily, the other reason he'd felt very nervous, was that for the entire time he'd been talking, or rather, answering pointed questions from Amanda's parents, their farmhand, dressed in oversized overalls, floppy, knee-high boots, and wearing a beekeeper's hood, had stared at him from the kitchen doorway.

Johnny had felt certain that the farmhand had been staring at him because the front of the beekeeper's hood had been facing in his direction.

So far, it seemed that neither the farmhand nor Amanda's parents approved of her choice of a husband, then Johnny winced and tensed up a bit when Frank came back upstairs, handed him a beer, shook his head slowly as he looked at Johnny's sweat-soaked shirt, then he walked away without speaking.

Johnny had brought three bottles of liquor with him to give to Amanda's parents, however, after meeting them, he decided to keep two of the bottles in his room and drink them himself.

He sorted through one of his suitcases, picked up his bag of marijuana, kissed it, then put it back in his suitcase. He hung his clothes on a hook near the window, put his light cotton robe on, and went looking for the bathroom to have a shower.

Johnny was elated when he saw two cans of air freshener in the bathroom, so, now he could take one to his room, roll a joint, sit by the open window, and spray the air occasionally to disguise the odor of marijuana.

If ever he needed a couple of big, strong drinks and a joint in his life, it was now, so that he could get through dinner buzzed and smiling if or whenever Frank or Edith spoke to him.

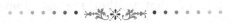

He felt quite refreshed after his shower and he'd made sure that the water wasn't cool so that when he finished his shower, he could appreciate the slightly cooler air in the house and stop all his sweating, which had been caused by the high heat and Frank's chat with him.

Edna called upstairs to tell him that dinner was ready, and Johnny smiled from the buzz that the two stiff drinks and the thick joint had given him.

He felt higher than he'd planned to get, and he knew that he'd have a difficult time concentrating on their conversation, as well as probably suppressing the occasional giggle during dinner.

Johnny walked into the dining room and smiled at Frank and Edna, then he almost burst out laughing when he saw their very odd-looking farmhand, then noticing Edna and Frank glaring at him, Johnny tried very hard to suppress the urge to burst out laughing as he sat down at the table.

For some inexplicable reason that Johnny wasn't about to question, the farmhand had put on a Groucho Marx mask, and the large nose and big, bushy mustache on the mask was making it quite difficult for Johnny not to start giggling.

The farmhand stood watching them from the kitchen entrance, and besides the funny mask, he was wearing a large, crumpled, dark gray fedora, a baggy, long-sleeved, plaid shirt that was obviously three sizes too big for him, and quite big, very dark sunglasses, then Johnny quickly pretended that he was coughing to disguise a guffaw.

"Oh, I forgot to tell you. That's Wham," Frank told him as he nodded at the farmhand.

"Nice to meet you, Wham," Johnny said, trying not to laugh.

"Wham! Are you going to sit down and eat with us, or not?

Wham? I bet you've been smoking that wacky-tabacky again. Wham? Well, say something!" exclaimed Frank. "You look like hell in that get-up, but I suppose you think you're being funny! Well, I don't think it's funny, at all! You're not being polite by staring at Mandy's future husband. Wham? Okay then, be that way, damn it. Go ahead and pass Johnny the potatoes, Edna, and to hell with Wham. You like mashed potatoes, Johnny?"

"Oh, yes, I love them, thanks, uh, Frank," he replied.

"Hmmm, pass him the ham, Edna. You like ham, Johnny?"

"Yes, I do, sir. Thank you."

"Pass him the broccoli, Edna. You like broccoli, Johnny?"

"I love it, thank you," he said while suppressing a giggle.

"The peas and carrots come from our garden. Pass him the veggies, Edna. You get fresh veggies in the city?"

"Yes, we do, sir. Not fresh picked, though."

"Uh-huh. Didn't think so. Pass him the sauce, Edna. She made it herself for the ham. Go on. Put some on your ham. Yeah, that's it. Now taste it. You like that?"

"Mmmmm," replied Johnny, hoping he wouldn't start laughing.

"You must really like your food because you're smiling a lot more than when you first got here, soaked in sweat, and dripping all over my nice, upholstered armchair that I...Well, I *used* to love so much, but now it's...Oh, well," said Edna, frowning as she heaved a big sigh.

"Mmmmm," Johnny murmured while stifling a giggle.

"Does Wham staring at you make you uneasy?" asked Edna.

"Oh, not at all," Johnny said, coughing to disguise his giggles.

"Well, it upsets *me*," said Edna, pouting. "Wham, take off those awful sunglasses and that silly mask. Wham? I have no idea what you're up to. Aren't you hungry? Wham? Oh, well, just stand over there, then, and don't say anything. Be like that. See if I care. You could've dressed up for Mandy's Johnny. Sometimes I just don't understand you. You can be so...Well, *odd* at times. What's wrong with the veggies, Johnny? Do you want more butter on them?"

"No thanks, they're just fine," he replied. "I like them over...I mean nice and soft. Very, very soft. Easy to swallow because you don't have to chew them. And from your own garden, too. Quite tasty. And they're not too soggy. Just...Uh, perfect."

"Edna's a wonderful cook," Frank told him.

Johnny realized that if he sat at the table any longer, he'd start laughing from the effects of the marijuana and the vegetables that were complete mush, so, he had to get back upstairs and have a nap, which he hoped would lessen the effects of the marijuana high he was on.

"I didn't realize I was so tired. I can hardly keep my eyes open, but I guess that's because of the long trip here, and the heat, too. This dinner is, uh, so good. Very delicious, but I hope you'll excuse me because I have to have a nap. I'm sorry," said Johnny.

"Fine by us. I'll wake you in a couple of hours, then I'll drive you into town, okay? Friday night, so, you'll want to have a good time. Lippert's bar and tavern has live music, and you can get to meet a few of our Mandy's friends. They've been asking about you, so, I told 'em I'd bring you in. But Edna and I won't be going because there's a good show on TV. One of our favorites. That bother you? Are you a bit of a snob, being a city boy, and all? You *want* to meet Mandy's friends, don't you?" Frank asked him.

"Oh, of course, I do. Uh-huh. You bet. Sure."

"And you don't have to dress up, either, to go to Lippert's tavern. Well? Go have your nap," Frank told him.

"Thank you," said Johnny. "Wonderful meal, Edna."

"You barely touched it. Well, thanks, anyway," she said.

He stood up too quickly and knocked over his chair, then feeling rather high, he almost lost his balance while leaning over to pick it up. Johnny apologized as he quickly shoved the chair back to the table, which had thin, flimsy legs on it, so, when the chair hit the table too hard, it caused the glasses of milk to topple over and splash on both Edna and Frank's dinner plates.

He grabbed his napkin, and when he reached across the table to mop up the milk around Frank's plate, his knuckles hit the plate and it slid off the table onto Frank's lap.

Johnny began rushing around the table to help clean up the food on Frank, however, his thigh hit the edge of the table, and dragged much of the tablecloth away, causing the bowl of Edna's sauce, the plate of food Johnny had been nibbling at, his glass of water, and several other things to crash onto the floor.

When Edna stood up to grab the tablecloth to stop it from

slipping further, her dish that was teetering on a gathered part of the tablecloth, fell to the floor and smashed.

Johnny's thoughts were whirling as he dashed forward to wipe splattered food off Frank's lap, and seeing Johnny coming at him, Frank turned to face him, and held up his hands to tell Johnny not to worry about what had happened.

Before Frank could say anything, Johnny stepped down hard on Frank's foot, causing him to cry out in pain. Edna shrieked, and when Johnny spun around to look at her, and find out what had made her cry out in alarm, his tightly closed hand that was holding his napkin swept up and smashed into Frank's jaw, knocking him backward off his chair, and he fell onto the floor.

He took a few quick steps toward Frank to help him up, but he stumbled over the toppled chair and fell over Frank, who began yelling and pounding on Johnny's chest as he struggled to get out from under him.

Edna hurried around the table to Frank and Johnny who were struggling on the floor, and she slipped on some mashed potatoes, fell over sideways, and land on top of the squirming men.

Johnny tried to get up onto his knees, and when he reached out for support, he accidentally clutched one of Edna's breasts, then she slapped his face.

Frank was swearing as he struggled to get out from under Johnny's body, so, Johnny tried to roll sideways to get off him. But his body hit one of the thin table legs, and the vase of flowers that had been dragged close to the edge, along with the tablecloth, toppled off the table, and landed on the top of Edna's head.

The pain of being struck on the head by the heavy vase made Edna burst into tears and screams as Frank laid on his back, pounding and kicking at him while he yelled at Johnny to get the hell off him.

Edna's hair and blouse were soaked with water from the vase, and she wept as all three of them struggled to get up on their hands and knees.

She screamed and cowered back from him when Johnny reached out to help her up, and then Frank shouted at him to leave his wife alone.

Johnny grabbed onto the edge of the table as he stood back up, then he turned around and looked down at Amanda's parents kneeling on the floor, splattered with food and sauce, and surrounded by broken glasses and dishes as they stared up at him in shock, anger, and fright.

"Oops! Uh...So, um, sorry about that. I...I think I'll go upstairs and, um, have that nap. Can I help with anything?" asked Johnny.

"Oh, God, no! Please don't!" cried Edna as she hugged Frank.

"I think you'd better just go upstairs. Please. Now. Just go away. Leave the dining room. Please," Frank told him.

"Sure, okay. As I said, I'm terribly sorry about the accident."

"Please," said Frank, glaring at him as he patted Edna's back.

"Well, if you're sure, um, well, okay, bye," said Johnny.

He backed away from Edna and Frank, stepped over the mess on the floor, then Johnny turned around and walked quickly out of the dining room.

"He's gone, hon, so, don't worry. You're going to be okay now. Shhhhh, stop crying. He won't be comin back because I hear him going upstairs. City boys. So strange," said Frank, scowling.

Johnny stumbled upstairs to his room, pulled off his food and sauce-stained clothes, put on his robe, and went down the hall to the bathroom.

He stepped into the tub and sighed as he turned on the shower, then after he'd closed his eyes and thought about the awful impression he'd made on Amanda's parents, he started giggling.

The water gushing down over his head made him feel much better, so, he lingered under the shower. Johnny pointed the nozzle away from his head, then closed his eyes, leaned back against the tiled wall, and began thinking about Amanda and wondering if most of her injuries had been caused when she'd fallen off the hospital's operating room table.

He decided to have the matter thoroughly investigated so that those types of accidents in hospital operating rooms could be avoided in the future.

He sighed as he pointed the shower nozzle back toward his head, then after a few minutes of letting the water rush over his head, Johnny turned off the water, and opened his eyes.

He reached for the towel, and it was then that he realized he hadn't closed the shower curtain. The floor was soaked with water, and as Johnny began mopping it up with all the towels he could find, Frank was pounding on the closed bathroom door and angrily shouting: "What in the hell happened? Jeezuz! There's water everywhere in the living room!"

"Oh, hi, Frank! I forgot to close the shower curtain, and I forgot I had the nozzle turned toward the outside of the tub! Sorry about that! I didn't know I got some water on the floor!"

"The water's ruined every God damned photo in Edna's album! It's totally soaked my armchair! I won't be able to sit in it for weeks because the material's like a God damned soaking sponge! God damned water everywhere! God damn it all to hell!"

"Oh, sorry! I won't do it again!" Johnny hollered.

"I guess not! You used up all the God damned hot water, now! Edna and I wanted to get off all this God damned muck you spilled all over us! God damn it!"

"Oh! Oh, no! Sorry about that, too, Frank! Really!"

"Aw, fuck ya! God damned city slickers are all alike!"

He wasn't able to hear the rest of the shouting because Frank had walked away from the bathroom door, so, Johnny continued sopping up water, and wringing out the towels in the bathtub.

After his nap, Johnny sat up on the bed and recalled what had happened at the dinner table, and then feeling rather embarrassed, he rolled another joint.

He sat beside the open window, blowing smoke outside while he wondered what Amanda's friends would be like when he met them at the tavern.

Frank hollered at him through the door, asking him if he was ready to go to town yet, and then Johnny yelled back that he'd be right down.

. . . . . . ⚜ . . . . . .

They didn't speak all the way to town as Frank sped along the two-lane highway, terrifying Johnny every time the truck dodged side to side as Frank tried to pass cars, and they almost collided head-on at times with two eighteen-wheelers and six cars.

The screeching of the wheels on Frank's truck as they came to an abrupt stop in front of the tavern was still ringing in Johnny's ears as he watched Frank hightail it back to the farmhouse. Johnny presumed that the reason Frank was in such a hurry to get back home to Edna was because their favorite television show must be starting at any minute.

He thought that although Frank seemed a little curt at times, he had shown how generous and kind he could be by driving him into town to meet a few of Amanda's close friends.

Johnny hadn't had time to explain to Frank that although he'd lived in the city for quite some time, he had bought a five-hundred-acre estate that had once had a few farms on it, therefore, he felt that made him a sort of farmer like Frank.

He hadn't told Amanda about the land purchase because he wanted it to be a surprise wedding gift for her, and to ensure that she'd love it, Johnny had spent almost two hundred thousand dollars for renovations on just the main house.

He had planned to buy and read books on how to grow his own vegetables, but he'd cheated a bit by hiring a butler whom was an avid gardener, therefore, most of the vegetable gardens would be started by the butler.

When Frank had asked him if he was a snob, Johnny had told

him he wasn't, however, he hadn't explained why he didn't feel he was a snob, which was because he'd always liked to socialize with every class of people, regardless of his wealth that not many people were aware of, including Amanda.

Johnny had never flaunted his money, and that's why he'd preferred to live in a modest, two-bedroom apartment. He realized that his great wealth would become noticeable to most people when he and Amanda married and moved into the enormous home that he'd had renovated on his new estate.

He'd become good friends with the children of his parents' former household staff, and they'd introduced him to Loreen, whom had once worked as a maid for Johnny's grandparents.

Loreen had mistakenly thought that because of the way he dressed, and because he was a friend of the staff, that Johnny also worked in some capacity as a household servant.

She had then quickly dumped him to marry a count in Europe whom she'd met on a vacation with a girlfriend. Johnny hadn't realized that Loreen was more interested in a man's wallet than the man himself, therefore, he often wondered if she'd left him because he'd been grieving too long over the death of his father whom had died fifteen years after Johnny's mother.

Now he felt so alone without parents, and because he was an only child, Johnny hoped that he and Amanda would have several children, as well as the kind of loving relationship that her friends had told him they'd had since the time they had married.

He heaved a sigh, then began walking toward Lippert's tavern and bar, and when he opened the door, he was met with the sound of loud music and laughter, so, Johnny smiled and looked around the crowded room while looking for an empty table.

Moments after he found an empty table, a waiter hurried to him, carrying a tray laden with big glasses of beer, so, Johnny bought two glasses.

He began drinking beer while looking at the two, fat, short men and a woman whom was heavier than both of her fellow musicians as the three of them played accordions while singing a cowboy song that included much yodeling.

Johnny felt glad that he hadn't overdressed for the occasion because almost everyone in the tavern had on plaid shirts with either denim overalls or jeans.

He blushed and smiled when he noticed all the women looking at him, so, he raised his glass and grinned at them, but that caused the men they were seated with to glower at him.

He felt a bit nostalgic when he recalled how his friends had often told him that he had the two best Ls, which were: "Looks and Loreen," but now Loreen was gone, and Johnny wished that that the L for Loreen had been replaced with an L for "Luck" because since the time he'd proposed to Amanda he'd been having so many accidents.

The accordion music and yodeling stopped after almost an hour, and by that time, Johnny had drank three beers, so, he was feeling comfortable and happy.

He went up to the bar and introduced himself to the bartender as Amanda's fiancé, and then the bartender told him that most of her friends had gone camping for a few days.

Johnny felt slightly disappointed as he sat back down at his table, then he gawked at the side door when he saw a startlingly beautiful young woman enter the tavern, then everyone laughed and cheered her as she walked over to the bar and bought a cocktail, and then she turned around, looked at Johnny, and smiled.

He was surprised to see such a well-dressed woman in the tavern because everyone else was dressed casually, and he stared at her marvelous figure that was admirably displayed by her clinging, hyacinth blue dress.

Her dark blonde hair was cut fairly short, but the style of it suited her very well, and her only jewellery consisted of a very thin gold necklace and a narrow gold bracelet, and Johnny thought she looked like one of his favorite movie stars.

He had never given much credence to the belief some people held that people could fall in love at first sight, but now, looking at her, he was having feelings quite similar to overwhelming affection as he looked at her, and he also felt as if this was the woman he'd been looking for all of his life.

He realized that the marijuana and beer had most likely enhanced his feelings, however, he was enjoying the delightful sensations as he stole glances at her.

She suddenly began laughing heartily, then after regaining her composure, she continued to smile at Johnny. Two men seated at the table next to him, noticed that Johnny was gaping at her, so, one of them leaned toward him and said: "She's really, really beautiful, huh?"

"She sure is," replied Johnny. "Amazingly beautiful."

"She's not just that, though. She's got the three Bs."

"Oh? What are they?" asked Johnny, still staring at her.

"Beauty, Brains and Bread. She's a doctor, and she's back here on holiday for a few weeks."

"Then she's been here before," said Johnny.

"She grew up here, and we love her because she's got a great sense of humor, and she's one of the best people y'could ever meet. Yep, she's got it all."

"Oh? Uh, what's her..." Johnny was about to ask.

Before he could finish asking what her name was, the men at the table beside him got up and went over to her. She hugged them, laughed, and kissed the older men on their cheeks.

While the men listened to what she was telling them, they

looked at Johnny, and then the two men suddenly burst into laughter. They put their caps on and walked by him on their way out of the tavern, then they stopped at the door to look over at Johnny and laugh again before they walked out of the tavern.

Johnny turned his head to look back at the beautiful young woman at the bar, and he gasped and almost dropped his glass of beer when he saw that she was now sitting across the table from him, and smiling.

"Hi."

"Uh, hello," said Johnny.

"As you can see, word spreads fast around here because within two hours, almost everyone heard about your accidents at dinner."

"Oh, hell, that was so embarrassing. Food and I spell disaster. I forgot that news travels fast in small towns, so, I guess my hosts were on the phone right after I was dropped off here in town."

"So, you're marrying Mandy, huh?"

"Yeah, I am. She's a nice girl."

"*Nice*? How overwhelming. Hmmm, all right then, I'd describe her as nice, too, because I like her. Well, *love* her, actually."

"Uh-huh, I see. She's in hospital, but I suppose you know that."

"I do," she replied.

"Um, about the accident...Or *accidents* I had at dinner, well, I don't mean to imply that Amanda's the cause of them, but it seems like ever since we decided to get married, I've had the worse run of bad luck. One accident after another."

"Oh, I'm sorry to hear that. When I heard you were marrying Mandy, I was rather surprised, but I'm really quite happy for her, and I'm sure she'll make a wonderful wife."

"I sure hope so. You see, we have very little in common, but I've started to become friends with her, and I'm sure that after we're married, I'll get to know her better, then I'll like her more. You know, after I find out what she likes and that sort of thing."

"Oh? She hasn't told you much about herself?"

"Not very much, at all. The only thing she's wanted to talk about since we met was us getting married and how happy we'd be after that. That's what her male friends told me, too. They're French, and married to French girls, and they said they didn't really love their girlfriends until after they married them. They assured me that after Amanda and I got married, I'd start feeling love for her, and as I said, she's nice, so, after we're married for awhile, then I probably might start loving her, and she'll start really loving me. Right now, the only thing she's interested in, as I said, is getting married."

"Hmmm, I see. How interesting. So, they told you that you'd love each other after you were married, huh?"

"Yes, and that she'd...Well, become more amorous. I mean, I know she likes me, but I expect that she'll love me after we're married, just like I'll hopefully love her, which I probably will because as I said, I like her, even though we're not that close."

"Uh-huh. Well, I suppose there *is* the possibility that you two could fall in love after you're married. Especially if, as you say, Mandy really wants to be married, but I'm old fashioned. I want to be madly in love with a guy before I marry him."

"Well, you certainly won't have any problem having many guys fall in love with *you* because you're very beautiful, and I was told by the two gentlemen you just talked with that you're very nice, too, and they also said you're quite intelligent."

"Thank you, and thank *them*. That's very, as you put it, *nice* to hear, and I just know that Mandy must be so pleased to be marrying such a handsome man. And a very *nice* man, as well."

"Um, should I call you, 'Doctor?'" Johnny asked her.

"Uh-uh, too formal. How about calling me, Wilhelmina? Because I haven't been called that around here for years. My name's a bit odd, but I'm sure *you* can pronounce it very well."

"Yes, I can. I'm Johnny."

"Oh, we all know that, Johnny. Accidents, remember?"

"Oh, man! And so many of them. Yeah, I suppose I've made quite an impression around here."

"You've impressed me, immensely, but then, you're getting married, so, I won't try to pick you up. How's that? Okay?"

"Oh? Oh, I see. Well, um, may I buy you a drink?"

"Uh-uh, no thanks. I have to go, but I'll be seeing you again."

"You're coming back?" he excitedly asked her.

"No, I meant tomorrow. We'll do brunch. Bye now."

"You're leaving? Wait! ...Damn! She's gone. Whew! She's so incredibly beautiful!"

Johnny gawked at her as she laughed and chatted briefly with many of the patrons before she left by the side door, and he suddenly realized that his heart was beating rapidly.

He'd never had a woman effect him as strongly as she had, then he began thinking about Amanda, and wishing that he felt more than casual like for her, and then he had a sudden feeling of panic when he thought about marrying her.

Now that he'd met Wilhelmina, Johnny realized he was making a terrible mistake by marrying a woman he wasn't sexually attracted to. He'd told Amanda that he *would* marry her, and he *had* met her parents because of their wedding plans, so, Johnny groaned while realizing it was too late to back out now.

He was about to get up from his table to ask the bartender if he knew Wilhelmina's phone number, when Frank walked into the tavern, and told him it was just after eleven o'clock, so, he was ready to drive him back to the farmhouse.

* * * * * * * ✄⚜✄ * * * * * *

He felt very relieved that Frank never spoke to him all the way back to the farmhouse, because Johnny was thinking about

Wilhelmina, and whenever he thought about marrying Amanda, he felt trapped and scared.

He knew that her parents weren't too pleased with him because he was a little accident-prone, as well as unable to speak French, and Frank and Edna had looked slightly disappointed when they'd called him a city boy, so, he'd be marrying a woman he didn't love, then have in-laws who didn't like him.

When Frank and Johnny entered the house, Edna hurried away to the kitchen, so, Johnny went straight upstairs to his room. An hour later, he felt hungry because he had eaten very little at dinner, and he thought that if he was very careful, he could go downstairs to the kitchen and make a sandwich, without having an accident.

He'd felt terrible when he had seen the big upholstered armchair with a puddle under it, sitting on the porch before he and Frank had come into the house.

He winced as he then remembered that he'd ruined all the family photographs when the water from the shower had leaked through the bathroom floor, and now Johnny hoped that he could make it to the kitchen without having another accident.

Frank and Edna looked rather wary of him as he passed them on his way to the kitchen, then they cowered away from him when Johnny returned to ask if it was all right to make a sandwich.

Frank told him to help himself to anything he wanted as long as he ate it upstairs in his bedroom. Johnny thanked them and walked back to the kitchen, and then after he picked up all the scattered slices of bread off the floor that had accidentally slipped out of the bag he'd been holding, he started looking inside the fridge.

He saw the partially cut, large ham sitting on a platter, so, he lifted it out of the fridge, then after turning around to carry it to the table, he bumped into Frank, whom Johnny hadn't noticed come into the kitchen.

The platter was knocked out of his hand, and then it smashed to pieces on the floor, and the ham skidded across the kitchen floor, through the slightly open door to the basement, and it tumbled down the steps.

"Oops!" exclaimed Johnny.

"Jeezuzz! I came in here to *stop* an accident, and *now* look!"

"But I didn't see you! How was I to know you were standing

right behind me? Or beside me? Or wherever you were!"

"You fuc...No, I better not let you know what I really think of you. Sit at the table. Please. Don't move, okay? Now I'm going to make you a peanut butter sandwich. Got that?"

"Oh, okay, thanks. I was going to ask you or Edna if you had another loaf of bread because I..." Johnny started to say.

"You don't like white bread? Tough, because it's all we have."

"Oh, uh, well, that's fine with me. Why I was asking is that I dropped a loaf on the floor, and the slices got dirty. I'd accidentally stepped on quite a few of the slices before I realized I was holding the bag upside-down. I'm so sorry about that. Really."

Frank's face turned red as he glared at him, but he felt determined not to lose his temper, and just find something for him to eat, then Johnny would be gone.

Frank sucked in his breath through his clenched teeth while forcing a smile, then he began to speak very slowly to Johnny.

"You dropped the bread. Just like that. And on the floor, yet. Uh-huh, *all* over the floor. Oh, and you stepped *all* over the bread, too. And that was the only loaf of bread we had in the house. Uh-huh, sure. Yes, and now, I can't...*Won't* have any God damn toast for breakfast! None! Get that, you stupid...Johnny? Unless I get into my truck, then drive *all* the way into town. Uh-huh, and now that *you're* here, I'll have to buy four...No, *five*...No, maybe *six* loaves of bread. Maybe *more* because you might drop *all* those *all* over the floor, and then step all over *them*, too. Right? Now, because there's no bread, thanks to you, I can't make you a sandwich. Now I'm *really* brokenhearted about you not getting a sandwich. Uh-huh. No sandwich. Nope. Not for *you*. But if I don't find something to stuff into your...Your *mouth*, you might come downstairs sometime during the night, then...No, I can't let that happen. No, uh-uh. I have to control myself. I won't get any madder. I'm okay. I can do this. Uh-huh. You keep sitting in that God damned...In that chair and...Please trust me...Yes...I'll find something. Oh, God, there must be *something. Anything* to stop you from...No, I won't say it. I'll just stay calm and hope I can find something for you to eat," said Frank, clenching his teeth.

"I hope I haven't upset you. Have I? After all, it *was* an accident. *Our* accident, actually."

"Yeah, sure, it was just another accident, Johnny. Another one, just like all the others. And that platter...That platter you, you son of a...That platter had been handed down through Edna's family for...Get this, you fu...For many, *many* generations. Uh-huh, yep. Edna's prize platter, but you, you piece of...No, it's too late. It's broken now, but that's okay. Yes. Oh, I know! I'll hide the pieces. The *smashed* pieces. I have to because I don't think Edna or I can handle too much more excitement today. No, no, I know *I* definitely can't. Uh-uh. Whew! Now, what to...To cram down your...Careful. Yes, I have to be careful. I'm okay. What to serve you. Something to stop you. A gun. No, not that. Hmmm, yes, something to stop all your...Your *hunger*. Hunger. Hung-grrrr. Calm. I've got to stay calm. Very calm. Uh-huh. I know I can do that. I can," he mumbled.

"Oh, anything'll do, Frank, so don't go to any bother. Pity about the ham, though, because I was looking forward to a nice ham sandwich."

"So was I. Uh-huh. A nice ham sandwich. But that's not possible. Nope. Because now the fuc...The ham's lying in the kitty litter box at the bottom of the basement stairs. You see, Edna called me upstairs before I could empty it, so, I left it there. Yes, I did. I mean, it seemed safe there for awhile. So very safe, so, what were the odds of something awful happening? The ham seemed safe in the fridge, too, but it wasn't. Not from you. No. Uh-uh. Oh, we all seemed so safe here in the house. Uh-huh, we did, but then suddenly, there was you, and now, there's no bread. None at all. No platter. Nope. No ham. All gone. Gone away."

"I beg your pardon? I didn't quite hear what you'd been saying because you had your back turned to me," said Johnny, smiling.

"No, no, you didn't hear me. Did *I*? What did you say?"

"I said, I didn't hear what you just said, Frank. Here, I'll come over there and..."

"No! Don't move! Sit! Oh, God, please sit. Yeah, that's it. Now stay there. Don't move an inch."

"I hope I'm not imposing on your TV time."

"You rot...Hmmm, no. Uh-uh. I wouldn't have it any other way. Now let me see what we have here in the fridge. Oh, no, the peanut butter jar is empty. Who would put that back in the fridge if it was empty? Who? I mean, it's empty. Now *it*'s gone, too. I'm not mad. No, I'm not. Hmmm, olives, and hmmm, oh, and some mixed pickles. Orange Jello. Half a grapefruit. Lettuce. Uh-huh. Yes! That's it!"

"You found something?" asked Johnny.

"Yes, thank God. I'll make you a lettuce and pickle sandwich with mayonnaise."

"Uh, Frank? There's no bread. Remember?"

"No bread? No bread! You...Edna!" yelled Frank, rushing out of the kitchen.

Johnny had frowned while watching Frank running out of the kitchen, and he presumed that Frank had to use the bathroom, and that on his way back, he was going to ask Edna to make him something to eat.

He felt relieved that Frank hadn't been too upset about the ham accident, and that Edna was now feeling better about the dinner accident, and while thinking about that, Johnny saw Edna's head poking around the side of the kitchen entrance.

"Oh, hi, Edna! We had a slight accident. Awfully sorry."

"Please. Please, stay there. I'll get Wham. Wham can make anything. Frank needs Wham to talk to him. Wham will calm him down. Just stay in the chair 'til Wham gets here. Please? Just keep sitting right there in that chair. Oh, please," she pleaded.

"Oh, of course, and I hope you don't have to get Wham out of bed. I mean, I can always...Edna? Oh, well, I guess she's gone to get Wham. Hmmm."

He smiled as he waited for Wham to prepare a snack for him, although he felt a little embarrassed about imposing on his hosts and their farmhand so late at night.

Johnny looked around the kitchen, then he got up from the chair and began picking up pieces of the broken platter. Frank had told him that the platter had been one of Edna's favorites, so, Johnny had to find a place to hide the broken pieces before she saw them, and he sensed that Edna would dislike him even more if she found out that he'd accidently broken her favorite platter.

He hurried to the basement door, looked for a light switch, and when he couldn't find one, he stepped carefully down the dark staircase, holding his arms out in front of him so that he wouldn't bump into anything.

Then oops! He stepped off the last step and onto the roast of ham in the kitty litter box. The ham wobbled, causing Johnny to lose his balance, and start falling forward, then after he slammed down onto the basement floor, he laid sprawled out on his stomach, and moaning.

He heard screeching and howling and he hoped that he hadn't stepped on the cat instead of the ham. Crawling around on the floor on his hands and knees, he felt the bottom of the staircase, then he blew out a sigh of relief when he found it wasn't closed-in, so, he tossed the platter pieces under the stairs. He intended to pick up all the broken pieces of the platter sometime during his visit, and try gluing the platter back together.

Johnny could see a bit of light from the kitchen coming through the slightly open door to the basement, and he started to limp back up the stairs while hoping that he'd only sprained his ankle, and not broken it.

He stepped back into the kitchen, then wiped sweat off his

forehead while hoping he wouldn't have another accident during the rest of his visit with Frank and Edna.

He looked down at his soiled clothes, and began trying to brush off damp kitty litter that had spilled out of the box when he'd fallen onto the basement floor, then he sighed and sat back down on the chair to wait for Wham.

Johnny scrunched up his nose from the smell of used kitty litter on his clothing, and he wondered if the stains from the used kitty litter and whatever Edna had coated the ham with, would come out of his clothes when they were washed.

After noticing a few scratches on the palms of his hands, he dared to rush over to the kitchen sink to wash them, and he winced as the water ran over the scratches, then he hurried back to the chair, sat down, and smiled.

He heard Edna and Frank talking loudly in French, so, Johnny assumed that they were talking about both the ham accident in the kitchen and about preparing something to eat for him, or perhaps explaining to to their farmhand how Frank had caused Johnny to drop the platter of ham onto the floor.

He then wondered if Edna and Frank would come into the kitchen and chat with him while they had a coffee and he ate whatever the farmhand prepared for him.

Because they still hadn't joined him in the kitchen, Johnny realized that Frank and Edna had decided to remain in the living room until he was served him something to eat, then they'd all sit with him in the kitchen.

Johnny toyed with the idea of putting the kettle on, then he decided he'd better not do that, then a moment later, Wham walked into the kitchen, and Johnny gaped, and then wham! His thoughts began whirling wildly.

"Again? You certainly won't be forgotten when you leave here, Johnnycakes. Hmmm, considering all that's happened, I think you and everyone else in the house will feel so much safer if you checked into the hotel in town, immediately. What do you think? Good idea or what?" Wham asked him.

"Uh...Uh...It's you! Frank...He...I, um...Oh, it's...He...I...Oh!"

"That's not quite right. It's 'E–I–E–I–O,' then 'Old McDonald had a farm, E–I–...' Come on. Sing the chorus...'E–I–E–I–O!'"

"I...Oh, my...It's you...I...It's...I...Oh!" exclaimed Johnny.

"Aw, forget it, if you can't remember the lyrics. Now what to feed you? Hmmm, I'll throw a salad together, okay? Tuna or salmon? Let's see what's in the fridge. Hmmm, ah, good. I'll boil a few eggs, cool them in ice water, then throw them in the salad. Well, maybe after I make the salad, the warm slices of egg on top might be nicer. Oh, good, there's plenty of salad dressing in this cupboard. Thank God the jar of dressing wasn't open and in the fridge because if it had been, there's no telling what you would've done with *that*. Hmmm, now what else can I make for you?"

"Wham? Oh, my God! Wham?"

"Shhhh, I'm thinking. Hmmm, oh, yes, there's celery in the small fridge outside that door beside you. And some radishes, tomatoes, cucumbers. But don't you move out of that chair. I'll get the things out of the small fridge on the back porch. You hear me?"

"Yes. I mean, no, I won't move. Wow! Wham!"

"I can't hear you! Just a sec!" yelled Wham from the porch.

Wham walked back into the kitchen, carrying vegetables, and smiling at him.

"Okay, here we are. Now for the salad."

"Where are Frank and Edna?" asked Johnny.

"Gone to bed. Here, I brought two joints downstairs with me because I had an idea you needed one. Light one up for us because I could use a toke, too. Gawwwd! I know how you feel. I can't last longer than an hour here with them, without a joint."

"But...But the hat. The sunglasses. The...Why?" he asked.

"Well, you see, I thought you were expecting to see a weird country bumpkin sometime when you arrived out here among mostly farmers, hoedowns, quilting bees and all that, so, I decided not to disappoint you. You were hilarious at the table, so, thanks for adding some excitement. I had to run out the back door before I began laughing because I was *so* stoned! I loved your ridiculous accidents. They were the highlight of my day."

"Oh, yeah? Well, look at my hands. I scratched them after I fell over the kitty litter box at the bottom of the basement stairs, and now I'll probably get an infection. Well, I don't care if I do because I'd rather die than marry Amanda. I'm sorry, but I don't love her, and she does nothing for me sexu...I mean, in any way."

"Aw, Johnny. Let me see your hands. Hmmm, good, you washed them. The floor of the basement is very clean, and the linoleum is spotless. Hmmm, there's no kitty litter in or near your scratches. Oops! Bad news, man. You're going to live. Bong! Bong! Bong! Hear those wedding bells? If I were you, after you finish smoking the second joint, I'd pack my things and run back to the city. Nobody's holding a loaded gun to your head, so, if you don't want to get married, then don't. Stop feeling so damned guilty, and get your life back—or together. You hear me?"

"Yeah, I hear you. You make me feel all the things I wanted to feel for Loreen or Amanda, or any woman I ever met in my life."

"Oh? Hmmm, interesting. Now whatever will Mandy say? Well, lots, probably. Tears for sure. But that's all right because she'll latch onto her true love in a week. In the meantime, she'll be a little miffed for a couple of hours, then Mandy'll be just fine. Honestly. Now, you just get yourself mellow, and then after you eat, start packing your suitcases, and then I'll drive you to the airport. Okay?"

"But it's almost forty miles from here!" exclaimed Johnny.

"So? I'll be okay. Hardly any traffic for at least twenty miles. Now when you get back to the city, and Mandy goes on and on too long, then you call me and I'll have a talk with her. Okay? She listens to me, and besides, she only ever wanted to marry Jimmy Glenford. She's always wanted him, but he wasn't divorced yet, and now he is, and he's hot for Mandy. If she'd known he was free, she would've dumped you so fast. Got that? So, get over it. Feel better, now?" asked Wham, smiling at him.

"Oh, yeah! Thanks! Oh, man! Thank you!"

"Good. Now let's get you something to eat."

Johnny hadn't been able to take his eyes off Wham, and he knew for certain that he'd fallen head over heels in love, but he wasn't sure if Wham felt the same way about him.

"Uh, doc? I, uh, I'd like to know if...Um, would you think about...Never mind," he said, blushing.

"Doc? Around here, you call me, Wham."

"Okay. Wham is a bizarre name," said Johnny, smiling.

"I have no idea why mom and dad gave me such an odd name. Oh, well, there's probably some German in our family somewhere,

I suppose. Wilhelmina was too difficult for my playmates to pronounce, so, most of the kids started calling me 'Wham,' and now it's a permanent nickname."

"So, your Amanda's sister. Man, I never thought that knowing her would lead me to you, then I saw you, and then—*Wham!*"

"I'm sure that the reason you've been having so many accidents is because you don't want to marry Mandy.'""

"You think so?"

"Uh-huh. Simple psychology. However, don't ask me to let you drive us to the airport or anywhere else 'til we're sure you're over this fun, but almost deadly phase of clumsy accidents. Hmmm, I'd better check up on you now and then. I'll be back in the city in about two days, so, I'll call you a few times a week until you've stopped having all these ridiculous accidents. Okay?"

"Really? Um, maybe you should also check out my apartment to make sure everything's okay. Okay?"

"Well, if you insist. You're so pushy," she said with a smile.

"Great! Thanks, Wham!"

Johnny arrived back in the city, however, when he went to the hospital to visit Amanda, he was told that the doctors had given strict orders that she couldn't have any male visitors, which Johnny thought was rather unusual.

He tried to phone her, but apparently she couldn't receive phone calls from males, either, so, Johnny sent her flowers with a note, wishing her a speedy recovery.

When Wham came to visit him, Johnny thought it was rather strange when she told him that Jimmy Glendon had been allowed to visit Amanda. Wham then explained to him that instead of bringing Amanda flowers, Jimmy had brought her an engagement ring, and now that they were making wedding plans, Jimmy was the only male allowed to visit Amanda in the hospital.

Of course, Wham didn't tell Johnny that the real reason he'd been told that no males were allowed to visit Amanda in the hospital was because Amanda was just as terrified of Johnny as her parents were.

Wham had been right about his problem because Johnny stopped having accidents, the longer he was around her, so, he continued seeing her almost on a daily basis, then two months later, he was ecstatic when Wham agreed to marry him.

* * * * * * ⁓⧉⋇⧈⁓ * * * * * *

Johnny was surprised that he was included in the wedding invitation that Amanda sent to Wham, and he hoped that he wouldn't have or cause an accident sometime before, during, or after the wedding ceremony.

On their way to Amanda and Jimmy's wedding, Johnny felt ebullient as he looked forward to his own marriage to Wham. His happy mood was suddenly overclouded with trepidation as he drove nearer to his future in-law's property and he saw Frank. Edna, Amanda and Jimmy standing on the farmhouse porch.

"Uh-oh, they don't look too happy, Wham," said Johnny.

"Oh, now don't feel that way, gorgeous. You've stopped having all those accidents, and my parents know that, so, just relax."

"Uh, yeah, sure, okay. Sure are a lot of people here, huh? Look at that huge tent they've put up. It must be at least a hundred feet long and about thirty feet wide."

"That's not a tent. It's a canopy, and that's where Mandy and

Jimmy will be exchanging their vows. Hmmm, it's a great day for it. Lots of sunshine."

"Yeah, but let's hope there won't be a sudden storm."

"Don't be pessimistic," Wham told him as she smiled.

"It's hard not to be after all the accidents I had until I met you, and now everything's great," said Johnny, grinning.

"So, keep thinking that there won't be anymore accidents, and I'm sure you won't have any. Not as often, anyway."

"Yeah, I keep trying not to think about that terrible run of bad luck I had. Hmmm, just to make sure that I don't have an accident while we're here, I'll stay out of the way of tables and any other wobbly objects while I'm mingling with all the guests, but I'll say hello to your parents, first. Amanda and Jimmy, too."

"Whatever makes you feel more comfortable. Oh, dad's coming over. I guess he's going to show you where to park."

"Either to do that, or to shout at me, and ask me why the hell I came here."

"Johnny, you've got to try to forget what happened when you were here before. Just put it all in the past."

"I'm trying to, beautiful," he said, forcing a smile.

"Now keep smiling."

"Oh, gawwwd. I hope he says something nice to me, instead of yelling at me and calling me a jerk," whispered Johnny.

When Frank reached Johnny's car, he suggested that Wham get out of it, and go greet her mother while he told Johnny where to park his car.

Wham winked at Johnny, and before she got out of the car, she leaned over and whispered to him that her father had forgotten all about the accidents that had happened during Johnny's first visit. He smiled at her and felt much more confident, then Johnny's smile faded when he turned his head to look at Frank.

"So where's this big fancy trailer Wham was telling me all about? Bet you didn't hitch it up right, and it came loose on the way here, and shot across the highway, and crashed head-on into the car of some family, killing them all," said Frank.

"No, not all. There's no reason to hook up the trailer 'til we go on our honeymoon," Johnny told him.

"I'm still trying to talk Wham out of that because I'm really, and I mean, *really* worried about her gallivanting across the country with you at the wheel. Especially with a big fancy trailer in tow because I can just see it now. You trying to keep control of the car on a mountain pass while your big fancy trailer's skidding left and right, then all of sudden, you go off a cliff."

"Oh, don't worry about that because I test drove the car with the trailer attached to it, and I handled it pretty well."

"Yeah, but you probably just drove around the block, but just wait 'til you take it on the highway. I keep seeing headlines about a huge pile up on the highway caused by some idiot's loose trailer, and there's blood and guts scattered all over the road, and twenty or thirty people dead," said Frank.

"Uh, I really *did* make sure I didn't have a problem driving with the trailer attached to my car. Honest."

"Oh, yeah? Just a sec."

Frank walked around to the back of Johnny's car, then he walked back, and said: "The trailer hitch looks okay to me. Who put it on?"

"The maintenance men where I bought the trailer."

"Oh, yeah? Y'sure you didn't try to save a buck or two by having some unemployed neighbor of yours put it on?"

"No, I didn't. Honest," replied Johnny.

"Hmmm, I'm still worried about my daughter."

"Oh? Which one?"

"Wham! Why? You thinking about talking Mandy into going with you? She's getting married today!"

"No, I meant...Well, I thought you were worried that Mandy might be making a mistake."

"Wham's the one making the mistake! And it could cost her, her life! But she won't listen to me! She's...hmmm, what's the use? I tried my best to raise them, then some stu...City slicker comes along and...and....Aw, to hell with it. I'll get you parked, then you can wander around here, and when you do, try to act normal. I don't want everyone knowing that Wham's marrying a walking bundle of impending disasters. Okay, now follow me."

"Okay, sure," said Johnny, getting out of his car.

"What the hell are you doing? I meant follow me in your *car*! Jeezuz! God damn city slickers!"

"I thought you wanted to show me where to park, then I'd walk back here and drive my car there."

"With all these cars scattered everywhere, and you behind the wheel trying to get by them? I'm not dumb enough to let you do that! Just get in your car, and *then* follow me, okay? Jeezuz!"

"Sorry. I'll be right with you," said Johnny.

"I shiver every time I think about Wham, you, and that big, fancy trailer of yours out on a busy highway."

"Pardon me? I didn't quite hear you."

"I said I shiver when...Aw, forget it! You ready?"

'I'm ready, Frank."

"Now watch me, and do what I say."

Frank walked slowly alongside Johnny's car, asking guests to step out of the way as he directed him toward the rear of the very big canopy, and as Johnny drove slowly by the crowd of guests, he made certain that he followed Frank's directions, precisely.

When he was nearing the canopy, Johnny could see dozens of tables and chairs set up beneath it, and there was one very long table with a bar near the middle of it. At the other end of the canopy, there was another very long table that had many plates and bowls of food on it, and in the middle of that table, Johnny saw the tall wedding cake, and he decided that he and Wham would have a wedding cake three times that size when they got married.

"Hey! Pay attention, you stupid...Whatever!" shouted Frank.

"Oh, sorry. I was just looking at the setup under that tent."

"It's not a tent! It's a canopy!"

"Right. That's what Wham told me. Sorry."

Johnny quickly applied the brakes when laughing children ran out from between two cars, and Frank shouted at them as the kids continued laughing and running toward the canopy.

"I'm surprised to see that so many guests came," said Johnny.

"Whaddaya mean by that?" shouted Frank. "Everyone likes our Mandy, and that's why so many people came!"

"No! I just meant that I didn't know so many invitations had been sent out."

"Yeah, even *you* got invited, but I guess that happened because someone figured you'd be part of our family if Wham didn't change her mind before Mandy's wedding."

"Uh-huh. I'm sure glad she didn't change her mind, or won't change her mind," said Johnny.

"You're not married to her, *yet.*"

Johnny wondered if Frank would ever accept him as a son-in-law, then he decided he didn't care as long as Wham continued loving him as much as he loved her.

"So many God damned cars here today, that I've spent all day finding parking spaces for them," said Frank. "At least you haven't bumped into any cars, yet. Okay, keep coming this way. That's it. Very slowly. Those God damned idiots over there parked their cars too God damned close to each other. Must be English people."

"Oh? There's other English guests besides me?" asked Johnny.

"How the hell do I know? I didn't invite any, but seeing the way those two cars are parked too close to each other, I bet a few of the English people from town sneaked over here to help themselves to free booze and food," said Frank, scowling.

Johnny noticed two parking spaces up ahead, and directly across from each other, then he stopped the car when Frank hurried toward him while holding up his hands.

"Hold it!" yelled Frank. "Don't move!"

"Okay. *Now* what?" asked Johnny.

"Now turn your car around so that you can back up into that parking space on your right."

"Okay, right away."

Johnny backed his car up very slowly as he looked in the side-view mirror, and Frank kept telling him to drive even slower. He noticed one of the other cars was parked at an angle that wouldn't allow him to back the car up any farther, so, he stopped, and turned off the ignition because he thought Frank wouldn't mind the front half his car poking out from between the other two cars.

"Well, don't stop, completely! Why the hell did you do that? You fuc...Aw, to hell with it!" Frank yelled.

"The back of that car on the right's parked at an angle, so, if I'd backed up farther, I would've scraped the side of it."

"Bullshit! Y'think I don't know how to tell you to park? Just a sec! God damn it!"

Frank peered between Johnny's car and the one beside it, then he glowered at Johnny, and said: "Okay, so you found that out, but that doesn't mean I was wrong. Okay? I was just testing you to see if you could figure out for yourself that there wasn't enough space between your car and this one. Well? What the hell are you doing just sitting there gawking at me? Start the God damned car!"

"Oh, sure. Sorry," said Johnny.

He started the car again, drove out of the tight parking spot, then he forced a smile for Frank.

"There, is that all right?" asked Johnny.

"Yeah, but it's hard to believe, considering what a...Okay, now come toward me. *Slowly*, God damn it!"

Johnny apologized to him, but just to soothe him because the front of his car was at least six feet away from Frank. He drove very slowly toward cars that were parked haphazardly, and Johnny had to keep veering slowly left and right to get past them.

Frank kept slowly backing away from him, then Johnny stopped the car again when Frank held up his hands.

"Okay, now that you're past those jerks, try to squeeze by the next cars we're coming to. But maybe you won't be able to figure out how to maneuver that God damned car of yours past them."

"What cars do you want me to squeeze by?" asked Johnny.

"I'm getting to that, okay? God damn it! Just past that red car, you can make a turn! Okay?"

"Yeah, okay."

Frank walked backward in front of the car, gesturing Johnny to follow him, then he pointed to an open space, and Johnny felt relieved that there was plenty of space between the cars.

He began slowly turning the steering wheel as he backed up his car, and he'd just started to back up between the two cars when Frank held up his hands and shouted: "Stop!"

Johnny stopped the car, then he wondered if Frank had changed his mind about where he could park.

"Is something wrong?" asked Johnny.

"Yeah! You were backing up so fast that you could've hit one of the cars!" shouted Frank.

"But there's lots of room on each side of me."

"That wouldn't stop you from having an accident, though! I don't want you putting dents in anyone's car, so, back up real slow! Okay? *Real* slow!"

"Yeah, sure, okay."

Johnny began backing up much slower as he kept looking into both the side and rear view mirrors.

"Slower!...Careful!...Slower!...That's it!" yelled Frank.

He felt like telling Frank that there was no way he could hit the sides of the cars he was driving between, but Johnny didn't want to upset him anymore than he seemed to be already.

He kept inching the car backward, then Johnny stopped when he looked at the canopy, which was a short distance behind him.

"Oh, I never noticed that before."

"What's that?" asked Frank.

"Most of the back of the tent is covered in."

"That's to make a wall, okay? We needed something to hide at least *some* of these God damned cars, okay? And it's not a tent! It's a canopy, okay? Jeezuz! How many times do I have to...Aw, fuck it! Okay, now keep backing up, but to your right. That's it. Now pull over closer to the tent."

"Canopy, remember?" Johnny reminded him.

"I said that! Think I don't know English? Hah! Now turn to your left. *Left*, God damn it!"

"But you just told me to move to my right, a second ago."

"That was then, this is now, okay? I had to get you to move to your right so you could get by that car, and now I want you to move your God damned car to the left! Okay?"

"Yeah, okay. Sorry," said Johnny.

"Sorry? I'll bet you spend every hour of your life saying your sorry about some God damned thing or other."

Johnny had very slowly backed up, and he was still only halfway into the parking spot, but he knew that Frank would become even angrier if he drove slightly faster.

"Hold it! Stop!" shouted Frank.

"Stop? Okay, there. Now what?" asked Johnny.

"Now back up, slowly. Careful!"

"I'm barely moving the car."

"Think I don't know that? I'm the one directing you! You just drive, and let *me* do the thinking! Not that *you* do too much of that! Okay, now keep going back 'til I tell you to stop."

Johnny backed up his car, very slowly, then he heaved a big sigh when he felt certain that he could now get out of the car.

"What the hell did you shut off your car for?"

"Because I thought I'd backed up far enough."

"No, damn it!" shouted Frank.

"Okay, then I'll back up farther," said Johnny.

"No! I don't want you to back up anymore! That space you're in now, is for the bartender's car! Jeezuz!"

"Oh, sorry, but it's just that when you told me to..."

"I was just getting you into position, okay? You see that parking place directly ahead of you?"

"Yeah, I do," replied Johnny.

"That's where I want you to park, okay? Now that the front of your car's pointing right at it, that means you can drive straight ahead, and into that parking space, without banging the hell out of any cars on the way there. If I'd asked you to just pull right in there, I knew you would've banged the hell out of at least five cars, so that's why I had you back up into the bartender's parking place so that you could drive straight across to that parking place."

"I see," said Johnny. "But you know, I'm not a bad driver, so, I could've easily parked over there in the first place, and without bumping into any of the cars beside that spot, so, instead of going through all the problem of backing up into this spot where the bartender parks his car, I could've just..."

"Jeezuz! Blah, blah, blah! Will you stop yakking and just start your God damned car again? *Please!*"

"Right," said Johnny.

He looked in the rear view mirror again, then in the side-view mirror, and then Johnny frowned, and opened the car door so that he could lean out to have a closer look at the canopy behind him.

"What the hell are you doing *now*? The side of your car's miles away from the one beside you!" yelled Frank.

"Yeah, I know that. I was just looking at the canopy ropes."

"Jeezuz! Y'mean to tell me you've never seen a God damn rope before?"

"Of course I have. It's just that I thought it was sort of odd the way they're tied," said Johnny.

"Odd? *You're* odd! Jeezuz! Okay, what's odd about them?"

"Well, it's just that all the ropes stretched out from the tent are...Oops! I mean, *canopy*, are the same length, except for one, and that one's really *much* longer, and whoever put up the canopy, wound up the excess rope, and then tied it about a foot up the rope, instead of winding it around the stake in the ground in the same way as the others. I don't see why they didn't just cut off the excess rope, or wind it around the stake like the other ropes, instead of tying it up the rope a bit, so, it just struck me as sort of odd, that's all," Johnny explained.

"So what? What difference does it make if the God damned excess rope is wound up a few times, and then tied a foot above that God damned stake, instead of just being wound around the stake? Jeezuz! Just back up your God damned car! *Now*! I haven't got all God damned day!"

"Back it up? But why don't you want me to drive forward?"

"Because if you drive forward, you stupid, fuc...Never mind! You can't do that because the way your car's angled, it'll scrape the back of the car beside you! Okay?"

"Uh, I thought I *could* get by it because there's...Never mind.

Sorry. Okay, I'll back up," said Johnny.

"Thank you! Jeezuz! You finally get it!"

Johnny backed up past the backs of the cars beside him, then he stopped his car again.

"Okay, there. *Now* what?" asked Johnny.

"Look ahead of you. What do you see?"

"The parking spot that you wanted me to park in, instead of here in the bartender's spot."

"Is the parking spot ahead of you, a wider one?" asked Frank.

"Yeah, it's even wider than this one."

"Now doesn't that set a bell off in that...In your head?"

"Yes, of course it does."

"And do you see any other cars in your way?"

"No, I don't," replied Johnny.

"Then there's no reason to drive slow now. Right?"

"No, there's not, but I had to drive slowly on the way to this area because I had to squeeze by so many cars while you were..."

"Jeezuz! Are you going to sit in that car of yours and blab on and on, or are you going to gun the motor and get that car of yours parked? I haven't got all day, you know!" shouted Frank.

"All right, I'll park it over there, but you'll have to move out of my way."

"How rude! You could ask me politely, you know!"

"Sorry. Will you please move a..." Johnny started to say.

"I'm out of your way, okay? Satisfied? Jeezuz! God damn city slickers! Well, at least you're the only one here today. I hope. Why are you still sitting there? Move that thing, and fast! Gun the God damn motor and burn rubber! I've still got to walk you over to the reception area, then that's it! No more you for hopefully two God damned hours! So, move it! Jeezuz!"

"Right. Here goes," said Johnny, perspiring.

He felt so nervous, and he wanted to make sure he followed Frank's instructions, exactly, so, Johnny stepped down hard on the gas pedal, the car jolted forward, and he began speeding toward the open parking spot directly across from him.

That was the beginning of the next disastrous accident. It had been set into action when Johnny had backed up his car past the back of the cars beside him to get into position in the bartender's parking spot before driving straight ahead into the parking spot where Frank had wanted him to finally park his car.

He had seen that the excess rope attached to the canopy had been wound up into a big coil, then tied a foot above the ground, however, Johnny hadn't known that the large loop part of the tied rope had slipped over the hitch ball for his trailer.

Frank gasped in shock when Johnny's car sped away from the canopy, dragging much of it away while the rest of the canopy began rapidly collapsing.

Edna and Amanda had been showing six of the guests around the area beneath the canopy, and those guests were admiring all the decorations, vases of flowers, and the tall wedding cake, when suddenly, the canopy collapsed onto them.

Johnny gaped in astonishment while watching the rest of the canopy falling, and he heard all the screams and shouts rising up from under the collapsed canopy, as well as excited shouts from wedding guests who had started hurrying toward the now almost completely flattened canopy.

Edna was on her hands and knees, crawling through the

crushed wedding cake toward the end of the fallen canopy while Amanda sat weeping and looking down at her wedding gown splattered with food and sauces, then she began picking food out of her ruined coiffure, and wiping sauce off her face.

Her fiancé, Jimmy Glendon, had rushed to the fallen canopy, lifted part of it, then laid on his stomach to start squirming his way under the canopy to get to Amanda while hoping that she, Edna and any of the guests hadn't been seriously harmed.

When the canopy collapsed, Wham had suddenly realized that only one person could've caused that accident, therefore, she had hurried around the crumpled mess, and seen Johnny blushing and frowning as he looked at the collapsed canopy.

Frank had run over to help guests pull the canopy off the people trapped beneath it while he yelled obscenities at Johnny whom stood gaping at the collapsed canopy.

Wham grabbed Johnny's arm, and then they shouted apologies as they ran to his car, got into it, and sped away past guests who were throwing their beer bottles at them.

Regardless of the many mishaps that had led him to Wham, they married and lived happily ever after without anymore clumsy accidents. Well, there really were more clumsy accidents now and then, but Johnny always felt relieved that they were never truly disastrous ones.

The End